IN TWILIGHT'S HUSH

A Gabriel McRay

Published by FYD Media, LLC

IN TWILIGHT'S HUSH

A Gabriel McRay Novel

By Laurie Stevens

Copyright ©2020 by Laurie Stevens

Published by FYD Media, LLC

www.fydmedia.com

ISBN print book: 978-0-9970068-2-7

LCCN: 2020901996

In memory of Cindy Zarzycki
And a case once cold, now closed.

ACKNOWLEDGMENTS

I would like to thank the following people for their valuable contributions to this book: the talented Scott Templeton who designed the cover, Dr. Stephen Kibrick for his assistance in all things psychological, along with author and therapist Dennis Palumbo, Sarah Carter, William Carter, fellow authors Connie DiMarco, Kim Fay, Diann Adamson, team members Jody Hepps, Alan Nevins, Diane Golden, Ray Hoy of Misty Mountain Productions, and Ken Mindar of Photo ER. Steven, Jonathan, and Alanna, thank you for providing the foundation of love on which I can build my creativity. I could not do this without you.

PRAISE FOR THE GABRIEL MCRAY NOVELS

"Top-notch psychodrama suspense at its best!" – *A Bibliophile's Reverie*

"Stevens sets the stage for graphic sensory details and fast-paced, tantalizing mystery that utilizes her passion and research in forensics and psychology."
 – *Kirkus Reviews (a starred review)*

"Frighteningly great Indie title. Make sure to leave a light on." – *Huffington Post*

"Stevens deftly intertwines McRay's childhood trauma with the crimes taking place in the present, intensifying the emotional force of the story. The characters have depth and personality, and their internal conflicts are portrayed in a wrenchingly human fashion."
 – *IndieReader.com*

"The ultimate cat-and-mouse thriller; a genre that has shown Laurie Stevens to be the leader of the pack."
 – *Suspense Magazine*

"Stevens does a masterful job of developing both the characters and the plot."
 – *Sheila Rae Meyers, Shelfari Reviewer*

CHAPTER ONE

"The wind is powerful and causes my clothes to flap. Up here, I can climb aboard the air current, and let it carry me to parts unknown. Perhaps I can ride the wind into the origin of my dreams and forget all I've lost."

Carmen Jenette sat on a tangerine-colored couch with her eyes closed. Words tumbled from her mouth, but they were not her words.

"Below is a fantasyland," she continued in a soft voice. "The pedestrians appear like tiny movable dolls, and their cars look like toys. From this vantage point closer to heaven, I am removed from their fractured world. Although a wave of vertigo causes me to sway, I stay close to the edge." The volume of Carmen's voice rose. "I face the next wind gust with a hearty, *All Aboard*."

Carmen opened her eyes and blinked slowly at the woman sitting on the couch next to her. "Your brother committed suicide, didn't he?"

The woman, stout in body, but frail in spirit, regarded Carmen in confusion. "No."

No? Carmen's eyes scanned the studio audience, where she saw the eager ovals of two hundred faces waiting for the Psychic to the Stars to continue the reading of one of their brethren.

"He didn't jump from a building?"

The woman, who only moments before gave her name to Carmen as "Becky," shook her head and nervously touched the microphone attached to her shirt collar.

Carmen's tongue ran along her lip, a movement designed to hide her surprise and embarrassment. She took Becky's meaty paw into her hand and closed her eyes.

A moment later, Carmen felt her hands tingle as if the vision inside her mind wished to poke through her pores. The prickle at her nerve endings served as the physical signal of Carmen's second sight.

"I see a pickup truck."

Becky gasped and then bowed forward. Her parched, shoulder-length brown hair hid her tears as her body shook with emotion. "That's how Dan died."

Out in the audience, the gasps and murmurs coalesced into one vocalized body, which filled all four corners of the sound stage.

Carmen Jenette released the woman's hand in relief. Why she'd envisioned a man on a ledge, Carmen didn't know. Swallowing her puzzlement, she continued Becky's reading. "Dan knows you are suffering."

"We had argued the day before." Becky's head sunk between the brackets of her shoulders. "I never got the chance to tell him I was sorry."

"Dan understands," Carmen assured the woman.

"Can I tell Dan that I love him?" Becky sniffled.

"Of course." Carmen handed the woman a box of

tissues. "Dan wants you to know that he is in a good place. He –"

The car door closes, and we are alone. We are supposed to be making plans, but then the car revs, and we take off.

Carmen's words killed themselves abruptly, and she became mute in the wake of their death. Where did that random thought come from? Did it have to do with Becky's brother Dan? Did it have to do with the building-jumper?

Driving somewhere was not part of the plan.

Carmen cleared her throat and addressed the sister-of-the-deceased before her. "Dan wasn't a passenger in that truck, was he?"

Tears made swollen paths of water down Becky's cheeks. "No. He was walking across the street as the pickup raced with another car. I don't think he saw it coming. I hope he didn't." Becky suddenly dipped her face into the Kleenex. "I need to know Dan is okay."

"Your brother is at peace," Carmen told her. "He loves you very much, but cannot go forward until he knows that you –"

The handle of the car door is gone. Why is the handle missing?

Carmen felt her heart quicken with something she labeled "Panic by Proxy." She sensed the intimate fear experienced by another coursing through her body. A pitcher of dread poured into Carmen. Something horrific had happened to this other person.

The woman across from her, Dan's sister, pulled a lock of dry hair from her face to better regard the psychic. Out of the corner of Carmen's eye, she caught the show's producer mouthing, "What's wrong?"

Carmen could not reply. She sat immobile in her chair in front of a live studio audience as her pulse continued to rise.

The car has stopped, and I'm frightened. It's pretty, but I don't belong here. I want to go back.

Carmen shut her eyes and soundlessly asked the question: Who are you?

I want to go home.

Who are you?

I can still taste the ice cream on my lips.

Carmen Jenette's green eyes fluttered open. Emotions, like tributaries branching from a flowing river, encircled her heart in sorrow, her belly in fear, and her mind in curiosity.

Lifting her gaze, Carmen looked past the bewildered audience members to the clock hanging across the studio floor. The medium made a mental note of the time: 3:15 pm.

At the back of a designer stationery store on Montana Avenue in Santa Monica, a saleswoman with strawberry blonde hair and bold eyelashes watched the Psychic to the Stars freeze on television. The saleswoman looked over to a prospective bridegroom picking out wedding invitations. "Did you see that?"

Detective Gabriel McRay stood behind a long glass counter spread with an array of catalogs and cards. "She got stage fright," he said without interest.

He held a sample invitation in his hand. On its face, a bride and groom, dressed in the style of the belle époque era, sat in a café and shared an ice cream sundae. Gabriel tossed the card onto a growing pile of rejects.

The saleswoman shook her head. "Carmen Jenette doesn't get stage fright. She's a pro. Don't you watch her show?"

"Never saw it until now." Gabriel felt a tap on his shoulder and turned around.

Dr. Ming Li, Gabriel's fiancée, handed him a standard white linen card with an overlay of lace adorning the corners.

"This one's called Lovely Lace," Ming said. "What do you think?" She gauged his reaction and chewed on a fingernail.

The nail-biting had recently developed, the byproduct of an insecure side of Ming unfamiliar to Gabriel.

He shrugged. "I don't know." Glancing up at the TV, Gabriel saw, not the cute psychic, but a commercial for an erectile dysfunction drug that promised sexual bliss, but warned of diarrhea as a possible side effect. Nothing like the runs to get you in the mood. For the first time all day, Gabriel grinned in amusement.

Ming's fingernail dropped away from her mouth. "Will you pay attention? It's your wedding, too, you know."

Gabriel pulled his eyes from the commercial and studied the invitation. When he saw the price tag of Lovely Lace, his breath escaped in a whistle.

The saleswoman approached the couple. Her long, maroon fingernails tapped against the glass counter. "Isn't that card beautiful?"

"It's pretty steep." Gabriel heard his fiancée sigh at his sentiment and faced her. "Why don't we take a trip to the courthouse, babe? No fuss, no muss. No overpriced lace."

With a flick of his wrist, the invitation joined its fellows on the reject pile. The saleswoman batted her eyelashes in displeasure and retreated to her television program.

In response to Gabriel's suggestion of a quick legal

union, Ming handed him another invitation. This one featured wildflower seeds embedded in compostable paper.

"It's good for the environment." Her eyes darted between the invitation and him.

Gabriel's cobalt blue eyes appraised Ming. Despite her jangled nerves, his fiancée managed to look beautiful. A clip dammed the ebony waterfall of her hair, but the few escaping strands framed Ming's high cheekbones and emphasized the rosy pout of her mouth. Small diamonds twinkled at each earlobe, and a solitaire diamond engagement ring glittered on her surgeon's hand. The jewelry had been a gift from Gabriel. Ming's thick hair, along with her curvaceous figure, had been a gift from her Mexican mother. Ming's Chinese father had bestowed to her those intelligent, almond-shaped eyes. In a few days, Gabriel would be meeting Ming's parents for the first time.

If he had to guess, Gabriel would bet the fingernail gnawing stemmed, not from the wedding preparations, but mom and dad's impending visit.

"Here's a photo invitation." Ming slapped a new card into Gabriel's hand, and then suddenly gasped. "Oh, my God!" Her brows furrowed as though she'd been smacked between the eyes. "Did we set the date with the tuxedo shop?"

"You've asked me that ten times."

"Well, did you set it?"

"Yes." Gabriel set the invitation down and put his hands on Ming's shoulders as if to steady her. "Baby, let's get out of here. How about a beer? How about a glass of wine?"

"It's the middle of the afternoon."

"You need it."

She ducked out from under his hands. "What I need is to

get shit off my to-do list." Her eyes, wet and weary with anxiety, found Gabriel's. "Help me. I'm drowning."

Grinning, Gabriel put a gentle arm around his fiancée and steered her out the door.

They went to Ye Olde King's Head Pub and sat at a table near the window. A strand of purple and orange lights hung above their heads, and stickers in the shapes of ghosts and witches adorned the window glass. Gabriel ordered beers, a Dos Equis for him, and a local craft beer for Ming.

"Are you hungry?" he asked.

The waitress, boasting several ear and facial piercings and a jet-black Betty Page hairstyle looked questioningly at Ming, who shook her head.

Gabriel's fiancée stared dispassionately at a distant corner of the restaurant. In Ming's role as the Los Angeles County Medical Examiner, she could study maggots feasting off a corpse with ease. Planning their wedding, however, had hurled her analytical brain into a panic.

"When do your parents get in?" Gabriel asked.

The reaction on her face told him the question was a direct hit. "Tomorrow night. What am I supposed to do with them? You and I were supposed to meet them at the airport, but I told them to rent a car."

"That wasn't very daughterly of you."

"Everyone knows you need a car in L.A. They can't expect me to shuttle them all over the place, 24/7."

The Betty Page waitress set down two ice-rimmed glasses along with two beers.

"You should pick them up." Gabriel poured Ming's beer into one of the glasses and pushed it toward her.

Ming's obstinacy toward her mother and father perplexed him. She hadn't seen her parents in a couple of years, and Gabriel imagined that the trio would be happily anticipating a reunion. Dr. and Mrs. Li intended to throw Gabriel and Ming an engagement party, and some of their friends were making the trip across the country to attend. To him, that seemed generous.

Ming took a sip of her beer, and then wiped the wetness from her lips with her sleeve. "They can rent a car. I'm giving them a free place to stay."

Ming lived in a Spanish revival-style home not far from the Greek Theater in Los Feliz. The neighborhood possessed a stately grace, a feel of 1930's Los Angeles. One could easily imagine a star of the silent screen traipsing down the tiled staircase in Ming's home, wearing an art deco gold lamé gown and entertaining Hollywood's elite in the great room, with its arched stucco doorways and wrought-iron chandeliers. With five bedrooms, Ming's place offered plenty of room for guests. Where else would her parents be expected to stay?

Gabriel had recently bought and renovated a "tear down" in Santa Monica. He'd gone beyond his budget to purchase the home, although everyone told him what a steal the bungalow had been. At any rate, Gabriel liked it. The beach was within walking distance, and the ocean served as a calming friend to him.

"Aren't you happy to see your folks?" Gabriel asked. "It's been a long time."

Ming didn't reply.

He took that as a 'no.' "Should I be worried?"

"My mother will love you." Ming sipped her beer. "She's a doormat basically and has no opinions."

"Ming, that's terrible."

"It's the truth. My father completely cows her. He worries me. If he says one nasty thing to you, I want to know about it. Promise me you'll tell me everything he says."

"I'm not going to promise that."

Ming gave her lover a disparaging grin over the rim of her glass. "You have this weird sense of right and wrong, Gabe. You feel you have to be respectful to him because he's my father. But he's a tremendous asshole. He's going to give you crap about still being a detective."

"*Still* being a detective?"

"He wants to know why you haven't made lieutenant in the bureau yet."

Wow. Gabriel shifted in his chair and held the beer bottle for support. That came from left field. His career had been a topic of conversation. No, his lack of promotion had been the topic.

"Los Angeles is a big pool," Gabriel said and tested the bottle against the edge of the table. "Not everyone becomes a big fish overnight." *Although Ming was one.*

He took a reassuring swallow of beer.

"My dad will bring it up." Ming drained three-quarters of her glass. "Now you know why I live across the country from them." She hid her mouth behind her hand and belched quietly.

"I think I can handle your father," Gabriel told her.

Ming guffawed. "You think."

His gaze traveled through the thick pane of the window. Outside the pub, tourists cluttered the street, perhaps heading toward the Third Street Promenade, a store and restaurant-filled enclave that attracted shoppers and the homeless alike.

Glancing once more at his nail-biting, beer-swilling girl-friend, Gabriel took another swallow of the cold, amber liquid to soothe his nerves. They were beginning to fray.

At home, Gabriel went into his study and opened the window. Technically, a second bedroom, he used the space as an in-home office. Two armchairs, which converted into twin beds, were positioned against one wall and had been bought for Gabriel's niece and nephew. The two children didn't visit as often as he would have liked because they lived in Seattle with their parents.

He'd placed a desk next to the window so he could feel the incoming sea breeze while he worked. Across the room stood a barren bookcase, like a lone soldier standing sentinel. The empty shelves threw questions at Gabriel like *"What kinds of things do you enjoy collecting?"* And even worse, *"Who are you?"*

Someday, Gabriel would purchase items to fill the void, just as soon as he learned what interested him.

The breeze from the nearby ocean arrived like a caring friend and brushed away the frown line from between his brows. Ming had successfully dropped a pebble of fore-boding into the well of Gabriel's mind, and now ripples of worry washed through him when he thought about his future in-laws.

Taking a seat at the desk, Gabriel placed a paperweight, a small but solid Buddha head, over a sheet of paper that fluttered in the moving air. Ming had given him the Buddha as a reminder to view situations, specifically tense situations, with a calmer mind. If anyone needed to get Zen, however, it was the Bridezilla who insisted on throwing a monster wedding.

Gabriel didn't want a large formal affair because neither he nor Ming had a lot of friends. In regards to family, Ming was an only child, and Gabriel's entire clan consisted of his mother, father, his sister, and her family.

Janet, Gabriel's sister, had two children to contend with, and Gabriel's father had early-onset Alzheimer's. Gabriel had no intention of insisting his family participate in a barn-burner. And whom would Gabriel choose to be his groomsmen? His closest friend was his psychiatrist (if that didn't speak volumes), and the one who would have stood as his best man idled in prison.

Michael "Dash" Starkweather had been Gabriel's partner in the homicide bureau for years. Gabriel would never have imagined Dash absent from his wedding. But then, he never imagined his partner would become a felon serving time for planting evidence.

To avoid further thought on that matter, Gabriel reached for a case file.

The nearly forgotten criminal cases belonging to the Unsolved Crimes Unit brought to mind the withered tombstones found in old cemeteries. The ambiguity of death lay among their yellowing papers and dried-out evidence bags, yet the surroundings were deceptively peaceful.

Gabriel had been relegated to the Unit after a particularly brutal experience with a serial killer named Victor Archwood. Among those forgotten cold cases, Gabriel could utilize his skills as a detective while he recovered personally from the torment he'd endured at Archwood's hands.

A corner of the folder ripped away, torn by Gabriel's fingers. He advised himself to forget about Victor Archwood and opened the folder. A teenage girl smiled at him from the square of a Polaroid picture. He pulled the photo free from its paperclip bond and studied it in the afternoon quiet.

The girl wore her blonde hair cropped in a popular 1980s style. A wedge cut, Gabriel believed they called it; short at the back of the neck, longer at the forehead. Her shirt featured a cutout collar that left one shoulder winsome and bare. What truly arrested Gabriel were the girl's sparkling blue eyes. They looked out at him from across the decades with a fecundity of spirit and an easy-going maturity that belied her youth.

Her name was Nancy Lynn Lewicki, and the Polaroid, taken in 1988, was the last known photograph of her. Nancy had been fifteen at the time. Gabriel turned the photo over. In a faded script, he read, *"4 Punkin."*

Who's Punkin? Gabriel wondered.

Placing the photo aside, he pulled a brittle missing person's report from the folder.

Missing from: Liberty Canyon/Agoura, California.

Time and date last seen: April 19, 1988.

Someone, at some point in time, must have placed a coffee mug on the report. A tan ring encircled the words "Description of Teeth." There followed choices to mark off: braces, caps, protruding, gapped, chipped, and decayed.

Nothing had been checked off. Gabriel glanced at the Polaroid. Nancy's smile boasted naturally straight, white teeth.

Under "Special Identifiers," the choices listed were

eyeglasses, facial hair, scars, marks, and tattoos. Someone had typed: *A small birthmark on upper right thigh.*

Gabriel continued to scan the missing person's report until his eyes halted on Mental State: *Agitated.*

He viewed Nancy's picture again. The breeze ruffled Gabriel's dark curls as he contemplated what might sour such a carefree expression. On a whim, he rose from the chair and propped the Polaroid on his bookcase. Nancy livened up the otherwise empty shelf.

Returning to his desk, Gabriel read the detective's report to see what his predecessors had gleaned from the case. Nothing much. Nancy had left school one afternoon and did not return home. Detective Harris Brody, who worked Missing Persons in the eighties, wrote that Nancy had been a popular girl who had a large circle of friends. She did not indicate anything being amiss on the day she disappeared. In fact, Nancy had been planning a surprise party for her best friend and, per one schoolmate, seemed "totally into it." When the school day ended, Nancy told her friends that she needed to run errands for the party. No one ever saw her again.

Gabriel leaned back, crossed his arms, and regarded Nancy's photo once more.

For the sake of the bright essence captured in a long-ago smile, he made a silent promise to find out what happened to a girl who disappeared when Gabriel was a boy.

CHAPTER TWO

That's what I like about you, Wally Palmar. You can hear me talking in my sleep anytime you want. We're dancing to the beat, and I'm telling the crew we'll be up on that stage someday. A girl in front of me tosses her hair, and it gets snagged on my lip-gloss. Gag me with a spoon!

Strands of hair and song notes wove together to form ethereal sheet music, which drifted at the edge of Carmen's inner vision. The tops of Carmen's hands tingled, and music whispered in her ear.

I hear the secrets that you keep.

Carmen Jenette tried to piece together the fragmented messages, but they made no sense.

Standing at the reception desk in the Hollywood community station on Wilcox Avenue, she felt caught between the pull of the stranger's voice and the pushback coming from two LAPD cops. The officers regarded Carmen with doubting eyes and pursed lips.

"I'm sure it's a girl," she told the two cops. "The voice feels female. She's lost and can't find her way home."

The desk sergeant, a young African-American with a boyish, polite face and long limbs, raised his eyes to the older, uniformed cop standing next to him. That one was of a saltier variety, a man with thin lips and a pitted face seasoned enough to be cynical.

"Are you reporting a missing person, Ma'am?" the salty, pitted one asked.

"No," Carmen replied. "I'm not reporting a missing person. I'm looking for a missing person. I may be able to help with the investigation."

The desk sergeant accessed his computer. "Name?"

"I'm Carmen Jenette." She felt slighted that the two men didn't recognize her.

"Not your name," Salty-Pits told her squarely. "The name of the missing person."

"I don't know her name. I only know she's a female."

"I'm sorry," the boyish desk sergeant said with a shake of his head. "I don't understand. You are looking for someone you don't know?"

Carmen sighed. Her fame as a television personality usually opened doors for her. These two *idyos,* as her Creole grandmother would say, apparently didn't watch TV.

"I'm looking for a missing female." Her arms rested on the countertop. "The girl is lost, and I'm sensing a lot of time has passed. My name is Carmen Jenette, the medium. Have you seen my show? Psychic to the Stars?"

The two cops stared at her, a duo of open mouths.

Carmen tried again. "The LA Times recently ran a feature story about me in the Calendar section. I mean, they featured my show."

Carmen's *grandmere*, a Cajun *traiteuse* or faith healer, had warned her pretty granddaughter to watch her ego. It's your *defo*, your flaw, *Grandmere* told her. A flaw is a rip in your soul. You must do the work to stitch it closed, otherwise evil will creep into the space the way bacteria infects an open wound.

Salty Pits looked at his wristwatch, apparently done with the conversation. "You'll have to check the Missing Persons' list, Miss Janet."

"Je-*nette*," Carmen told him.

The man didn't seem to hear her. "We only have about 90,000 missing persons in the USA on any given day. Figuring half of them are female; that should narrow your search down to 45,000. And if you're talking about someone who made the lists years ago, well..." He smirked at her once again. "Better get out your crystal ball."

Carmen had learned to expect this treatment, although these days, with the success of her show, she rarely received the brushoff. A few years back, she had worked with detectives on their investigations. The passing time, however, had transformed Carmen from a hayseed clairvoyant yearning for big city aplomb into a bona fide celebrity, engrossed in Nielsen ratings and the marketing of her brand. Carmen abandoned her role as a police assistant.

The resulting guilt over that decision, along with her grandmother's warning, brought Carmen to the desk of these two yahoos. Leaning toward the two men, giving Salty-Pits a chance to view her cleavage, Carmen said, "The way this works is when someone, usually within the police department, revives something that has lain dormant, such as an old case, the action kicks up on my end. Something forgotten is now remembered, and the recollections stir the pot. Do you understand?"

The two men blinked and said nothing.

Carmen sighed. "Can you at least put me in touch with the LAPD or Sheriff's Department detectives who are handling old cases involving missing females?"

Glancing at his older cohort for support, the desk sergeant said, "You'll have to contact both Missing Person's units, Ma'am."

No, Carmen decided. She had other avenues at her disposal. Her brother-in-law worked in the District Attorney's office. His name was Donovan Thorne, and Carmen would ask him to pull a few strings for her.

"She'd gone to a concert the night before at UCLA. I forget the name of the group."

Nancy's mother, Pauline Lewicki, rubbed the fingers of her plump right hand against her thumb, as if the movement, like the rubbing of a magic lamp, would bring forth the unrecalled band's name. The apples of Pauline's Slavic cheekbones went rosy when the genii of memory materialized.

"The Romantics! That was the name of the group." She addressed Gabriel, who sat on her living room couch. "Does it help?"

Pauline's eyes were blue like Nancy's, but melancholy weighted them, and they appeared heavy upon her face.

"Everything helps," Gabriel said. "I appreciate you going through all this again with me."

"I appreciate that they've reopened the case."

Gabriel wanted to interview Nancy's surviving relatives and friends, and the first order of business was to call on the missing girl's parents. They lived in a condominium on

Bundy, near Wilshire Blvd. Nancy's father, unfortunately, was not at home.

"Len is sorry to miss you, but he's over at our son's place," Pauline explained. "A last-minute emergency..."

A shadow moved over her features, and Gabriel wondered if the passing darkness referenced Len's missed meeting with Gabriel or the son's last-minute emergency.

"The report indicated that Nancy's state of mind was agitated," Gabriel said. "Why was she agitated?"

Nancy's mother sighed deeply. "Nancy was grounded at the time she went missing. She wasn't supposed to go to that concert. She'd asked for our permission, and we said no. I was a bit overprotective of her, I guess. I didn't like the idea of a fifteen-year-old girl going to a university concert." The woman paused and then shook her head. "Look where all that caution got me. Look where it got her."

She offered Gabriel a sad smile, which he did not return. In a case such as this, he had to consider all possibilities. A parent as a perpetrator wasn't beyond the realm of possibilities.

"Where do you think it got her?" he asked and gauged the woman's reaction.

Blotches of indignant red burned the pale of Pauline Lewicki's face. Gabriel instantly regretted using the tact. In a previous life, Gabriel would tough it out with the violent offenders while Dash handled the more sensitive situations. Interviewing a parent of a missing child classified as a sensitive situation. Dash, however, was no longer his partner, and Gabriel needed to pull the reins on his aggressive approach.

"I'm sorry," he said.

"I'm sorry as well, Detective. I did not harm my daughter. That particular ground was covered years ago, by the way. I was hoping to break new ground with you." Pauline strode to the front door. "I think this interview is over."

Gabriel stood rooted to the spot. He didn't want to leave. Leaving would mean getting hassled by his superior for blowing the interview. While Gabriel viewed Miguel Ramirez as a friend, he knew the feisty Lieutenant enjoyed keeping his underlings in line and would welcome the opportunity to berate Gabriel. Lacking a more redeeming excuse for his behavior, Gabriel settled on the truth.

"Look, I'm not used to working missing persons cases," he confessed.

"Then why did they put you on one? I know it's a cold case, an old case for you, but for me, Detective, time did not heal all."

Nancy's mother opened the door wide, a clear indication of his dismissal.

Gabriel didn't budge. "My superiors gave me Nancy's case because they feel I shouldn't handle my regular work-load right now."

Pauline Lewicki shifted in front of the door but said nothing. Gabriel took her silence as a cue to explain why they'd transferred him.

"I had an experience last summer with a suspect who beat a murder charge. I was the investigator who tried putting him behind bars. The man wanted revenge and took it. So, with me, Mrs. Lewicki, as with you, time has not healed all."

Gabriel tried to smile, but like her earlier grin, it held no concrete joy and broke apart on his face.

The woman's fingers left the doorknob to point at Gabriel. "I know who you are. You're the detective who was taken prisoner by that maniac Victor Archwood. Oh, my

LAURIE STEVENS

goodness." Pauline Lewicki gawked at Gabriel in stunned silence for a moment and then allowed the front door to close.

"Call me Pauline." She beckoned Gabriel over to the couch. "Please sit, Detective McRay. Let's you and I start over."

Gabriel followed her and decided he liked the woman. Pauline seemed a genuine sort, one who had little time for meaningless conversation. With her, raw emotion lingered under a thin scab of normalcy, and he could relate to that. Gabriel knew he could safely open up to Nancy's mother. His ordeal with Victor Archwood was no secret anyhow, as her recognition of it firmly attested.

Thanks to Dash for planting evidence, Victor Archwood had walked away a free man from his trial. Archwood's acquittal had been bad enough, but Gabriel had no idea what the cunning killer had in store for him. Memories floated down like confetti, like pieces of horrific theater that landed on Gabriel's conscious mind: Archwood killing a young woman, whom he then impersonated. Archwood poised with a syringe as he approached Gabriel, who lay chained to a bed.

Gabriel could recall the sting of the needle and how the drugs released terrible recollections from his childhood. Memories of an abuse he'd rather forget.

Giving Archwood a mental kick, Gabriel reclaimed his seat on the sofa and pulled a pen and a dog-eared notepad from his jacket pocket.

"It must have been awful for you." Pauline studied him as she sat down.

"I was up close and personal to a very disturbed person."

Pauline Lewicki's blue eyes grew distant. "But you got away."

Gabriel nodded. He had physically escaped Archwood. Mentally—only time would tell. Still, Gabriel was determined to prove that Archwood had not won, that he could perform his job, get married, have a beautiful life, and remain unaffected.

His mind laughed at him.

"You grounded Nancy the night before she disappeared, correct?" Gabriel asked. "When she came home from the concert?"

"Yes," Pauline confirmed. "Can I get you something, Detective? Anything to drink?"

Gabriel shook his head. "No, thank you. Please continue." He took notes as Nancy's mother recounted what occurred in the spring of 1988.

"On Sunday evening, Nancy said she was going to a church study group. When it became late, Len and I started worrying. The kids didn't have cell phones back then. We called the church, found out there was no study group, and then we called her friends. Nobody knew where Nancy was. Finally, we got a hold of a friend's mother, who told us the girls were at a concert. Nancy could be sneaky when she wanted. Her father and I were pacing the floor at two in the morning when she finally strolled in. We grounded her on the spot. No going out for a month."

Pauline bit her lower lip and studied the floor. Gabriel wondered how many times the woman regretted punishing Nancy. How often did Pauline blame herself for making the last conversation between them an argument? Probably countless times.

"How angry was Nancy at being punished?" he asked. "Furious? Mildly upset?"

Pauline held up a plump hand. "Please. I know where this is going. You think she might have run away."

"These things happen," Gabriel offered.

"Your predecessors suggested the same thing. It is true Nancy was upset, and it's true she sometimes lied to us. Len and I were strict, but we had a good home life. We were a happy family. People argue, Detective McRay, but they don't run away. I know Nancy didn't run away from home because she wouldn't have left Clifford."

Gabriel looked up from his notepad. "Clifford?"

"The Big Red Dog. The cartoon. You see she had a stuffed animal, a Clifford dog that was hers since she was a baby. She slept with it every night. Here, I'll get it for you."

Gabriel wanted to tell her not to bother, but Pauline jumped up and jogged up the stairs. Left alone, Gabriel put his notepad aside to survey the Lewicki home.

The condo appeared tastefully decorated, but without character. A framed photograph of a blond man with Pauline's eyes stood on the table next to Gabriel. The professional shot included a woman—his wife, Gabriel assumed, and two smiling, tow-headed boys. In the photo's background, stood a lit Christmas tree, a typical studio holiday prop. A crease running along the upper left-hand corner of the picture resembled the white line of a scar. Other than the damaged image, no other indicators of the 'happy family' adorned the condo.

The small living room in which Gabriel sat faced the front door. He swiveled his head to look behind him and saw a dining room with a dark wood table and six chairs. A table runner held a vase filled with fake yellow roses covered in shiny plastic dewdrops. Beyond that, there was a small kitchen with a butcher-block island, upon which sat a ceramic pumpkin, the only seasonal decoration Gabriel could spot.

The narrow, beige-carpeted steps Pauline had ascended must lead to the bedrooms upstairs, from where Gabriel heard the muffled creaks of someone moving about. The condo seemed to be a home on hold, a way station. Underneath the staged display, Gabriel sensed an oppressive atmosphere. The years had passed, but as Pauline had pointed out, the family's wounds had never healed. They had continued to bleed until the pain congealed into a palpable presence, which Gabriel bet even the dullest of visitors could sense. It made him want to leave.

Pauline padded down the steps and handed Gabriel a small, stuffed dog. "Nancy would never go somewhere overnight without it. Her girlfriends knew all about Clifford. They would laugh. Nancy would laugh with them."

Gabriel inspected the stuffed dog, made of squeezable red plush worn bald in various places.

"She slept with it every night." The weight momentarily lifted from Pauline's eyes and was replaced by a soft reminiscence. "Nancy wouldn't run away and leave Clifford behind." Pauline regarded Gabriel in earnestness. "She wouldn't have run off and left us behind."

Gabriel passed the toy back to Nancy's mother. He believed her.

CHAPTER THREE

Carmen Jenette shook hands with the lawyers at her brother-in-law's office on West Temple Street. Donovan had worked as an Assistant District Attorney for most of his career. He was a smart, elegant-looking man who had pepper-colored hair with salt at the sideburns. Donovan made an effective prosecutor and was well respected among his peers.

He introduced Carmen as his sister-in-law without mentioning her renowned alter ego. The entire office staff, however, already knew of the psychic's fame and loitered around in breathless excitement.

"Carmen," Donovan began, "this is Anne Nolan."

Carmen shook the hand of a giggling reed of a woman wearing a snappy gray suit. The thin woman gushed. "I love your show."

Donovan prodded Carmen along the row of those waiting to meet her. "And this is Marty Riskin."

A rotund man with a full black beard who reminded

Carmen of a pirate gave her a wide, genial smile. "My wife is a big fan."

"Not you?" Carmen asked him coyly.

A sheen broke out on the Pirate's forehead. "Ah, I'm not much of a believer."

"Give me your hand," Carmen demanded with a flirtatious grin.

Marty the Pirate shot out his hand, and Donovan gave Carmen a push toward his office.

"She's off the clock," he said.

Once through, Donovan closed the door and let out a big breath. "Look, I'm doing you a favor, but don't push it, okay? Everyone's already wondering why you're here."

Carmen put her hands on her hips but didn't argue.

Donovan waved his hand over a stack of papers on his desk. "Here they are. Twenty-seven new and reopened old cases regarding young females that might fit the description of your…"

"My visions."

Carmen found this squirrely act of Donovan's tiring. Out of sight of his co-workers, both Donovan and his wife Desiree sought her services. Desiree, Carmen's older sister, came with an open mind, having been nursed on the same magical milk as Carmen. Donovan, on the other hand, submitted to a reading only after he'd had a few drinks. Carmen supposed he needed liquid fortification to accept her unique approach to managing life's challenges.

She leaned over the stack of papers that contained the photographs of girls and case descriptions. Flipping through them, Carmen hoped one might arrest her attention.

They heard a knocking, and Donovan's door swung

open. A man in his mid-forties, handsome in a soft way, peered inside.

"I hope I'm not interrupting."

Donovan eyed the visitor with the worshipful expression of a mutt that rolls over for the alpha dog. "Not at all! Come in. Carmen, this is Brad Franklin."

Carmen didn't need an introduction. The District Attorney had earned the nickname The White Knight, which reflected his solid track record. During Brad's tenure as DA, the city's overall felony conviction rate peaked to its highest point in twelve years. Under his leadership, the office doubled the number of serious and violent offenders sent to state prison, convicting more than 1,200 rapists and sexual predators.

Setting the papers down, Carmen smiled and shook the hand of The White Knight. "I know who you are."

"And I, you, Miss Jenette." Brad held onto her hand. "I'm a fan. Tell me, will I make Attorney General?"

Carmen took a lavish intake of breath. "I see in your future –" She then grinned. "I need my tarot cards. But I'm happy to do a free reading for you if you –"

Donovan suddenly blathered something incomprehensible and shook his head. "We're in the middle of something, Brad."

"It's okay, Don." Brad seemed amused at Donovan's evident unease. "I'll get out of your hair." As he released Carmen's hand, he said, "I watch your show whenever I get the chance, Miss Jenette. I wouldn't miss it."

Carmen's grin widened. "Super."

"Well, I'll leave you to the something you're in the middle of." Brad winked an eye and whisked out the door.

"*Super?*" Donovan faced Carmen. "Did you actually say that?"

Carmen watched Brad's departure through the office window. "My, he's fine. And he's single, isn't he?"

"His marital status is public knowledge. Put him out of your mind, Carmen. Brad is too low-key for you. He doesn't care about the red carpet treatment."

"Is that why he's running for Attorney General? Because he shuns the limelight? Don't be a fool, Don." Carmen giggled and returned to the desk and its papers. "I could get down with an Attorney General."

"Honestly, Carmen. You're so thirsty for fame; it's not funny."

"Me? What about you? You cry if a week goes by without seeing your name in the papers."

Donovan scowled at her, but no real malice lay behind the expression.

"Quit being embarrassed by me," Carmen admonished her brother-in-law. "It doesn't look good on you."

"Ah, the All-Seeing Carmen." Donovan nodded to the papers. "Well? Are you getting anything?"

Carmen took the hint. She picked up the papers once more and shuffled through them. No visions of ice cream or music grabbed her. No cars with missing door handles sparked from the pages. Could she have misunderstood the call for help? Carmen could hear the tapping of Donovan's impatient foot. Perhaps she needed the aid of more companionable surroundings. Carmen didn't have to be psychic to see that Donovan wanted her to leave.

The sausage squeezed out of its casing, prodded along by Gabriel's pressing fingers. The meat dropped into a cooking pot where it joined diced onions and garlic. Using a wooden spoon, Gabriel pressed the sausage into small chunks. He then crushed a few basil leaves from a plant that grew in his garden. Gabriel derived a lot of pleasure cultivating herbs in his backyard.

"That's an awful lot of sausage you're using."

Behind him, Ming was chopping vegetables for a salad. The knife made staccato music on the cutting board.

Gabriel's broad shoulders shrugged. "I like a thick sauce. We'll freeze whatever we don't use. You can take some home with you."

The chopping sounds ceased. "Am I going home tonight?"

"No, but when you do, you can take some." He threw the basil into the pot and felt Ming's eyes on his back.

"Eventually, we're going to have to make a decision, Gabe. We can't live in two separate houses. We're going to have to sell or rent one out."

Gabriel's stomach clenched at her words, which surprised him. He thought about the garden out back where bunches of mint reached toward the sky along with chili peppers and basil. He'd bought seeds to grow lettuce and three different kinds of heirloom tomatoes for the summer. Cucumbers and squash already stretched along the backyard wall, behind the Jacuzzi tub he recently installed. This winter, Gabriel planned to build a decorative arch to support grapevines.

"I like Santa Monica," he told Ming.

His fiancée resumed her task, only this time she chopped with more ferocity. "You know this house is not big enough for a family, and mine is. If you don't like Los Feliz, then let's sell both houses, pool our money, and get something different."

"Where?"

"I don't want to be too far from work. How about Echo Park?"

Gabriel moved the sizzling meat around with a long spoon. "No."

"You haven't even looked there. It would be an easier drive to Commerce for you. Besides, it's a happening spot. They have nice places near the lake. And what about Mount Washington? That's family-friendly."

"No." Gabriel shook his head. "I don't want to think about moving right now. I just bought this place. And by the way, lots of families live in apartments and small homes. Not everyone has to live in a mansion."

Ming sighed. "What is it, really?"

Gabriel didn't answer because he didn't know how to verbalize what he felt. How could he explain that his identity had been stolen the summer he turned seven? That was when his across-the-street neighbor molested him. Whatever path to adulthood Gabriel might have taken skewed after that, and he grew up hiding behind walls of shame. He didn't have the mental freedom to find himself. Before therapy, Gabriel pretended invulnerability and used rage and anger to provide him an illusion of strength. Looking back, he could see he lived in a chaotic thunderstorm of pain. Ordinary occurrences would trigger terrible memories that hit like lightning strikes and cut Gabriel to his core. Diligent self-work had helped him creep out from under that black cloud of self-loathing, but Gabriel didn't know himself. He hoped to find his reflection mirrored somewhere—within his home perhaps.

If he moved in with Ming, Gabriel worried he would feel cheated; for Ming's place was all Ming. Her study brimmed with medical books, classic literature, even books written in Latin if that weren't enough to intimidate the average tenderfoot. Ming knew her likes and dislikes. To be truthful, her strong sense of identity attracted Gabriel.

As he sautéed the meat, Gabriel contemplated his inability to express himself to his lover. He worried Ming would view his self-scrutiny as a sign of weakness.

Just then, Ming's slender arms wrapped around his waist. He felt the familiar curve of her body as she pressed close and smelled the herbal scent of her hair. Gabriel's shoulders relaxed, and his breathing evened out. Ming always managed to reassure him. How could he hold back and risk losing her?

"We'll work it out, babe," he offered in a bumbling, hopeful way to put her at ease. He kept his eyes on the sauce.

Ming's chin nuzzled the back of Gabriel's shirt between his shoulder blades. On the heels of that, he felt a simultaneous awakening in his slacks.

"I know," she murmured. "We always work it out. As long as we have each other, everything will fall into place."

Gabriel pivoted around and took hold of Ming's arms, wrapping them more firmly around him. "How do you put up with me?" he asked. "Why do you do it?"

"You're not so hard to get along with." Ming smiled at him.

Gabriel tilted his face down to hers and gave her a long kiss. The softness of her tongue, the tenderness of Ming's lips, caused the pressure in his pants to grow into a more urgent need.

"Did I push too hard?" she asked, angling her face away. "To get married?"

"No," he said firmly. "I didn't have to be pushed. You're the best thing that's ever happened to me."

Ming glanced at the pot hissing behind him. "Your sausage is ready."

He smirked. "I know." Gabriel backed her body up against the counter.

"Easy, cowboy." Ming reached behind her to pick up a large can of diced tomatoes. "Toss this in. I've been waiting patiently for your special spaghetti sauce. Then we can explore other ways of feeding your libido."

Gabriel eyed the cooking pot over his shoulder, gave Ming's body a squeeze, and then relented. He opened the cans of diced tomatoes, sauce, and tomato paste and mixed all the ingredients. Wiping his hands on a towel, he turned around to find his fiancée with her blouse and bra removed. Her breasts perked up merrily under a suggestive grin.

"Who cares about spaghetti?" Gabriel commented appreciatively and went into her waiting arms.

CHAPTER FOUR

"Hey, there he is!"

Gabriel walked into the homicide bureau and was greeted warmly by his fellow detectives and the various clerks. Upon seeing Gabriel enter, Lt. Miguel Ramirez exited his office.

Short, but tough, reminiscent of a Pit Bull with an intemperate attitude and a biting mouth, Ramirez made his way toward Gabriel, carrying a medium-sized box.

"How's it going with the Lewicki case?" He set the box down on Gabriel's desk.

"A little more mellow compared to the rat-race I usually run."

"Don't get too comfortable," his Lieutenant told him. "There's a lot of rats in this city. You'll get plenty of homicides to work in the future."

"And besides," a female voice intervened, "I miss you hassling me."

A stocky, African American woman poked her head around the wall separating her cubicle from Gabriel's. She sat at the same desk that used to house his friend Dash before they terminated his employment. Jonelle Williams was Gabriel's new partner, and they had worked only one case together before he'd made his temporary transfer to the Unsolved Unit. While Gabriel felt gladdened to hear both Jonelle and Lt. Ramirez discuss a future that placed him back in action with current crimes, he didn't mind the more sedate pace of working with unsolved crimes. Although no press and public pressure surrounded a cold case, their faded reports typed on extinct typewriters still cried out for justice.

Ramirez tapped the box on Gabriel's desk. "I checked this out for you from the property room. Get it back to them whenever you're finished."

"Thanks," Gabriel said. "I need to contact the detective —Brody, I think it was? He's probably touring the country in an RV these days, but I'm going to have to track him down."

Ramirez leaned against the gray textured wall separating Gabriel's cubicle from Jonelle's. "You won't be able to contact Brody."

"Why not?" Gabriel regarded his superior.

"He's dead."

Although stated bluntly, Gabriel sensed unmistakable sorrow behind the words, "He passed away a couple of months ago." Ramirez allowed a moment to pass. "Did I ever tell you about where I grew up?"

Gabriel shook his head.

The Lieutenant rolled a chair over. The squeaking wheels protested as he spun the chair around and took a seat. Ramirez normally made an effort to shield his private life from the office gossips. Rumor had it that he had sprung from a tough East Los Angeles neighborhood. Other than that, the rest of the man's past was the stuff of myth and legend.

Smoothing his shiny, short black hair, Ramirez then picked a piece of lint off his shirtfront. He seemed to be working up the bravery to open up. Gabriel felt strangely honored.

"I won't bore you with details, but my dad worked all over the city as a *jornalero,* a day laborer, and my mom cleaned house for some rich dude in Pasadena. My parents were *nunca están en casa.* Never at home. I made friends, you know? Not the good kind.

"I went to school, but getting street cred was more exciting. Anyhow, this cop, this detective—an older guy, would come around the high school as a community service thing. Giving back is what he called it. He'd hang out with us *chavos.*"

"That was Brody?" Gabriel asked.

"Yeah, and he took a special interest in me." Ramirez grew quiet, lost in thought. He then said, "Harris Brody got me interested in fighting crime instead of committing crime. He's the reason I wanted to become a cop. He was at my graduation from the Academy. When I made detective, he was the first one I called."

"I'm sorry for you that he's gone," Gabriel told him.

Ramirez nodded slowly. "The Nancy Lewicki case was the one that got away. It always weighed on Harris. When he died, I decided to reopen it. I'm giving it to you because I want you to help me honor a good man."

Gabriel surveyed the cardboard evidence box. "Did he tell you anything about the case?"

"No. Just that it frustrated the hell out of him. They

treated it as a missing person at first but then upped it to critical. A couple of homicide guys were assigned to put together a task force. All that effort went nowhere. They exhausted the few leads they had, and the case went cold. It never left Harris; that's all I know." Ramirez extracted a note from his pocket. "You call Margery. That's Harris's wife. Maybe he told her something he didn't tell me. Here's her phone number."

Ramirez handed the paper to Gabriel and pushed off the chair, causing it to roll across the floor with a noisy screech. "Make us look good, McRay."

Gabriel watched Ramirez head back into his office. His testy boss had confided in him. What a miracle. Gabriel had indeed risen in Ramirez's esteem.

Gabriel broke the seals off the evidence box and peered inside. Nothing much had been collected. Detectives and evidence room personnel continually evaluate the necessity of maintaining and storing items. They make every effort to return the personal property to the family. A few things still remained in the box, however, and these Gabriel proceeded to take out one by one.

The first item was a single label that must have been affixed to a piece of evidence. The date read 4/29/88. The URN or unique reference number appeared on one line, and the agency to which the evidence had been assigned was on another line, in this case, SIB, or Sheriff's Department Information Bureau. Below that was a description of the item: DIARY.

On the DISPO line, 'Release' had been circled. That meant they'd returned the diary to the family, Gabriel presumed. He made a note to ask Mrs. Lewicki for the diary.

Putting the label aside, Gabriel drew from the box a

receipt from a party store. The date of the receipt was 4/18/88. The ink on the original paper had faded and was illegible, but Brody had wisely made a decipherable copy. On the bottom of the copy, he'd written: *Store receipt found in Nancy's bureau. Brody, 5/04/88*

On the receipt copy, Gabriel read cups, napkins, plates, birthday banners, candy, party favors, and various themed decorations. The bill came to $74.25.

Someone lightly kicked Gabriel's chair, and he jumped. Turning to look behind, he saw Detective Rick Frasier, who laughed.

"Sorry, man. I didn't mean to scare you."

Gabriel held out a hand to Rick, who shook it. "With that face, you'd scare anybody."

It was a joke, of course. Rick had a handsome, boyish face. He had started as Gabriel's adversary back in the day— a cocky, yuppie detective with a penchant for wearing topsiders and preppie blazers. Gabriel used to tease Rick about his blow-dried hair. Time had passed, and along with it, their mutual dislike for each other.

"Glad to see you back in action," Rick told him.

"Glad to be back," Gabriel said.

"You okay?" Rick asked in a hushed tone. "I went and checked on the bastard. Personally, I'm glad you beat his face in."

Victor Archwood.

"He asks about you," Rick continued and kept his voice tactfully low. "He wants to see you. I told him where he could stick that request."

Gabriel did not comment, so Rick changed the subject and said in a more distinct voice, "Hey, congrats on you and Dr. Li tying the knot."

"Thanks."

"I wanted to ask you, has anyone offered to handle your bachelor party?"

Gabriel hadn't thought about that. He shook his head.

"Well, a couple of the guys and me were talking about it, and we want to give you a last hurrah. Only thing is…" Rick looked behind him and then leaned toward Gabriel. "Ramirez wants an invite. Dude, you know we can't party around him."

Gabriel didn't reply. He was too busy being surprised and pleased that Rick wanted to throw him a bachelor party. And did Rick say there were a "couple of guys" that wished to partake in the festivities as well? Maybe Gabriel's days of being a pariah were over. He found his voice and asked, "Ramirez wants to come?"

"Yeah, I mean, are you okay with that?"

Ever since Gabriel forayed into hell with Victor Archwood, Ramirez had displayed to Gabriel a much kinder side. Today's unbosoming of his history and relationship with Harris Brody testified to that. Come to think of it, Gabriel couldn't remember the last time he fell victim to Ramirez's usual abrasiveness.

Gabriel shrugged. "It's okay with me if he wants to come."

The preppie detective cocked his head and stepped away. "It's your funeral. I'll make some plans and keep you posted."

Gabriel turned back to the evidence box, still impressed that he might be popular enough to warrant a party. He would have taken pleasure in that factor if Rick hadn't blown the moment by bringing up Archwood. *He wants to see you.*

Gabriel cleared his throat and phoned Harris Brody's widow.

A woman answered, "Hello?"

"Hello, Ma'am, I'm Detective Sergeant Gabriel McRay with the Los Angeles County Sheriff's Department. I work with Lieutenant Miguel Ramirez. Is this Margery?"

"It is."

Gabriel voiced his regret over her husband's passing and then told Margery Brody why he was calling.

"I remember that case," she told him. "Harris always said that every detective has a case that stays with him, one that he will never forget. The Nancy Lewicki case was his. It always upset Harris that he couldn't find the culprit."

"Culprit?" Gabriel honed in on that. "Your husband never listed any offense in regards to Nancy."

"Oh, Harris always believed that something bad happened to her. Most everyone assumed she was dead. Whether it involved one suspect or two, he didn't know, but Harris was convinced of foul play. A popular, healthy girl just doesn't disappear into thin air. But she was never found. Nor anything belonging to her."

Gabriel confirmed that and then said, "I'm sorry to burden you with these questions. I know Detective Brody's passing was recent."

Margery paused, and Gabriel wondered if she were too grief-stricken to continue. To his surprise, Margery Brody continued in a clear and steady voice.

"Miguel told me he was going to reopen the case. It means a lot to me. I know it means a lot to the Lewicki family. Ask me anything you like, Detective McRay. Harris loved his work."

Gabriel decided to plow forward. "Did your husband

have any hunches about the case? Anything he discussed with you?"

"Well, like I said, Harris always felt that there had been foul play. Nancy had too much going for her and was an overall happy girl. He also believed that whomever Nancy had fallen victim to was known to her."

"What made him think that?"

"From what Harris could gather, Nancy Lewicki may have been young, but she wasn't foolish. Nor was she the type to frighten easily. Supposedly, Nancy talked with confidence and walked with confidence. She skirted around her parents' strict rules and came out smelling like a rose. Harris didn't think she was the type that would fall prey to a random killer."

Thinking of Victor Archwood, Gabriel said, "Some criminals are very savvy. And very brutal. They don't wait for someone to become vulnerable."

"That's true," Margery said. "But Harris was convinced that a girl of Nancy's type would not let her guard down unless it was with someone she trusted. Of course, he had no proof of that. He had nothing, and it bothered him long after he retired."

Gabriel thanked Mrs. Brody for her time and hung up the phone.

She walked with confidence.

Nancy had been fifteen years old with short blonde hair and a cheerleader's smile. A little sneaky, she knew she could undermine her parents, but remain the apple of their eye.

Gabriel reclined against the chair back and let a clearer picture of Nancy Lewicki take form in his mind, like a ghost slowly materializing.

Carmen viewed the amulets before her and tried once again to summon the lost girl. Laid out next to the photos of the missing females were talismans employed by generations of Carmen's family. An animal bone. A sprinkling of herbs. A tiny, yellowed scroll, which held a verse from the Quran. Muslim culture had influenced many early Africans, so it wasn't unusual to employ Islamic phrases.

A silver disc with the visage of the Ifa, the goddess of destiny and prophecy warmed Carmen's palm, and a crystal of quartz, for the purpose of enhancing spiritual energy, completed the collection.

Carmen's ancestors were brought to the United States on a slave ship from Senegal. Along with rice, corn, indigo, and tobacco to plant in the fertile soil of Louisiana, the slaves brought with them the talisman magic of their homeland.

Her ancestors believed in one God, but they cherished goddesses as well, which suited Carmen fine. The divine females, however, were conveniently laid to rest when the patriarchal religions took predominance in history.

Grandmere had passed the amulets down to Carmen's father, who then bestowed them to Carmen. Each generation handed the rituals and teachings to the opposite gender. Ideally, Carmen's son would next inherit what she called, the "tools of her trade."

At twenty-nine, Carmen considered herself a blossoming flower and had no wish to clip her petals to nurture a child. Although she rejected motherhood, Carmen didn't balk at the idea of becoming a wife.

She'd grown weary of the single life with its blissful, yet

meaningless post-coital morning-afters. Carmen wanted a partner, a hand-holder, a forever friend, but she couldn't afford to cater to a man who would resent the demands of her skyrocketing career. Carmen needed a man as driven as she.

Sighing, she dropped her eyes to the photos of the missing females. Why did nothing tug at her?

Carmen had carefully designed her home to boost the efficacy of her gift. Here, surrounded by the things she loved the most, her mind should have been able to open. The little West Hollywood home boasted as much of New Orleans as she could recreate. Carmen loved Mardi Gras masks, and they adorned her walls, from sequined and feathered eye-coverings to Venetian Jester heads that cost hundreds of dollars apiece. Scented candles filled the rooms with exotic aromas like frankincense and patchouli. Bookshelves of venerable wood contained tomes with such titles as "Dragon's Blood Potions" and "Sexuality and Oshun."

Carmen especially loved antiques because she enjoyed reading the imprint of the souls who once made use of the objects. Sensations would sometimes overwhelm her when she purchased a piece. Her living room boasted an old pub bar from a café in the St. Bernard Parish that had been destroyed by Hurricane Katrina. Carmen had salvaged the carved wooden bar and had it imported to Los Angeles. When her handyman reconstructed the piece, so many visitations and images flooded Carmen; she had to do a leveling prayer to ask the many spirits attached to the bar to retreat.

Visitors often commented that they felt transported to another world when they entered her home, and that's precisely the atmosphere Carmen wished to create.

What she couldn't recreate was the sultry air, the secretive wetness that hung about New Orleans like a sensual shawl. Carmen missed the south.

She closed her eyes and let her mind's eye roam the photos of the missing girls again. Nothing.

Disappointed, Carmen could not understand why she didn't get a bead on the voice she heard. Perhaps none of these cases involved the one reaching out to her. She decided upon a process of elimination. Carmen would personally contact the families of each girl and hope that at some point in the parley, her mentalist's bell might begin to ring.

CHAPTER FIVE

3/30/1988

I *went to May Company and saw the bitchenest mini that will look so perf over my black leggings. It's got this ruffled hem made with a thick lace. So adorable! Gramma says she'll buy it for me cuz she knows I'm saving for my synth. She's so totally awesome. Abby wants to come over to do our hair before the party, but there has to be a party first. And no lie, I don't know if I want her to come over because last time she broke my blow dryer and used all my Dippity Do. As if I'd want to get ready with her again!"*

Gabriel had returned to the Lewicki's. He held Nancy's diary, opened to an entry made two weeks before she went missing.

"That would be Abby Underwood," Pauline said to Gabriel. She sat next to Gabriel on the couch with a stack of yearbooks on her lap. A rare smile framed her face as she gazed at the diary passage. "She was one of Nancy's good friends. And Gramma would be my mother. She and Nancy were close." The smile slowly faded from her face. "This shattered my mom. The strain wore her down. She..."

Pauline could not continue. Gabriel cut her a break by asking a question.

"Did Abby go to the concert with Nancy that Sunday night?"

"No, I don't think so." Pauline flipped through a glossy yearbook. "I'll find Abby's picture for you."

She halted on a page of black and white thumbnail photos and pointed to one girl. Gabriel could see why Abby had used up all of Nancy's styling gel. Abby's dark hair may have only been shoulder-length, but she had teased her long bangs high off the top of her forehead. The girl looked like she could saw wood with that starchy hair.

"Do you know if Abby is still in town? Do you keep in touch?"

"I wouldn't know. For a while, people kept in touch. All of Nancy's old friends called. She had lots of girlfriends. They would send me cards on her birthday, which I appreciated. And then, by and by, the friends dropped off. It's a disturbing thing for people to deal with, I suppose. No one likes being near a tragedy. Life goes on, Detective McRay."

But it didn't for you, Gabriel thought pensively. Aloud, he said, "Please call me Gabriel."

Nancy's mother offered him a grateful smile. "You can keep the diary for as long as you need it. I do want it back, of course."

He nodded. "Is there anything inside it that stands out to you? Any indication of something Nancy might have feared?"

"No," Pauline said with some nostalgia. "Just the trials and tribulations of a happy-go-lucky teenager."

"How about the mention of anything out of the ordinary? A new person at school, for instance. A new friend?"

"No."

"A chance encounter with a stranger? Someone who showed interest in her?"

Pauline Lewicki shook her head. "If Nancy did run into trouble with someone, then it must have been a stranger. One of the detectives, back when Nancy disappeared, mentioned a serial rapist roaming the city at the time."

Pauline's hands twisted together at that, but her tone was brave. She'd gone through this before.

"I'll check into that possibility," Gabriel promised. "In the meantime, I'm going to read Nancy's diary cover to cover. Sometimes, what passes for normal trials and tribulations masks a deeper issue."

A man with bristly-short gray hair entered the room. He might have been muscular and tall once, but now his body bent over like a crowbar. Despite the cowed posture, Gabriel felt the man couldn't be much older than his wife.

"This is Len. Nancy's father."

"Nice to meet you, sir." Gabriel stood and shook the man's hand. Len's grip was firm at first but fell apart under Gabriel's steady hand. Len Lewicki bade Gabriel sit down.

"Detective McRay and I have been going through Nancy's diary," his wife told him.

Nancy's father scratched at a five-o-clock shadow. "What do you hope to find?"

"Anything." Gabriel nodded to the picture of the family posed under the Christmas tree. "You mentioned having a son. I'm assuming that's him?"

"Yes, our son, Paul. He's younger than Nancy by four years. You'll meet him at some point." Pauline regarded the photo tenderly. "Paul grew up under the shadow of all this. We tried to lead a normal life, but you see, we continued to wait for Nancy. This was not good for our boy."

"Pauline," Len admonished her lightly.

"Well, it wasn't easy for Paul."

"I didn't read much about your son in the report," Gabriel said. "Did Detective Brody interview him?"

"He was only eleven years old."

Eleven years old, Gabriel reflected, *but not a baby*. The boy could have carried key memories with him into manhood. "I'd like to talk with him," he told the Lewickis.

Pauline exchanged a tense glance with her husband.

When Len spoke, he appeared to choose his words carefully. "Nancy's disappearance is a sore subject for Paul. He and his sister were close, and we, Pauline and I... Well, our little family sort of fell apart. Paul eventually married, but –"

"We have two adorable grandsons," Pauline interjected.

"What about Paul's wife?" Gabriel asked.

"They're divorced."

Gabriel nodded his understanding. "I see. Still, maybe your son remembers something pertinent from around the time Nancy disappeared."

"He doesn't." Pauline closed the yearbook and held it to her breast. "We nearly drove Paul insane, badgering him. Did Nancy say anything to you? Did you see anything? Hear anything? Anything at all? I think he was tempted to make something up, just to shut us up. We were grasping at straws, you understand. It was a lot of pressure for a boy to deal with, along with his private grief."

"I understand." Gabriel decided to leave the matter alone

46

—for now. He regarded Nancy's father. "What about you? Did Nancy confide anything important to you that you can remember?"

"Nancy and I didn't share the kind of intimate talk she did with her mom. But I do know one thing. Nancy had lots of girlfriends. You ought to talk to them."

"All of her friends appear to have been interviewed." Gabriel pulled out his notepad. "Nancy was planning a party for a friend. For whom?"

"Jenna Goldman," Mrs. Lewicki said. "Jenna was Nancy's best friend. Oh! I think it was her—the friend she went to the concert with."

Gabriel made a note of it. "When was she having the party? The date?"

Nancy's mother shrugged. "I'm not sure of the exact date. Nancy didn't invite us. Does it matter?"

"Everything matters. I want to get a clear picture of everything going on in Nancy's life at the time of her disappearance. That way, I'll have the birds-eye view I need to catch any inconsistencies."

"And what about that—that person who terrorized the neighborhood?" Mrs. Lewicki hugged Nancy's yearbook more tightly.

Gabriel saw the dread in Pauline's eyes. *She doesn't want to say the word "rapist."*

"I promise you I will look into it," he told her. "So, when do you think the party was planned for? Take a guess. The following weekend? The following month?"

"About a week from the time she went missing. That's another reason why I know she didn't run away, Detective. I remember Nancy being excited and nervous. She said she had a lot to do because she wanted the party to be perfect. That was Nancy. She was a planner and a good one."

"Nancy had a lot to do," Gabriel repeated, more to himself. "For a party. Where was it to take place?"

Calamigos Ranch flashed briefly in his mind. Ming planned on dragging his ass there tonight to tour it as a possible wedding venue. "Was Nancy scoping out various places?" Gabriel shrugged. "Restaurants, maybe? A particular salon or room to rent that she might have visited?"

A laugh erupted from Mrs. Lewicki. "You don't have children, do you, Detective? On her chore allowance, Nancy couldn't exactly afford to rent a hall." The chortle ended in a bleak grin. "Nancy was going to have the party at Jenna's house."

Something snagged on Gabriel's memory, but when he threw a mental spotlight on it, the recollection darted away like a mouse. Shaking it off, he made a note to hunt down Jenna Goldman.

Len walked Gabriel to the front door. The phone rang, and Pauline went to answer the call.

"I'll keep you posted," Gabriel promised and crossed the threshold into the sunlight. As the front door closed behind him, Gabriel heard Pauline say to the caller, "Carmen, who?"

A few hours later, Carmen Jenette sat in the Lewicki's living room. The husband Len scrutinized her with squinty eyes, apparently not buying what Carmen was selling. The wife's eyes, however, held out hope. Carmen inclined her body more toward Pauline.

Len's eyes didn't leave her. "How did you find us?" he asked.

"I work with local police agencies." Carmen offered a sympathetic smile.

Donovan would go berserk if a victim's family filed a harassment complaint with his office because he referred a psychic to them. Better to keep his name out of it. So far, Carmen had visited or spoken with nine of the twenty-seven missing girls' families and had scored zero.

"We're not paying you," Len Lewicki told her. "If that's what you're looking for."

"Oh, no, sir." Carmen sat up straighter. "I don't charge for my help. Not on cases such as this."

"How do you make your money then?"

"Len…" Mrs. Lewicki brokered a contrite smile. "Miss Jenette is a famous medium."

"I have a very select clientele who seek out my services on everyday matters," Carmen told Len. "That's how I make money, although the television deal is very nice."

She heard, in her grandmother's distant Creole, "*Sispann.*" Stop. Truth is humble, *Grandmere* said to Carmen. If you are a seer, you will be humbled under the banner of truth. Carmen, however, felt anything but humbled.

"A select clientele?" Len gave her a dubious look.

"Some names you would recognize. Other names that you wouldn't. Either way, I'm sure you can understand that these people would rather not publicize their meetings with me. If I were to work with you, I would, of course, consider it pro bono."

Carmen tossed her mane of brown curls over her shoulder and eyed the front door. She had made a mistake. Nothing in the condominium ignited the flame under her psychic abilities. Without another word, she rose from her seat on the couch and regarded the older couple. Time to move on.

"I'm terribly sorry. I believe I've wasted your time."

"You're not going, are you?" Pauline asked.

"I'm afraid I need to continue my search. Unfortunately, I'm not getting any information about your daughter. I do apologize." Carmen headed for the front door. Pauline followed her and wrung her hands.

"Oh, but you can't leave. We'd welcome your help, wouldn't we, Len?"

Len said nothing. Carmen read the words, *crackpot, charlatan,* and *loony tunes* coming off his gaze. Pauline, however, trailed Carmen and implored her to help them find Nancy. Although Carmen empathized with the Lewickis, she needed to find the true source of the call that tugged at her.

To Carmen's surprise, Pauline blocked her path. "You said you worked with police agencies. Perhaps you know the detective working Nancy's case, Sergeant Gabriel McRay. He's a good man, I can tell. Wait, I'll get his card, and you can call him."

Unseen hands gripped Carmen's shoulders, causing her to pause. She glanced at the tops of her tingling hands. *Something here,* she thought.

Carmen watched Pauline bustle about the kitchen, rifle through a pile of papers, and curse her forgetfulness. She then found the card in plain view, leaning against a landline telephone. Carmen softened, touched by the woman's heartrending eagerness.

"I've got it!" Pauline proudly held up the business card.

Something here… Carmen glided so swiftly toward Pauline the older woman took a startled step backward. Taking the business card from Nancy's mother, Carmen read the lettering on it. Once again, pins and needles pricked her flesh. "Yes," Carmen murmured. "I do believe I will contact Detective Gabriel McRay."

———

Calamigos Ranch lay in the middle of the diminutive Malibu wine-growing region of the Santa Monica Mountains, where entrepreneurs had cleared the hills of chaparral to make room for grapevines. Elegant tasting rooms and restaurants with reservation wait-lists now competed for space against the canyon's hippie enclaves.

The Santa Monica Conservancy continued to purchase land in the mountains surrounding the sprawling metropolis of Los Angeles to preserve open space. Gabriel, who found solace in the hills, had joined the Sheriff's Department because the LASD maintained substations within the parkland. Ridged against the Pacific coastline, the Santa Monica Mountains had housed and fed the Chumash Indians, and then later abdicated its terrain to the Hollywood film industry. Remnants of both cultures remained in its oak-studded hills, from arrowheads to abandoned movie sets. Leave it to Ming to choose a site like Calamigos Ranch. She knew the location would appeal to Gabriel and hopefully arouse his interest in planning their wedding. He had to give Ming credit. It was a good strategy.

"This is our Birchwood Room with a maximum capacity of 140 guests." The venue's saleslady was a trim twenty-something. She wore a pencil skirt with a matching jacket over designer pumps. Her flawless makeup and tidy hair bun reminded Gabriel of a flight attendant from the nine-teen-sixties.

"As you can see, it's very intimate here with the waterfall and the weeping willows. They are over one-hundred years old."

"I think we'll need something bigger," Ming commented, and Gabriel gaped at his fiancée in astonishment. How many people did she plan to invite?

"Then, you've got to see our Redwood Room." The saleslady gestured for the couple to follow her, as she expertly navigated a narrow rock path in her high heels. "That's the salon where the lights drip from the trees at night. It's simply magical."

Ming trailed the woman, but Gabriel paused to gaze at the row of willow trees and the gentle bowing of their branches in the evening breeze.

"Gabriel?"

He pulled his eyes away to see Ming standing on the path, waiting for him. Leaving the dancing arms of the willows, Gabriel joined his fiancée.

"I like the bigger salon because those lights will make a spectacular entrance," Ming told Gabriel after the tour of the facilities.

The couple sat in matching Adirondack chairs. Flames from a private fire pit warmed them against the coastal breeze. The Malibu Café was on the grounds of the Ranch, and patrons could eat outside on a wide expanse of lawn that boasted fire pits and pool tables lit by crystal chande-liers hanging from trees. Nearby, ducks swam in a lake.

Ming looked longingly through the capering flames toward the rental salons beyond.

"That's assuming it's a night wedding," Gabriel told her. His pager went off, and he called his work. After listening to a message, Gabriel shook his head.

"What is it?" Ming asked.

Tucking his phone away, Gabriel muttered, "The Lewickis want me to work with a psychic. They can't be serious."

"Those poor people." Ming picked up a poker and gave the burning wood a nudge. "They're so desperate, Gabe. What are you going to tell them?"

"If it makes Len and Pauline feel better to consult a fortuneteller, that's their business. I'll have nothing to do with it."

The fire jumped with new life. Ming set aside the poker and handed Gabriel a brochure. "Here, have a look at the catering menu."

Gabriel took the brochure from Ming's hand. "If psychics could find a missing person or even a lost sock, don't you think everyone would use their services?"

"Well, it might help the Lewickis from an emotional standpoint."

"And that's fine with me." He shook the flyer open and tried to read the lettering in the firelight, only he felt personally affronted by the Lewickis and had a difficult time concentrating on the brochure. Why did they hire a psychic? Gabriel had only recently begun his investigation. Nancy's parents should at least allow him to make some progress. And what could a circus performer do except sully the works?

At that moment, the evening breeze kicked the flames,

sending fireworks of sparks into the air. Ming marveled at the light show. Gabriel's eyes caught a willow tree standing near the edge of the vast lawn that appeared to wave at him through the blurry heat rising from the fire pit.

A waiter came over bearing two heaping plates, which he set down before them.

"Get this," Gabriel said as he dragged his eyes from the willow tree. He unfolded his napkin and revealed the cutlery ensconced within. "Some of the guys want to throw me a bachelor party."

Ming spread a napkin over her lap. "Wonderful! Who's throwing it?"

"Rick."

"Rick Frasier?" She grimaced as she brought her plate closer. "Please tell me you're not going to do the whole stripper thing. That's so frat house."

"Knowing Rick, it will probably involve a country club or a fashion show."

Ming cut into her smoked tri-tip. "True. He's such a face-man. But it's nice that he wants to celebrate you. Doesn't that make you feel good?"

Gabriel nodded and saw Ming grinning at him through the flying sparks. As he reached for his meal, the branches of the weeping willow made whispering sounds that, strangely, Gabriel could hear above the crackling of the flames.

CHAPTER SIX

I nterview with Jenna Goldman, May 7, 1988.

Miss Goldman states that she had been Nancy's friend since the 2nd grade, and they were very close. Miss Goldman insists that Nancy would not have run away because they had plans to start a band. They recorded music together. Nancy had a tape recorder (found in the bedroom, empty of tapes). Jenna mentioned that Nancy was into music and carried a Walkman (not found) everywhere she went.

Gabriel paused and set aside the typed sheets of Brody's interviews. He sat in his home office and wrote a reminder note to ask Mrs. Lewicki if Nancy walked or hiked wearing her Walkman. The predecessor to the iPod, the Walkman, when first introduced with its electronic skip protection, lightweight headphones, and "turbo bass," was ground-breaking in that people could listen to their favorite tunes anywhere they went without carrying a boom box.

If Nancy had been prone to jogging or walking alone wearing her earphones, it was feasible that someone could have crept up on her. Gabriel needed to know where Nancy liked to hike if indeed she did.

Nancy Lewicki, captured in the aged Polaroid, viewed him from the bookshelf with secrets secured in her smile. Gabriel regarded her as well and reflected how different Nancy's world was compared to that of a modern teenager.

Countless digital platforms made themselves available for a social exhibitionist to display his face, his wants, needs, loves, likes, and commentary. Today, Gabriel would have a reliable timetable of Nancy's personal life online. Not only that, but CCTV cameras, installed almost everywhere nowadays, provided readily available surveillance videos. Cell phones could be tracked. He could check the recent activity of bank and credit card accounts. Gabriel would have an avalanche of information if he were investigating a modern-day teenager.

All he had to assist him in Nancy's case was a hand-written diary.

Pulling his gaze away from the Polaroid, Gabriel wrote on his notepad; *ask Pauline if she has Nancy's cassette tapes.*

A yawn escaped him, and Gabriel covered his mouth with his hand. A mockingbird called outside the window, mimicking his feathered friends. Gabriel leaned back in his chair and listened to the birdcalls. The ocean breeze caused the window shade to sigh against the sill, and Gabriel's eyes began to close.

A stream ran in his mind. He heard the sound of trickling water and the crunch of footfalls over stones and dirt. Gabriel walked a mountain path, bordered by oak trees, and carpeted in miner's lettuce. His hand skimmed over gray-green sage and he could smell the aromatic brush. The sun felt warm on his back. A drop of water hit his cheek, and

Gabriel looked up to see gray clouds collecting in the sky. All at once, he tripped, fell in the dirt, and came nose-to-nose with a human skull. Instead of a skeletal grin, the two rows of teeth turned downwards into a toothy frown.

The phone rang, a persistent bleating. Gabriel awoke to feel his heart bumping against his chest. On his lap, rested the case file. Stamped in his mind was the footprint of a nightmare. From across the room, Nancy Lewicki looked at him from a three-inch square. Gabriel answered the phone.

"Gabe," Ming said on the line.

"Hey." He tried to compose himself. "Yes. The answer is yes. I went to the market and picked up the food for tonight."

"That's not why I'm calling. I want you to turn on the TV."

Still a little breathless, Gabriel trekked into his living room and switched on the flat screen. "Where are you?"

"In the hospital cafeteria," Ming answered, and Gabriel caught amusement in her voice. "Guess what show the staff tunes into every day? Go to channel four."

Gabriel flipped through the daily diet of talk shows, soap operas, and drug commercials. On channel four, a stunning-looking woman in her late twenties spoke directly to the camera. Her dark hair fell in tight curls around a heart shaped face in which two green eyes regarded the world with a near arrogant posture. Gabriel could see more chocolate than cream in the woman's café-au-lait skin and guessed some African ancestry figured somewhere in her genealogy.

The Psychic to the Stars said, "Nancy Lewicki disappeared over thirty years ago, and now her heartbroken parents have asked for my help. What happened to Nancy?

Join me on this important journey as I work with investigators to find the lost Lewicki girl. Already, I have sensed valuable information relating to the case, which I am sharing with law enforcement officials. If any of you have knowledge concerning Nancy Lewicki's whereabouts, please call the hotline number you see at the bottom of your screen. And of course, your prayers and positive thoughts are welcome. Together, we will give Pauline and Leonard Lewicki the closure so long denied to them."

Gabriel stared at the woman on television. "So much for my low-key case," he said.

"Don't have a fit," Ming warned him. "You've got to be on your best behavior tonight."

Gabriel eyed the phone in annoyance. Did Ming think he was that inept? *No, she just knows you well.*

"Don't worry about me." He hung up and then frowned at the regaling visage of Carmen Jenette. What "valuable" information did the psychic have? The woman's brazenness astounded him.

Don't have a fit, Gabriel reminded himself as his finger jammed the "off" button on the remote control.

Ming's father held out his hand to his future son-in-law.

Gabriel stood in entryway of Ming's Los Feliz house like an awkward teenager. He gripped a bouquet in one hand and a bursting bag of groceries in the other. He placed the bag on the tiled floor, where it promptly fell over and spilled its contents. Ignoring the spillage, Gabriel shook the hand of Ming's father. He aimed to make a good impression.

"Nice to meet you, sir."

Dr. Li gave him a brisk nod and viewed the mess on the floor, which Ming rushed to remedy.

"I'll put these in the kitchen." She hurriedly replaced the items and hoisted the bag upwards. "Wow, this is heavy. Gabriel is so thorough when it comes to cooking. Gabe, this is my mom, Elena. I mean, Mrs. Li."

Ming tossed Gabriel a look that said, "you're-on-your-own" and then escaped into the kitchen.

"Elena is fine." Ming's mother gave Gabriel a grateful smile as she took the gladiolas from him. "How nice. Ming must have told you these are my favorite flowers."

He nodded.

"I'm so happy to meet you, Gabriel." Elena embellished his name with a pleasant hint of her Hispanic accent. "Tom and I have heard so much about you."

Mrs. Li had full lips like Ming's and brown eyes that blazed when she smiled. Her hair was thicker than her daughter's and her skin browner. She stood at least a foot shorter than Ming but shared her daughter's beauty. Elena did not seem to fit with her trim and dapper husband. While she exuded warmth, the senior Dr. Li gave off drafts of cold air, at least to Gabriel.

Ming had crowed so prodigiously to her parents about Gabriel's cooking that his future in-laws requested he prepare a meal for them. As if Ming's exalting prelude about his culinary skills wasn't enough to intimidate Gabriel, she insisted they eat at her house. Gabriel rarely cooked in Ming's kitchen and worried he might bungle the job.

He'd chosen pork tenderloin *en croute* accompanied by sautéed green kale for tonight's menu. The three Li's followed Gabriel into the kitchen, where he unpacked the grocery bag. He didn't relish the idea of people ogling him while he cooked, but after a few minutes, Ming and her mother gravitated into the adjoining dining room to talk. The two sat side by side and spoke in earnest and hushed tones, at times giggling and at other times pausing to regard each other wistfully. Mother and daughter appeared to be healing some shared wound, and Gabriel had the good sense not to interrupt their conversation.

Unfortunately, their departure left him alone with Ming's father, who sat on a barstool in the kitchen and studied Gabriel as if he were an unusual zoological exhibit.

Dr. Tom Li was a retired endocrinologist. Gabriel was aware that he had raised his only child to excel at everything from violin lessons to a brag-worthy career. Always the dutiful daughter, Ming had obliged. The fact that Ming had developed little-to-no social skills, barely had any friends, and appeared awkward and uncomfortable around her own father didn't seem to faze the senior Dr. Li at all.

"Can we help you with anything?" Ming's mother called to Gabriel from the dining room. Ming, too, leaned over to peer through the open doorway. She appeared content.

"No, thanks," Gabriel answered. "I've got it under control."

But he didn't. Ming's top-of-the-line appliances vexed him. The oven sported more digital controls than the space shuttle. Besides that, Gabriel couldn't shake his irritation with the famous medium. Carmen Jenette had essentially thrown his case into the limelight, and Gabriel detested public attention.

Floundering about the kitchen, wishing he could be anywhere else, Gabriel began to receive the heat treatment from his fiancée's father.

"Did you ever go to college?" Dr. Li asked. "What did

you study? What year did you join the police academy? How old are you again?"

Gabriel felt like a suspect in an interrogation room. Don't-throw-a-fit, he silently repeated, and it became a mantra. He chopped mushrooms to keep his hands busy and constructed his answers in a self-promotional context in order to present the Best of Gabriel McRay. The questions rattled him, and he couldn't concentrate on the meal prep. Pausing over thawed sheets of puffed pastry, Gabriel asked himself, *what are these for?*

Ming's mother appeared at the kitchen doorway. "You should help your future husband." She directed the statement to Ming but lay her gaze on the struggling, waffling chap dicing kale and trying not to cut his hand. Mrs. Li must have overheard her spouse's rapid-fire questions and decided to rescue Gabriel.

"If I help, we won't be able to eat." Ming walked over and wrapped her arms around Gabriel's waist. "I can't cook anything edible."

"A wife should learn how to prepare meals." Her mother gently chided.

"In what century?" Ming asked.

The senior Dr. Li spoke up then. "The new way is for the wife to earn money, I suppose?"

Now it comes, Gabriel thought. The Fit. He seasoned the tenderloins with a show of force and glanced over his shoulder at Ming.

Ming caught her lover's glower. "Excuse me," she said to her father. "Both of us work, but I do not cook. I buy my meals from restaurants. Since Gabe's cooking puts most restaurants to shame, call me a lucky lady."

She glared at her father, daring him to comment. He did not.

Changing the subject, Gabriel addressed Mrs. Li as he carefully enveloped the meat in the pastry. "Ming tells me you are originally from Jalisco."

"Yes." Ming's mother said. "I still have family there, but I–we haven't seen them in a long time."

"I've never met them." Ming kept defiant eyes on her father.

Gabriel felt the underlying tension building amid the Li family. Around his waist, Ming's arms tightened to the point of discomfort. Gently freeing himself from her grasp, Gabriel said, "Someday, I'll have to make you my Jalisco specialty: *birria*. Of course, I don't have an underground oven, but I can get goat meat to be mighty tender just the same. You ask your daughter."

"Goat meat?" Dr. Li asked from his seat.

"Would anyone like some wine?" Ming went over to a built-in wine cooler and plucked a bottle. She pulled four glasses from a shelf.

Gabriel continued his dialogue with Mrs. Li as he ladled the mushroom stuffing onto the tenderloins. "You'll have to try my version to see if it can rival your own."

Ming's mother smiled apologetically. "Oh, I don't cook Mexican food. It bothers Tom's stomach."

The room went quiet. Gabriel knew that Mrs. Li suppressed her Mexican heritage. Her Chinese husband preferred it that way, which made no sense to Gabriel. After all, the man married a Latina.

Gabriel also knew that as an incoming relative, he should mind his own business and play neither peacemaker nor provoker. Still, he couldn't help himself.

Placing the tenderloins in the oven, he said, "What a pity. Mexican food is our favorite, and I cook it all the time. In fact, Ming and I thought the beaches of the Yucatan would be a great place for a honeymoon."

Ming swiveled her head in his direction. They'd never discussed their honeymoon, not once. Gabriel winked at her. True, he made a jab at Ming's father, but only because Tom Li played the Inquisitor General. Gabriel used to manage tough situations with his fists. He found making mental warfare a more civilized way to fight.

The tactic worked. The older man appeared to respect Gabriel's effort and refrained from further cross-examination. Feeling a mollifying sense of triumph, Gabriel concentrated on sautéing the kale.

Carmen Jenette used a terrycloth hand towel to wipe the perspiration from her brow. Her footfalls pounded on the moving belt of the treadmill and coalesced with the general din of the fitness center. Off and on the crash of the metal weight bars meeting support struts pierced the ongoing white noise of the gym.

Regular workouts not only moved Carmen's *chi*, her energy, but also helped maintain her excellent figure. A sucker for southern delicacies like shrimp *etouffee* and bread pudding, Carmen needed to exercise to fend off the extra pounds. She had a photo shoot coming up in a couple of weeks for a spread in a self-help magazine and wanted to drop a pound or two.

Carmen adhered to a strict daily regimen and was a familiar face around the gym. She often took classes.

Slowing from a brisk run, Carmen diminished her speed to a leisurely walk and cooled down. She then made her usual tour through the weight machines.

With endorphins cruising happily through her body, Carmen went to the locker room to retrieve her purse. She felt ebullient from her exercise and the securement of her participation in the hunt for the Lewicki girl. Aiding in a police investigation would add an exciting element to her show. She figured millions of viewers from the crime series demographic would tune in, and her ratings would soar.

In the lobby, two women sharing a purple-colored smoothie stood near a sign that advertised an upcoming Halloween party. They followed Carmen with wide eyes.

"Isn't she…?"

"I think she is."

Carmen smiled and sashayed out the door, exuding vitality in her wake.

Outside, the air was crisp with November's approach. A new moon kept the sky indigo and allowed the stars to shine brightly. Carmen walked fast through the parking lot with her keys at ready in her hand. West Hollywood evoked images of trendy cafes and clubbing, but as with any big city, an element of danger existed. A man sporting a long gray braid exited the gym along with Carmen, the sixty-going-on-twenty type toting a Coach leather gym bag and yakking on his iPhone to somebody named Tony. He ambled toward a red Maserati, which Carmen noticed, hogged two spaces. She pointed the key fob at her Audi and heard the reassuring warble as the door unlocked. Gripping the door handle, Carmen made to open the door when

Why is the handle missing?

The question popped uninvited into her head, reminding

Carmen of her first encounter with the one who sent the sixth sense SOS. Fingers of ice did an arpeggio along Carmen's spine. The tops of her hands tingled.

Light from the metal-halide lamps reflected against the Audi's tinted windows and sequestered the car's interior, making it black. Carmen saw her disquieted face cast against the pitch.

A scream of burning rubber startled her, and Carmen swerved her head to see the Maserati roar out of the lot. The Italian-made torpedo blasted down the street and left a denuded silence in its wake.

At the end of the row of cars, half masked in shadows, stood a man; or what Carmen assumed was a man. His head appeared misshapen, but that might have been a trick of the light. Although she couldn't see the man's eyes, Carmen sensed him watching her. A moment passed, and he walked out of view.

Carmen's insides felt inexplicably loose, gelatinous. Something was off-kilter in the parking lot. Slowly unfurling clammy fingers from the lever, Carmen backed toward the gym's entrance and kept her eyes trained on the parked cars. Above her head, moths plinked against the lamps, their hectic enterprise fraught with futility. *Directionless and frantic,* Carmen thought, *one will never capture the light.*

She turned and fled into the gym. Her heightened senses rebelled against the onslaught of normal activity, and the musty smell of chlorine and sweat burned her nostrils. Human conversation and clanging machinery assaulted her ears.

Carmen fought the urge to hide and, instead, approached the front desk receptionist. "Do you have a security guard?"

"We do, Miss Jenette." The receptionist was dressed like

a man but wore the makeup of a diva. "Would you like someone to accompany you to your car?" He picked up the phone ahead of her reply.

"Yes," Carmen said, and then held up her finger. "Wait. Do you have cameras outside?"

The man nodded and his glamourized face glowed. "I have to tell you; I *love* your show."

Unable to travel on her usual ego trip, palsied by an unnamed panic, Carmen asked, "Could I view the video?"

———

Seconds later, Carmen was upstairs with the security guard observing the parking lot on closed-circuit television.

"There's my car," she said, pointing. "The Audi."

"What are we looking for?" the guard asked. Unlike the receptionist, this one was every bit meat-eating American male with steroid-enhanced muscles and a dimpled chin set in a strong, masculine jaw.

"I don't know," Carmen told him. "I had a terrible feeling."

"I'd be happy to walk you down, Miss Jenette, and get you safely into your car."

"Not yet. I want to watch the parking lot for a couple of minutes."

"Did you see someone suspicious-looking?" He tried to adjust the angle of the camera lens remotely on a computer.

"There was a man, but he walked away."

"We get a lot of transients. They're mostly harmless, but every now and then a druggie breaks into a car to steal something. Is there any shattered glass around your car?"

Carmen wished the man would shut up. She'd been dealt

a hand from a deck of vibes and needed quiet to play them. At that moment, on the video monitor, Carmen saw the rear door of her car swing open.

"Wow," the security guard said, surprised. "Someone's in your car. Are they supposed to be there?"

Carmen pursed her lips together, and the guard quickly picked up the phone to call 911. As Carmen stared at the live feed, the figure emerged from her Audi. A dark hoodie covered the intruder's head. Dark pants. Gloves. A man? He'd hid in the backseat of her car. Why? Frigid fingers plucked at Carmen's spine.

While the guard spoke with a police dispatcher, Carmen watched the figure lope out of sight.

CHAPTER SEVEN

Gabriel sat in his cubicle in Commerce with a phone to his ear. The city lay east of downtown next to its equally industrial brother, Vernon. Mostly made up of warehouse buildings and train tracks, Commerce housed the homicide bureau of the Sheriff's Department.

When his call ended with Jenna Goldman's father, Gabriel hung up the phone and tapped impatient fingers on his desk. Jenna's dad said that the girl was now Jenna Klein, a married mother of three. She lived in San Diego but was currently in Europe on vacation. Gabriel would have to wait until she returned to talk to her. Never one to wait, Gabriel sent Jenna Goldman Klein an email and hoped the woman would reply.

Adding to Gabriel's frustration was the fact that Pauline Lewicki told him none of Nancy's cassette tapes survived. They'd stored the recordings, along with the tape player, in the garage of their previous house. A water pipe had burst in 1993, soaked the storage box, and destroyed its contents.

"What's happening with the Lewicki case? Anything?"

Gabriel looked up to see his Lieutenant hovering above him. With a shake of his head, Gabriel replied, "I guess you didn't hear the news. A psychic is on board."

"A psychic? You mean like a ghost whisperer?" Ramirez seemed fascinated.

"I have no idea," Gabriel answered, and then waited for the expectant wisecrack to spout from Ramirez's mouth. When, to Gabriel's surprise, none came, he said, "Whatever she is, I'm not going to allow her to mention me or my progress on her show."

The Lieutenant shrugged. "A little publicity can't hurt after all these years. Maybe a new lead will shake loose."

"Maybe. I'm about to check ViCap for a serial rapist who ran amok in the valley at the time Nancy went missing. Maybe that'll shake something loose."

"Good." Ramirez nodded a little too vehemently. "You wanna catch some lunch?"

"Sure." Gabriel glanced at his wristwatch. Only ten o'clock. "A little later?"

Ramirez didn't answer him. He stood by, loitering, letting his eyes travel over Gabriel's desk, the corners of the cubicle—anywhere but on Gabriel.

Observing the other man's visible affliction, Gabriel asked, "What's up?"

Ramirez crossed his compact, muscular arms and blurted, "Am I invited to your wedding?"

From a distance, another voice asked meekly, "How about me? Are you inviting people from work?"

Gabriel turned to see Jonelle Williams sticking her head around the corner of his cubicle. He'd never seen the tender stamp of vulnerability on that woman's normally stoic features, but there it was, plain as day.

Jonelle was a tough, big-boned lady who didn't take flack from anyone. She'd earned her self-possessed stripes from time spent both as a homicide investigator and as a single mother trying to raise a teenage boy in a formidable city. Jonelle didn't talk about her son's father, only to say that she hoped her boy wouldn't turn out like him. Now, this stalwart woman was asking Gabriel if she would make his guest list.

"Of course, you're both invited." Gabriel scratched his skull in a sudden bout of angst. "Ming and I will send invitations out to all the guests, just as soon as we choose them. The invitations, I mean."

Jonelle, satisfied with his answer, disappeared behind the partition separating her desk from Gabriel's. Ramirez nodded and headed in the direction of his office.

How odd, Gabriel mused as he watched the other man's departure. Did these two suffer from a bankrupt social life? Most likely, Ramirez did, but Jonelle? Reputedly, she enjoyed a wide circle of friends, so why did she feel the need to attend Gabriel's wedding?

For many years, Gabriel had worn the scarlet letter of "pariah" at the bureau, and he had done little to change his co-workers' opinion of him. His black sheep status seemed to have changed, though. Pleased by that possibility, Gabriel turned his attention to the ViCAP database.

The Violent Criminal Apprehension Program served to link homicides, sexual assaults, missing persons, and unidentified human remains. Primarily an FBI maintained database, over five thousand law enforcement agencies spanning the country participated in ViCAP. Upon its creation in 1985, only FBI personnel could access the program. When Nancy went missing, extrinsic agencies were required to submit their case information to Quantico through the mail. It was an arduous process.

Now ViCAP Web could be accessed through an online portal, which made it easy for other agencies to compare, update, and add new information. Gabriel logged on to ViCAP to input the details of Nancy's disappearance. He searched the database for similar cases and reviewed separate historical cases. He soon confirmed what Harris Brody had researched.

A series of rapes did occur in the valley around the time of Nancy's disappearance. A wormy-looking suspect named Dale Meyerlink had eventually been caught and convicted. The authorities questioned Meyerlink about Nancy, but he denied any involvement. While Brody referenced Meyerlink in the report and suggested that poor Nancy might have crossed paths with the man, no evidence existed to substantiate that claim.

Like Brody before him, Gabriel had his doubts. No one ever accused Meyerlink of murder. Apparently, he was a creep, but not a killer. A whiny, undersized man by all accounts, Meyerink got his jollies by breaking into houses in the dead of night and pointing a pistol in the faces of the sleepy residents. He would then bind the husbands and rape the wives. The press labeled him "The Silent Stalker" because his attacks were swift and quiet. Meyerlink had never abducted anyone. Nor had he ever molested or attacked any minors asleep in the home. He left his victims traumatized but alive.

Gabriel read that after Meyerlink's arrest, he told detectives that he avoided houses with dogs and kept to neighborhoods that abutted the Ventura Freeway. In particular, he broke into homes on street corners for quick getaway access. Unfortunately, Gabriel would not be able to talk to Meyerlink because in 1997, while serving his prison sentence, the man suffered a surprise nighttime attack of his own. He died in his cot when his gut exploded from an abdominal aneurysm.

Karma may be slow, Gabriel asserted, but it's a feral bitch.

Gabriel then researched the ViCAP database for any other crimes involving young girls in Nancy's locale in the late eighties. He then widened the range to include the entire Los Angeles basin. Gabriel couldn't find any crimes that could conceivably connect back to Nancy. Just Meyerlink's.

Gabriel decided to check out Nancy's old house to see if it fit Meyerlink's bill. He emailed Pauline Lewicki for the address and asked if she had a photo she could scan and email him of the prior residence. After receiving her reply to the affirmative, Gabriel gathered his effects and headed toward the exit.

Carmen Jenette waited for Gabriel in the lobby. Wearing a calf-length silky skirt and a tight blouse that showed off her well-defined bust, she approached him and offered her hand in greeting.

"Detective McRay?"

"Yes?" Gabriel recognized the Psychic to the Stars, but feigned ignorance of her identity.

"I'm Carmen Jenette," she said. "It's nice to meet you."

Gabriel lightly shook her hand and did not reply.

She stepped in front of him to make her point. "I was wondering if we could have a word."

He waited.

"Perhaps you've heard of my work?"

Gabriel shrugged and looked off in the distance. The psychic bristled at his speechlessness. "I'm a medium. I'll be working with you on the Lewicki case."

"Sorry, but I wasn't informed about that. Have a good day." Gabriel walked into the sunshine of the parking lot. Carmen stayed right by his side.

"Look, if you could spare a moment..." She touched his sleeve and halted in her tracks.

The light entreaty on his jacket caused Gabriel to feel a smidgeon of guilt for stonewalling her. The young lady was only trying to help. He faced the psychic and was startled by the unblinking intensity of her green eyes.

It took an effort to keep his voice firm. "I heard what you said on your show, Miss Jenette. As of right now, I don't need a co-investigator. And if I need help, my partner is back in there." He cocked his thumb over his shoulder in the direction of the bureau.

The medium's eyes, nearly chartreuse in the sunlight, held Gabriel in their grasp.

"Do you understand?" he asked pointedly. Why did she stare at him like that?

Carmen took a sudden intake of breath, and her posture relaxed. "I'm sorry. I believe it's quite important that you and I work together, Detective McRay. I promise I can help you. All my guides are urging me on this."

Gabriel frowned and headed toward his car. Carmen, reanimated, ambled along beside him. "You're on your way to do something in regards to Nancy, aren't you? Please let me accompany you."

"You're a psychic," Gabriel stated as he arrived at his car and unlocked the door. "You say you can be of help. Tell me, where is Nancy Lewicki? What happened to her?"

"It doesn't work like that, Detective."

Gabriel nodded. "I thought as much. Now, if you'll excuse me."

As he drove off, Gabriel glanced into the rearview mirror and saw Carmen Jenette standing motionless in the parking lot, still fixated upon his person.

Nancy had lived in Liberty Canyon, a neighborhood in Agoura just beyond the San Fernando Valley, a vast suburb of Los Angeles. Nancy's neighborhood featured single-story tract homes with swimming pools. Located close to the freeway, the community would have served as a decent hunting ground for the rapist Meyerlink.

Gabriel pulled up and parked in front of Nancy's house, which lay at the end of a tree-lined cul-de-sac. He viewed the printout of the photograph Pauline had emailed. The picture had been taken on Halloween. Fabric ghosts, caught by the photographer in mid-sway, hung from the tree on the lawn. Jack-o-lanterns lined the walkway up to the house, while life-sized plastic skeletons stood on the front porch, posed in various affectations.

The family, wearing their costumes, had posed among the skeletons. Paul Lewicki, only eight or nine years old at the time, was dressed as a Pac-Man. Len wore an Alf costume, a character Gabriel remembered as a moose-faced extraterrestrial that took television by storm in the early eighties. Len had made a hefty Alf, strong, built like a moose himself. It took the disappearance of his daughter to bend all that tough metal into a crowbar.

A younger, thinner Pauline donned the outfit of a generic gypsy, with a long, rustling skirt and a red scarf tied around her straw-colored hair. Her smile was radiant. She stood over the family's Golden Retriever, who wore Mickey Mouse ears.

And then there was Nancy.

She'd dressed as Princess Leah from Star Wars. A brunette wig of winding braids hid her blonde hair. Loose white pants and a matching tunic offered a fair imitation of the Star Wars character. Nancy had her fingers raised in the "Vulcan Salute," a tribute to another famous space epic. She looked to be about thirteen. Like a sculpture waiting to be fired in the kiln, Nancy's face had not yet set into the confident cast displayed in the Polaroid at Gabriel's home. Still, her smile sparkled.

Gabriel regarded them all — the complete family. A happy family. His eyes then fastened on a plastic skeleton standing behind Nancy. This particular one reached a bony arm toward the girl. Like an ominous portent of the terrible events to come, the skeleton resembled the Grim Reaper about to tap Nancy on the shoulder.

A shiver ran through Gabriel. He wondered if the Lewickis had ever noticed it. Probably not, but that gaunt figure poised behind the carefree young girl disturbed him.

Tucking the photo into his jacket, Gabriel exited the car to view Nancy's house in real-time. The current residents had also decorated for Halloween, which created a surreal overlay in Gabriel's mind. The surrounding scenery developed a dreamlike texture, as if it were woven into a tapestry.

Foam gravestones poked out of the drought-dead lawn at crooked angles. A noose hung from the rafters over the porch. A rubber cadaver, with bulging eyes and a neck encircled by the rope, twisted on the Santa Ana breeze.

Surveying the porch, Gabriel could not shake the image of the skeleton reaching for Nancy.

Her family had lived here and left no trace. Nancy had played on this lawn and then disappeared. A detective in another decade stood at the edge of Nancy's lawn, and it might as well been a precipice. Although Gabriel perceived he had his feet planted on terra firma, he worried there existed no real space to inhabit.

We cling to the delusion that we matter, he thought. *Our only reality is our collective yearning, and even that is temporary, for it dies when we do.*

Depression gripped him, and Gabriel struggled out of its grasp. He had to, or he might debate whether marriage or anything else mattered. To put a halt to his dismal, runaway thoughts, Gabriel looked beyond the holiday decorations and studied the place with an investigator's eye.

The remodeling of the house reflected the ebb and flow of changing fortunes. Built originally as a one level ranch style home, someone, at some time, had added an upper story and a Spanish tiled roof. These enhancements forced the modest home into a Mediterranean "McMansion," a design widely popular in the nineties. The cobblestone driveway, while attractive, didn't match the house. The only thing that remained of the original home was the grand and glorious weeping willow on the front lawn.

At least the successive homeowners had the good sense

to keep it, Gabriel thought. On a whim, he walked over to the willow and stood under its flowing green canopy. The breeze made tranquil whispers through the leaves, and he felt its delicate boughs trace his arms and dance along his cheekbones as if nature was writing calligraphy upon his person.

"Can I help you?"

Standing on the front porch of the home was a barefoot, skinny man wearing baggy sweats, a stained white t-shirt, and an Angel's baseball cap over short red hair and a substantial red beard.

Gabriel pulled out his badge and walked over to the man. Seeing the instant alarm break onto the homeowner's face, Gabriel reassured him. "I'm working a cold case that involved a missing person who lived here many years ago. Maybe you heard about her?"

The man, relieved, gave the rubber cadaver a spin and casually turned on the garden hose. He began to water a group of azaleas planted near the front door. "I did hear something about that when we moved in. They have to disclose that sort of information, don't they?"

"I wouldn't know," Gabriel replied. "I just wanted to get a feel of the place."

"Well," the man said as he turned off the hose valve. "You are more than welcome to come inside."

Gabriel appreciated the generous offer but shook his head. From the looks of the house, he doubted if anything original remained from the Lewicki's time. Besides, this home did not fit the description of the type Meyerlink preferred. Although the neighborhood abutted the freeway, Nancy's house nestled between two other residences and shared fences. On top of that, the Lewickis had owned a dog

— a big dog. Gabriel felt reasonably sure that Nancy did not come into contact with Meyerlink, and that put him back to square one.

As he returned to his car, Gabriel once more regarded the waving branches of the willow tree. The branches dipped and flowed in a hypnotic waltz, the music provided by the breeze. The gracious tree had withstood the test of time, unlike the rest of the house, which had been sacrificed to the caprices of changing tastes. Nancy had looked upon this tree. The willow forged a bridge between them.

If only you could talk, Gabriel wished silently.

CHAPTER EIGHT

It's him, Carmen thought. The detective is the conduit, and he doesn't know. Most likely, Gabriel McRay wouldn't accept the fact, even if she made him aware of it.

Vodka sloshed colorlessly into the tumbler Carmen had pulled from the shelf of the reconstructed pub bar in her living room. She usually preferred wine to hard alcohol, but the antique steam valves, the stained glass, and brass foot rail of the carved wooden bar invited her to step up and *laissez les bon temps rouler.* Let the good times roll.

To a nonexistent barkeep, Carmen said, "Men like McRay need a spiritual awakening. They have no clue how to work with the natural world and instead want to dominate it. Well, here's to you, asshole." She knocked back the drink and set the empty glass down on the bar top, whose old wood bore the marks of countless rings. Ghosts of libations past.

This bar had calmed many fears and eased troubled minds. A variety of elbows once rested on the countertop. The sweat and perfume emanating from the pores of countless patrons had seeped into the fibers. Carmen sensed the despair of some folk but tingled with joy at the celebrations of others. The vodka enfolded her in a warm serenity, and so consoled, Carmen found herself humming Lucinda Williams' "Crescent City," a fine tribute to New Orleans. She smiled at the invisible barkeep. "How about another?"

Carmen let a moment pass and then reached for the vodka bottle. "Don't mind if I do."

Her cell phone rang, and Carmen sighed. Grabbing the phone, she eyed the display: Donovan Thorne. She weighed whether or not to answer, and then relented.

"Hi, Don. What do you need?"

"What's up?" he cried out joyfully.

Carmen rolled her eyes. Evidently, her brother-in-law was making use of a cocktail hour. The background resonated with loud music and voices.

"I'm here with my man, Brad," Donovan said. "He's a fan. Here, talk to him."

Carmen heard Brad's swift, "No—oh, come on," and then an awkward, "Hello? Miss Jenette?"

Taking a sip from her refreshed drink, Carmen said, "Yes?"

"I'm sorry," Brad told her, now that he was fully on the phone. "It's Friday, and we won a complicated case. We're kind of celebrating at the Redwood."

"No apologies necessary," Carmen assured him.

From the background, Carmen heard Donovan yell, "Ask her for a date!"

The conversation grew muffled as if Brad covered the phone, and then he was back. "I'm sorry."

"It's okay." Carmen smiled. "You can ask."

Brad laughed. "Not like this. But I'll call you. I promise."

"Okay."

She heard an accompaniment of raucous cheers, and then the phone went dead. Well, Carmen reflected, it looks like I might go out with the District Attorney. Donovan, as much as he hassled her, had looked out for Carmen. Smiling, she lifted the drink to her lips. She could see herself arm-in-arm with the future Attorney General. Why not? Brad was a fan, wasn't he? That probably made him more accepting of her spirituality. In Carmen's eyes, that made Brad a more courageous man than Donovan who had to drink to believe in Carmen, and Gabriel McRay, who refused to acknowledge her.

To his credit, the detective possessed striking cobalt eyes that drilled right through a girl. Those eyes were a plus. And Carmen got the warm, sensual feeling that underneath his suit jacket, Gabriel harbored some strong muscles. He wore his black hair slightly longer than most police officers, but it curled handsomely around his face. She didn't sense any real malice behind Gabriel's annoyance with her. Carmen felt he used his gruff attitude as a front, something to present at will, like a business card.

A pronounced creaking sounded from the kitchen. Carmen inclined her head toward the sound. A few years back, she had ripped out the stone tiles the previous homeowner had installed and imported old wooden floorboards from a burned-out church in Palmetto. Some of the boards even sported scorch marks; an addition Carmen found delightfully unique. The old Louisiana floorboards creaked, but only when someone walked on them.

She sat on the barstool and listened. As she waited, the melting ice shifted and clinked in her glass. Carmen didn't fright from things that went bump in the night. In fact, the pokes and nudges from beyond the horizon of the physical world pleased her. She continued to listen, but no further noise came from the kitchen.

Carmen took a languid sip of the vodka and closed her eyes. What she couldn't see, she might sense. Carmen's hearing sharpened, and she became aware of a gentle tinkling sound.

Opening her eyes, she let them run the length of the bar, rove over the cabinet brimming with books and the mélange of crystals, gris-gris bags, and the many accouterments of the Wiccan trade. She scanned the small round table where she read tarot. Nothing lay there but a deck of tarot cards and a white candle that smelled of patchouli. Carmen rose from the barstool and, holding her drink, stood in the center of the room.

After a moment, she discovered the source of the chinking. A row of masks hung on the wall between the kitchen and the living room. Carmen's eye fell upon one of her more exceptional pieces, an elaborate white and gold Venetian jester mask, handmade in Italy.

She wandered over to the jester's head and contemplated the glib and frozen half-smile, the black and fathomless eyes. One of the bells dangling on the jester's conical cap quivered.

As the bell clinked, a slight breeze tickled her cheek. A window left open, perhaps – no big deal, except that the flesh on her hands began to creep.

Carmen re-entered the living room and halted in her tracks. Seated at the bar was a man, facing the back mirror. He could have been an ordinary man bellying up to the bar, except that no drink rested before him, and a red cavern comprised the right side of the man's head. Carmen swallowed. She could see gray stripes of the brain and crushed pieces of bone within the wound. Realizing she was in the presence of the dead, Carmen reassessed the man.

Whoever he was, he never saw death coming. The guy had received one hell of a wallop, from, Carmen intuited, some type of accident. His face, though damaged, did not bear the sorrow and condemnation of a murder victim. In the dim light, Carmen couldn't make out much more except that he wore a work shirt soiled with blood. His dirty work boots rested on the brass foot rail. The man's remaining eye stared at her from his reflection.

"What is it?" Carmen asked.

A breeze caressed her back and caused her skin to prickle with goosebumps. She glanced away and reminded herself to close that window. When Carmen looked back at the spectral injured man, the barstool was vacant. He was gone.

No bother, she thought. Carmen walked into the kitchen and saw, not the window, but the backdoor standing wide open. The open door unnerved her more than seeing a ghost.

When she moved forward to close it, Carmen's shoe crunched against something on the wood flooring. She looked down. Glass littered the floor. One glance at the door, and she saw a pane broken out. *Shit.*

Carmen pivoted around. The kitchen appeared empty, but that factor did not stop a ball of fear from rolling through her body.

Carmen. Run.

She heard no sound but felt sure that the ghost at the bar had accompanied someone very much alive.

Run.

Instead, she grabbed a knife from a drawer and returned to the living room. Carmen's eyes ran over each nook and cranny. The tumbler on the bar shed water droplets, and the ice shifted. From the corner of her eye, Carmen spied a mask coming toward her. The mask depicted a skull with an upside-down grin, and a stranger wore it.

Carmen whirled around, raising the knife high. In an instant, the masked figure grabbed her arm and twisted it hard. The knife she held clattered to the floor.

He's strong, Carmen thought wildly.

The intruder whirled her body around and immediately swung an arm under Carmen's chin and across her neck, putting her in a chokehold. From his touch, images, like separate coaches of a train, assailed her. *The thumping of a stuck door trying to open. The shrill and unusual timbre of an alarm.* The mental coaches rumbled along a track, but Carmen's panicking mind prevented her from putting them into one cohesive train of thought.

Gusts of breath hit her ear, and Carmen smelled the brutish musk of her attacker. His arm, so tight under her chin, crushed her throat. She couldn't breathe. Carmen knew she had a minute, perhaps only seconds, before she passed out.

Frantically reviving techniques from a self-defense class, Carmen grabbed at the attacker's forearm and violently pulled down to create space. To her instant relief, the movement worked. She hiked her shoulders, which managed to block his grip on her. Carmen quickly gasped in a much-needed breath and steeled herself for the next move. Twisting to the side, facing him, Carmen glimpsed two angry brown eyes. She didn't waste precious time trying to understand his intentions. Carmen delivered a quick palm to the man's nose and heard a satisfying snap under the mask. She followed that with a knee to his groin. Her attacker doubled over. Carmen ran to the open door in the kitchen and screamed through bruised vocal cords, "Help me! Someone call the police! I'm being –"

Suddenly, she felt her head yanked painfully backward. The man held her by the hair and pulled Carmen from the doorway. Her head twisted this way and that. *Stop his hand!* Stop his hand before he slams your head into something unforgiving.

Carmen dug her fingernails into the man's hand, and for a split second he couldn't pull her head at will. She then punched her fist as hard as she could in the shallow just above his elbow. The man's fist fell away from her hair. Carmen threw herself toward the knife she'd dropped, but the assailant, having had enough, ran through the door. He left Carmen gasping above the scorch marks on the wood floor.

CHAPTER NINE

Pauline Lewicki had given Gabriel a large plastic bin filled with odds and ends she'd saved from Nancy's old bedroom. It was a forlorn box, Gabriel decided as he lugged it inside his home and set it down on the carpeted floor of his study. Imagine all the things emblematic of our lives too easily shoved into a single container.

Removing the blue lid, Gabriel sat beside the box and peered inside. On top was the Clifford dog. Gabriel put that aside and pulled out a few framed photographs. One showed Nancy and Abby Underwood, arm in arm. Gabriel recognized Abby from her big hair. The rest were of Nancy and another friend, a bony brown-haired girl boasting the tight curls of a permanent wave and spray of brown freckles across her nose. Her lively smile was hampered by a retainer, which made a metal line across her teeth. On one of the photos, the word "Jen-Jen" was printed in block letters underneath the girl. Gabriel surmised this was Jenna Goldman. Written under Nancy's visage was the name

"Punkin." That solved one mystery. Punkin was Nancy's nickname.

Setting the framed photos down, he pulled out a folded up poster and spread it out. It showed Michael Jackson dressed in black leather, his hair Jheri-curled and shiny around a handsome face only partially touched by a plastic surgeon's knife. Pinholes pierced the four corners. Another folded poster opened to reveal a publicity shot from the movie "The Lost Boys." Pinholes marked this one as well. Gabriel pulled out a dry, blue Esprit tote, which was empty save for an ancient Beaman's gum wrapper and a movie ticket to see "Beetlejuice." Another purse, this one made out of blue jean material and suede fringe, held only a dime with the mint date of 1979 and a hot pink rabbit's foot keychain.

The next item out of the container was a small, white wooden cabinet—a jewelry box. A line of pink trim surrounded two doors. These opened to reveal three little interior drawers. Gabriel slid open the first and withdrew a boxy pair of earrings, multi-colored squares that looked like something out of a Mondrian painting. The studs had tarnished. He saw a couple of rings, each with a fake colored gem bordered by two fake diamonds; the kind of adjustable rings they sold in discount stores like the TG&Y in Gabriel's old neighborhood. As a boy, Gabriel would sneak into the TG&Y and spend every penny in his pocket on candy.

He'd been heading home from the TG&Y when his neighbor Andrew Pierce pulled up in his car. Andrew offered Gabriel a ride home, and Gabriel had taken the offer.

Turning away from the memory and the other recollections it might ignite, Gabriel opened the second drawer of the jewelry box and lifted out a charm necklace. This one was no fake. The chain looked like real gold. He wondered why Pauline Lewicki would remand something valuable to storage, but then realized—what value did this gold necklace have without the wearer?

Curious, Gabriel studied each of the charms. They appeared to be made of gold as well. One was a tiny horseshoe; another an astrological sign that looked like the letter M with an arrow at one end. Gabriel double-checked the symbol on the Internet and learned that it signified Scorpio. Also attached to the necklace was a small horn, which Gabriel dimly recalled as an Italian horn, popular at the time. Another charm was a gold heart with a tiny diamond in it. He turned it over but saw no inscription. Returning the necklace to its compartment, he opened the last drawer. Tiny pieces of paper stuffed the space, fortunes from fortune cookies. Gabriel read some of the life-coaching phrases.

The success you desire will be yours to achieve

Miles are covered one step at a time

In the end, all things will be known

Gabriel smiled pensively at the collection. As if life's mysteries could be solved in a tiny rectangle of paper.

As if!

A shudder ran through him. That was not his way of speaking, but the phrase tagged Gabriel's brain like a sudden spray of graffiti. His finger slowly pushed the drawer closed. He sat in the security of his home, yet the personal belongings of a long lost stranger cast an eerie hue about the place.

Gabriel set the jewelry box aside and lifted a pocket-sized scrapbook from the plastic container. Each page held a Polaroid photograph, and someone had written "Mammoth Lakes" on the cover in what appeared to be red nail polish.

Gabriel opened the small book and saw photos apparently taken on a summertime trip to Mammoth Lakes.

Mammoth, a popular Southern California ski resort, received a better snowpack than the other local mountains. Although better known for its winter sports, Mammoth sustained an equally excellent reputation when the snow melted because the warm weather revealed the sparkling lakes.

The Lewickis must have rented a cabin on one such lake. From the look of the family members in the photos, Gabriel surmised they'd taken the trip not long before Nancy went missing. He glanced at her picture on the bookshelf and determined that Nancy's hairstyle and facial features were the same.

In one photo, she wore belted shorts, high in the waist, so different from the current fashion. Nancy also wore a tucked-in shirt and tan hiking boots. Timberland, maybe, the kind that laced up the ankle. A Dodger baseball cap crowned her short blonde hair.

Gabriel could discern the bulge of breasts under Nancy's shirt and noted that her legs were shapely if a little coltish. Although she'd developed the body of a young woman, the smile on her face and the laughter in Nancy's eyes held the effervescence of a child reared in wholesome abundance.

She must have been some kid, Gabriel thought. She would have grown up to be some woman. Nancy would have been a little older than him now.

Gabriel considered the idea that Nancy was still alive. Had she sustained an accident that left her suffering amnesia? Had she been kidnapped, brainwashed, and raised by a stranger?

He lay back on his elbows and mulled over the possibility. Could someone intimidate and brainwash a teenager? Could someone force a new identity on Nancy? Elizabeth Smart had been kidnapped as a teenager and fell prey to the threats of her abductor. He dared to venture out in public with her, and Elizabeth did not run away. Gabriel himself had struggled against a perverse, growing dependency on Victor Archwood last summer when he'd been his prisoner.

And there were other tricks the mind could play. Gabriel knew them well. At seven years of age, his mind decided that he should shut down his memory.

Gabriel had lived in San Francisco with his parents and his younger sister, Janet. On one side of his Sunset District neighborhood, the sea rolled with the fog. On the other, Golden Gate Park beckoned. A young man named Andrew Pierce lived across the street from the McRay's. Gabriel's mother called him a "drop-out." Each afternoon, Gabriel would wait on the front steps for his mother to come home from work. Lonely, and with nothing better to do, he'd watch Andrew tinker with his car. Gabriel thought the older boy was cool. One day, Andrew asked Gabriel if he would like to come over and play.

Gabriel brought himself forward. Dr. B had helped Gabriel remember what Andrew had done to him. Victor Archwood, the serial killer who tormented Gabriel last summer, helped him remember anything the therapy left out. Archwood had done a damned good job of squeezing any leftover repressed memories out of Gabriel's head. Now, all that was left were his fresh recollections of being trapped in a secret room with Archwood.

Stop. Walk away from this.

Gabriel cleared his throat and turned back to Nancy's scrapbook. He viewed photos of mountains, a pretty lake, and a sign that read, "Devil's Postpile." The family must have visited an Old West town because the next few shots depicted abandoned buildings on dusty roads. One photo depicted Nancy hugging Paul as he grinned under a cowboy hat. They stood in front of a slatted wood building next to a sign reading "Saloon." Another photo taken indoors had grown dark and murky with time. Still, Gabriel could make out the saloon bar with its rickety stools and big gilded mirror behind the long wooden counter. The reflections in the mirror were indecipherable. The rest of the Polaroid photos—three of them to be exact, had stuck together. Gabriel tried prying them apart until he realized they were starting to tear.

He needed to see them. The middle photo showed Nancy standing next to a painted, life-sized effigy of a cowboy. Somebody else stood on the other side of the cowboy, but Gabriel could only make out that person's elbow. After making one more attempt at separating the photos, he gave up with a grunt of frustration. He couldn't risk destroying them. With the voyeur in him fully tantalized, Gabriel deposited the melded photos into a bag to take to the forensic lab.

A pronounced ping issued from his cell phone—an alert Gabriel had set as a reminder to get ready for his date with Ming's parents. Reluctantly, he left Nancy's belongings and walked out of the room to take a shower.

A minute or so passed and the sound of running water permeated the small home. The slanting sunlight fell across the bookshelf and bathed Nancy's face in a golden glow. In the plastic container, an overstuffed three-ring binder shifted to reveal the edge of a yellow and brown folder.

Gabriel met the Li family at Napa, a wine bar on Hollywood Boulevard, not too far from Ming's home in Los Feliz. The place had lots of wines available plus a tasty menu. Ming and her father were trying to decide if this would be a nice venue for the engagement party.

Nobody asked Gabriel's opinion. Ming buzzed about the place, bent on impressing her father. Pleasing daddy had taken a toll on his fiancée, Gabriel could tell. Her voice was shrill, and Ming seemed irritated and out of sorts.

"I like this place well enough," Dr. Li said and then pointed a finger at his daughter. "You've got the invitations handled, right?"

"Right," she answered. "And I'll get them out tomorrow."

Always the high-achieving daughter, Gabriel thought. He and Ming hadn't even looked at engagement party invitations and she already had it "handled." Wishing he could have ordered a whiskey with dinner, Gabriel kept his mouth shut by eating.

When he reached for the tab at the end of the meal, Dr. Li grabbed the check before Gabriel could.

"It's okay," Ming's father announced. "You're on a policeman's salary. Save your money for the honeymoon."

Ming shot Gabriel a worried look. "Dad…"

"It's okay!" Dr. Li exclaimed. "How often do we see each other? It's my pleasure."

Notwithstanding the pleasantry in his tone, Dr. Li had managed to insult Gabriel. Ming's past words, *tremendous asshole*, lay in Gabriel's gaze as he regarded the older man.

Elena Li seemed aware of the offense. "Tom," she said to her husband, "I think if Gabriel would like to take us out, you should let him."

"It's not a big deal." Dr. Li made a show of plucking a sleek wallet from his suit pocket.

Ming took Gabriel's hand as if that made everything okay. "Well, thanks, Dad."

"Yeah," Gabriel echoed hollowly. "Thanks."

CHAPTER TEN

Y*ou're on a policeman's salary.*

What a dick. Gabriel pondered what kind of hell would break loose if he skipped his engagement party. He briefly considered voicing his hesitancy about the wedding to Ming, and then thought the better of it. Gabriel loved Ming, but the idea of committing himself to a lifelong relationship caused the breath to catch in his throat. He feared to open his life and his heart completely to Ming. What if he lost her to a terrible fate? Bad things happened all the time.

Although it was well past midnight when he returned home from the restaurant, Gabriel sought to find solace in his work. He plopped down on the carpet in his study and foraged through more of Nancy's belongings. His eye caught an overstuffed school binder of white vinyl, worn down to the cardboard in one corner. A beige and brown Pee-Chee folder peeked out. Curious, Gabriel pulled the folder loose.

Hand-drawn hearts and cubes adorned the folder along with a cartoon musical group, which had been sketched at the bottom right. Two stick-figure guitarists, a drummer, seated behind a drum kit, a keyboardist, and a singer standing beside a microphone completed the crude rendering.

As Gabriel ran his finger over the drawing, the pages of an imaginary calendar flipped backward and came to rest in the year 1988.

Gabriel envisioned Nancy sitting, bored in class, with her blonde head bent over the same Pee-Chee folder. A teacher stood at the blackboard writing in chalk, "No man is an island, entire of itself." Ensconced in her private world, Nancy mindlessly doodled and daydreamed.

Look up, Nancy. Can you see me?

Gabriel smiled at his whimsy. What an imagination. That's what working late at night will do. Leaving the imagined classroom in his head, Gabriel opened the Pee-Chee folder. He thumbed through a couple of English assignment packets and a few tests. All the papers were marked with an "A." One test, stamped with an "A+," was entitled "For Whom the Bell Tolls."

No man is an island, entire of itself, the poem began.

For all her daydreaming, Nancy Lewicki had made good grades. Gabriel tucked the exam back into the folder, and as he did so, his eye fell on a folded piece of lined paper peeking from behind the flap. He wrestled it free and read what appeared to be a note passed in class.

Mr. Colliard called me a bald-faced liar.

The statement was written in a girl's neat and curling handwriting. In the days before texting, kids had perfected the stealthy art of exchanging notes. Below that, in black pen, and in a different script, *It's bold-faced, you dork.*

Underneath, the first girl wrote,

No, he said bald-faced. As if I can have a bald face.

The words suddenly reminded Gabriel of the grinning skull behind Nancy in the Halloween photo. A bald face indeed.

I shined on first period cuz I didn't wanna take that test, but Colliard caught me at Alpha Beta during lunch. He saw me at check-out! Can you believe it? He asked why I wasn't in class this morning, and I told him I was sick, and he called me a bald-faced liar.

Gabriel smiled. Nancy had ditched school. The friend wrote,

Oh, burrnn! Are you in trouble?

No, he's too much of a dweeb to do anything. How's the bod doin?

Totally awesome. I picked out th—

The rest of the note was gone, ripped away. Gabriel wondered who the friend was. He figured that friend was exercising to "workout tapes by Fonda." An amused grin broke across Gabriel's face. Isn't that what people did in the eighties to get a hot bod?

At work the following day, Gabriel received a call from Donovan Thorne. Gabriel didn't have any pending affidavits with the DA's office and wondered why Donovan would want to talk to him.

After the men exchanged the usual pleasantries, and after Donovan congratulated Gabriel on his impending marriage (good news travels fast, Gabriel thought), the lawyer explained the reason for his call.

"Did you know that Carmen Jenette and I are related?" he asked.

"No, I did not."

"My wife is her sister."

Gabriel chewed his lower lip. Was Thorne going to reprimand him for being rude to a relative? As Gabriel's brain stumbled around in search of an adequate rationale for his behavior, Donovan spoke first.

"Listen, I know Carmen has been trying to talk with you about the Nancy Lewicki case. Carmen is good, Gabriel. Sometimes she comes up with uncanny revelations. It couldn't hurt to let her tag along, could it?"

His request surprised Gabriel. Thorne was a prominent prosecutor with the District Attorney's office. Why would he ask a detective to work with a psychic? Was Thorne innocently supporting the career of a relative or connecting the dots between his position, an ongoing investigation, and the inevitable publicity that could be garnered by linking all points to a television personality?

Gabriel knew that the dynamic attorney enjoyed basking in the limelight.

"Look, Donovan, like I told your sister-in-law. I don't have a problem with –"

"Did you know someone assaulted her last night?"

Gabriel paused. "What happened?"

"A guy broke into Carmen's home and tried to strangle her."

"Was he apprehended?"

"No. But he left a couple of blood drops behind. Could you at least speak with Carmen? I know it would make her feel better."

"Why me? She made a report didn't she?"

"Carmen specifically asked to see you. Do you have time today?"

Thorne acted expediently when investigators came to his

office in search of affidavits or warrants. Gabriel decided to meet with Donovan's sister-in-law in the spirit of good public relations.

"Give me her phone number," he said.

The cars inched along the freeway during the drive from Commerce to West Hollywood, which made the drive seem to last forever. At last, Gabriel arrived at the appointed meeting place, a coffee house on Santa Monica Boulevard that specialized in organic cold brew. Gabriel didn't understand what that meant.

The only cold brews he enjoyed were of the beer variety, and the idea of cold-brewed coffee seemed to have the word "trend" written all over it. Gabriel disliked trends and purposely avoided following them. Stubbornly, he ordered coffee made the old-fashioned way.

Carmen Jenette waited for him at a small table, adorned in her usual habiliment of a long, fluid skirt and a tight chemise. She waved him over, but Gabriel pointed toward the coffee counter. Did she want a cup? Carmen nodded eagerly, evidently pleased at his gentleman's manner.

A few minutes later, with coffee mugs in tow, Gabriel approached the psychic and fought the urge to ask Carmen if she had predicted the traffic would make him late. He kept his mouth shut in deference to Donovan Thorne.

"I heard you were assaulted, Miss Jenette." Gabriel placed a mug of coffee before her and took a seat in a rickety wooden chair that creaked under his weight. "I'm sorry to hear about that. Did you file a police report?"

"Of course. My brother-in-law is –"

"I know who your brother-in-law is," Gabriel said and then reminded himself to be kind. "Donovan and I go back a few years. Who did they assign to your case? Which detective?"

"A man named Adam Bonin from Robbery/Assault. Have you heard of him?"

Gabriel nodded, sipped his coffee, and found it flavorful and hot. Still pondering what cold brew meant, he said, "I'm sure you're in good hands."

"The man who broke into my home was wearing a grinning skull mask. Only it didn't grin. It frowned. Like this..." Carmen pulled the corners of her mouth downward.

Gabriel regarded the psychic through the steam rising from his cup. The sounds of the coffee house faded as his dream of the grimacing skull moored in his head and dropped anchor. To change the subject, he said, "Donovan says the thief left his DNA."

"The police found a few drops of blood. I smacked the guy pretty hard in the nose."

Gabriel nodded appreciatively. "They'll run the sample through a database and hope for a match. You're a lucky woman, Miss Jenette."

"Luck had nothing to do with it. I took a series of self-defense classes at my gym. They paid off."

Gabriel half-smiled. He had a new respect for the Psychic to the Stars. "Smart," he said. "But you're still lucky. A lot of people get killed when they surprise or fight a robber."

"I didn't have a choice. He came after me."

A couple, a sleek thirty-something yuppie and his wife, hip and slender despite the newborn baby nestled into the futuristic stroller that she pushed, approached Gabriel and Carmen's table.

"Are you Carmen Jenette?" the woman with the stroller asked.

Carmen smiled and nodded.

"I am absolutely in awe of you." The new mother glowed.

Her husband leaned into the conversation, tanned, buff. "We're huge fans. Huge."

The yuppies were positively gushing, and Gabriel guessed it took a lot to impress them. Even the baby, dressed in a posh bodysuit, smiled for Carmen. Or maybe that was merely gas.

"Can I ask you to sign my..." the new mother looked around fretfully and then finally settled on her Louis Vuitton diaper bag. "Would you autograph this?"

Carmen seemed only too happy to oblige. She produced a pen out of nowhere and signed her name on the fabric with a flourish.

"Oh, thank you." The woman looked at Carmen as if the psychic had just saved her from drowning. The husband offered a broad smile and a slight bow of the head. The couple, charmed and happy, pushed the stroller out the door.

"Damn," Gabriel said, marveling at the show of idol worship. "What is it like to be adored?"

Carmen lifted her coffee mug with a grin. "Don't you know?"

"I haven't exactly built a large following of fans in my lifetime."

Taking a sip, Carmen said, "Well, adoration aside, all I'm doing is trying to help people."

Gabriel didn't buy it. Carmen's attempt to sound humble failed miserably.

"Did you know my car was broken into a week ago?" she asked.

"No, I hadn't heard."

"I was in the parking lot of my gym, about to get into my car, when I felt this terrible sensation of danger."

Gabriel kept a poker face at the precognitive reference. He wasn't here to laud the famous psychic. The couple with the baby had already given Carmen her daily dose of ego.

"I knew without a doubt something was wrong," Carmen said. "I didn't figure the danger was in my car because I knew I had locked it."

"Do you use a remote key fob to lock your door?" Gabriel asked.

Carmen nodded.

"Jamming devices are popular with carjackers," he explained. "They stake out parking lots and wait within fifty feet of a car. When someone gets out of her vehicle and locks the car using the remote, the suspect's device jams the signal, and the car doesn't lock."

He watched Carmen take a sip of her coffee. The mug shook in her hand.

"From now on," Gabriel told her, "press the button on the door to lock your car."

"You don't understand, Detective McRay. The person in my car wasn't trying to steal it; he was waiting for me to get inside."

"How do you know?"

"I don't, not for sure. I can only assume. When I ran back inside the gym, he left and didn't take anything. I saw him on camera."

"Do the police have the footage?"

"Of course."

Gabriel reflected on that and then asked, "Would the person in your car happened to have been wearing a skull mask?"

"No," Carmen answered. "He wore a hoodie over his head like the Unibomber, and hid his face from the security camera."

"What makes you think it's a male?"

Carmen shrugged. "His posture, his gait... I know it was a man, just like I know he was purposely waiting for me. Honestly, I don't want to think about what would have happened if I'd gotten into my car that night."

Gabriel studied her. "Do you think the two incidents are related?"

"Yes."

"Do you feel that the person waiting for you in your car was the same person who broke into your house?"

"I do."

Gabriel might have to agree. Two attacks in one week didn't feel like a coincidence, and he didn't believe in coincidences any more than he did in ghosts. Carmen was famous, young, and pretty. He figured she had a stalker on her tail.

"Miss Jenette," he began.

"Carmen."

"Okay, Carmen. You are a celebrity, so you must know the pitfalls. Someone has become fixated on you. Not only are you famous, but you're good-looking."

Carmen lit up at his words. She possessed a slightly crooked canine tooth that gave her smile character. Noting the sudden light that turned on in her emerald eyes, Gabriel wished he could retract the compliment.

"All I'm saying is that your popularity comes with risk. I

suggest you get a temporary bodyguard and a dependable alarm system for your home."

Gabriel picked up his coffee cup and added, "Your stalker ought to know who your brother-in-law is."

The smile stayed on Carmen's face as Gabriel took a drink. "And that I work with a very handsome and capable detective from the Sheriff's department."

A dribble of coffee spilled on Gabriel's shirt. "We're not working together. But feel free to let me know if you get..." He waved his hand in the air in front of Carmen's face. "Information about Nancy."

She nodded and took a sip of coffee.

Gabriel watched her. "Out of curiosity, do you have any sensations about Nancy? Just out of curiosity."

Carmen grew animated now that Gabriel showed interest in her abilities. "It's the strangest thing. I get messages here and there, but they're vague like they're filtered. I do, however, pick up strong signals from you."

Gabriel averted his eyes. He should have never complimented the psychic on her looks. If Ming got wind of it, the next time her parents wanted dinner, she would serve Gabriel's head on a platter.

"You've connected with me, Detective. Maybe by watching my show?"

"If that were the case," Gabriel said. "You'd connect with thousands of viewers every day."

Carmen's finger made a lazy circle around the rim of her cup. "But it's happening only with you. There's a reason for it, I'm sure. I believe you're the filter. Would you come to a séance, if I hold one for Nancy?"

"No." Gabriel's eyes found the exit. "I'm afraid that's not my thing."

"But you must come. This time, Detective McRay, I'm not the one connecting with unseen forces. You are. You're the one Nancy is reaching out to."

"Unseen forces?" Gabriel returned his gaze to the young woman seated across from him.

"Guides, angels... The dead."

"The dead? Let me tell you something, Miss Jenette."

"Carmen."

Gabriel sat back in the creaking chair and gave her a patronizing smile. "In my profession, if I could talk to the dead, I would have the number one homicide solve rate in the country. Unfortunately, I don't."

Carmen's green eyes remained fixed on him. "Yet, you have an incredibly good track record. Donovan told me about you. You don't think intuition plays a part?"

"You didn't mention intuition. You mentioned talking to the dead."

"You're the one getting the clues from Nancy, but you don't know how to read them. That's where I can help. This is my area of expertise, Detective. If you knew how many letters and emails I receive from people begging for my help..."

Gabriel blew out a big breath. This conversation had gone AWOL. What did he expect? Los Angeles attracted all sorts. This girl had done pretty well for herself. She'd achieved the rank of celebrity; only Carmen's success didn't guarantee she wasn't an egotistical nutcase.

Standing up, Gabriel tossed a couple of dollars onto the table as a tip and then issued a warning to the psychic. "Don't mention me on your show, Miss Jenette. You are not to do anything that interferes with my investigation. Do you understand?"

"You need to attend the séance, Gabriel. Can I call you 'Gabriel?'"

He regarded her blandly. "Would you like any more advice regarding your break-ins?"

"No, thank you."

"Good. Please tell your brother-in-law I said hello." Gabriel finished the dregs of his coffee and then headed out the door.

CHAPTER ELEVEN

4/1/88

A*pril Fools! I wish I could think of a good one to play. The only thing I could come up with was making a time capsule. Went up Summit-to-Summit road and walked down to the cement pad. At the fence facing the Valley, I buried it. I will come back here as an old lady, and I'll laugh at myself.*

Gabriel stood on Summit-to-Summit Road with a shovel in his hand. The dirt pathway served as a fire road that connected the neighborhood of Calabasas to Old Topanga Road. It was a well-used hiking trail, not too steep and wide enough for a fire truck. A couple of huge houses had been built in the passing years along its route, but for the most part, the landscape looked much like it did in Nancy's day.

Gabriel walked the dirt road, and the sweeping suburban

vista known as the San Fernando Valley opened up before him.

The cement pad Nancy referred to in her diary had been the foundation of an old house. The scarred and pitted driveway sprouted weeds. A fence, overgrown with Poison Oak, enclosed the entire property. Gabriel hated Poison Oak. He could merely walk by the innocuous-looking shrub, and angry itching welts would appear on his skin.

Might as well get to it.

Gabriel threw over the shovel, hopped the fence, and tried to steer clear of the branches of green and red leaves that reached out venomous fingers.

As he walked along the ruined driveway, an intense sun toasted him, and Gabriel removed his jacket. Some autumn we're having, he thought. The stubborn summer never loosened its hold on Southern California without a fight. This year seemed particularly brutal because of the drought. A crunchy dryness lay on the land, and if the rain didn't come soon, no wildflowers would bloom in the spring. Only the damned Poison Oak seemed impervious to the dry weather. It was just as lush as it could be.

Tucked between a coastal live oak tree and laurel sumac, Gabriel spied a crooked metal post that reminded him of Len Lewicki's bent posture. He scanned the area, and sure enough, about ten feet away, another post poked from the rocky soil. These had to be the remnants of the old fence. Gabriel walked over to the first post and paused, shovel in hand. *Now, what?* The time capsule, if one existed, could be anywhere.

He felt foolish. Gabriel wasn't mandated to walk down every avenue of Nancy's life. He should stick to interviewing friends and family members—any possible witnesses. But what if Nancy had left a trail of bread-crumbs? They could exist in any niche or cranny. Gabriel needed to place himself in Nancy's footsteps at the time of her disappearance, and if it meant standing on a fire road in the middle of the Santa Monica Mountains on a hot day, then that's what he would do.

You're the one getting the clues from Nancy.

No, Gabriel inwardly argued. I'm nosing through her diary, that's all. We'll see if that effort provides me with a lead.

A breeze came up then, cooling the sweat on his brow. Gabriel rolled up his shirtsleeves and laid his jacket on the first post. Nancy claimed to have buried her time capsule on April Fool's Day. For what Gabriel knew of the prankster in Nancy, he could imagine that she'd written that diary entry for the sole purpose of fooling her parents, if they dared to delve into her private journal. Instead, the joke was being played on a detective more than thirty years in the future.

Ah, what the hell... Gabriel took up the shovel and hit hard, resentful earth. He began perpendicular from the old foundation to the fence post, figuring if Nancy did plan to revisit sometime, she'd need a marker. She mentioned the Valley, so Gabriel shoveled dirt at a spot with the best view of suburbia. He didn't dig too deep. A young girl wouldn't have had the patience. Had the ground been so hard then?

Nancy dug here in the springtime, and perhaps green grasses blanketed the area, the soil rich and soft from good winter rains. This sun was relentless. Gabriel grew thirsty and berated himself for not bringing along bottled water.

Just then, he hit pay dirt. About a yard away from the fence post, at about a foot in depth, he felt something crack under his spade. Using his hands to toss the earth aside,

Gabriel uncovered a Rubbermaid container about the size of a shoebox. Something was inside. The brittle lid, already fractured from Gabriel's efforts, disintegrated into shards when he opened the box.

He lifted out the bundle, and his hands trembled in anticipation. The wrapper turned out to be a blue jean jacket. As he unfolded the jacket, he found the material stiff and unyielding. *Like a body in rigor mortis*, he thought.

Despite its protest, the jacket succumbed to reveal the secret inside: a Jack-in-the-Box.

Gabriel inspected the toy in the bright sunlight. It was well preserved, considering the three decades it lay underground. The square box displayed circus scenes, which were slightly rusted and faded. He turned it over in his hand to view each side and beheld a Merry-go-Round, a circus performer riding an elephant, a trapeze artist caught in mid-air, and a lion who snarled at its chair-holding, whip-wielding tamer. The closed lid beckoned to Gabriel.

Moving under the shade of the oak, Gabriel wiped sweaty fingers on his shirt and carefully turned the crank. He heard a tinny rendition of the familiar "Pop Goes the Weasel" tune. The lyrics surfaced to his mind. *All around the mulberry bush, the monkey chased the weasel. The monkey thought t'was all in fun...*

The song was about to end when—Pop! Up sprang a painted-faced clown, and mice ran down Gabriel's spine.

The clown triggered a terrible memory. Victor Archwood had thrown a party at his home and insisted that Gabriel attend. Itching to access the killer, Gabriel neglected to consider the possibility of a trap and accepted Archwood's taunting invitation. Costumes were mandatory, or a guest could not enter. Gabriel recalled Archwood wearing the accouterment of the Grim Reaper, a black-robed skeleton—appropriate for a killer.

Gabriel, who had refused to dress up, was handed the costume of a clown upon his arrival at the party. Having no other choice, he'd worn the costume to gain entrance.

Gabriel could remember very little of the party. He only remembered waking up from a drugged sleep, bound and gagged, and hanging by his arms from a meat hook.

Gazing now at the jovial clown with its outstretched arms, Gabriel thought of Nancy's words, *I'll laugh at myself.*

A tiny pink paper was pinned to the clown's baggy pants. Swallowing his dread, Gabriel unpinned the doll-sized note and unfolded it. In neat handwriting were the words, "Are you still afraid of me?"

He brought the toy with him to Commerce and placed it on his desk. Keeping one eye on the closed lid, lest the clown jump out bearing more bad memories, Gabriel picked up the phone and called Jenna Goldman Klein.

A message machine answered, so he tried her cell phone. No answer there either. Gabriel hung up and dialed the Lewicki household. As he listened to the ring tones, his thoughts went back to the blonde teenager who buried an object of her fear and dared herself to return to it. What a personality Nancy possessed. How could she know, at her young age, that time might be an ally in conquering her fear?

And the fact that she left bits and pieces of herself around... Keeping class notes, burying the Jack-in-the-Box.

It's as if she knew, Gabriel mused. It's as if Nancy needed to leave a mark of permanence before she vanished.

Pauline answered the call. "Hello?"

"I found a Jack-in-the-Box," Gabriel blurted and then wished he had more tact. "I think it belonged to Nancy. She buried it and wrote in her diary where to find it. I hope I didn't cross a line or anything."

"What?" Nancy's mother asked in confusion. "She buried something? I don't understand."

"A Jack-in-the-Box," Gabriel repeated and worried he'd violated some sacred code by digging up a time capsule. "A pop-up thing with circus scenes on it."

"Oh, that." Pauline seemed relieved to quit the subject of something buried. "I remember now. Nancy hated that thing. She'd gotten it as a birthday present when she was little and swore it played on its own. I used to tell her that it was only a cheap toy with a defective mechanism. If it bothers you so much, I said, throw it out. I guess she did."

Gabriel laid his palm on the toy's lid and imagined the clown crouching inside, coiled and ready to strike.

"Is there something else, Gabriel? Did you find anything more?"

"A jacket," he mumbled. "I'll return it to you."

"Please do." Pauline paused. "Gabriel, I have a special favor to ask."

He hoped the favor had nothing to do with a séance.

"Carmen is holding a séance at our house, and I want you to come."

Before Gabriel could protest, Pauline continued. "Carmen says you must participate. She says you hold the key to Nancy's whereabouts, but she must be the translator."

The caustic words that threatened to burn through Gabriel's mouth, he would reserve for the Psychic to the Stars. Nancy's harrowed mother, however, required a gentler approach.

"Pauline," he began, "if I had any idea as to where Nancy was at this moment, I would already be there. This woman, this medium, is nothing more than a TV personality. Please consider that when speaking with her."

"I want you to participate," Pauline begged. "If Carmen is some sort of fake, then isn't it better for you to be there, playing advocate for us? You would do that for Len and me, wouldn't you?"

Gabriel's hand went to his forehead. Nancy's mother certainly knew how to push his buttons. "Okay," he consented. "I'll be there."

"I'm so glad. Carmen wanted to know if she could bring in a camera crew."

"Mrs. Lewicki."

"I'll tell her 'no.' It's not a problem. I'll see you tomorrow at six-thirty."

When the call ended, Gabriel's eyes fell on the Jack-in-the-Box and its four circus scenes. Now, he was going to attend a performance worthy of a Big Top. He picked up the toy and turned the crank.

All around the mulberry bush—there existed horrors far more frightening than a bullshit session with a Ouija board. *The monkey chased the weasel.* Gabriel recalled how the area rug in the living room of a child molester felt against his face. *The monkey thought 'twas all in fun.* He considered how a serial killer named Victor Archwood went, in the course of one evening, from being Gabriel's prey to Gabriel's predator.

The clown suddenly popped up with a small bang. *Are you still afraid of me?*

Gabriel's throat felt dry. He set the toy down and walked over to get himself coffee. Rick met him at the machine.

"Okay, Gabe," the younger detective started in immediately. "I think the Lucky Strike downtown will work. It's a bowling alley, but I can get private lanes, and I'm pretty sure they sell booze. Or we can keep it close to you in Santa Monica at the Fairmont Hotel's Bungalow. That's a little more chic if you prefer something classy."

It took Gabriel a moment to figure out what Rick was talking about, and then he remembered—the bachelor party.

"I don't have a preference," Gabriel told the younger detective.

"I do," countered Ramirez, who had magically appeared behind the two men. "What kind of bachelor party doesn't have women?"

"Well..." Rick began, surprised to see his superior standing there. Had Ramirez been watching and waiting for a bachelor party conference?

"Bowling?" Ramirez barked. "Are you for real? And why would we want to go to some stuck-up bar? 'Oh, let's drink a cognac overlooking the ocean.' Fuck that. Let's see some titties. What are you, Frasier? Some kind of *maricón*?" He turned to Gabriel. "I'm taking over your party."

With that, Ramirez splashed some coffee into a mug, threw both Rick and Gabriel an exasperated look, and strode back toward his office. The two detectives stared after him.

"You're in deep shit," Rick said.

Gabriel sighed. "I was okay with bowling."

CHAPTER TWELVE

A t the end of her taping, Carmen rose from her chair as the audience clapped. Today, she had acted as the liaison between a man and his deceased father, and then she had performed a reading on a famous comedian, who had lost a beloved cousin to a car crash the year before. With the final tear wiped from his eye, the comedian thanked Carmen profusely, claimed she had set a part of him free, and walked off the stage. The Psychic to the Stars now stood alone to address her audience.

"I am excited to give you an update on the Nancy Lewicki case," Carmen said. "The lead investigator has agreed to join me in a séance."

The members of the audience gawked at Carmen, enraptured.

"You see," she continued, "while witnesses age and forget, and forensic evidence dries to a powder, the spirit world remains eternal. Nothing is forgotten. This is where we are going to find the resolution to Nancy's case. If people are responsible for her disappearance, rest assured their secrets will be uncovered at last. That is my promise. Light will fall where shadows hide the truth."

The audience broke into applause, and a few people hooted. Carmen put up a palm to quiet her devotees. "The detective and I plan to make contact with our spiritual guides in the hopes that they lead us to Nancy's whereabouts. I, of course, will keep you continually posted on what we learn about Nancy. Check my Twitter and follow me on Facebook. They say it takes a village, so I am asking you to send me your prayers and positive energy. Together, let's bring a lost girl home."

Carmen allowed the audience to show their admiration by clapping loudly. The taping ended for the day, and Carmen departed for her dressing room.

Once inside, she checked her cell phone and was delighted to see that Brad Franklin had called. Carmen immediately phoned him back, but the call went to voicemail. To avoid coming off as desperate, she did not leave a message. Carmen needed to play her cards right.

Brad and she would make an excellent match. A man running for political office wouldn't question Carmen's success. Instead, he would be proud to link himself with a celebrity. Carmen imagined the two of them together at society events, winking at each other from across a crowded room, anticipating the hour when they would shed their clothes and fuse their bodies.

Smiling in her reverie, Carmen sat primly at her makeup table and reached for a facial cleansing towel. As she wiped the studio makeup from her skin, Carmen's mind drifted to Detective McRay. She hadn't forgotten his little compliment about her looks. Gabriel, though, didn't strike her as the flirtatious type. In fact, Carmen sensed the presence of a significant other, but she also sensed hesitancy. Was Gabriel unhappy with his significant other? If only she had the opportunity to learn a little more about the detective.

Carmen remembered leaning toward Gabriel as they sat together over coffee. She'd caught a subtle hint of his cologne and under that, the crispness of a freshly laundered shirt. A woman would have to hold Gabriel very close to capture his essence.

Why did he wrap himself in so much protective insulation? Carmen longed to perform a reading on the detective. Besides the fact that he mystified her, Carmen couldn't shake the feeling that Gabriel had connected to Nancy. Why or how the two were connected, Carmen did not know. They could be long-lost relatives walking the same genetic road, calling out to each other through the chains of DNA. Perhaps Nancy and Gabriel had forged a meaningful relationship in a past life. If Nancy hadn't disappeared, would they have met again in this one?

Or perhaps there was something about the detective that attracted wayfaring souls. Maybe Gabriel functioned like an astronaut's flag planted on a lonely plain of the moon. Maybe his presence reassured the lost, and he served as a signpost to point the way home across seemingly endless space. The more Carmen considered it, the more she grew certain that Nancy Lewicki had reached out for help across the spheres of human consciousness, and Gabriel McRay grasped her hand.

And the mindless man didn't even realize it.

In a way, Carmen envied Gabriel. His blindness made his intentions pure. Not so for other people. Carmen eyed her image in the makeup mirror and reflected on her rise to stardom. *No,* she thought. *You had better close the door on that particular reflection.*

A foot of shame crossed the threshold and blocked the psychic from shutting out her memories. She began her career as a petite Creole girl who accompanied her salesman father to Hollywood, California for an Amway convention. Her father, blessed with second sight, read tarot when he wasn't selling personal care products. Faith healers credit God with their cures, so he took no money for his spiritual services. Carmen had considered that irresponsible.

While in California, an amused cohort of her father's introduced the two of them to a famous playboy. Carmen had pulled out Daddy's tarot cards and gave the playboy a reading. The *bon vivant*, beguiled by the young and pretty occultist, asked her out on a date. Carmen's father had been indignant. "You're too young for him," he said.

Carmen, however, snuck out of the hotel room to meet the playboy and soon discovered how hard that boy could play. She said goodbye to the south and took up residence in the man's Beverly Hills mansion. Carmen didn't tarry there long, for she met other important men who were more than delighted to dip their wicks in her brand of exotic wax. Those gentlemen helped to move her career along.

In no time, Carmen became the in-crowd's best-kept sensation. She was a jet setter, reading the palms of the European elite—once even for a reckless sheik in Dubai. Carmen's ambition knew no bounds. When celebrities began touting her abilities, Hollywood came calling. Although she would admit this to no one, money and fame became Carmen's most precious amulets.

Grandmother's warning of Carmen's *defo*—her tragic

flaw grew distant in the face of all the accolades. Carmen was having too much fun to worry about a fall from grace.

And then she met Gabriel McRay, who unknowingly raised a mirror to Carmen's insolent face. Reflected in that glass was not the celebrated clairvoyant idolized by audiences around the world, but the willful little hick who'd slept her way to the top.

"I call to you, Nancy!" Carmen smacked her lips shut in embarrassment. Why did she shriek like that? Thank God she had a private dressing room.

The truth is humbling. Covering her face with her hands, Carmen whispered, "I call out to you to give me a sign, Nancy. Make me legit. Tell me where you are."

When he left work for the day, Gabriel carried with him both the Jack-in-the-Box and Ramirez's threat to plan the bachelor party. He pondered calling his boss to propose that the men have a casual night, a dinner out perhaps, but then Gabriel imagined the backlash he'd receive from such a suggestion.

As his car crawled along the congested freeways, Gabriel decided that he hated parties. *All* parties. Having no one else he could vent to, Gabriel called Ming but found his fiancée as agitated as he. Ming had been calling bakeries all day and needed to know what flavors Gabriel liked and which days he would be available to go cake tasting.

Gabriel couldn't end the call fast enough.

As soon as he stepped through the front door of his house, Gabriel poured himself a glass of Jameson and downed the whiskey in one swallow. He decided to spend the night in front of the television and took the whiskey bottle with him.

A few hours later, Gabriel roused himself from the couch, locked up the house, and began his usual nightly routine.

He undressed, hung his tie on the rack, did the same with his belt, and tossed his dirty clothes into the laundry basket. He laid out his work clothes for tomorrow, brushed his teeth, and set the alarm.

Would his routine change when Ming came to live with him? Her toothbrush already cozied up next to his in the bathroom drawer. Her shampoos, conditioners, salt scrub, and body oil took up most of the space in his shower. He figured things wouldn't change that much. Or would they?

Gabriel went to the bedroom window and opened it. It was almost Halloween, and the weather remained warm. After climbing into bed, he reached his hand toward the opposite side where Ming usually lay. Thoughts of her smooth skin and the way her hair draped about her face when she slept comforted him. Gabriel watched the moon make a slow trek across the night sky until sleep closed his eyes.

A sound, profound and abrupt, startled him awake. Sitting up, Gabriel looked at the bedside clock, 3:15 a.m. He waited, listening, and then heard a single knock at his front door—loud and hard.

The cop in him was immediately suspicious, the victim

in him, paranoid, and with newfound adrenaline, Gabriel launched himself out of bed. As he walked toward the front of the house, he fought the temptation to get his gun.

Gabriel opened the front door. No one stood on the threshold. He stepped outside, and the ocean breeze stroked the curls of his dark hair. Oddly, it wasn't dark out. Nor was it light. Gabriel felt caught between night and day, in a sort of twilight.

Santa Monica never slept. The distant sound of neighbors' voices, cars, planes, and the occasional siren produced a constant hum. Tonight, however, a hush fell over the city. The only sound Gabriel heard was wind chimes. Ming had hung the deep bass kind out front and a smaller set in the backyard. The long chimes rang in a low, resonating peal.

Send not to know for whom the bell tolls. It tolls for thee.

An unwelcome hollowness filled Gabriel's chest. Sure that he'd heard a single, deliberate knock, he scanned the ground to see if someone had thrown a rock at his door. No stones littered his porch, and no scratch marked the entry. Figuring he'd dreamed the sound, Gabriel pivoted back into his house and froze.

A hideous figure, a corpse so rotted that the gender was unrecognizable, stood on his wood floor. Clothed in rags that were dripping wet, the figure stood motionless. As Gabriel stared dumbstruck, water swelled the dead flesh. Fissures broke through on the skin, and dark water poured from them. The facial tissue peeled away in thick clods to reveal a white, grinning skull.

Gasping, Gabriel jerked back and his head hit the bed's headboard. Clutching his aching skull, he realized he'd been dreaming.

No dream. That was a nightmare. Had Victor Archwood returned, dressed as the Grim Reaper, to haunt Gabriel's sleep?

"Jesus," Gabriel muttered and looked at the clock. The numbers glowed red: three-fifteen.

CHAPTER THIRTEEN

4/4/88

S*at under my tree tonight and had to do it. I can't keep it to myself anymore, and now it's out there.*

Gabriel sat hunched over the diary in the semi-privacy of his work cubicle. He absently rubbed the tender spot where his skull connected with the headboard last night and turned the page of the dairy, eager to discover what "it" referred to. Instead of elaborating on the secret she could no longer "keep to herself," Nancy had written a new entry.

4/7/88

Creamed by schoolwork, but getting excited. I'm counting down to the big day!

The following page was blank. Gabriel thumbed through the rest of the diary, but only empty lines met his eyes. Surprised at how dejected he felt to see no further entries, Gabriel closed the little book and gazed at its faux-leather cover and tarnished brass lock.

He wondered what Nancy felt compelled to do that long-ago April fourth.

His cell phone chirped with an alert and glancing at it, Gabriel put the diary away. It was time for his therapy session with Dr. B, and after last night's dream, Gabriel did not want to miss this appointment.

In Monterey Park, about a twenty-minute drive from Commerce, the departmental psychiatrist Dr. Raymond Berkowitz welcomed Gabriel into his office. A few years back, Internal Affairs had mandated that Gabriel go to therapy. Now, his visits were purely voluntary. Dr. B, as Gabriel called him, now seemed more like a friend than a therapist.

"Let's talk about you for a change," Gabriel told him when he'd settled in his usual chair.

"Fine." Dr. B grinned from the opposite armchair. "I'll come to your house and usurp the entire conversation, but while we're on your dime, I think it's okay to discuss you."

Gabriel didn't argue, although he wished he could once and for all shed the issues that dominated his conversations. Every time Gabriel reached a point of strength and felt empowered enough to end his therapy, a challenging event or a simple negative word would trigger his self-doubt. Even the clown in Nancy's Jack-in-the-Box had managed to shake him up. Gabriel didn't like the idea of psychoanalysis functioning as a lifelong crutch after he married Ming. He should be stronger than that.

"Excited about the wedding?" Dr. B asked as if reading Gabriel's mind.

"Of course." Then, Gabriel added, "And don't try to find anything wrong. We're all good on that front."

Dr. B's features remained passive. He was a lanky man in his fifties who wore wire-rimmed glasses that he rarely bothered to adjust. When he bent his face down, they slid down the bridge of his nose or fell off. The lenses magnified his brown eyes, which didn't bother Gabriel because those eyes were always warm and attentive.

"It's a big step," Dr. B stated.

"You're fishing, Raymond."

"That's my job. Is everything truly all quiet on the marriage front?"

"Nice war analogy." Gabriel sighed. "You know me better than anyone. I'm trying to figure out why the prospect of marriage scares the hell out of me. Sometimes I think it's because I don't want to give up my home, my privacy—but that's not it. I miss Ming when she's not around." He paused to think. "Maybe it's the idea of a long-term commitment."

"What about committing bothers you?" Dr. B asked.

"I don't know. Maybe I'm not capable of it."

The psychologist shrugged one shoulder. "I think anyone who envisions a long-term commitment is going to be intimidated. The way I see it, Gabe, you commit to a lot of things. Every time you take on a case, you commit. Every time you wake up in the morning and brave the traffic to work, you commit. As inconsequential as it seems, planning and cooking one of your gourmet meals is a commitment. You've told me you recently committed to a vegetable garden because you wanted to grow your ingredients. I don't see you as fearful of commitment at all. Could it be that you are afraid of being responsible for a wife?"

"No," Gabriel answered, and then recalled Ming's father picking up the dinner check because Gabriel earned a "policeman's salary."

"What do you think is behind the fear?"

Fear. Why did every negative emotion seem to stem from fear? Gabriel figured Dr. B knew but wanted his patient to pinpoint the source of the discomfort. The fear must be very deep-seated, because every time Gabriel got close to it, his mind ducked and ran for cover. Even now, merely discussing marriage caused a pit to form in his stomach.

"Marriage is a big step," Dr. B prompted. "Not only are you trusting that Ming will not hurt or betray you, but you are also trusting that life will provide you with a happy ending."

Immediately, the pit in Gabriel's stomach widened into a chasm.

Dr. B stood up and walked to the water pitcher. He poured a glass for Gabriel, who accepted it. Dr. B then reclaimed his seat.

"Let's explore the fear. Is it something about a happy ending?"

Gabriel thought of Nancy Lewicki, and his throat momentarily constricted. How did her parents live with that kind of pain?

Dr. B's glasses slipped, and he pushed them up the bridge of his nose. "Loving someone puts you in a very vulnerable position, doesn't it? Do you feel it is better to be alone on an island where no one can hurt you? Where nothing can touch you. Do you think that would protect you?"

No man is an island, entire of itself. John Donne's poem, along with Nancy Lewicki, stepped into Gabriel's mind.

"Gabe," Dr. B said and leaned forward. "You have been making strides to get off that lonely island since the day I met you. Your desire to work toward being happy is one of your best traits, and why you've progressed so well."

Gabriel said nothing, but the black hole in his gut began to diminish.

Dr. B continued, "Think about the wonderful progress you have made, and in the meantime, we'll explore the fear. Marriage is a big commitment, and it's okay to feel doubtful. Do you know what the German folklorist Walter Anderson said about the subject?"

Gabriel chuckled and waited. Dr. B was fond of quotes.

"'We're never so vulnerable as when we trust someone. But if we cannot trust, neither can we find love or joy'." Dr. B sat back in his chair, satisfied. "So, what do those sage words mean to you?"

"Take the risk," Gabriel answered.

The therapist grinned, which caused his glasses to slip again.

"Speaking of the wedding..." Gabriel shifted in his seat.

"Yes?"

"How would you feel about being my best man?"

Dr. B righted his spectacles and shook his head. "Gabe, I would feel honored, but unfortunately, I cannot be your best man. It's a conflict of interest."

Gabriel again thought of his ex-partner, Dash, who would have been his first choice. Dr. B was right, of course. A friendship would conflict with their professional relationship. Unfortunately, that presented Gabriel with another dilemma. He could not think of one person to stand up for him at his wedding.

As he collected his jacket, Gabriel said, "I'm amazed at

how this marriage business manages to spotlight all my deficiencies."

"You are not deficient," Dr. B said and accompanied his patient to the door. "You have a very level head on your shoulders."

"But I'm having nightmares again. I thought I was past all that PTSD stuff."

"And then Victor Archwood came along."

"I need to get past it. I can't bring it into a marriage."

"Give yourself time to process everything, okay? Ming knows who you are." Dr. B clapped him on the back. "Any exciting plans for the evening? Where are you off to now?"

"I'm off to a séance where I'm expected to commune with the dead." He gave his therapist an exaggerated wink. "How's that for my level head?"

CHAPTER FOURTEEN

As Gabriel drove to the Lewicki condo in West Los Angeles, some idiot texting in the car behind nearly slammed into him. The sudden screeching of brakes caused Gabriel's already tense shoulders to bunch up and ache. On top of that, Gabriel suspected that tonight's séance would be comparable to taking an innocent walk and stepping on dog shit.

Once Pauline showed him inside, Gabriel handed her Nancy's jean jacket without fanfare. Not a sympathetic move, he quickly learned, for Pauline froze when she grasped the article of clothing. Her fingers traced the threads of the coarse fabric as if they could string a path to her missing daughter.

Reluctantly, Pauline released the jacket to her waiting husband. When Len's once-powerful hands made contact with that strayed memento of Nancy, his angled posture bent earthward another few degrees.

Gabriel looked beyond the living room to the small dining room, anything to avoid watching Len and Pauline's heartstrings plucked by a musty jacket. The dining room table, he noted, now sported a velvet, wine-colored cloth.

"Gabriel, I'd like you to meet our son, Paul."

Nancy's mother gestured toward a man who hovered like an apparition in a corner of the living room. Upon seeing him, Gabriel would have indeed thought he'd encountered a ghost, except that Nancy's brother appeared burdened by pure mortal hell.

Thinning blonde hair topped a sun-peeled forehead. Paul's red-rimmed eyes possessed a wild look that reminded Gabriel of the drug-addled or the insane. Although Gabriel figured Paul Lewicki to be in his late thirties, he seemed old, aged before his time.

"How do you do?" Gabriel held out his hand to the man.

Paul gave him an inimical handshake as if touching Gabriel would prove unhealthy.

"How do you do?" The words fell out of Paul's mouth like crumbs.

As Pauline headed toward the dining room, she said, "Nancy was like a second mother to Paul, and Carmen hopes that their close sibling connection will get us good results."

Gabriel tried not to roll his eyes. Instead, he studied Paul Lewicki. If mannerisms indicated a person's mindset, then Paul's body language spoke volumes. He fidgeted like a five-year-old and appeared to be afflicted by a nervous tic that caused the left side of his mouth to twitch. Gabriel noticed that Len and Pauline tiptoed around their son but didn't take his plagued demeanor too seriously. Perhaps they considered Paul more a millstone around their necks than a serious family calamity. Gabriel would advise them to think otherwise.

Carmen Jenette exited the kitchen, holding a glass of water. When she saw Gabriel, she lit up. "You made it. Thank you for making an effort."

Yeah-let's-get-this-over-with. Gabriel returned her greeting with a half-hearted wave of his hand.

Carmen moved over to Len. "Is that Nancy's jacket? May I see it?"

Len handed her the blue jean jacket. Gabriel glanced over at Paul. Nancy's brother flinched to see the psychic caress the cloth.

"This will help us," Carmen told Len, and then addressed the others. "Why don't we all take our seats now?"

Nancy's brother, father, and mother headed into the dining room. Gabriel lingered behind and followed Carmen as she turned off the lights.

"Did you get a proper alarm system installed in your home?"

"Not yet," Carmen replied, "but I've made some calls. Do you know if a DNA profile has been done yet? You know, on the blood found in my house?"

Their shadows grew more pronounced along the walls with each dying light.

"Detective Bonin could give you a time frame. Have you two been in contact?"

"He says he's hoping to have the results soon, although I'd appreciate it if someone could rush the testing. You don't know anyone working in the forensic lab, do you?"

As soon as Carmen asked the question, she paused, and then faced Gabriel. *"Do you?"*

"My fiancée is the county M.E."

A knowing smile extended across the psychic's face. Her

hangdog tooth gave her grin a playful twist. "Ah. I knew something was there. I guess I didn't want to delve too deeply into your love life. You and I will just have to remain friends."

Gabriel kept his expression serious. He figured Carmen fell naturally into the role of a coquette, but he wasn't game for her manipulation. Carmen, failing to get the reaction she'd expected, cleared her throat. "It's time to join the others."

The dining room had been transformed for the evening's special paranormal event. The flame of a pillar candle threw dancing shadows on the walls and emitted a strong-scented smoke. Various amulets rested on the table, a few crystals, and something that looked like an animal bone.

When Gabriel and Carmen entered the room, Len and Pauline took their seats. Heeding a non-verbalized signal, Paul sat between his parents.

"Gabriel?" Carmen gestured to the open chair between herself and Pauline. "I need everyone to join hands."

Gabriel took off his jacket and hung it over the chair back. Sitting, he took the hands of the two women on either side of him. He noticed Nancy's jacket lay across on Carmen's lap.

Carmen, controlled and in her element, said, "I need everyone to clear his or her mind of any straying thoughts. Just concentrate on your breath. Everyone take a deep breath and let it out slowly. Relax."

Next to him, Gabriel heard Pauline take a shaky inhalation as if her body would not hold air. On the opposite side of the table, Len Lewicki seemed to be barely breathing. Paul kept his bloodshot eyes on the candle. His lips pinned to a horizontal line.

"Visualize bright, white light," Carmen murmured in a voice smooth as the velvet cloth. "It is surrounding you. Let it clear your mind. Breathe."

The words struck a familiar chord with Gabriel. He tried to remember where he'd heard similar phrases.

"Take deep breaths and let them out slowly. Visualize the light."

Then Gabriel remembered. A couple of years before, he had sat with Dr. B and received the same directive. *Watch the light. Listen to my voice. Take slow, deep breaths.*

Was Carmen trying to hypnotize the present party? Is that how psychics pulled off their stunts? Gabriel focused on the candle, which was sending a thin plume of smoke into the air. Through the flame, Gabriel saw Paul Lewicki shake like a volcano about to erupt until his father threw him a fierce look, which quelled the trembling.

"I see mountains," Carmen said.

Pauline nodded and whispered, "Nancy loved the mountains."

Paul's lips moved as he muttered under his breath. Gabriel reckoned that a man with a fragile mental state probably should not be exposed to a gathering of ghosts.

Carmen's brows furrowed in concentration. "I'm not getting a clear picture."

She gave a small shake of her shoulders and sat up straighter in the chair. "We are seeking the help of our spiritual guides to lead us to Nancy. We want to focus only on those who can enlighten us about Nancy. Come forth."

A silence fell upon the room. Gabriel's eyes shifted

toward Paul Lewicki. He was shaking his head, and his face screwed up as if he were about to cry.

Carmen's grasp of Gabriel's hand suddenly tightened, and she sucked in air. She held her breath for what seemed an extraordinarily long time and then slowly released it.

"I see an ocean." She gripped Gabriel's hand more firmly. "Gray water—not blue. Cold."

Pauline Lewicki gave a little gasp, and Gabriel felt her fingers tremble in his. He knew what she was thinking. She anguished that her daughter lay in some cold, disconsolate ocean.

Grief is a taxing burden to bear. Unrequited hope is tortuous. Gabriel witnessed each of the Lewickis displaying the strain. He fired a disparaging look toward Carmen, but the psychic did not notice. Her eyes were shut, and words floated from her mouth in a hushed monotone.

"I smell pine trees and damp air. I feel concrete underneath me—no, granite. I can see the variations in the stone. Gray, black and white. Smooth to the touch. There's a rumbling on the street where I sit. A trolley car."

Pauline Lewicki opened her eyes and looked beyond Gabriel to her husband. Len's eyes were open wide, and the couple shared an anxious glance. Between them, Paul Lewicki sat still as stone, except for that tic agitating the corner of his mouth. The poor wretch seemed distracted by the candle, whose dancing flame mocked his misery.

"The granite steps lead to the front door of a house," Carmen whispered. "There is loneliness here and the fear of being alone."

Paul's eyes shifted to Carmen. Pauline's hand squeezed Gabriel's as if holding on for dear life. And there was something else, something that dragged Gabriel's heart down to the pit of his stomach.

Carmen shook her head. "A terrible danger is close and hidden within the guise of a friend."

Len Lewicki blurted out, "Where are you, Carmen? Can you see? Can you see any street signs? Anything?"

The medium, her eyes still closed, shook her head fervently, not in response to Len, but against some unseen terror.

"A smiling, brutal friend," Carmen said. "Callous. Selfish with an insatiable need."

Gabriel watched a tear make a track down Pauline's cheek.

"Nancy," Pauline whispered, and her nose began to run. "Where are you, Sweetheart?"

For a terrible moment, Nancy's mother reminded Gabriel of the watery corpse of his nightmare, filled with a flood of sorrowful emotion. A deluge so overpowering, that when it broke, it would leave nothing behind but a blood-less shell. All at once, Gabriel broke his handhold with Pauline and Carmen and stood up.

The psychic kept her eyes shut, but Nancy's mother looked at Gabriel in concern. He would stay no longer. The only valid means of returning Nancy to her family, dead or alive, was gumshoe detective work. Not psychic phenom-ena. Not hocus-pocus. Certainly not this debasing tribute to Carmen's ego.

"We're done," Gabriel announced and addressed the closed-eyed psychic. "Don't you think this family has been tortured enough? What exactly are you trying to accom-plish, Carmen? You see mountains. You see oceans. What's next? The fucking rings of Saturn?" He tossed an apologetic face toward Pauline and Len. "Pardon me."

Facing Carmen again, Gabriel shook his head. "Getting visions from the great beyond about Nancy... What are you really after?"

The shades of Carmen's eyes rolled up, revealing two emeralds that glittered at Gabriel. "The messages I'm receiving today are not about Nancy, Detective. They are about you."

Gabriel shivered involuntarily but held his defiant posture.

"The granite stairs. The duplex. Your childhood home, correct?"

He held his tongue.

"And the false friend was real, wasn't he? He was a monstrosity that burned a brand onto your psyche. I saw what that man did to you, and now I understand."

Gabriel felt his face go ashen. The room seemed a dead weight around him, a crush of heavy stones on his chest. Len and Pauline regarded him with a mix of compassion and curiosity. Nancy's brother gaped at Gabriel with an expression Gabriel couldn't decipher, for humiliation blotted out his senses.

Carmen's voice soothed like a soft cloth. "Your suffering gives you great empathy for the victims of the cases you work, Gabriel. Perhaps this is the reason Nancy sought you out."

"You'd better stop while you're ahead," he told her in a voice prickling with menace. He pulled on his coat and then addressed the Lewickis. "Give me time. That's all I ask. But please, do not ask me to participate in any more of this lunacy."

Outside in the fresh air, Gabriel leaned over his car and took a deep breath to clear his head. Clouds rolling in from the cold north sheathed the horizon in a brilliant sunset.

The front door of the Lewicki's condo swung open, and Gabriel saw Carmen hustle down the walkway toward him. She had a nerve, that one. Gabriel yanked open his car door and slid inside.

"I didn't mean to offend you." Carmen came to the driver's side window. The sky glowed orange and pink behind her brown hair, which made the young woman appear otherworldly. "I'm sorry. You have to understand; I cannot help what I see."

Gabriel eyeballed her but kept quiet.

"We called upon those who could enlighten us to find Nancy, and you appeared. As I said, you're the one getting the clues."

With his database of snide responses completely disabled, Gabriel pushed the key into the ignition and started the car.

"What's expensive?" Carmen asked as the sky bled scarlet around the halo of her curls.

"What?" Gabriel asked her.

"I don't know." Her eyes dropped to her feet as if she'd suddenly grown shy. "I'm reading off of you that something is expensive. Are you thinking of buying something?"

Again, Gabriel found himself unable to speak. *I saw what that man did to you.*

"Not in the market for a new car or wristwatch, are you?" Carmen looked up and offered Gabriel a cordial smile in a vain attempt to lighten his mood.

"No," he answered gravely and put the car into gear. As he pulled away from the curb, his cluttered mind begged for a reprieve, and his heart twisted up in his chest.

———

Gabriel ended up driving to Nancy's old house in Liberty Canyon. He had to take a drive. Carmen had successfully dug a peephole into his soul and peered through his defenses. Gabriel didn't relish the idea of going home and bleeding out his bad memories alone. He could have called Ming, but visiting with her meant visiting with her parents, and Gabriel couldn't fathom doing battle with Tom Li while feeling eviscerated. He would find shelter in his work instead.

Gabriel exited his car. Above him, a few stars lay scattered near a doleful crescent moon, fighting for relevance against the overwhelming San Fernando Valley lights. He thought he might take the opportunity to canvass the neighborhood and see if any of Nancy's neighbors still lived in the surrounding houses. He'd probably find more residents at home in the evening anyhow.

Gabriel walked toward the house next to Nancy's, but the Weeping Willow on her lawn snagged his attention.

Once again, Gabriel stood at the edge of the lawn and surveyed the tree in the moonlight. Why did it mesmerize him? Out of the corner of his eye, Gabriel spied the red-bearded homeowner staring at him from the window.

Gabriel looked expectantly at the front door. Sure enough, a moment later, Redbeard threw the door open and strode outside.

"You again. Why are you watching my home? What do

you want?" He planted himself on the lawn opposite Gabriel and put his hands on his hips. "I have a gun, you know. Inside."

Gabriel pointed innocently toward the street. "I was planning to interview your neighbors."

"Oh, yeah? Lemme see your identification again."

Gabriel produced his identification. The man carefully inspected the badge and then handed it back.

"I'll ask you again. Why are you watching my house?"

Gabriel glanced at the willow. "I don't know. The girl I'm looking for, Nancy Lewicki, used to live here and wrote about a tree in her diary. I thought maybe this was it."

The red-bearded man didn't seem to buy his explanation. Gabriel didn't blame him. Sanity, ever-elusive, seemed to have abandoned Gabriel altogether. "Sorry to have bothered you."

He headed down the sidewalk and then paused. "You wouldn't happen to know which of your neighbors are long-time residents, would you? Maybe some of them remember Nancy."

"Nancy." The homeowner thoughtfully pulled at his ginger beard. "Sorry. I only know there are lots of families on this street with teenagers. They drive you crazy with their parties. Say, I can call the cops if they get too loud, right?"

"Why not?" Gabriel grinned and began walking toward the next house.

"You know," Redbeard began and waggled a finger in the air. "I'll bet those initials are hers. There's an 'N' there."

Gabriel swiveled around to view the man. "What initials? Where?"

"Just on the other side of that tree." Redbeard gestured to the willow.

Gabriel's feet moved quickly across the grass. His eyes scanned the trunk.

"Hold on," the homeowner said. "I'll grab us a flashlight."

Gabriel discerned some sort of indentations under the moonlight, but the shadows played tricks. The homeowner soon returned with a good strong light and trained the beam on the tree trunk. Etched into the bark were the barely perceptible initials *NLL*.

Gabriel reached out, and his fingernail traced the grooves in the wood. Touching the letters, he could almost picture a lazy afternoon with birds chattering and the sound of a distant lawnmower. *Nancy sits with her back against the tree, and a diary on her lap. She chews on a pen and contemplates life under the flowing branches. The leaves tickle the top of her head. A feeling so powerful, so forbidden, overtakes her, and she must do something to release it. Getting a screwdriver from her dad's toolbox, Nancy returns to the tree, and leaves an impression in the wood. The tree shares her secret.*

NLL

Gabriel's heartbeat quickened, but it was not due to the carved remnant of Nancy. Under her initials, he viewed the scraped symbol of a plus sign and, underneath that, the letters BOD.

CHAPTER FIFTEEN

As soon as he tossed his keys onto the kitchen counter, Gabriel strode into his study and dug through the plastic container holding Nancy's effects. He searched for the Pee-Chee folder with its hand-drawn hearts and the stick-figure band. Finding it, Gabriel reread the note passed between Nancy and her friend. He held Nancy's diary entry next to the note and compared the handwriting of both.

Although he was no forensic document examiner, Gabriel had shadowed enough professionals in his career to understand the significance of key signs. The characteristics examiners considered when conducting handwriting comparisons were not necessarily identical letters. Any decent forger could trace or mimic someone else's writing. Professionals looked for the subtle, subconscious habits of the writer, and observed the formation and spacing of the letters, even the pen pressure. By comparing Nancy's diary entries to the note passed in class, Gabriel could now see that he mistakenly assumed Nancy had written the first sentence of the note.

The friend had been caught for ditching school. It was the friend who asked how the "bod" was doing. "Bod" did not reference a body. The letters B-O-D were someone's initials.

Gabriel rifled through the plastic container, searching for Nancy's school yearbooks. He found the one dated 1988 and flipped it open. His eyes scanned through all the names in Nancy's grade and found no one, neither a boy nor a girl, with the initials B.O.D. Gabriel then checked all the other classes. No B.O.D.

He picked up his cell phone and texted Pauline Lewicki, asking her if Nancy had a friend, most likely a male, who had the initials B.O.D.

While he awaited her reply, Gabriel searched the box for other yearbooks, and picked through each class, searching for last names beginning with a "D."

His phone chirped, and he read Pauline's text. She could not outright remember any friend of Nancy's having those initials, but they could have belonged to an acquaintance from school.

Curious about the initials, Pauline questioned Gabriel about their importance. He remained vague. What if his discovery had no value?

Nancy's mother sent Gabriel another text, this one asking if he was okay. *You can confide in me. I will understand.*

Gabriel's ears reddened at the idea that a stranger could peer into his private life—thanks to Carmen Jenette. He replied to Pauline that he was fine, thanked her for her concern, and then swallowed the embarrassment clogging his throat. He promised to keep her updated on his progress.

As he set down the phone, Gabriel felt his admiration for

Nancy's mother grow. Pauline put aside her own plight so she could deal with his. Red capes didn't always identify a heroine.

He looked over at Nancy's picture. "Your mom is a good person," Gabriel told her. "I don't know why bad things happen to good people."

From his bookshelf, Nancy smiled.

The remaining yearbooks lay on the carpet in front of him, awaiting his attention. Sighing, Gabriel pulled one to him, determined to ferret out the identity of B.O.D.

"I'm sensing mountains," Carmen said on her show the next day. "I'm getting a strong connection between the outdoors and Nancy Lewicki. I believe she went to some sort of mountain area. There are trees."

Dr. Ming Li, wearing scrubs and sitting across from Gabriel in the L.A. General Hospital cafeteria, viewed the television.

"What is she? The Magic Eight Ball?" Ming stuck a forkful of skillet potatoes in her mouth and talked as she chewed. "The answer is unclear. Check back later. Hey, pass the salt."

Gabriel reached for the saltshaker and watched Carmen's televised image.

"I picture Nancy," the medium said and held up her hands. "And I get a strange flowing sensation, as with an air or water current."

"Jesus, she's vague." Ming took the salt from Gabriel and liberally dosed her potatoes. "I could do a better job, and I'm about as clairvoyant as a crab."

Gabriel did a double-take at the amount of salt Ming poured. "Take it easy with that, babe. I'm getting high blood pressure just watching you."

Ming laughed and traded in the salt for a squirt of Tabasco.

Gabriel picked up his fork and dug into his chicken potpie. "She's in a bind. She announced to the entire world that she would single-handedly solve the case."

"No," Ming countered. "She said she was working with *you*, and the two of you were going to solve the case."

"Looks like we're both lost then."

"Why? Aren't you keeping her updated on your progress?"

"What progress?" Gabriel said with a full mouth. "All I have is the hunch that Nancy might have had a crush on someone with the initials B.O.D. And I can't find a kid with those initials. I tried."

Ming waved him off. "Quit spitting on me. You're talking with your mouth full."

Gabriel opened his mouth to tease her and then nearly choked when he started to laugh. Ming frowned at him.

"I won't save your life, you know. Not if you're going to be gross." Her frown morphed into a smile. "You'll find what you're looking for. You always do. At any rate, you're doing better than her." She lifted her chin toward the television.

Gabriel's laughter faded, and he looked pensively at his meal. "I don't know. Carmen did a pretty good job on me at the séance. She described my home in San Francisco right down to the color of the front steps."

Ming sat back and gazed at her fiancé.

Gabriel speared a piece of chicken with his fork. "Strange that she'd focus on the steps."

Gabriel had been sitting on the stairway the day his neighbor Andrew waved to him from across the street. He had invited Gabriel to come over, like the proverbial spider to the fly.

"Carmen said she saw what Andrew did to me." He stabbed the chicken again.

Ming's gaze did not waver, but her voice went soft. "Phonies can uncover a lot through research. Maybe she studied up on you. Did she give you the details? I mean, did she tell you exactly what she supposedly saw?"

"Nope."

"Well, there you go." Ming took up her fork. "Want me to beat her up?"

Gabriel grinned. "No."

"You sure? I'd be happy to punch her lights out."

Gabriel surveyed his lover from across the table, the torn hangnail on an otherwise smooth-skinned hand. The obsidian wells of Ming's eyes glittered with merriment and wisdom. Gabriel envisioned the tantalizing curves beneath her clinical scrubs.

"I miss you," he said.

"You don't have to be a stranger, you know."

"I'm giving you space to catch up with your folks."

"Bullshit. You hate my father."

"Hate is a strong word." Gabriel glanced at his watch. "I gotta go." He rose from his chair.

"I love you, my husband."

He bent down and kissed the top of her head. "Did I miss the wedding?"

"No," Ming replied, smiling. "But doesn't it sound nice? Don't you like hearing me refer to you as my husband?"

Gabriel ruffled her long hair. "I do. Listen, I've got to run and get a couple of photos to the lab. Speaking of lab work, the DNA profile on Carmen's attacker—could you check on the status of that?"

Ming's smile wilted like a dying rose, the petals of it falling from her face. "Sure. I'll check. Why are you so interested? This has nothing to do with your case, does it?"

"No. I'm curious, that's all."

Gabriel left Ming in the cafeteria and wondered how his heart could be so cruel. Why did he continually deny his fiancée the chance to be excited about their upcoming wedding?

The Hertzberg-Davis Forensic Science Center resided on the Cal State Los Angeles campus. The facility contained photography and digital evidence studios, where Gabriel hoped to find assistance in salvaging Nancy's photographs. As he pulled into a parking space, a call came through on his cell. Gabriel picked it up.

His Lieutenant spoke, "I got it all planned out, McRay."

"You've got what planned out?"

"Your bachelor party, dumbshit."

Ramirez. What a gem.

"I'll email you the details, but I'm throwing your fiesta at Jumbo's Clown Room in Hollywood."

"Jumbo's Clown Room?" Gabriel repeated.

"Something wrong, McRay?"

"No, but I have a thing about clowns."

"Well, don't worry. You can drown your fear in booze and strippers."

Ramirez hung up. Gabriel tucked away his phone, shook his head, and killed the engine of his car.

Once inside the studio, Gabriel presented the criminologist, Martin Lopez, the three melded photographs. "Can you get these apart without ruining them?"

Lopez shrugged. "No problem."

Gabriel watched as he soaked the photos in a mixture of water and Photoflo, a product that, according to the Kodak Company, claimed to be wetter than water. With scrupulous hands, Lopez pulled the photos apart until he met with resistance. Taking up a small baster, Lopez applied a squirt of liquid and continued peeling them away from each other. He then dried the photographs and presented them to Gabriel.

They could now view the middle picture in its entirety. A boy stood on the other side of the cowboy figure from Nancy. Unfortunately, part of his face was a ruinous mass, the result of its fusion to the other photographs.

Seeing Gabriel's disappointment, Lopez assured him. "Not to worry, Detective."

The criminologist scanned the photograph into his computer. He duplicated the left side of the face and then flipped it to the right.

"Human faces are basically symmetrical," Lopez explained. "We've got algorithms for facial image recognition that are implemented through computerized symmetry sensing. What I'm doing is superimposing the questioned image over a control image, which gives me a projective symmetry. I'll make a composite image from the superimposed image, and that should provide us with a reasonably accurate identity establishment."

Gabriel held out his hand. "Just give me the damn photo."

Lopez laughed and strode over to his printer. "Rumor has it that you're having a bachelor party. You getting married?"

Jumbo's Clown Room clunked into Gabriel's mind. "That's the usual prerequisite for a bachelor party, isn't it?"

The criminologist walked over to Gabriel and handed him an enlarged version of the restored photograph.

"I like parties," Lopez stated. "It would get me out of the lab."

"True." The tie around Gabriel's neck suddenly felt too tight, and he pulled at it. "It's fine with me if you'd like to come. Talk to Lieutenant Ramirez. It's his show."

"I will. Thanks for the invite, Gabe."

Sure thing, Gabriel thought wearily and didn't bother to readjust his tie. He watched a contented Lopez return to his computer and the digital riddles therein. Gabriel then dropped his eyes to the reconstructed photograph.

Standing on the opposite side of the cowboy effigy was a young man. Athletic and handsome, he had sand-colored hair and the gawky smile of a boy riding the tail end of adolescence. Gabriel shifted his gaze to the exultant smile on Nancy's face.

He felt confident that if no cowboy stood between the two young people, hands would be held and bodies would touch. Gabriel couldn't say how he knew this; perhaps the glint in Nancy's eye afforded him insight. She did, however, hide one arm behind the statue, and one could easily imagine her reaching around and resting a hand on the boy's backside. At any rate, Gabriel could see that Nancy Lewicki was in love.

Pulling out his cell phone, Gabriel called Pauline and told her they needed to talk.

CHAPTER SIXTEEN

The space around Carmen felt deadened, gravid, like a swollen corpse. The oppressive atmosphere enshrouded her in such lethargy, when Carmen's cell phone rang, she couldn't answer it.

She stood in her dressing room and stared into her open purse. The feeling had plagued her throughout the entire taping of the show. Carmen might have considered the possibility of a physical malady, except that she knew better. The vacuum, the deadness, was a warning.

Carmen heeded its counsel but didn't know what she should avoid. A part of her wanted to investigate the danger like a moth that, yearning for the light, risks peril at the flame. For now, Carmen resisted that particular calling and summoned up the energy to answer the phone.

"Carmen? It's Brad Franklin. I hope I'm not disturbing you."

"Not at all," she said, grateful for the interruption.

"I've been thinking about you."

"Nothing bad, I hope."

"All good. I wanted you to know that I keep my promises. Are you free tonight?"

"I am."

"Would you like to meet for drinks? Dinner?"

"I could use a drink right now."

"Really? Well, I'd like to hear why. Name the place and the time."

Carmen paused a moment, thinking. "How about the Formosa Café at eight?"

"You got it," Brad said. "I'm looking forward to seeing you."

The DA hung up. A serene smile shaped Carmen's lips as she wandered from her dressing room into the hallway. Normally a hub of activity, the studio seemed deserted. Well, she thought, the weekend was coming up. Carmen couldn't blame the interns and crew for cutting out quickly.

Entering the soundstage, Carmen strolled through the empty set, thinking of Brad Franklin and turning her back on the ominous feeling. She imagined that dating Brad would lend legitimacy to her work, especially after he made Attorney General. What a power couple they would make!

Swinging her purse over her shoulder, she traipsed toward the exit. The cameras stood silent around Carmen, the lenses of their eyes blackened and closed. The lights, usually bright and intrusive, hung in suspended dispassion.

She hopped off the stage into the well of audience seats. As Carmen made her way through, a man pounced behind her and clamped a hand over her mouth.

Panic tore through her. Carmen pulled against the stranger, but his fingers smashed against the southern hemisphere of her face. Not again, she thought. Not here! This was her world.

The man's touch rained a storm of sensations upon her. A useless thought—nearly laughable at this point, rose above the din of her internal alarm bells: she should have carried pepper spray.

"Why won't you let her sleep?" The man's voice shredded the air between them. "Why are you doing this?"

His breath was hot in Carmen's ear, and his body emitted a desperate sweat. The hand crushing her lips felt pasty and thick.

"Let her alone! Leave us in peace!"

Carmen gathered her wits together and plowed her elbow into a surprisingly soft belly. A pneumatic hiss erupted from the man, and he fell away from her. Carmen didn't waste precious time to view her attacker. She ran, like a wild animal, down the corridor and screamed.

CHAPTER SEVENTEEN

Gabriel pulled the restored photograph of the unidentified boy out of his jacket pocket and held it in front of Pauline Lewicki's eyes.

"Who is this?" he demanded. "Is this someone with the initials B.O.D.?"

Pauline took an involuntary step back, and Gabriel retracted his hand—somewhat. His overenthusiastic approach did need curbing, but this new lead had galvanized him.

The condo smelled comfortably of supper and seemed to reproach Gabriel's churlish entrance.

"I don't know." Pauline squinted her eyes at the photo. "I've never seen that boy. I don't remember."

"Are you sure?" Gabriel pressed. "Because I found it in an album called 'Mammoth Lakes,' and I'm assuming you were there with Nancy."

Len Lewicki rose from the dining table, where two plates strewn with half-eaten food lay amid crumpled napkins. He plucked the photo from Gabriel's hand and went to study it on the couch.

Reaching into his jacket once more, Gabriel produced the miniature photo album entitled "Mammoth Lakes." He handed it to Pauline.

"Can I get you something to eat, Gabriel?" she asked as her eyes fell on the photo album. "I made pork chops."

"No, thank you, I'm…" Glancing once again at the couple's partially eaten supper, Gabriel felt a cloud of shame descend upon his head. "I apologize for busting in like this."

"Are you kidding?" Len called from the couch. "We welcome your updates at any hour."

Pauline moved over to her husband's side on the sofa and deflated against the cushions. "These were taken in Mammoth Lakes," she murmured as her index finger traced the edges of each picture. "We used to rent a cabin on Lake George every summer."

Gabriel seated himself in the armchair across from the Lewickis. He leaned forward, elbows on his knees. "You went the summer before Nancy disappeared?"

"Every summer," Len affirmed as he studied the restored image of the boy.

"I want to know who he is." Gabriel waved a finger at the Polaroid. "I looked through all of Nancy's yearbooks. I couldn't find anybody with the initials B.O.D. I need to know if they belong to this kid. You must know him."

The Lewickis shook their heads in unison, and Pauline spoke up. "I can't recall any boys Nancy would have met on our trips to Mammoth. But it was so long ago. Nancy didn't take any boys along with her; just a girlfriend once or twice."

"We've been to Bodie, but I don't recall Nancy meeting anyone there."

"Bodie?" Gabriel asked.

"That's where the picture was taken. Bodie is the ghost town." Len Lewicki handed the photo to his wife. Pauline examined it and nodded her agreement.

Gabriel blinked at Len. The wheels turned in his mind and gathered speed.

Bodie. Bo-D. *B.O.D.*

Not initials, but a nickname? Could B.O.D. stand not for a boy, but a ghost town? Would Nancy have kept this person such a secret she would have assigned him a code name? The boy had not traveled with the family but somehow appeared in their photos. This meant that Nancy either met the young man in Bodie for the first time or arranged to meet him there. The body language between the two young people made Gabriel suspect the two already knew each other.

He'd hunted through all the names containing the letters B.O.D in Nancy's yearbooks. Now, Gabriel knew he'd have to inspect all the boys' pictures in the hopes of identifying the mystery male.

His cell phone vibrated in his pocket, but Gabriel ignored it. "The summer when that photo was taken, would that have been in 1987?"

"Might be," Len said, viewing the photo once more.

"You went to a ghost town called Bodie in 1987. You don't remember Nancy meeting anyone there?"

Again, the Lewickis shook their heads.

"I wonder who took the picture, if not you…" Gabriel blew out a frustrated breath and glanced at the recent calls on his phone. "Excuse me."

Gabriel walked away from the Lewickis and returned Ming's call.

"Hey," he said when she answered.

"I've pushed the biological reference sample left by your palm reader's perpetrator up in rank," she told him.

"That's one mouthful," Gabriel said.

"Welcome to my world. We'll get a DNA profile sometime this week.

I also contacted Detective Bonin for you and told him you were 'curious' about the suspect's identity. He says he'll contact you as soon as the sample has run its course through CODIS to assuage your curiosity."

A sprinkling of sarcasm on a well-intentioned cake killed the sweet flavor.

"You okay?" Gabriel asked his fiancée and quickly deduced that she wasn't.

"Just peachy. I've got a postmortem to do. See you later."

Gabriel chewed at the side of his mouth. Trouble brewed. Could Ming be jealous of Carmen, a woman he could barely tolerate? Or had Ming finally wearied of Gabriel's lack of enthusiasm for their wedding? A small, insidious voice whispered inside him; *you want that, don't you? You want to push her away.*

His phone pinged again, a message from work, which thankfully interrupted the slanderous whispering in his head. After placing a call to his office, Gabriel learned that Jenna Goldman Klein had left a message for him. She was available to meet at any time.

Gabriel retrieved Bodie's picture from the Lewickis and bade them goodbye with the promise of keeping them posted on the identity of the boy. As soon as he entered his car, Gabriel returned Jenna's call.

For someone so pivotal in Nancy's life, Gabriel requested a face-to-face meeting. He offered to drive to San Diego the very next day, with the fragile hope that Nancy's best friend would give him information she was unable to provide thirty years before.

"Why didn't you go straight to the police?" Brad Franklin asked Carmen.

"I knew I would see you," she told him. "Who better to hear about this than the District Attorney? Besides, the studio security guard reported it."

Carmen and Brad were seated in a cozy red booth under the black and white visage of Frank Sinatra. Brad set his cell phone down next to two Singapore Slings and an untouched plate of chicken dumplings.

"And the guy escaped again," he muttered.

"I admit I was a bit hysterical. I guess while I was trying to make myself understood to the guard, he slipped past us."

"Well, your Detective Bonin knows about the assault now."

"What did he say?" Carmen asked, glancing at the phone on the table.

"He says he'll call me as soon as they get a profile on the suspect. If they get a profile."

Carmen raised her green eyes to Brad's. "The guard at the studio thinks the man had a reserved ticket, joined the rest of the audience, and hid himself away at the end of the taping."

"Well, that may work to our advantage," Brad said.

"We'll view the footage of the audience, and you can pick him out."

Carmen shook her head. "I didn't see him. I know that sounds stupid, but I panicked and ran. I didn't want to stay around and look."

"Surely, you must have seen something."

"I'm sorry. It happened so fast."

"You're not safe, Carmen. You should get a bodyguard."

"That's what Detective McRay says. He thinks I have a stalker." She reached for her beverage and held it to her lips. "Do you know Detective McRay? He's investigating a cold case, the police case I've talked about on my show. The Nancy Lewicki disappearance from the late eighties."

"I know of him," Brad said. "People in the public eye, people like you and me need to take extra precautions for our safety."

Carmen shook her head. "I'm not going to be followed around by some hulk." Taking a sip, she said, "The man who grabbed me tonight asked why I wouldn't leave her alone. Do you think he was talking about Nancy?"

Brad looked confused. "What makes you say that?"

"He told me to—to let her sleep. That's how he put it."

Brad reached for his frothy drink. "The guy could be talking about any one of the guests you've had on your show —or their dead folk."

"But when I calmed down, I asked my spiritual guides for help. They referenced Nancy to me. Who is he, that he would know her?"

"You couldn't identify him?"

"I don't know."

"He's most likely a deranged fan of yours. God only knows what he was talking about." Brad took a swallow of his drink. Finding the beverage too cloying for his liking, he grimaced, which caused Carmen to smile.

Setting down the drink, Brad appraised his tablemate. "It's nice to see you smile. Thanks for keeping our date. I would have understood a cancellation."

"Like I said, who better to save me than The White Knight?"

"Aren't you afraid, Carmen?"

She watched the condensation form on her glass for a moment. "I'm feeling tangled," she said, at last. "Uneasy. I can't shake it."

"Well, given what's happened to you..."

Carmen shivered. When she looked at Brad, there were tears in her eyes, like sparkling dewdrops on two fields of green. He reached across the table and clasped her hand.

"Maybe you shouldn't go home alone tonight," he suggested.

"Where can I go?"

Brad flashed her a canny wink and asked the waiter for the check.

Gabriel returned home from the Lewickis, enveloped in fatigue, but unable to sit still. He burned to know the identity of Nancy's enigmatic male friend and hoped the meeting tomorrow with Jenna would bear fruit.

A text from his office appeared on his phone. Gabriel considered ignoring it for the night but then changed his mind.

Detective Bonin from Robbery/Assault had left a message regarding Carmen Jenette. Someone had attacked her again, this time at the television studio. Bonin also informed Gabriel that he'd entered the DNA profile from the sample found in Carmen's home invasion into CODIS, the Combined DNA Index System. The process might take up to two weeks, but Bonin promised to make it a high priority.

Gabriel plugged his cell phone into the charger and then wondered what he could do to relax. Deciding a soak in the hot tub would make him drowsy, he stripped off his clothing and headed outside.

To keep his nakedness private, Gabriel turned off the backyard lights and lifted the lid from the hot tub. The water inside appeared black. Climbing in, Gabriel sat back, heaved a sigh, and closed his eyes. He could hear the low bass of the wind chimes hanging in the front yard. More distinct was the second set of chimes. They made a light, fluttering sound. Why Ming insisted the house needed two sets of chimes, Gabriel didn't know. Perhaps it was her way of staking a claim to his property.

The hot water lapped against his body, and Gabriel felt his shoulders loosen. His features relaxed, and his breathing evened out. The sounds of the city began to fade away. A plopping sound accompanied by a small splash made him open his eyes. He viewed the dark water but didn't see anything unusual. Above, dark clouds crept slowly across the plain of the sky and slowly consumed the moon.

A jelly-like object passed against Gabriel's calf, and he jumped. His eyes pierced the water. *What was that?*

All at once, the tub's jets activated, and a slick and bloated corpse upended next to Gabriel, with swollen, milky-blue eyes and a yawning mouth.

"The fuck!" Gabriel cried. He grappled for the edge of

the spa, but his hands slipped, and he fell back against the corpse. To his horror, the roiling water stripped sheets of dead flesh away until nothing remained but bones.

Coughing, Gabriel opened his eyes and righted himself from where he'd slipped under the water. The jets were stilled. The water lay calm. Gabriel's heart, however, surged as he turned on the spa lights and searched for the dead body. He saw nothing. There was nothing to see.

How long had he been asleep? Gabriel climbed out of the tub and wiped his mouth with a shaky hand. Trekking into his bedroom, he noted the time on the bedside clock: three-fifteen. As he climbed into bed and hid under the covers, Gabriel wondered whether or not he should check himself into a psych ward.

You're the one getting the clues from Nancy.

No, he told himself. The sodden corpse was no message from a phantom. Nightmares had beset Gabriel in the past. This head-trip merely constituted one more manifestation of a mind he continually tried to mend, which stubbornly, sadly, defied Gabriel's best efforts.

CHAPTER EIGHTEEN

"I wish you'd told me you were going to Carlsbad. The two of us could use a getaway," Ming said over the phone.

Gabriel pulled into the parking lot of Vigilucci's on the coast highway in Carlsbad, a beach town just north of San Diego. He used Bluetooth to talk to Ming, a standard feature on his new car. For years, Gabriel had driven an ancient Celica whose best function was an air conditioner that only worked when driving downhill. The last time Gabriel had seen the Celica was the night he began his descent into hell with Victor Archwood. Having no idea what Archwood did with the car, Gabriel purchased a Mazda sedan.

"I'm not staying overnight," Gabriel told her. "I'm interviewing one of Nancy's girlfriends and then heading back to LA."

He parked and held the phone to his ear as he walked toward the restaurant. "How about staying over at my place?" he asked.

"I can't. I was only fantasizing about a getaway. There

are a lot more details to hammer out before tomorrow night. You do remember our engagement party, don't you?"

He ignored the venom in Ming's question. "I thought your parents were throwing the party. How did the planning fall on you?"

"They're from another state, Gabriel. It's hard for them to plan something from far away. They're paying for the party, and that's enough."

Gabriel glanced at the ocean, his constant friend that sparkled like a sapphire as it played on the sand to his left. He never asked Ming's parents to pay for anything. The engagement party had been their idea.

"It's a lot of pressure to put on you." Gabriel refused to feel indebted to the Li's.

She did not respond.

"Ming?"

"I'm here."

Gabriel paused at the café's entrance. "Can't we simplify things?"

"We could call off the marriage," she answered. "That would simplify things."

Glancing once more at the blue water, Gabriel wondered why life couldn't roll as naturally as the waves to the shore. His hot tub hallucination and this fight with his fiancée were wearing him down, and Gabriel felt his temper twitch.

"I wish you would get into this wedding a little more," Ming said. "You don't seem excited to marry me."

"I'm excited."

"Listen to you! You sound like a frigging lobotomy victim."

"I'm tired, okay?" Gabriel groused. "I didn't sleep well. Look, I've got to go. I'm at the restaurant."

"Have a wonderful dining experience, asshole."

Ming hung up. Gabriel wiped his brow, though no sweat moistened his skin, and deposited the cell phone into his pocket. He moved to the hostess counter to ask for a table.

Vigilucci's served classic Italian fare. The weather was temperate despite the season, and the hostess seated Gabriel on the outside patio, which afforded him a nice view of the water. Watching the surf, he reflected on his conversation with Ming and felt culpable, although he failed to understand the exact nature of his crime.

Gabriel only knew that he shied away from the marriage. He'd been doing that since Ming said yes to his proposal. Why? Why did he want to sabotage a union with the woman he loved?

Gabriel brushed aside the troublesome question to read the menu. After making a food choice, he looked up to search the faces of the patrons as they walked into the restaurant. He wondered if he'd recognize Jenna Goldman Klein.

Gabriel's image of Jenna was that of a teenaged girl with freckles, a bright smile, and chestnut hair styled in a permanent wave. A girl whose body had been prepubescent—thin, boyish, with womanhood still far on the horizon.

A female entered the restaurant wearing plus-size jeans and a loose blouse. A large tote burdened one shoulder. She paused and looked around, and Gabriel lifted his hand in a hesitant wave. Was she Jenna? The woman walked over to him.

"Detective McRay?"

"Yes." Gabriel rose in a gentlemanly way as Nancy's old friend took a seat. Jenna's hair, from-the-bottle red, showed gray at the roots. A carpal tunnel support encircled her right wrist, and a Band-Aid covered a vein on her left arm. She wore sporty sunglasses in an attempt to splash beach city vogue on an otherwise afflicted appearance.

Gabriel handed Jenna his business card, which she carefully inspected and then deposited into her handbag.

"Thank you for driving all this way," she said as she removed her sunglasses. "I know the traffic can be horrid."

"Not a problem." Gabriel reclaimed his seat. Eyeing Jenna, he searched for the teenaged girl in her features, behind the jowls that pulled on her face and the brown and white spots that marked her décolletage, courtesy of the California sunshine. He tried, but couldn't find her—the youthful Jenna, the girl with the buoyant smile. She wasn't there.

Fear slithered into the seat next to him and elbowed Gabriel. *Nothing lasts forever*, the fear whispered and pointed a bony finger toward his union with Ming.

"So," Jenna began. "What did you need to talk to me about?"

"Ma'am, do you remember your friend, Nancy Lewicki?"

"How can I forget her?"

A waitress strolled over and addressed Jenna in a cheery voice. "Would you like to see a menu?"

Jenna shook her head and ordered a decaffeinated coffee. Gabriel ordered a prosciutto sandwich with a side of soup. When the waitress left, he said to Jenna, "There was a boy that Nancy met in Mammoth one year. Did she mention him?"

"Bodie?"

The corners of Gabriel's mouth dragged down. *That simple*, he thought. If only he could have talked to Jenna sooner.

"Was that a nickname?" he asked, stewing in his juices.

"I believe so."

"What was his real name?" Gabriel brought out his notepad and pen.

Jenna shrugged. "I don't know. I only knew him as Bodie."

Staving off his frustration, Gabriel pulled the restored Polaroid from his jacket pocket. "Was this him? Was this Bodie?"

Taking the picture from Gabriel, Jenna studied the boy captured on film. "I think so. I can't be sure. It was so long ago. I believe that's him."

"Who was he?" Gabriel asked. "Do you know anything about him?"

"A cute guy who Nancy liked. That's all. It wasn't a big deal. Is this what you came all this way out for?"

"When Nancy went missing," Gabriel said, and his irritation began to pierce the conversation. "How come you didn't come forward to tell someone about her friend Bodie?"

"Why would I?" Jenna asked, defensive. "He was only a kid, just like us." She paused a moment to think. "I think he might have been slightly older. That's right. He was a sophomore at Taft. I think Bodie was a jock. At any rate, Nancy had this huge crush on him and knew her parents would think she was too young for a boyfriend."

"Taft?"

"Taft High School in the Valley."

The food arrived, and Gabriel picked up a spoon to sample the minestrone. "You recognize his picture, so you must have known him. What do you remember about him?"

"Nothing." Jenna poured two packets of sugar substitute

into her cup. "We'd meet and hang out at Topanga Plaza. That was the big mall back then. Bodie had some cute friends that he'd bring along. I had a crush on one of them —Toby." She paused to smile as she stirred her coffee. "At any rate, Bodie always treated Nancy with respect. It was obvious that he liked her a lot, and she liked him. Nancy had planned a sixteenth birthday party for him."

The spoon froze near Gabriel's mouth. Jenna's words caught him off guard. "The party she was planning wasn't for you?"

Jenna sipped at her coffee. "We only told Nancy's parents it was for me. They would never support her having a boyfriend, much less throwing a party for him."

"Christ... And you didn't think this was important?" Gabriel put down his spoon and stared at the woman across from him.

Jenna seemed perplexed by his reaction. "I never gave Bodie a second thought. My God, you don't think he –"

"Your best friend goes missing, and a mysterious boyfriend isn't anything noteworthy to bring up?"

"He wasn't mysterious!"

"Except for his identity, which was a secret, correct? Nothing mysterious about that."

"Excuse me, Detective. I don't like your tone." Jenna jammed a lock of flame-colored hair behind her ear and then rubbed at her supported wrist as if it pained her. "You're not going to play the bullying dick with me because I have access to good lawyers. I have zero tolerance for cops like you."

Gabriel stayed quiet. He perceived Jenna Goldman Klein to be a lady accustomed to getting her way by employing sharp tongue or—he glanced at the Band-Aid and wrist support, by gaining sympathy for a variety of ills. While his assessment of the woman might prove incorrect, nothing in Jenna's present demeanor negated that judgment.

"I'm trying to be helpful here," she continued. "Don't you think I've racked my brain for over thirty years trying to figure out what happened to Nancy? There, but for the grace of God, go I. It could have been me, Detective. Why was it her?"

Jenna swallowed hard as if Nancy's disappearance represented a bitter pill. Her head drooped, and she concentrated on her coffee. "Nancy was my best friend. One day, here, the next moment, gone. I mean, vanished from the face of the earth. Everyone knew something bad had happened; only nobody could figure out what. I kept thinking I was next. I slept in my closet, but that wasn't the worst. You see, Nancy and I had plans. All of us were going to start a band. With Nancy around, anything was possible. She had this contagious enthusiasm. She embraced life, then just disappeared."

Jenna's voice hitched, and Gabriel watched her dig through her purse. "Sometimes, I dream about her. In my dreams, she's the fearless leader, and I'm her follower. I loved Nancy. She lit up the room when she walked in. If a light like that can go out, then what's left for the rest of us?" Jenna extracted a tissue from a pack and dabbed at her eyes. "It stays with you, you know. The guilt, the fright, the strangeness—all the emotions turn into little ghosts that haunt you."

Jenna went silent and waited for Gabriel to offer his sympathy. He didn't.

Nancy shouldn't be blamed for ruining Jenna's life.

Gabriel speculated that Jenna perceived Nancy's disappearance as the first paving stone on a path of woeful events.

Gabriel could have played the victim countless times, but he rejected the idea of presenting himself as a hapless man, a ghost fleshed with a human form. Even Pauline Lewicki, a grieving mother, could put aside her misery to care about the feelings of a stranger.

Jenna seemed to realize that Gabriel had interpreted her inner self, and her cheeks flushed a little red. "But we're here to talk about Nancy, aren't we?"

Gabriel didn't reply, so Jenna continued. "Bodie couldn't have had anything to do with what happened to Nancy. He was out of town at the time she disappeared."

"How do you know that?"

"I tried calling him right when –"

"You have his phone number?"

"I *had* his phone number. Bodie was in Texas with his relatives at the time of Nancy's disappearance. I remember he was in Texas because I thought it was such a long distance for a kid to fly alone. I can tell you that when we finally talked, he sounded very upset. I'd never heard a boy cry before, and it made an impression on me. Bodie and I never spoke after that."

"And you never learned his name?"

Jenna shook her head. "He liked his nickname and referred to himself by it."

Gabriel contemplated the calm ripples of the ocean beside them. "Tell me about your plans that spring with Nancy."

"After Bodie returned home from Texas, we planned to have him meet us at my house, and then go together to the mall. Of course, upon his arrival, all of his friends would be waiting as a surprise, and we'd have the party. It was a simple plan."

"Did Nancy have a list of his friends?"

"She must have. She would have called them to invite them."

Gabriel hadn't found any such list. Not in her diary, not in her photo album, nor anywhere among her personal items. Of course, over time, her parents could have thrown out a random piece of paper.

"Why is Bodie so important to you, Detective?"

"He's the only lead I've got," Gabriel answered honestly. "In my world, you look for the things that stand out. A new friend with no name stands out. Whether he was in Texas or Timbuktu, I'll put Bodie to rest when I'm satisfied that he's a dead end."

Jenna Goldman Klein nodded in understanding. "So you're going to find out his name and talk to him?"

"Absolutely."

She reached into her purse. Instead of pulling out another tissue, she pulled out a padded envelope and slid it across the table to Gabriel.

"Then maybe these will come in handy."

Gabriel took up the envelope and opened it. Inside were cassette tapes.

Jenna smiled, and for a moment, Gabriel caught a glimpse of the carefree teenager. "I kept them," she explained. "Not all of them, of course. Some of the tapes went bad. I listen to them now and then. Nancy envisioned me as the lead vocal, but I don't think I ever would have made it to Carnegie Hall. Nancy played keyboards, but she could sing, too. You'll know her on the recordings because she's the one with the better voice. She told me to keep the tapes at my house because Bodie is on a lot of them. Nancy knew how to cover her tracks."

"Thank you, Mrs. Klein."

The interview was over. Jenna stood up, and her red hair netted the sunlight. She put on her sunglasses and hoisted her tote onto her shoulder.

"Do let me know what happens, Detective. Perhaps then I can put all the little ghosts to rest. The ones that have haunted me all these years are relentless."

CHAPTER NINETEEN

Early the following morning, Gabriel phoned the school's registrar and asked to access the district's database. Taft High School was located in the San Fernando Valley, about ten miles away from Nancy's neighborhood. As Gabriel sat in freeway traffic, he called Ming and hoped to make amends.

After answering his call with the expected brusqueness, Ming softened, and asked how his interview went with Nancy's friend. He relayed to her what Jenna had told him about Bodie and her relationship with Nancy.

"Jenna sounds like a follower," Ming said.

"She admitted as much."

"I guess Nancy was pretty popular with lots of friends."

"I guess," Gabriel said. "Did you have followers?"

"I wasn't popular," Ming said without sentiment. "Nor did I have any friends."

Gabriel guffawed behind the steering wheel. "I have a hard time believing that."

"It's true. I was the girl who was invited to the parties

but could never attend. Too busy with extracurricular activities."

"Setting the world on fire."

"Feeling the burn," Ming admitted.

Thanks to Daddy Dearest, Gabriel added silently. He pulled up into a parking space under a covered lot. A large red and yellow sign above him read: Taft High School.

"Can you meet for lunch today?" Ming asked over the car's speaker. "Say you will."

"I will."

"Great," she said. "I'll come to your office."

"Sounds good."

Five minutes later, Gabriel stood in the high school's administrative building and explained why he was there. The school's principal showed him into an empty office, and Gabriel began to research the photographs of sophomore boys from the year 1988. It didn't take him long to find Bodie.

The boy in the picture with Nancy, the boy tagged with the initials BOD, was named Christopher Rand. Gabriel also learned that his last known address was only a few streets away.

After thanking the school administrators, Gabriel navigated to the Rand home. No one answered when he rang the doorbell, and a surreptitious glance in the mailbox told him that new residents lived there. The Rand family had moved on.

Deadlocked, Gabriel returned to his car. He very much wanted to speak with Christopher, aka Bodie. Perhaps the reason nobody knew what happened to Nancy was because nobody knew about Christopher Rand. Maybe the young man was in Texas at the time Nancy disappeared. Maybe he wasn't. Gabriel intended to find out.

When he was settled once again in his cubicle in Commerce, Gabriel researched Christopher Rand on the Internet. More males with that name existed than he imagined. After hunting through DMV records and probing Google for all Christopher Rands who fit within the correct age range, Gabriel hit upon Bodie. He identified the young man through a picture attached to an obituary notice. *No!* Gabriel smacked his desk with a fist.

Christopher Rand had died of leukemia in 2004 at the age of twenty-eight. Frustrated, Gabriel double-checked the information and then rechecked it. He gazed in defeat at the monitor — *all the little ghosts*. The deceased Christopher Rand was indeed the same young man pictured in Nancy's photo.

A true dead-end.

Gabriel dragged himself into his superior's office to give Ramirez the dismal news. He'd gotten nowhere. Maybe a psychic could do better than he.

After Gabriel gave him the update, Ramirez got to his feet and came around the desk.

"Don't give up, McRay," he said, facing him. "There's got to be something that we missed. You can find it."

Ramirez's portrayal of a supportive friend flummoxed Gabriel. Usually, he exchanged a more acerbic dialogue with his superior. Naturally falling into the role of defending himself, Gabriel complained. "My one lead is dead. What am I supposed to do?"

"What's your gut telling you? You've always had good hunches."

"You sound like Carmen," Gabriel muttered.

"Who?"

"The psychic the Lewickis want me to work with."

Ramirez leaned against his desk. "Is she as hot as she looks on TV?"

"Yeah, but…" Gabriel gave his superior an annoyed look for trapping him. "No."

Ramirez stepped closer. "You sure? What kind of women do you like anyhow?"

Gabriel's eyebrows knitted together. Had he missed something?

"Dr. Li is Mexican," Ramirez said. "But she's also Chinese. I take it you like ethnic-looking women. Fine by me, but you wanna try a blonde on for a change?"

The bachelor party. *God…*

"I don't want to try on anyone for a change," Gabriel told him. "I'm with Ming."

"Pussy." Ramirez reverted to his old unlikeable self. "You've had your head shrunk by Dr. B for too long. You need to loosen up. This is good for you. Trust me."

"Lieutenant, do you want me to be divorced before I'm married?"

"That's up to you, *vato*. You got to keep your woman in line."

Behind Ramirez, Gabriel saw Ming appear at the doorway. He'd nearly forgotten about their lunch date. Gabriel couldn't get a warning out fast enough, so Ramirez rambled on.

"Let me give you some marriage advice. The man makes the rules; the woman follows. Get that?"

At the doorway, Ming crossed her arms and glared at the back of Ramirez's bristly black-haired head.

Gabriel lifted his chin toward the doorway in warning, but Ramirez didn't catch the cue.

"Always remember, McRay, you're the man. Women like being dominated. Like little bitch dogs, the male puts 'em into heat."

Heat. Gabriel could swear he saw steam rising from his fiancée's scalp.

"Now, I know Ming," Ramirez said, unaware of the female broiling behind him. "She thinks she's a real smart-ass. Got a big mouth on her. If she gets in your face too much, don't be afraid to –" He lifted the flat of his palm into the air and grinned, joking.

"To what?" Ming charged forward into the room.

Ramirez jumped and, seeing the fiery medical examiner, put a protective hand over his heart.

"What would you do, Macho Man?" Ming inclined her head toward him. "Come on and astonish me. Boy, you sure do fit the bill of something that would attract a dog. Well, you know what they do to male dogs that get too feisty." She moved right under Ramirez's nose. "They cut off their fucking balls!"

The Lieutenant escaped behind his desk. "Keep away from me."

Ming turned her back on him to address Gabriel. "I'm here for lunch, but also to make sure you leave on time to get ready for the party." She tossed a withering glance toward Ramirez. "A party to which you're not invited."

Gabriel nodded and ushered Ming out the door. "I'll meet you back at my desk, okay?"

Ramirez watched Ming depart and then regarded Gabriel with something like pity. *"Aye, Cabron. Esa mujer…"*

Gabriel informed Ming that he didn't appreciate her flexing her muscles around his boss.

"Don't worry," Ming brushed him off. "Miguel gets me. We go way back. And why do you care if I get in his face? He's always gotten into yours."

"I can stick up for myself."

"Of course, you can, but you don't have to consider yourself as his inferior."

"He is my superior, whether I like it or not."

Ming twirled a chopstick between her fingers. They sat in a Chinese restaurant called Mama Lu's Dumpling House in Monterey Park, eating pork dumplings and stir-fried udon. "What I mean is, you can think beyond your current status. You may have his job someday. One never knows."

"Is this you talking or your father?" Gabriel asked.

Ming's cheekbones reddened. Answer enough. Gabriel speared a pork dumpling and shoved it into his mouth. Chewing, he asked. "Any updates on the DNA profile for Carmen Jenette?"

Ming pushed her plate away and lay her hand on the table palm-up as if in supplication. "Can I ask you something? Why are you so interested in the identity of some random woman's attacker, and yet you act so completely disinterested in our marriage?"

Gabriel shrugged. "What do the two have to do with each other?"

Ming gazed at him, and he saw defeat steal the sparkle from her eyes. Gabriel looked down at her vulnerable hand and knew he should take it. He ought to kiss her hand and tell Ming that he loved her. A stifling stubbornness, however, prevailed upon him, and Gabriel sat like a cold statue.

Ming sighed. "Are you having second thoughts about us?"

"No," Gabriel replied.

If only he could talk to Dash. Gabriel used to rely on his ex-partner for advice on sentimental matters. If only his emotions weren't at odds. Gabriel missed Dash's friendship but resented the man at the same time. Gabriel loved Ming but kept a padlock on his heart and refused to give her the key.

"Tell me what's wrong," Ming pleaded.

Gabriel couldn't pinpoint a reason. He felt knotted up and didn't know how to unravel himself. *Don't push her away.*

"I don't know," Gabriel answered.

Ming's eyes glistened but she placed a tight hold on her emotion. She sat back in her chair, retracted the hand resting on the tabletop, and whispered, "I see."

At the day's end, Gabriel took a quick detour to Monterey Park for a non-scheduled appointment with Dr. B. Before either of the two men could sit down, Gabriel brought up his discussion with Ming.

"I don't know whether the case is getting to me, or it's the wedding," he said. "But if I don't work things out soon, I'm going to lose Ming."

Dr. B settled into his usual chair. "What is it about the case that gets to you?"

Restless, Gabriel stood behind his chair and lightly drummed his fists against the seatback. "Everyone is older or dead."

Dr. B gave him a benign smile. "That tends to happen with a thirty-year-old case."

"I know, but it's different." Gabriel wiped his brow with the back of his hand. "It's depressing. Nothing lasts in this world. There's no solid ground."

Dr. B leaned back. "Why don't you sit down and elaborate."

Gabriel came around the chair and took his seat. "Nancy disappeared without a trace decades ago. The boy who might have known something died pitifully young from cancer. Then there are these dreams I'm having of dead bodies and skeletons. Everywhere I turn, even in my sleep, there's death, dying, loss, and heartbreak."

"Well," Dr. B said with slight amusement. "You are a homicide detective."

Gabriel smiled wearily. Dr. B knew how to deflect his drama. "I get it. Look, the negative shit I see every day has always bothered me, but for some reason, it feels personal now. I don't know why."

"Maybe that's a sign of progress, Gabe. You don't feel detached any more. You used to walk around with protective walls around you."

"Well, I need 'em back. I can't do my job if every bit of bad news is going to floor me. Ming senses I'm pulling away from her. I don't know why." Gabriel shook his head, agitated. "Maybe I'm just beat. These dreams make me not want to sleep."

"Tell me about them."

"They're basically the same. Water and bones. That's strange, isn't it?"

Dr. B removed his glasses and cleaned them on his shirt. "Dreams are where we work things out, and you have a lot to process these days. Our busy schedules don't allow us the time to examine our inner workings, so we do it at night. Although, I will venture to say that this particular dream, this vision you have of a skeleton –"

"And water," Gabriel added. "Always something to do with water."

"Think about it, Gabe," Dr. B said as he positioned the glasses on his nose. "This is most likely a mental leftover from your tortuous experience with Victor Archwood. Before Archwood abducted you, when you were in his house for the costume party, wasn't he dressed as the Grim Reaper? And didn't he wear a skull mask?"

Gabriel nodded.

"Someone cannot go through what you experienced without having been affected. Cut yourself a break. This reaction, while uncomfortable, is normal."

A reflective moment passed, and then Gabriel regarded his therapist. "Carmen says I'm communing with the missing girl. Do you believe in that kind of thing?"

"Who's Carmen?"

"A famous psychic."

The psychiatrist clasped his long fingers together. "I

don't discount the possibility of a highly intuitive person, and I do respect other people's beliefs. But I would advise you to watch out for a sales pitch."

"What do you mean?"

"People who have suffered trauma tend to be more susceptible to the beliefs of someone else, especially if those beliefs offer a convincing explanation of why bad things happen."

"You make me sound pretty feeble, Raymond."

"You're not feeble, nor are you weak. You have successfully integrated catastrophe into your life and are drawing strength from it. That makes you a survivor. There will, however, always be a part of you that questions why bad things happen. All I'm saying is that you don't have to adopt someone else's ideology to answer that question. Carmen is human like the rest of us, and in her quest to 'see light,' she is not exempt from darkness. Consider that, okay?"

"Carmen says my bad experiences are blocking my psychic ability."

Dr. B regarded him carefully. "Do you feel the need to have such an ability?"

Gabriel gave a half-hearted chortle. "I'm not yearning for importance, Raymond. I'm not interested in reading minds. She simply brought up some interesting points."

"Interesting points that only she can enlighten you about, I presume."

Gabriel said nothing.

Dr. B continued. "Perhaps Carmen has some deep-seated psychological reason for needing to appear all-knowing. Trust me; I've seen the need in one form or another sitting right there in that chair."

Gabriel nodded. He understood.

"You mentioned that nothing lasts. I think we ought to talk about your issues with Ming. What's going on?"

"I don't know."

The therapist pushed his lenses up the bridge of his nose. "You said you were going to lose her. Why?"

"She's unhappy that I'm not excited about the wedding."

"You're not looking forward to it? Why not?"

"It's not that I don't want to marry Ming. I do. But she's insisting on a big celebration. The whole nine yards. For me, that includes a bachelor party, which, by the way, Ramirez is planning."

"Yikes."

"Exactly," Gabriel said. "Miguel wants everyone to get drunk and do the whole stripper thing, and I—well, you know. I'm a little picky in that arena."

Dr. B understood. As with most survivors of sexual abuse, the borderlines between sex, perversion, affection, and friendship had blurred for Gabriel, and sexual intimacy had made him uncomfortable for years. Therapy had helped Gabriel put each into its appropriate category. Still, the psychiatrist understood his patient's hesitancy to partake in what most males would consider lusty fun. Sex was strictly a private enterprise with Gabriel, and he was particular regarding any invasion of his personal space. Dr. B also perceived that Gabriel wouldn't want to look weak in the eyes of the other men and would go along with it if he had to.

"Why don't you tell Ramirez to lose the lap dances?"

Gabriel shook his head.

"It's your party, Gabe."

"And I'll cry if I want to? No, thanks." Standing up, Gabriel pulled on his jacket.

"Where are you going?"

"I gotta go and get ready for my engagement party. Do I look excited?"

Dr. B stood up and walked over to his patient. "I think we need to continue this conversation. There's a reason for your apathy. We'll find it."

Gabriel nodded, headed for the door, and then paused. "You wouldn't happen to have an old cassette tape player lying around, would you?"

CHAPTER TWENTY

Dr. Tom Li welcomed the guests as they walked into Napa's private party room. On the surface, Ming's father appeared the model of generosity, a magnanimous father-of-the-bride. Gabriel watched his future relative from the sidelines (where they'd relegated him as an inconsequential groom), and decided that Ming's father was a big blowhard. Clearly, this was Dr. Li's party, and Gabriel didn't appreciate the man using him as a means to show off.

The appointment with Dr. B hadn't done much to lighten Gabriel's mood. One of the few plusses of tonight's affair, however, was the presence of Gabriel's sister Janet and her husband, Michael. The couple had flown in from Seattle that afternoon to attend the party. Gabriel's niece and nephew, much to his disappointment, had been left with a sitter at home.

Janet wove her way through the guests toward him. His sister wore a conservative brown jacket over a tan skirt, and the overhead light cast gold onto her reddish-brown hair. She looked good for a woman who chased after two young kids everyday and kept her appearance like her household, tidy, with nothing out of place. When she arrived at Gabriel's side, she wore an amused grin.

"You look pissed off." Janet nudged her brother. "Smile. It's a party."

Gabriel lifted his chin toward the senior Dr. Li. "Can you imagine growing up with him as a father? Dad was so cool compared to him."

Janet observed Ming's father, a short man whose personality managed to tower over those around him.

"Speaking of Dad, I'll be bringing him and Mom in for the wedding. I've handled all the arrangements, so don't worry about a thing."

Gabriel put an arm around his sister and nodded. He wanted his father to be present at his wedding. "Thanks, Janet."

Ming surfaced next to them, smiling too widely, standing too close, and wobbling slightly on her shapely legs.

"Having fun?" She smelled like gin.

Janet put a steadying hand on Ming's upper arm. "It's a great place. I love the ambiance."

"Wait till you taste the food." Ming's short, clingy green dress showed off her curves, and her hair fell like a black silken veil down her back. She swung her arms around Gabriel's neck and gave him a cross-eyed stare. "How about you? Tell me you're having fun."

He winced under Ming's breath. "Last call for alcohol, babe. How much have you had?"

Ming blew a raspberry. "I lost count. Will you please mingle?" She waggled a reprimanding finger in Gabriel's face. "How can people meet my fiancé if he doesn't mingle? Come on."

Ming took Gabriel's hand. Giving Janet a wink, Gabriel allowed his tipsy fiancée to tow him through the crowd.

He chatted with Mrs. Li, who introduced him to her friends. They seemed nice enough, but Gabriel felt like a specimen under a microscope all the same. He put forth a valiant effort to appear confident and every bit Dr. Ming Li's equal.

Finally, the senior Dr. Li announced that the guests should take their seats. When everyone had settled down, he raised his glass.

"I want to thank you all for coming here tonight. Elena and I appreciate that so many of you came from far away to partake in our celebration. Mr. Zhang, you spent hours teaching Ming to be proficient on the violin. With your help, she performed her first classical recital at only seven years old."

Mr. Zhang, an aged pensioner with spiky white hair and enough wrinkles to impress a Shar-Pei, raised a trembling glass in acknowledgment and smiled, showing off yellowish teeth.

"And so we should celebrate this milestone in Ming's life together," Dr. Li continued. "Please, join Elena and me in toasting the marriage of our daughter."

Janet exchanged an indignant look with her husband, who pointedly rose from his chair, intent on making another toast, one that would include the groom.

As Michael was halfway out of his seat, Dr. Li wisely added, "To her union with Gabriel McRay, her partner in criminology!"

The assembled party, except for Janet, Michael, and Gabriel, laughed at Dr. Li's play on words and cheered the couple.

When the waiters brought out the dessert, the guests gasped and murmured their approval. Ming had ordered customized miniature wedding cakes for each person. Mr. and Mrs. Zhang received cakes with a candied violin at the top. Ming's mother received one with a tiny bouquet of gladiolas fashioned from colorful fondant. Ming placed a small cake before Gabriel, which made him smile for the first time all night.

Two tiny figures, molded from marzipan, resembled shadowy detectives from a 1940's noir novel. The taller one, a male character, wore a fedora and overcoat. He embraced the female figure, who wore a trench coat cinched tight at the waist to accentuate her femme fatale curves. Their faces touched in a kiss.

"How do you do it?" Gabriel asked her in amazement. "You think of everything." He leaned over like the detective on the cake and gave Ming a real kiss.

"Cut it open," Ming said excitedly.

One of the guests teased, "This isn't an autopsy, Doctor."

Gabriel took up a knife and carefully cut open the cake. Inside was a tiny, sugared skull redolent of *Dia de los Muertos*. Delicate lines of black filigree and colorful flowers adorned the skull in typical Day of the Dead fashion.

"It's edible." Ming beamed at Gabriel.

Knowing all eyes gawked at him, Gabriel drew his fiancée close and pretended to be impressed. The skeleton, however, reminded him of his nightmares.

"I love it," he said and gave Ming another kiss, this one a crowd-pleaser.

Everyone clapped heartily. Michael drummed the table with a primal beat to cheer Gabriel on, and Janet hooted.

When the staff cleared away the dessert plates, and the last of the party guests exited, Ming sat on Gabriel's lap and rested her head against his shoulder. All the planning had worn her out. Gabriel kissed the top of her head.

"Someone's got to put you to bed,' he said.

"Okay." She yawned. "As long as it's you."

Dr. Tom Li stood above the couple and said to Gabriel, "How about joining me in the bar for an after-dinner drink?"

Gabriel glanced at his weary fiancée and then regarded the older man. Ming's father seemed determined, so Gabriel gently nudged Ming, and the two of them stood up. Ming went to find her mother, who was finishing a cup of tea at the table.

Tom Li and Gabriel went to the bar where the older man ordered them each a glass of twelve-year-old Glenlivet. Gabriel could see Ming across the restaurant, sitting with her mother. Senior Dr. Li looked at Ming as well.

"You see my daughter?" he said with pride. "She holds one of the highest positions in one of the biggest cities in the United States."

"Ming is very accomplished, sir. She is famous in her field."

"That's right." Dr. Li glowered at Gabriel over his glass. "You are somewhat famous, too."

Gabriel kept his back straight and maintained a calm expression, although his insides started to ferment.

"My wife told me not to say anything, but this concerns my daughter's future, so I have to speak."

"Speak then." Gabriel took a swallow of the scotch.

"I've read some news items about you that I find disturbing. First of all, it's no secret that you've killed people. One could argue that you did so in the line of duty, except that you received public reprimands for your actions. I also read that the city had to settle a multi-million dollar lawsuit because you struck an old lady."

Gabriel kept his voice level. "That incident happened a long time ago when I was in uniform, Mr. Li. It involved the grandmother of a drug dealer, who wasn't much of a lady."

"But the city lost the suit, which meant they found you found liable." The small man seemed pleased that he'd outwitted Gabriel. "You see, I worry that you have a problem with violence. Even now, I hear a man is in the hospital because of you."

Victor Archwood. Gabriel nearly laughed. A man? Try a sadistic serial killer with a penchant for impersonating his dead victims.

"Mr. Li…"

"It's Doctor Li. I worked very hard to earn that title. What assurance do I have that you won't use your fists on my daughter someday? It concerns me to know that you are under the care of a psychiatrist."

Gabriel fought the urge to jump up and give *Dr.* Li a taste of his fists but figured that would be a decidedly wrong move, considering the topic of their conversation.

Allowing himself a little verbal leverage, Gabriel said, "For someone so concerned about your daughter's welfare, where have you been all her adult life? You haven't been the one to pick Ming up when she's fallen. I have. I don't see her running around with a black eye from me, but she's got plenty of scars left by you. That, by the way, is what seeing a psychiatrist enables me to do. I can identify the scars."

Dr. Li's lips pressed together in a thin line. His eyes threw daggers at Gabriel.

Gabriel downed his drink—it was too good to waste. He then thanked Dr. Li for the party and moved off the barstool. He'd probably end up *persona non grata* with his in-laws from now on, but he'd had to defend himself lest Dr. Li think Gabriel was a wimp as well as a wife-beater.

The whiskey he poured himself when he returned home wasn't quite on par with the Glenlivet Gabriel had imbibed at the restaurant. However, the bottle belonged to him, bought on his 'policeman's salary.' Gabriel threw the liquor into his mouth, where it sizzled down his throat.

What a bunch of crap, he griped. Thankfully, Ming had been too wasted to see the line drawn in the sand between her father and him. She'd gone home with her parents, satisfied with the evening.

Still muttering, Gabriel refilled his glass and pulled from a plastic bag the dusty cassette player he borrowed from Dr. B. The words REWIND, PLAY, STOP, and FORWARD were printed under a toggle switch. If only life could be as simple as toggling between those four words.

Feeling the liquor warm his blood, Gabriel carried the tape deck and the drink into his study, although to listen to Nancy's tapes at this point seemed futile. Any information gleaned from the recordings about Christopher Rand would prove useless, seeing that the boy was dead and gone.

All around the mulberry bush.

Gabriel stopped in his tracks and cocked his head. He thought he'd heard music, but silence surrounded him. Moving into his study, Gabriel flipped the light switch.

The Jack-in-the-Box lay on the carpeted floor, square and

innocent. No music played. The crank was still, but Gabriel felt something winding up all the same. He pictured the crouching clown, hidden inside with a big painted grin. *Who's under the makeup? Andrew Pierce? Victor Archwood? Dr. Tom Li?*

When the lid popped open would Gabriel be yanked into the past with all hope for a happy future lost?

Damn Ming's father. He'd had to bring up Gabriel's checkered past. Now, doubts and insecurities goose-stepped in Gabriel's mind like enemy soldiers with raised bayonets. He glanced at the bookcase, and Nancy Lewicki's smile encouraged him. *Don't give up.*

Placing the tape player on his desk, Gabriel sat down and reached for the envelope containing Nancy's recordings. Dr. B claimed to have purchased the Philips tape player in 1991. Not sure if it would work, Gabriel plugged the cord into a socket and pressed the PLAY button. Sure enough, the rollers began to turn. He stopped the machine and inserted one of Nancy's tapes. Dialing up the volume, Gabriel pressed PLAY.

CHAPTER TWENTY-ONE

A terrible caterwauling filled the study. The tape recording resembled a demon talking backward. Gabriel shut off the awful sound, and, unnerved, exchanged the warped tape for a different one. He touched PLAY and steeled himself for another go-round. This time, Gabriel lowered the volume.

Amid crackles and a prominent buzz, he heard the strumming of an acoustic guitar. A girl began to sing, and a piano played. Another female voice chimed in. Superior to the first singer, this girl sang with more confidence. She belted sometimes and then went soft and mysterious. Her voice reminded Gabriel of the wind chimes at his home and in his dreams—Nancy.

Gabriel looked at her photo. Nancy's smile and blue eyes twinkled over her bared shoulder. The room filled with recorded giggles as the guitar player hit a wrong chord.

Ugh, not again! I think we ought to harmonize on that last stanza to bring it out more.

Good idea. A separate girl's voice agreed.

I'll bet we could play the Roxy.

No way.

Then the Troubadour, for sure.

Your parents won't let you.

My parents won't know. Come on, Jen-Jen!

Gabriel let the tape play to the end. He listened to their music and eavesdropped on their girlish banter. Punkin and Jen-Jen. Gabriel could see why Jenna's memories of Nancy carried such weight. Nancy sounded passionate about their musical endeavor, sure she could make it happen. The songs were quite good, too.

Gabriel switched out the tape for another. This one began with Nancy quietly counting off.

A one, two, three…

Nancy began to hum along to a guitar. Then Gabriel heard a rough, off-tonal singing, a boy's voice, deepening into manhood. Someone different attempted to sing with Nancy. *Bodie. Christopher Rand.*

Gabriel leaned forward in his chair and listened attentively. The boy's voice cracked suddenly, and Nancy and Christopher burst out laughing. Nancy's laugh was exceptionally high and giddy in this recording. The precocious giggle of a flirt.

"Nice, Bodie!"

"Hey," the boy on tape said, *"This is your thing, not mine. No one said I was Jon Bon Jovi."*

"It's your thing, too. It will be all of ours."

So, they were planning to play the Roxy with Bodie on board. Gabriel smiled at the youthful dreams and ambitions circulating on the tape deck's rollers. Resting his chin on his hands, he wondered if he should tell the Lewickis about their daughter and her boyfriend from Taft High School. Did it matter? Would the knowledge shake loose a valuable recollection? At any rate, Gabriel felt he should disclose that he had Nancy's musical recordings. Her parents would want to know.

Blood, even a dime-sized spot, provided decent quality DNA for forensic analysis. When Ming explained the science behind DNA profiling to Gabriel and used phrases like "variable number of tandem repeats" or "STR markers on loci," she lost him. All he wanted to know is whether or not he had a candidate match.

When Detective Bonin called to tell Gabriel they had a DNA profile on Carmen's attacker, Gabriel went over to Robbery/Assault to check the results from CODIS.

CODIS contained several databases, such as indexes of missing persons or unidentified human remains. It also included the National DNA Index System. NDIS held DNA profiles of convicted offenders (CO), arrestees (AR), and forensic unknowns (FU), which were samples taken from crime scenes, as in the case of Carmen's attacker.

Bonin, a wild-haired gamin in his late twenties, sat casually at his desk in Converse shoes, a black t-shirt, and skinny jeans. He reminded Gabriel of punk rocker Joey Ramone.

"I originally entered the profile in FU." Bonin pulled up a screenshot on his computer. "Then bounced it against AR and CO, and that's where I got a hit. The lab confirmed it, and here's our guy."

Gabriel leaned over Bonin's shoulder. The convicted offender who'd left his blood at Carmen's house was a man in his early thirties named Joey Bowles. In the photo, Joey sported muscles, a gangbanger crew cut, mean-looking eyes, and the tattoo of a cobweb on his elbow, which signified having done prison time.

"Do you have his arrest record?"

Bonin handed a paper to Gabriel, which he read.

Joey Bowles had acquired a lengthy juvenile record for robbery. He'd been a suspect in a homicide when he was seventeen, but prosecutors dropped the murder charge. As an adult, Joey spent a year in the county jail for assault with a deadly weapon and was still on probation.

Gabriel chewed his lower lip. It made no sense that the ex-con would risk a home invasion while on probation. Then again, if Joey had evolved into a stalker, sensibility played no part.

"We've got probable cause to get a saliva swab from this douchebag," Bonin said. He swung his Converse-covered feet onto the desk. "I've already paid a visit to the address on record. Not surprisingly, our boy is nowhere to be found. Give me a few days, though, and I'll track him down."

"Have you been in touch with Miss Jenette?"

"Carmen?" Bonin sniggered. "She's a hottie, isn't she?"

Gabriel stayed quiet.

"She specifically asked if you would get in touch with her and give her the update."

Without acknowledging the other man's leer, Gabriel asked, "Have there been any similar break-ins in Carmen's neighborhood?"

Bonin shook his head. "No guys wearing Halloween masks if that's what you mean. Carmen told me you suspect he's a stalker, and I'll approach Mr. Bowles from that angle."

"So, Bowles switched from being a thief to a stalker."

Gabriel let the statement dangle before the other detective, inviting rebuttal.

"Why not? He's a career criminal. Nobody says he has to stick to one job."

"Let me know when you find him." With a copy of the suspect's record in hand, Gabriel went out the door and phoned Carmen.

CHAPTER TWENTY-TWO

The psychic acted differently. She and Gabriel sat in the cold brew coffee place, and Carmen's green eyes glinted with secrets. A coquettish smile played at the corners of her mouth. Carmen didn't appear to Gabriel like a woman recovering from an assault; she acted like a woman in love.

Evidently, she'd ended her petty flirtation with Gabriel because she could barely stay focused on him. Instead, Carmen continually replied to texts on her cell phone.

Gabriel slid a photograph of Joey Bowles across the table. "Has this man approached you in any way in the past? Talked to you? Have you seen him hanging around?"

Carmen, with that impish smile twisting her lips, lifted her eyes from the phone and inspected the photo. She shook her head. "I've never seen him." She went back to typing. "Was he the man under the mask?"

"He left his blood at your house. Look, would you mind putting away your phone? I'm here because you requested that I inform you personally about your assailant."

Carmen dropped the device into her purse. "Sorry."

"The suspect's name is Joey Bowles. He's an ex-con, a burglar, not someone I would peg as the type to stalk celebrities, but you never know. When Joey was in your house, did he try and talk to you?"

"He tried to choke me."

"To kill you or subdue you?" Gabriel asked. "There's a difference."

"I have no idea what his plan was."

Gabriel, irritated, sat back in the chair and crossed his arms. "What was your sense? You're a psychic, aren't you?"

Carmen must have sensed the ire in Gabriel's tone, for she quieted down and closed her eyes in an attempt to remember. "It felt like he meant business. I'm pretty sure he wanted me dead."

Gabriel reflected on that. He didn't reckon that a man having wet dreams about a pretty starlet would choke the life from her. Spy on her, yes. Fantasize about her, yes. Try to convince the object of his desire to take part in his fantasy, maybe. But murder her right off the bat? That was an extreme introduction.

Carmen examined the visage of Joey Bowles more closely. Her gaze traveled over his build; the raffish tattoos patterned along his arms and up to his neck. "He looks strong," she told Gabriel. "He could be the man who was in my house, and maybe he's the guy who hid in my car, but he's not the man who grabbed me at the studio."

"How do you know?"

"The guy at the studio was weak, mentally and physically. I could tell."

The waitress refilled Gabriel's coffee cup. He nodded in gratitude, waited for her to traipse off, and then regarded

Carmen, "You could tell the guy was weak. What else? What about this sixth sense you claim to have? What do you do with the gift you're so famous for?"

Carmen bristled at Gabriel's tone and affixed her green eyes on him. "I can decipher dreams."

The detective's look of surprise satisfied Carmen. It happened like that sometimes. She would say things without knowing why she said them. Words without premeditated thought flowed through Carmen as if she were a river that linked a physical sea to a cosmic ocean. Carmen had learned to follow the waters to see what direction the conversation would take. This current river flowed in the direction of the detective's dreams.

Her bruised ego likewise tugged at her, and Carmen desired to show Gabriel that she was no charlatan. The detective made her feel like a child. Brad Franklin, on the other hand, made Carmen feel like a goddess. The DA worshipped her in bed by devoting himself to every avenue of her body. A tingle of pleasure raced through Carmen at the memory of last night's date. Even now, her solar plexus vibrated along with her cell phone as she received another racy text from Brad.

"You seem surprised," she said casually. Carmen couldn't stop herself. Ego, again.

Gabriel said nothing, but the perturbed look on his face told Carmen she'd won that round.

"Tell me about your dreams. I'm sensing that they distress you. Do they have a common theme?"

He crossed his arms. "Maybe."

"That's important," Carmen told him. "Do they frighten you?"

"No."

"Are you sure about that?"

Gabriel swallowed and said, "The dreams feature dead people."

"Anyone you know?"

He shook his head.

"What happens in the dreams?"

"The same thing happens. I see sopping wet bodies that are decomposed beyond recognition. Water deteriorates them into bones. I've never had this type of dream before."

"Well," Carmen began carefully, "I don't blame you for being spooked. Sometimes, when life challenges us, our spiritual guides give us symbols to help us better understand what we're up against."

Gabriel regarded her, although not in a hostile manner. He seemed interested, so Carmen continued. "Water, for instance, is symbolic of emotion. If you dream about a flood, you are emotionally overwhelmed. A tidal wave can represent unresolved feelings of stress and unhappiness in your life. Rain, though, can represent an emotional cleansing and the healing of unresolved sorrows or wounds."

Carmen studied Gabriel's guarded blue eyes. "But because these dreams are the same and are new, what I believe is that someone is sending you a message."

"I like the idea of healing sorrow better."

Carmen laughed, relieved that she might have felled the skeptic in him. "I've told you before that the messages are filtered through your fear, so things may appear scary. I've also told you that I can help you with that."

Gabriel's smile withered.

"Honestly, if you doubt my abilities, go ahead and ask the millions of people who watch my show for a reference."

His silent lips pulled down at the corners, and Carmen regretted bringing herself into the equation. Gabriel produced his wallet and laid a couple of dollars on the table.

"If you open your mind," she said, "you won't be frightened. The messages are not meant to scare you." Carmen watched Gabriel tuck his wallet away. "Messages are often sent through wildlife," she continued in desperation. "The spiritual world works hand-in-hand with the natural world. Butterflies, for instance, make beautiful messengers. They carry a note of comfort from someone who wants you to know that he or she is okay."

Gabriel rose from his chair, and his eyes were already on the exit. "And here I thought that all butterflies wanted to do was flit around and make little caterpillars."

"Can't you believe in something beyond your five senses?"

He regarded Carmen with a deadpan expression. "I'm sure there is a long Latin name for the disorder you have, Miss Jenette."

"Open your mind, and your eyes will open to see life more clearly."

"Oh, I see things clearly." Gabriel leaned over the table toward her. "I see that you are a performer."

"It's true I have a show, but I –"

"You're a hoax." His blue eyes drilled through her. "If you could truly see into my past, you'd understand that I deal with *memories*, not messages. If you had a third eye into the present, you'd quit trying to be a superstar and tell me where I can find Nancy. And if you could predict the future, you'd know if someone like me can actually sustain a marriage."

Carmen watched Gabriel struggle to jettison the raw susceptibility that overtook him. She plainly saw the devastated child who clutched at his grown man's heart. Carmen felt ashamed that she toyed with him for the sake of her pride.

"Gabriel," she began.

He put up a hand to interrupt her and shook off his discomfort like a tattered coat. "Perform all you want, Miss Jenette, as long as you do it for your paying audience. Leave the Lewickis alone. You've no right to build your act on the misfortunes of good people."

With that, Gabriel turned from her and exited the café.

CHAPTER TWENTY-THREE

The full, round moon shone bone-white through the arched window in Ming's home library. Gabriel gazed upon its brilliance with some wistfulness. The natural world beckoned to him whenever the material world grew too suffocating, and he felt suffocated.

Not only did he sit surrounded by wall-to-wall books, evidence of his fiancée's intelligence and extensive education, but his future in-laws sat opposite him armed with venue brochures and catering menus.

"What do you think of this?" Ming handed her father a menu. "It would cost about one-hundred and eighty dollars per person, but that includes wine and beer."

Gabriel pulled his gaze from the moon. "That's too expensive."

Everything about this gala affair went beyond his budget. Buying a new home had depleted his savings, and Gabriel wanted to recover financially, not splurge on a party. Carmen came to mind—how she asked him what was expensive. She must have honed in on the price of the wedding. Gabriel might have to credit her psychic ability, after all.

Ignoring Gabriel's comment, Tom Li said, "You must offer a full bar. People like to drink at weddings."

Ming shook her head. "If we go with a full bar, it costs an additional three-thousand dollars."

Elena Li wore reading glasses as she perused another flyer. "Here's one that offers a free wedding coordinator." She eyed her daughter above her small lenses. "Don't you want someone handling the details, honey? Especially the day of?"

"We could hire an independent bartender," Ming said to her father.

Gabriel grimaced. Didn't Ming hear her mother's question? He glanced over at Elena. The woman seemed used to playing second string to the Doctor Li Duo because she continued to study the brochure without demanding a response. Well, Gabriel wasn't going to stand for that nonsense.

"Ming, your mother is speaking to you," he said curtly.

His fiancée blinked in surprise. "Sorry. What'd you ask, Mom?"

Mrs. Li shrugged. "It's not important. I'm dizzy from all these choices."

Gabriel caught the senior Dr. Li's frown. Most likely, the older man didn't appreciate Gabriel reproaching his daughter. Maybe he worried Gabriel would wring Ming's neck. Feeling the need for fresh air, Gabriel rose to his feet. "I'll be right back."

The three Li's watched him exit onto the patio. He stood on the cement, which was awash in cool moonlight that soothed his hot head. He heard the door swish open, and Ming sidled up next to him.

"What a beautiful moon." She slid an arm around Gabriel's waist.

He nodded.

"Sweetie," she began, "you have to come back. We need your help."

"Isn't this supposed to be about us getting hitched?" he asked. "I don't get why we need a party."

"We don't need a party; we want one. And we've got to make reservations a year in advance and if we –"

"Whoa." Gabriel turned to face Ming. "What do you mean a year in advance? I thought we were going to get married in a couple of months."

"A couple of months?" Ming's eyes went wide. "Jesus, my dress won't even be ready for another four months."

"You do know that my father is ill, right?"

Ming bit her lower lip in reply.

"I don't have a year to wait," Gabriel told her. "And if we're going to have a wedding, then I would like my father to be present. It's important to me."

"Of course," she said. "It's just that we're not prepared for a quick wedding."

"Then let's go to the courthouse."

"No," Ming insisted. "I can pull it off."

"But what about the cost? It's getting out of hand."

Ming dismissed him with a wave. "We don't have to worry about that. My father has offered to pay for the wedding."

Gabriel's mouth fell open. "Why? We're not eighteen. Tell him thanks anyway, but we can handle it."

"He's trying to be involved, Gabe."

"He's a little late, isn't he? For as long as I've known you, you've avoided your parents, and now suddenly they're this big part of your life."

"Is that bad?"

"It wouldn't be bad if you didn't feel the need to please him."

"Oh, brother. Here comes the psychology." Ming tossed her dark hair. "You know, you've been nothing but cranky, Gabriel, and I feel like I have to drag you to the altar. If you don't want to marry me, then say so."

"I want a simple wedding," he argued. "Your plan is too complicated and too expensive."

"Then let my father pay for it."

"I'm not going to let your father make our wedding his show. We're too old for that, even if you do revert to being a teenager around him."

Ming scowled at him. "Okay, Doctor."

"You know," Gabriel told her. "Every time I give my opinion, you pull this stunt. I have news for you, babe. I'm not going to roll over like your mother who –"

Ming covered her ears. "Stop playing therapist!"

Gabriel felt the rage jump, and he quelled it by backing away. "I'm done." He tried to keep his rabid tone in a cage, but the harshness escaped anyhow. "You want to handle everything? Fine. Handle everything. You want Daddy to pay for our wedding? Let him. What the hell do you need me for?"

He didn't bother going back inside the house. He strode to Ming's side gate, opened it, and then headed to his car.

Carmen's perceptive mind conceded to the baser act of sex. The thrust of Brad's hips against her pelvis pounded out any extrasensory vibrations. Brad was skilled in the art of love-making, and Carmen happily abandoned her higher self to her lower extremity. From the time he'd ripped the shirt from her breasts, an action that caused the breath to catch in her throat, and lifted Carmen's long skirt, his attention to his lover never faltered. Brad had a great body, too. He was toned and athletic, which allowed the couple to experiment with a myriad of positions. Brad and Carmen created a rough and tumbled flurry of sighs, moans, and twisting limbs, accompanied by the squeaks and protests of her antique bed.

Finally spent, the two lay with their arms draped about each other like bird's wings—caressing one another with light feathery touches.

"Care to give me a reading?" Brad asked.

Carmen giggled. She'd read every line of his body; that was for sure. "Would you like one?"

He murmured his approval. She snuggled against Brad and rested her head on the curly hair of his firm chest. The gentle beat of his heart rocked her with sweet comfort.

"Problem is, I need my tarot cards."

Carmen didn't want to get out of bed. She wanted to revel in the scent of Brad Franklin, to relive his electric touch and remember how his tongue felt on her flesh. He seemed to read her thoughts.

"Let's take a rain check on that," he said. "Don't get out of bed."

"Why don't you make it easy and tell me about yourself? What made you the White Knight of the City of Angels?"

Brad rubbed his eyes. "How much time do you have?"

"All night. Get as deep as you like."

"Let's see…" He let his gaze drift off. "My mother was bipolar and had a taste for prescription drugs, which made my childhood pretty erratic. My father did his best, but he had his own set of issues. I was never beaten, abused, or starved. I just became a byproduct, something my folks passed over to any willing friend who would babysit or pick me up from school." A wry grin broke on his face. "I became an adept politician at a young age because I survived mostly on the kindness of strangers." He glanced at Carmen. "That deep enough for you?"

Her green eyes showered him with compassion. "But look how you defied the odds and pulled yourself together. You went to law school, became the District Attorney, and now you're running for Attorney General. You're a success story, Brad."

He nodded wearily. "I didn't do it alone. I never had much of a home life with my folks, and in middle school, I glommed onto a family that I admired. They took me in. Any success I have, I owe to them."

"If you don't mind me saying so, I think the reason you're so vigilant with your work and prosecuted all those lowlife criminals is because of your past. Maybe because your mother abused drugs?"

"I've often thought as much." Brad rolled over on his side to face Carmen. "What about you? What got you to where you are today?"

"My bloodline." In response to Brad's curious expression, Carmen explained, "I come from a long line of psychics and healers."

"Being psychic is genetic?"

"Gifts are passed down through the generations. My

grandmother was a *traituese*, a faith healer, but she was a medium as well and could commune with spirits."

A wave of malaise rolled off of Brad and washed over Carmen. She squinted at him. "You're not a believer?"

"I am. I fully believe in the existence of other types of energy." His eyes met hers. "And I do believe that you can tap into that energy."

His assurance pleased Carmen. She traced a finger along the gentle lines of his face and then playfully tapped the end of his nose. "What is it, then?"

"What is what?"

"It. The thing that's on your mind."

Brad's hand moved under the sheets and crept between her legs. "I don't know, but maybe I'll find it here."

Carmen felt a delicious tingle and reached for her lover.

In Santa Monica, Gabriel trudged into his study and sagged into the desk chair. The wedding was supposed to unite Ming and him, not tear them apart. Feeling glum, he picked a cassette tape from Jenna's envelope. Written on the label in bold marker was the word "Rad!" He placed it into the deck and pressed PLAY.

"Jenna could do a guitar solo after the bridge."

Gabriel had learned to recognize Nancy's voice. He heard some shuffling in the background and the soft strumming of a guitar as if one person was pacing while the other gently played music.

"Aren't you going to start?"

"You first," Christopher Rand replied.

Nancy giggled. "You're staring at me again."

"I can't help it."

Gabriel heard what sounded like the squeaking of bedsprings and the soft smack of interlocking lips. Someone sighed, and someone else murmured. There was shuffling, and the brief purr of a zipper.

"It's okay," Nancy whispered. *"I want to."*

There are some moments that time cannot decay. The sweet innocence of Nancy and Christopher's union touched Gabriel as he witnessed the event decades after the fact.

Christopher suddenly gasped, *"Hey, is that thing on?"*

The recording ended with a sharp click, which startled Gabriel. He rested his eyes on the tape as it continued to circle the rollers and realized he had never experienced the dewy freshness of young love. He'd had sex with girls, mostly because his high school peers expected him to do so. But Gabriel hadn't felt the rapid heartbeat or the heady anticipation that accompanied first love. Sex elicited feelings of shame and doubt in him. He'd married a woman named Cheryl, and his lack of emotion in the bedroom killed their marriage. Only Ming managed to break through, with her quirky sense of humor and clinical approach to life. With Ming, Gabriel could let down his guard.

He remembered the look on Ming's face when he left her alone on the patio. His fiancée appeared stricken. Reaching for his cell phone, Gabriel called her. She didn't pick up. He knew he'd have to apologize, both to Ming and her parents. With a heavy sigh, Gabriel pressed PLAY.

"—I'm sure Jenna would," Nancy was saying. *"Did you ask about the drum kit?"*

"Yep," Christopher replied. *"I think I'm getting it for my birthday."*

Nancy squealed with pleasure. "Bodie! As soon as you've got it, we'll get everyone over here. I'll improvise until I get my synth."

There was a pause, and then Gabriel heard Nancy's voice again.

"Oops! We've been recording. Okay, so let's just take it from the bridge to –"

A hard, single knock was heard, interrupting Nancy's words, and a door creaked.

"Anyone want a soda?"

Gabriel quickly stopped the tape and rewound it. That last was a different voice—a man's voice. Len Lewicki? Gabriel played it back again.

"Anyone want a soda?"

The recording ended. Replaying it for the third time, Gabriel once again considered Len Lewicki, but then remembered that Nancy's parents didn't know about Bodie. The voice couldn't belong to Len, although it sounded to be that of an older male.

Something significant passed through the sky of Gabriel's memory, and he tried to snatch it out of midair. Of course, the second he reached for it, the itinerant thought disappeared under clouds of more pressing considerations.

Who was the man? Gabriel replayed the unknown male's voice again and heard the singular hard rap that announced his arrival. The knock sounded exactly like the one in Gabriel's nightmare, the one that heralded the coming of a decayed and soaking corpse.

CHAPTER TWENTY-FOUR

Early the next morning, Gabriel called Jenna Goldman Klein as he dressed for work. When she answered, he dove right to the point.

"Did your father ever meet Bodie when you practiced at your house?"

"Good morning, Sergeant McRay," Jenna said pointedly.

"Good morning, Mrs. Klein. Did he –"

"And I accept your apology for calling so early and waking me up."

Gabriel rolled his eyes. "Sorry. Did your father meet Bodie?"

"We never practiced at my house. Nancy played keyboards. Since her parents owned a piano, we practiced there. I never got the chance to play music with Bodie."

"Why?"

"What does it matter?" she asked.

"It matters."

"Can I call you back in an hour?"

"Please, just answer my question."

"God, you're pushy. Nancy had plans for us to form a band, but she was waiting until Bodie got his drum kit, and she bought her synthesizer. It would have come together; I'm sure, but then Nancy... Nancy vanished."

Gabriel thanked Jenna, hung up, and then realized he didn't say goodbye. The woman was probably cursing him. He reached for his shoes, and as he tied them, Gabriel set the scene of Nancy's life at the time she disappeared.

Nancy had a boyfriend named Christopher Rand, aka Bodie. She wanted to form a band with Bodie and Jenna, but they hadn't practiced together because they didn't have their instruments. Jenna and Nancy played music only at Nancy's house because the Lewickis owned a piano. Nancy and Christopher would not have played music together at Nancy's house because she kept Chris a secret from her parents. That meant only one thing. Nancy and Christopher practiced at the Rand home.

Gabriel walked into his study and picked up the file on Nancy. Was there anything in there about the Rands? Any clue in Harris Brody's report? There wouldn't be, of course, because Brody didn't know about Christopher Rand. Still, Gabriel wanted to make sure. As he reviewed the notes, his eyes paused on the receipt from the party store.

Carmen's voice whispered in his ear. *What's expensive?*

Nancy had purchased party goods totaling $74.25, a rather excessive amount for a kid. Gabriel retrieved the phone and called the Lewicki's.

When Pauline heard Gabriel on the line, she told her husband to pick up.

"Any news?" she asked, hopeful. "What have you found out?"

Gabriel, in his usual style, ignored her question in favor

of his. "Did either of you give Nancy money for the party she was planning?"

He held back from divulging the fact that the party was for Nancy's boyfriend. Why get a girl in trouble for lying to her parents after so many years?

"Oh, no," Pauline Lewicki said, going by rote into the role of strict stereotypical mom. "It was Nancy's business if she wanted to throw a party." Then she added in a smaller, more defeated voice, "I guess we might have if she'd asked."

"How much was her allowance?" Gabriel pressed. "Do you remember?"

Len Lewicki spoke up then. "A few dollars a week. What do you think, Pauline? Five? Ten?"

Pauline was about to give her best guess when Gabriel spoke first.

"Somehow she got nearly seventy-five dollars to spend on the party. That was a lot of cash for a teenager back then, wasn't it?"

Mrs. Lewicki was adroit. "Seventy-five dollars! That's practically all the money Nancy had saved. She wouldn't have spent every dime on a party. She was saving for some piano, wasn't she, Len? Gosh, I remember how she –"

"A synthesizer," Len interjected. "She used to go on and on about how an electric piano wasn't good enough. She wanted one of the newfangled ones with all the bells and whistles."

"That's right," Pauline agreed. "Nancy wanted one of those."

"Maybe one of her friends helped pay," Len offered over the phone. "Someone must have pitched in for the party."

Anyone want a soda?

The words fell before the headlights of Gabriel's mind

and stood illuminated. Gabriel now honed in on what had snagged on his memory when he first heard that adult male's voice on Chris and Nancy's tape. Someone, most likely an adult, had contributed money to Chris's party.

A shiver of realization ran through him. Had Christopher's parents given Nancy the money? Of course. That made the most sense. The party was for their son, after all.

Anyone want a soda?

Nancy had visited their home. The parents would have known her. Who else would be able to provide Nancy with the contact information for Christopher's friends?

On a list no one ever found.

What's expensive? Gabriel had a strange feeling that Carmen's question hadn't been about his wedding but about the party store receipt. Should he thank the psychic? No, he decided. Carmen would only brag about her indispensable aid. Forget about her.

Once Gabriel arrived at work, he picked through Nancy's case file and found Christopher Rand's obituary notice. The parents were listed as survivors, and Gabriel managed to trace the mother, Eugenia Rand, to Madison, Mississippi. He wasted no time in phoning her.

A woman answered his call. "Hello?"

"Is this Eugenia Rand?" Gabriel asked. "Christopher Rand's mother?"

"May I ask who is calling?" The woman drew out her vowels in a pleasant southern accent.

"Detective Sergeant Gabriel McRay with the Los Angeles Sheriff's Department. Ma'am, could I speak with Mr. Rand?"

"Mr. Rand and I divorced many years ago."

"Oh." Gabriel figured it wouldn't be easy. "Would you happen to have a phone number for him?"

"I would not."

"Would you happen to know whereabouts he's living? Is he living?"

"I couldn't tell you whether Walter is dead or alive. Frankly, I do not care. Can I ask what this is about?"

Gabriel had a lot of questions to ask. He wanted first to know what Eugenia knew about Nancy but needed to find out whom he was dealing with. He could tell one thing; the woman had a strong opinion of her ex-husband. That piqued his curiosity.

"Well, Ma'am, if it's all right with you, I'd like to ask you a few questions. Is this a good time to talk?"

"I don't give information over the phone. You say you're a detective in California, but how do I know that? Thank you for calling. I really do have to go."

The line disconnected.

Gabriel stared at the gray fabric wall of his cubicle. Since Eugenia assumed he was a scammer, Gabriel would have to contact her in person. In the meantime, he would research Walter Rand. If the male voice on the tape belonged to Christopher's father, then Walter knew Nancy.

The DMV records showed no current address for Walter Rand. Worrying that the elder Rand might be dead like his son, Gabriel performed a more diligent search online. He chanced upon a small article from the Los Angeles Daily News dated three years before. A local businessman named Walter Rand had been arrested for sexually assaulting a young woman.

CHAPTER TWENTY-FIVE

Gabriel put Walter Rand's information into ViCAP and learned that he was currently serving a two-year sentence at the Men's Central Jail in Los Angeles.

He's right here, Gabriel mused and continued to read about Rand. The man had lured a nineteen-year-old waitress named Meghan Wright into his car. There, Rand sexually assaulted her. Before the incident could escalate into a rape, the girl escaped and alerted the authorities. Rand was due to be released in sixteen days.

Gabriel pushed into Ramirez's office and recapped the information for his superior.

"He's going free in two weeks. Can we detain him as a person of interest in Nancy's disappearance?"

Ramirez picked up the newspaper clipping on Rand and perused it. "Don't jump to conclusions, McRay. We don't know he had anything to do with Nancy Lewicki."

"Come on," Gabriel argued. "This guy is ready-made. I seriously doubt that Meghan Wright was his first assault."

"But he's got no priors?"

"No."

"And he's not in for a 261?"

261, meaning rape.

"No," Gabriel answered. "He didn't even get attempted rape, just this couple-year stint for felony sexual battery. The Judge took his past with no prior convictions under consideration. Asshole paid a fine of five thousand dollars, and now he's due to walk."

Ramirez reached into his pocket and pulled out a pack of cigarettes. "How old was the victim at the time?"

"Nineteen."

The Lieutenant plucked a Winston from the pack despite the no-smoking policy. "He'll have to register as a sex offender." Lighting up, Ramirez added, "He won't be going anywhere you can't find him, so don't worry."

The words did not reassure Gabriel. "You know as well as I do if Walter Rand wants to disappear once he's paroled, he will."

─────

Ming sat on Gabriel's front porch and dangled her sandaled feet off the edge so they could warm in the late October sun. When Gabriel pulled into his driveway, he looked surprised to see her there.

"What are you doing?" he asked as he exited his car. "Why didn't you let yourself in?"

"Well, if we're not getting married," she said, "Then maybe I shouldn't use the key to your house."

Gabriel unlocked the door and held it open for her. "Don't be ridiculous."

Ming did not budge from the porch step.

"Come inside," he told her.

"No." She regarded him with sad eyes. "You said you were done, and I want to know if you meant you're done with us."

Gabriel pocketed his keys and studied the one woman who made him feel like a man. Ming's hair hung listlessly, and her eyes appeared swollen. Gabriel blamed himself for making this capable woman cry. It wasn't the first time. Perhaps he was an abuser like her father suggested.

Without another word, Gabriel swept Ming up into his arms. She squeaked and looked around, astonished. He carried his fiancée across the threshold and bumped the front door closed behind him.

Standing in his living room, holding his fiancée aloft, Gabriel said, "This is what happens after the wedding. I don't know about you, but I'd like to skip right to it. This is your home, Dr. Ming. Don't ever forget it. And if I act like an ass, lock me out."

Ming searched Gabriel's sapphire-colored eyes. "You're not done with us?"

Gabriel shook his head. "Never."

She smiled.

Gabriel carried his lover down the hallway and crossed into his bedroom. "Can you forgive me?"

She rested her head on his shoulder. "Always."

"Good." Gabriel promptly tossed Ming onto the bed.

"Hey!" She laughed as she bounced. "Can you try to be romantic? Just once?"

Gabriel jumped onto the mattress beside her. "Okay."

"Cuddle with me," she commanded.

He did.

The two of them held each other and lay quietly for a

moment. Gabriel could feel Ming's gentle breath at the crook of his neck and inhaled the perfume fragrance of her hair.

"Something brightened your mood," she said. "What happened?"

Gabriel kissed the top of her head. "You know me well."

"What's going on?"

"I've got a person of interest in the Nancy Lewicki case."

"Who?"

"Nancy's boyfriend's father."

Ming pulled away and regarded Gabriel. "Oh, no."

"Yeah. He's serving time right now." Gabriel lifted a lock of her silky dark hair and rubbed it between his fingers, comforted by its smoothness.

"Wow," Ming murmured. "I hope this is the break you've needed."

Gabriel let the lock of hair fall from his fingers and pulled Ming close again. "I have an idea. You wanna sneak away from your parents tonight? You could spend the night with your boyfriend."

Ming gave Gabriel a conspiratorial wink. "I might get in trouble for that."

He rubbed his nose against hers, and then their lips met in a kiss. Gabriel's fingers worked the buttons on Ming's shirt and he laid it open. He took the weight of her breasts in his hand. At that moment, her cell chirped, and Ming reached for it. Gabriel stopped her hand. There would be no answering to Daddy tonight.

Ming lay back, and Gabriel unwrapped her like a much-anticipated present. His fingers traced her flesh, and he kissed her palms, the crook of her elbow, and the gentle curve of her neck. He got achingly hard, but made each moment last. Gabriel then made love to Ming as if their sex was sacred and secretive. As if he touched her for the very first time.

The following morning, Gabriel drove downtown to the Men's Central Jail, which housed Walter Rand. The interview room held a small table and two chairs, neither very comfortable. A two-way mirror took up one wall, and a thermostat hanging on the opposite wall hid a small camera and a microphone. The smoke alarm on the ceiling concealed another camera and mic. In Gabriel's pocket, he held a small remote device that could "flag" a part of the recording for later reference, in case he wanted to review a particular point of the conversation.

Walter Rand lounged in one of the chairs. Gabriel had purposely made the inmate wait, hoping to shake him up and get the upper hand. Rand, however, seemed perfectly calm. He was a stout man with wet lips and a cauliflower nose. His eyes, a mix of blue and gray, seemed too sharp for his puffy face. Rand's soft, overweight body said pushover, but those eyes of his told a different story. They were alive, alert, and icy.

No shackles bound Rand. He wore a green jumpsuit and plastic sandals with socks.

Gabriel introduced himself and read the inmate his rights. If Rand called for a lawyer, so be it, but Gabriel hoped he wouldn't. Clicking the button on the remote control device hidden in his pocket, Gabriel again thought of Dash and wished he could have been here. His ex-partner remained civil during suspect interviews and knew how to cajole monsters. Gabriel had countered as the sour vinegar to Dash's smooth oil.

"Good morning," Gabriel said to the inmate in an attempt to be amicable. "Thanks for seeing me."

"What can I do you for, Detective?"

Gabriel pushed Nancy's picture across the table and gauged Rand's reaction. There was none. Rand looked questioningly at Gabriel.

"Do you recognize this girl?" Gabriel asked him.

Rand shook his head. Gabriel examined the other man's face, looking for signs of recognition, guilt—any emotion. Rand's face betrayed nothing. Gabriel wasn't fazed. He'd met many a criminal well versed in the art of concealment.

"She was a friend of your son's," Gabriel prompted. "Christopher, right?"

The first sign of emotion. A subtle wave of warmth rolled over those frigid eyes, then broke apart on the sands of Rand's camouflage.

"My boy had a lot of friends," he said. "I can't remember every one."

Gabriel pushed the photo an inch closer to Rand. "Nancy was a girl he knew in high school."

"Okay. So, what about her?"

"She's gone. Vanished. She was last seen in April of 1988. I was hoping you –"

Rand guffawed, his huge stomach hitched, and he shook his head. "They sure got you from the demotion line. Collecting dust from over three decades ago!"

Gabriel felt his anger slam forth, but he forced himself to hold back. He had to. Dash wasn't here to play the good cop because he now wore a jumpsuit similar to Rand's.

Gabriel decided to throw the dice. "I've got you on tape talking to Nancy Lewicki."

The statement was a gamble. He didn't have one shred of evidence that proved the adult male voice on the cassette tape belonged to Walter Rand. He only had Jenna Goldman's assurance that the boy featured on the recordings was Rand's son. Gabriel, however, had to try to find some way of breaking the veneer that protected his suspect.

"What tape?" Rand asked without worry.

"Your son made recordings with Nancy at your home. You're on the tape, so don't pretend you don't know her."

"Now, how the hell am I supposed to remember some friend of Chris's from the eighties? Give me a break."

Gabriel smiled darkly, and his finger tapped Nancy's photo. "Ah, come on, Walt. You wouldn't have noticed a pretty girl like this, considering what you're in for now?"

"Well, fuck you, Detective." Rand stood up, sending the chair backward with a screech. "If you're trying to stick me with some crime from yesteryear, you got another thing coming. You go ahead and prove I had anything to do with some little bitch disappearing back in the –"

"You've got a penchant for young ladies, Rand." Gabriel rose from his chair as well. "You know it, and I know it. So, let's talk about Nancy. Were you attracted to her?"

"I know my rights. You want to talk? It'll be with my lawyer present. Otherwise, go fuck yourself." Rand motioned for the guard. "Take me outta here."

Gabriel let the inmate leave and cursed his mouth. Dash hadn't been there to rein him in, and in typical form, Gabriel's aggression had mishandled the situation.

CHAPTER TWENTY-SIX

"Don't tell me you lost your temper, McRay."

"I didn't lose my temper."

Ramirez lit up a Winston in his already smoky office in Commerce. It was a wonder nobody arrested the Lieutenant for violating the smoke-free policy time and time again. Ramirez dragged on the cigarette and eyed Gabriel. "You know you're not going to nail this guy unless he outright confesses. You can't afford to alienate him."

Gabriel waved the smoke from his face. "I don't believe Mr. Walter Rand suddenly developed a taste for sexual assault in his later years. I bet he's made a career out of it, and he's been lucky 'til now." Gabriel paused a moment and then said with some disgust, "He had access to Nancy. He had it through his son."

Ramirez contemplated his cigarette. "Maybe you ought to interview Rand's ex-wife. Let's hear what she has to say about her former husband. She may give you something you can use against him. The dude claims to remember nothing from his past. Maybe her memory is clearer."

True to her word, Mrs. Eugenia Rand would not speak to Gabriel over the phone, so he received permission to pay her a personal visit. He booked a squishy coach flight to Jackson, Mississippi, and from there, Gabriel rented a car to drive to the suburbs.

As much as Jackson had a predominantly African-American population, Madison made a stark contrast. The difference in demographics struck Gabriel, along with the onslaught of corporate chain stores and restaurants. The sparkling shopping mecca appeared to burst out of nowhere. To Gabriel, Madison didn't seem to fit in with the somewhat impoverished state, which had the proud distinction of being the birthplace of the Blues. Gabriel decided he wasn't the only one redefining an identity.

Eugenia Rand met him at a café bakery on Grandview Boulevard. Mugginess held the outside air for ransom and clamped a damp hand on the back of Gabriel's neck. The inside of the restaurant, however, was so cold he shivered upon entering. Gabriel hoped to sample Southern cooking, but the menu offered the usual corporate fare, the same food served in a hundred other identical stores.

Swallowing his disappointment, Gabriel ordered only black coffee but invited Eugenia Rand to order whatever she liked. She ordered hot tea and a salad. She was a slim woman with silver-gray hair cut in a sophisticated bob that highlighted her hazel eyes. Unlike her ex-husband, Eugenia was polished and poised. She fit right into Madison.

"Thanks for meeting with me," Gabriel said.

Eugenia gave him a polite smile. "I'm sorry you had to

come all this way. I have trouble talking about private matters over the telephone."

"I understand."

"So tell me why a detective from California flew to Mississippi."

"I have a few questions about your son. First, let me say that I'm sorry you lost him so young, Ma'am."

He watched Eugenia deflate before him.

"I hope it's not too painful to talk about Christopher."

Her eyes drifted up to meet Gabriel's. "I don't mind talking about Chris. Talking about him is all I have. It keeps him alive for me."

Gabriel lifted the hot coffee to his lips. The woman's words gutted him, and he was reminded of the brevity of human happiness again. The liquid managed to burn the tightness from Gabriel's throat so he could speak. "Did Chris ever mention a girl from California, a girl he liked in high school?"

"No," Eugenia Rand answered. A waiter brought over her salad and iced tea, and she contemplated the meal without much interest. "He was closemouthed about that sort of thing. He was a nice boy, good at sports, but very reserved. Chris was only a visitor here during his high school years, but I know he never mentioned a girlfriend because that's something I would have remembered."

Gabriel observed Eugenia as she picked up a spoon and stirred her tea. Her boy never had the chance to become a husband. Gabriel realized that he was a lucky man, and the revelation surprised him.

"Tell me about Walter," he prompted.

A pallor swept across the woman's face at the mention of her ex-husband.

"We met at Ole Miss. He was studying business. I was out to get an MRS degree." She smiled at Gabriel. "That means earning, not a bachelor's degree, but a bachelor, and graduating with him as your husband."

"Do you know that Walter is serving time for sexually assaulting a nineteen-year-old waitress named Meghan Wright?"

Eugenia's smile fell to ruins. Her eyes dropped to her teacup. "When I met Walter, he was such a gentleman, holding the door for me, pulling out my chair. He was good-looking then, a strong, big fellow, and a member of the swim team. Chris was a swimmer, too. Did I mention that?"

Gabriel shook his head but recalled Jenna saying something about Bodie being an athlete.

"I think Walter grew up with some problems at home," Eugenia said. "I know he didn't get along with his mother, but I never learned the details. Men don't talk about their problems, you see."

Gabriel blanched slightly, but Eugenia didn't catch it. He dumped his issues on his therapist twice a month, sometimes more. *That's okay.* For many years, the prevailing attitude toward male sexual abuse went something like this: a real man can't be abused, and if he was, then he can't be a real man. A psychologist gave Gabriel the tools he needed to cope with that viewpoint.

"I only met Walter's kin once—at our wedding," Eugenia said. "I know they were loving grandparents to Chris. He used to visit them in San Antonio."

She took up her knife and fork and primly cut her salad leaves. Gabriel watched her for a moment and asked, "If Walt was such a gentleman, why did you divorce him?"

The knife and fork paused.

Gabriel only guessed that Eugenia had initiated the divorce. He surmised a man like Rand would want to keep his dirty inclinations concealed behind a Norman Rockwell portrait of a marriage. Eugenia left Walter, and Gabriel wanted to know why.

"We lost our son," she explained. "It put pressure on the marriage." Her cutlery made genteel clinks against her lunch plate again.

Gabriel's mouth slanted into a skeptical frown. "Chris passed away when he was twenty-eight years old. You and Walter had divorced long before then, right? So, why did you leave your husband?"

Eugenia set down her knife and fork. "I found pictures I didn't like."

Extracting his notepad from his jacket, Gabriel waited for her to continue.

"I was cleaning his desk," she said. "Walt usually kept it locked, but I found the key and opened the drawer."

"What kind of pictures did you find?" Gabriel asked, making notes.

"Pornography." The word spilled from her lips in a mortified whisper. "Pornography involving teenage girls."

Gabriel's pen pressed a bit too hard on the paper as he felt his private wounds reopen. Half of him wanted to celebrate that finally, after all these years, there was a solid suspect in the case of Nancy Lynn Lewicki. The other half began to bleed out. No matter how much therapy Gabriel underwent, a seven-year-old boy would continually cut out pieces from his heart.

"Some of the girls looked streetwise," she said. "Others less so. All seemed underage."

"Were the pictures cut from magazines or actual photographs?"

"Photographs." She gazed across the restaurant toward a family—a man, a woman, and a child. They were laughing at some shared amusement.

"Some things you try to forget," Eugenia murmured, "but you know you never will. Just at the edge of one photograph, I saw a hand, a pointed finger." She lifted a dignified finger and pointed outwards. "It looked as though the photographer directed the girl to pose a certain way. You could see the cuff of his shirtsleeve. The shirt had a distinct purple paisley print."

Eugenia's eyes searched the big room and then found Gabriel's. "I had washed that same shirt the morning I found the pictures."

She shook her head. "I never wanted Chris to come from a broken home. He was only a year old at that time. I confronted Walter about the pictures, hoping—I don't know what I was hoping for. He lied at first. He told me he'd gotten the photos from a friend, that he merely liked to look, and there was no harm in that. Then, when I told Walt I knew he took the photographs, he broke down and cried. He said that it was a bad habit, but only involved prostitutes. He paid them to pose for him, and that was that. He said he just liked to look as if that were acceptable. I mean, those girls are someone's daughters, too, aren't they?"

Gabriel nodded but did not comment. He suspected that jacking off to photographs hadn't been Walter Rand's primary goal.

"Where did you find the photos?" Gabriel asked as he wrote on his notepad. "In California?"

"No, here in Madison, but they were the reason we

moved to California. I wanted to run. I was ashamed of my husband and terrified my family would find out."

"And you moved to Woodland Hills, California?"

"That's right. Walter promised to change, and I thought maybe we could start life over."

"What happened?"

"He changed, all right. He told me he was no longer interested in having sexual relations with me, so that part of our marriage died. He acted like staying home with me was a chore. Then Walt started saying cruel things about my looks, about my abilities as a mother." Eugenia took a dainty sip of her tea, but Gabriel noticed her hands were trembling.

"My family was here, and I needed them. I decided to file for divorce and move back to Madison. Walt fought hard for custody of Chris. He was an attentive father if you can believe that. Our marriage may have been a farce, but Walt didn't put on an act when it came to being a parent. I remember, when we were married, he used to invite all the boys over for hamburger-eating contests and other games. Walt was a man's man. He enjoyed being around boys and doing outdoorsy things. But his attitude toward women was very denigrating. I thank God we never had a daughter.

"Chris ended up living with me during his younger years. Then, when he was about eleven, he told me he wanted to live with Walter in California. I let him go."

Gabriel gazed at Eugenia. Living in a prison of pain had undoubtedly caused that inmate pallor that dulled her otherwise attractive face. "Did Chris ever talk to you about Walter once he began to live with him? Did he ever mention anything odd going on in the house?"

"No. He seemed happy with Walt. Chris always told me I

shouldn't worry, that Walt was a great father, very support-ive, the kind of man who helped out neighbors and took in strays. He tended to all of Chris's needs, which made me think I imagined my ex-husband was a monster. Then, just before his junior year of high school, Chris wanted to move back to Madison. Of course, I welcomed him, but I was confused. Chris had made friends. If he'd stayed at Taft, he would have lettered in swimming. Something burdened him."

Eugenia took a sip of tea, which Gabriel thought must be cold by now. He signaled a busboy for a refill, but Eugenia shook her head and covered the top of the teacup with her hand. Gabriel let the busboy pass. Perhaps the woman felt she deserved her sustenance served cold.

"Once he was home with me, I used to ask Chris what was on his mind. I worried that maybe he'd seen something. Maybe he'd found pictures like I had—or something worse. But Chris never told me. Even when I urged him to see a psychologist, he refused. And then, of course, we had a bigger issue to deal with."

"The cancer," Gabriel said.

Eugenia nodded and sighed. "Chris fought it for nine years, Detective McRay. He could because he was young and strong. He received bone-marrow transplants and chemotherapy. My son fought hard, but it beat him down." She blinked a few times, fending off tears. "It was heart-breaking. That's the only word that can adequately describe it. I like to imagine Chris as he once was, swim-ming like he used to, smiling like he used to. Oh, he had such a sweet smile. And then I remember what that disease did to him."

Her mouth twisted, and tears escaped her eyes. Eugenia

picked up her napkin and held it to her mouth. *Heartbreaking.*

Love and loss again, thought Gabriel, as he watched the woman grieve. The thought of being a father and possibly experience grief like this terrified him. As a homicide detective, every case he worked dealt with human loss. Why didn't it bother him before?

"Christopher's death crushed Walt," Eugenia said, and her drawl was more pronounced after her show of emotion. "I'm not going to lie; I was happy to see Walter fall apart at the funeral. I resented him so much. And there he was, babbling over Chris's coffin like a lunatic. 'You didn't have to go,' he cried. 'It's my fault! I made you sick.' He pounded his fist against the casket and begged Chris to come back. Can you imagine such a display? It shocked everyone there to watch him."

Gabriel stayed quiet.

"He berated the doctors and yelled at me for not doing more for Chris. He said we should have contracted a witch to cast a healing spell or a revival preacher to perform a miracle. I had no idea what he was going on about. I didn't listen. This was the same man who had photos of naked teenage girls in his drawer. Chris's funeral was the last time I saw or spoke to Walt."

Gabriel's mind processed everything Eugenia had said. She'd given him a lot of information. Still, he had one more question to ask. Taking Nancy's photo from his pocket, Gabriel laid it down in front of Chris's mother.

"This girl is Nancy Lynn Lewicki. Are you sure your son never mentioned her?"

Eugenia shook her head. "Nancy Lewicki. I'm sorry, Detective McRay. Nothing comes to mind."

The woman had been so forthright with Gabriel that he believed her. Besides, she had been living across the country from Rand at the time of Nancy's disappearance. It made sense that unless Chris mentioned Nancy, Eugenia would not know of her.

Gabriel drove away from Madison feeling numb and not knowing why. Perhaps it had to do with Eugenia, Pauline, Len, Mrs. Li, and everyone else who had a reason to be depressed. Rather than head back to Jackson, Gabriel took the 49 east to visit with Christopher Rand.

CHAPTER TWENTY-SEVEN

The headstones jutted up from the ground at cockeyed angles, and Gabriel swung around monument after monument, in his search for Eugenia's son. How far the boy lay from the California prison in which his father idled. The moist grass sunk under Gabriel's footfalls and the air hung still and heavy with thermal damp. Clouds lolled against the green marshes surrounding the cemetery.

Christopher Rand's headstone stood more erect than the others because it was newer. No flowers adorned the grave. Gabriel, feeling rather ashamed to have arrived empty-handed, searched his pockets for a tribute. Finding nothing else, he finally arranged a few Tic Tacs on the grave. A young man could always use a breath mint, he reasoned. Dabbing at the nape of his neck with a tissue, Gabriel solemnly regarded the monument.

Christopher Paul Rand, Beloved Son

Give me a clue, Bodie, Gabriel asked in silence.

A rumble of thunder sounded—this one on the approach. The sky seemed to accede to the oncoming pressure. Having nothing else to gain by staying, except possibly, to receive a formidable drenching, Gabriel made his way back to his car.

He had no desire to return to Jackson. A bland hotel awaited him there. On a whim, Gabriel continued along Highway 49. He yearned to see one of the famed markers of the Mississippi Blues Trail, so he drove past Indianola—from where hailed B.B. King, and kept along the flat wetlands of the Mississippi Delta.

He called Ming to tell her about his interview with Eugenia. She and Janet were on their way to a spa in Ojai for a bachelorette weekend. Not wanting to interrupt the party, Gabriel told her to say hello to his sister and ended the call. He realized again how much he enjoyed sharing his work with Ming and felt a nudge of neglect because she wasn't available to talk.

Eventually, Gabriel arrived at a small, rundown town named Clarksdale. A signpost on a street corner read, "Blues Alley" and under that, "Delta." Among the boarded-up buildings and empty streets that saddened the heart, a small hotel advertised a vacancy.

After speaking with the owner of the inn, Gabriel booked a room for the night. The owner, an amiable woman, said that in a previous life, the hotel was the G.T. Thomas African-American Hospital. The woman gave Gabriel a tour and showed him the room where singer Bessie Smith died after the car accident that nearly severed her arm. She then led Gabriel to his quarters, a venerable location where Ike Turner had stayed to write music. Although there were no televisions in the guest rooms and the occupants shared a bathroom down the hall, the hotel was clean, the people were friendly, and the Wi-Fi worked.

Gabriel emailed Eugenia Rand and asked her to send him a photograph of Walter taken back in the day, figuring an early identification of the man might come in handy. Then, having worked up an appetite, Gabriel decided to get dinner. He walked along The Big Sunflower River, which flowed behind his hotel.

He entered a small barbecue joint that sold hot tamales. Unlike the Mexican tamales Gabriel ate at home, these delicacies were simmered, not steamed. They featured the pebbly texture of coarse cornmeal as opposed to *masa*, the finely ground meal used in Mexican cooking. This particular establishment smothered the tamales in chili and cheese. When Gabriel pulled the first tamale out of its steaming corn shuck and took a bite, pleasure burst through the numbness that had accompanied him from Madison.

To further uplift his mood, Gabriel went to a concert at a surprisingly crowded club called the Ground Zero, a lively place for a sleepy town. An African-American kid that couldn't have been over fifteen sang originals and classics such as "Born Under a Bad Sign" and "Statesboro Blues."

As he drank two beers and watched the young musicians play, Gabriel thought of Nancy and her fledgling band. He thought of Christopher and wondered what it was that caused the boy to return to Madison. Did Chris find photos of girls his age in his father's possession, or did Walt do something worse? Did it have to do with Nancy?

Perhaps the hasty retreat to Madison had been nothing at all. Then again, maybe Christopher sensed the hand of death reaching toward him like the ornamental Halloween skeleton poised at Nancy's front door. Perhaps that's why Bodie had run into his mother's arms.

Sad, Gabriel thought. The whole scenario plagued him.

He left the club in a funk and trekked through the dark, syrupy night to his hotel, where he hoped to find relief in sleep.

Dulled by the beers and the rain and the heat, Gabriel stumbled to the bathroom at the end of the hall, wearily dragged a toothbrush across his teeth, and walked the creaking wood floor back to his room. He fell into the simple bed, exhausted, and could swear, as he crossed the bridge between consciousness and sleep, that Ike Turner sat on a chair in the corner, guitar in hand, composing "Rocket 88."

The rain thrummed against the roof. From somewhere inside the house came the sound of water pattering. The river outside swelled and threatened to flood, and Gabriel's sleep was fitful, filled with blues music and grainy photographs. The twang of a steel guitar pecked at his nerves. A fifteen-year-old black kid sang the blues on a stage, and behind him, Christopher Rand beat the drums. Their song warbled as if it were an old recording from a long time ago.

Gabriel sat in the audience, fascinated to see Chris alive and vibrant, even if the music he made sounded like one of Nancy's warped tapes.

The singing ended, and the black kid walked off the stage. Christopher stood up from the drums and pointed at Gabriel.

Startled, Gabriel wondered why Chris singled him out and then realized that the young man pointed not to him but at the table. Gabriel lowered his gaze and saw a bowl of green ice cream speckled with dark bits. *Mint chip,* Gabriel thought and shrugged at Chris.

Only his eyes viewed an empty stage.

Chris stood next to Gabriel, close enough that Gabriel could see into the boy's plaintive hazel eyes. Green, with dark bits in them.

All at once, a terrible roar filled the hall, and the surrounding walls suddenly crashed inward. Water poured inside. The torrents of water hit Chris, and large flakes of the boy's flesh peeled away. Sickened, Gabriel watched the boy disintegrate until there was nothing left facing Gabriel except a wet, white skeleton, which then collapsed into the water swirling on the floor. The bones washed past Gabriel to points unknown.

Opening his eyes, Gabriel looked toward the window. Outside, the rain came down hard and threw a wet towel over the daybreak.

This isn't me, he thought, and then wondered why he thought that.

CHAPTER TWENTY-EIGHT

The Chandler way of interrogation, where a detective 'busted a perp's chops' belonged to the realm of noir movies. While Gabriel favored that particular approach, he knew he couldn't afford to further alienate Walter Rand.

When he returned home from Mississippi, Gabriel made a second visit to the jail. He dismissed the guards who accompanied Rand into the interview room. Rand took a seat at the table but appeared to be in an emotional lockdown.

Behind his steel doors of defiance, he said, "We don't talk until my lawyer gets here."

"That's fine," Gabriel assured him. "But before we put every word into legalese, I want to tell you that I was in Mississippi visiting your son's grave."

Completely thrown, the big man's lower jaw fell open. "Why the hell did you do that?"

Gabriel mustered up a casual shrug. "I needed to know about Christopher and got only a little information from his mother. I'm hoping you'll fill in the blanks."

"Chris was closer to me than to her," Rand pointed out. He then asked, "Were there flowers on his grave?"

Gabriel nodded and then fabricated a quick lie. "I put some there myself."

Rand murmured something that sounded like, "Thank you."

"You still need a mouthpiece?" Gabriel asked him. "Or can we talk like two civilized men?"

Rand settled more comfortably in the chair, and Gabriel hid a sigh of relief. The bridge had been crossed. He pulled his chair near to Rand's.

The position of the chairs was reminiscent of Gabriel's sessions with Dr. B. Adlerian psychologists created a friendly environment, one where patient and doctor existed on the same level. The interview room was set up similarly. The table stood off to one side to support elbows or hold cups of coffee. A good interrogator would slowly decrease the gap between himself and his suspect by inching his chair closer until the two were nearly nose-to-nose, deep within each other's personal spaces.

"Tell me about Chris." Gabriel leaned forward in his chair and pretended to be interested in nothing but Rand's son.

The inmate rested his hands on his protruding belly. "Chris was the best thing that ever happened to me. He had my genes, you know. He was an excellent swimmer. Could do the fifty-yard freestyle in less than twenty-six. I saw him win a lot of medals in high school, that kid."

"That's impressive," Gabriel commented.

"Damn right, it's impressive."

And did Chris score big with the girls? Girls like Nancy Lewicki? And speaking of Nancy, did you want her the minute you saw her in your son's bedroom? The questions pressed against Gabriel's lips, asking to be heard, but he pushed them down into his gut, where they waited, suspended on his disgust.

Observing Walter Rand, Gabriel suspected the man was a violent storm encapsulated in the guise of a calm dough-boy. The time would come to draw out the tempest, but not now.

"You used to go to his swim meets?"

"Every one," Rand answered. "Why are you so interested in my boy?"

Gabriel moved his chair another inch closer to Rand and realized, with some disgust, that he could now smell the other man. A yeasty smell combined with a pungent body odor. For Gabriel, the atmosphere of the room took on that of the Delta—wet, filled with the blues. Gabriel wiped the perspiration from his brow.

"Are you hot?" he asked Rand. "I'm sweating in here."

"Yeah." The inmate agreed. "It is a little warm."

Gabriel stood up and asked a guard to turn up the air conditioning. Rand had asked a question for which Gabriel had no answer. He wasn't interested in Chris; that was the problem. Gabriel's only interest lay in the relationship between the suspect and Nancy. Still, it was too soon to focus on that. He needed to gain the inmate's trust.

"Are you hungry?" Gabriel asked, figuring Rand wouldn't turn down an opportunity to eat.

"Always." The big man patted his belly. "What'd you have in mind?"

"What do you feel like?"

"A burger?" Rand asked, hopefully. "And some fries to go with?"

"Sure."

Rand pried a fingernail between his teeth to dislodge something. "The docs say I have diabetes. They tell me if I don't watch my diet, I'm going to rot from the inside out. I got a thing on my foot they say is going to kill me, and they want to amputate. Can you believe that? Like I'd agree to them cutting off my foot." He removed his finger from his mouth, flicked something off of it, and then leaned conspiratorially forward in his chair. "They want to cripple me so's I can't go nowhere when I'm outta here. But they're not getting one over on Walter Rand."

As if he expected Gabriel to applaud his acumen, Rand nodded, winked, and sat back in his chair.

"What if they're telling you the truth, Walt? What if you could die from your condition?" Gabriel asked. "Shouldn't you take the help?"

The other man guffawed. "Not that kind of help. So, what about those burgers, Gabriel? Can I call you Gabriel?"

"Sure."

"Chris and I used to wolf down those Tommy's original cheeseburgers. You ever had one of those?"

"Of course."

"You know the only ones you can really trust are the ones at Beverly and Rampart."

"I can make that happen."

"That'd be great," Rand said with something like adulation. "It's been a long time since I've had one of those burgers."

Gabriel compelled himself to smile. "You want chili on yours?"

"Is there any other way to take it?"

"Nope." Gabriel's smile felt so cold; he could swear his

teeth were going to freeze, crack, and fall out of his mouth. "I'll be back within the hour."

—————————

In his car, as he drove to Tommy's, Gabriel thrust the visor down against the presumptuous sun. Was the weather ever going to cool down?

He wondered what strategy to take in regards to Walter Rand. Gabriel would have to tread carefully because, in truth, he had no solid evidence against the inmate. Taking a shot in the dark, Gabriel called Carmen Jenette.

The psychic answered on the first ring. "Detective McRay?"

"Yeah," Gabriel said. "Am I disturbing you?"

"Not at all, although I'm surprised to see your name on the caller ID. What's going on?"

"Walter Rand," he replied. "Does the name do anything for you?"

Gabriel cringed at his idiocy. He couldn't believe he was consulting a spiritual advisor.

"Is he a suspect?" Carmen asked. "Could I meet him?"

"He's in jail."

"Fine. Which jail?"

Gabriel tormented a small spot on the steering wheel with his thumbnail. "Forget about it. I thought I'd take a chance and run the name by you."

"I'm not going to forget about it. Let me do a reading on him."

"No." Gabriel realized the mark on his wheel was now more pronounced and regretted that his malcontented finger had accelerated the depreciation of his new car.

"But maybe I owe you a thank you." Gabriel chewed on the offending thumbnail. "You asked me if something was expensive, and, indirectly, the suggestion led me to this person of interest."

"And his name is Walter Rand?"

"You are not to divulge that information, Carmen. Do you understand?"

"I won't mention him, but I'm thrilled that I was able to help. Truly, I am. Please let me say something about this on my show. People are interested in Nancy's case."

"You can say what transpired, just don't mention any names. And please let the Lewickis know beforehand. Tell them I'll be in touch to give them the details."

"Perfect!" Carmen hung up, sounding elated.

Gabriel pulled under the red awning of Original Tommy's restaurant and noticed red dripping from his finger. He'd bitten the nail to the quick. Why did he tell Carmen about his lead? Now, the whole thing might blow up in his face.

When they brought Rand back inside the interview room, Gabriel laid the burgers out on the table. He pushed his seat close to the big man as if they were two pals sharing some lunch.

"This is good," Rand said as he unwrapped the paper from the burger and licked the greasy goodness off his chubby fingers. "I appreciate it."

"No problem." Gabriel took a bite of his burger.

"First thing I do when I'm outta here is to eat a proper meal. Then I'm going out into the sunshine and water."

"The water?"

"To fish."

"Where do you go fishing?"

"Well, I used to fish out on the Gulf for many years. Then out of Baja. Cabo San Lucas."

"Chris ever go with you?

Rand chewed a bite of the burger as he spoke. "I gave him his first beer on a three-day trip out of Ensenada. We stayed a few days, partied around town, and then hit the water for marlin and tuna." He chuckled at the memory. "He ended up throwing that beer up over the edge of the boat."

Gabriel made himself chuckle as well. "Other than the vomiting, it sounds like a fun time. Nothing like a father and son trip."

"You betcha. I took him hunting, too. Young men thrive in the outdoors."

"Did you and Chris ever do any freshwater fishing?"

Gabriel hoped Rand would mention the Mammoth Lakes area, which would establish a tie between him and Nancy in the nearby ghost town of Bodie. It made sense that Rand was the one who took that photograph of Christopher and Nancy.

Rand fell into meditative silence and then gazed at the chipped corner of the table. "He died of AML, you know. That's acute myelogenous leukemia. It's called acute because of the cancer's rapid progression. That's how the docs put it: rapid progression. He was a good boy, my Chris. Had a big heart. I miss the hell out of him, but I'm glad he ain't seeing me in here."

For a moment, Rand looked childlike. Emotion clotted his features and made his thick lips even thicker. The bags under his eyes swelled into suitcases. "I'm glad a lot of folks can't see me in here. I was a law-abiding citizen, you know. A taxpayer. I owned my own business and was a respected member of the community. Now, because of some little..." Rand jerked his gaze to Gabriel, and his words changed direction. "Yeah. As soon as I'm outta here, I'm heading to deep waters to fish. The Philippines, maybe. Someplace where I can leave all this shit behind."

Gabriel swallowed a chunk of hamburger to cover his alarm. Although Rand would be required to register as a sex offender in the United States, some countries extended a welcome to American criminals. The Philippines, Gabriel believed, didn't ask any questions. Once Rand was paroled, he could travel to that country, board a fishing boat, and disappear into deep water forever.

CHAPTER TWENTY-NINE

"There's been a huge break in the Nancy Lewicki case," Carmen told her studio audience. "After nearly thirty years, authorities are questioning a person of interest. I'm not at liberty to say who it is at this time, but I will tell you that my spiritual guides referred me to a purchase of Nancy's. Yes, a simple purchase, which led the lead detective to a suspect at long last."

The audience broke into heady applause. Carmen put a hand up to calm her followers.

"And I predict that this case will be solved within three weeks."

More applause.

"I'll leave you with a special thought." Carmen sauntered across the stage as the camera lenses followed, and the silky skirt she wore swayed like an empress's train.

"It's the quiet voice inside that speaks the truth we need to hear. Yet, this voice is so easily drowned out. Why is the truth quiet? I don't know, but perhaps this is the reason." Carmen picked up a glass of water and eyed the director, who cued her toward a particular camera. Carmen then shook the glass and held it toward the lens.

"When the water is agitated and moves inside the glass, images behind it blur." Carmen allowed the water to still in her hands. "When everything calms, the images become clear, and we see what's behind the water. In the waters of our lives, we need to become quiet to illuminate the right path. Calm is often hard to come by in this hectic world. So, I wish you a very peaceful rest of your day."

The audience members clapped vigorously. Someone yelled, "We love you, Carmen!"

She smiled. The Nancy Lewicki case had hiked her show in the ratings, and Carmen couldn't be more excited.

At the end of the taping, she went to her dressing room to change out of clothing made too hot by the studio lights. A security guard waited outside her door because Carmen decided to take no more chances with her safety.

Sitting at her makeup table, she removed her ready-for-camera face and thought about Brad and how they would spend the evening. No doubt under the sheets or in the bathtub or on the carpet. Carmen grinned at the memory of their delirious "sexcapades." Delirious, because, with Brad, Carmen drowned herself in physical sensations and threw all caution to the wind. Sometimes it felt good being turned on rather than tuned in.

Carmen glanced at her watch. Before her marvelous union with Brad could take place, she arranged to meet Gabriel at the Lewicki home.

Carmen cracked open a bottle of sparkling water and took a luxurious drink. Wiping the bottle's condensation against her forehead, she wondered if Gabriel would apologize for doubting her abilities.

Probably not. The detective's stubborn side would no doubt prevail. Brad, on the other hand, had become a complete convert. Carmen could tell Brad wholeheartedly believed in the possibility of communing with the spirit world. He'd told her so.

Because she and Brad shared similar beliefs and meshed so well together physically, Carmen figured she had finally found her one and only.

Tightness suddenly constricted her chest, and Carmen nearly dropped the water bottle. Her heart seemed caught in a vice-like grip. Panicked, she inhaled and let the breath out slowly. Inhale. Exhale. The stifling feeling passed as quickly as it came. Taking another deep breath, Carmen picked up her purse and joined the security guard outside.

On her the way to the Lewickis, Carmen became aware of a dark green sedan tailing her. No matter what avenue she took, the sedan appeared in her rearview mirror.

Did she imagine the green car following her? Was her paranoia heightened due to her previous attacks? The sedan looked to be a perfectly ordinary car, not like a pimpmobile or a thug's black-tinted speedster. But there it was again!

Peering into the mirror, Carmen tried to discern the driver; only the car remained at a distance. The late afternoon sun glared against the windshield and obscured its occupant. Carmen suspected that the horrid feeling she'd experienced in her dressing room had to do with Mr. Green Sedan.

I'm not playing this game, she decided. Whether she imagined someone followed her or not, Carmen swung her car around the next corner and pressed on the gas. She ran a stop sign and blew through the next red light, which left a screeching of tires and a flurry of honking horns in her wake.

With her breath short and her heart hammering, Carmen reversed her car into the driveway of an apartment house. She idled there and kept a vigilant eye on the street in front of her. Taking her cell phone from her purse, Carmen readied the camera.

She would take a picture of the green sedan and capture the license plate. Then she'd give the picture to Brad and tell him to attack.

"Come on," Carmen whispered as she held the camera out the window. "Let me see who you are."

Would it be Joey Bowles behind the wheel?

The green car, however, failed to appear.

CHAPTER THIRTY

W hen Gabriel arrived at the Lewicki condominium, he saw Carmen Jenette seated with Len on the couch. He intended to give the psychic an earful for bragging that her reference of an expense had all but solved the case, but Gabriel noticed how Carmen's green eyes appeared haunted. She crossed her arms and legs in a protective, unyielding manner. Something happened, he thought. Maybe she'd been attacked again.

Before Gabriel could talk with Carmen, Pauline surrounded him and wore a strained smile that barely masked her anxiety.

"Have you got some news for us, Gabriel?"

Len stood up from his seat on the living room couch, ready and waiting. How many times had Nancy's parents jumped up from their seats in anticipation of long-awaited information about their daughter?

"I've been interviewing a man," Gabriel said, without preamble.

"A suspect?" Len asked.

Gabriel didn't want to commit yet. "A person of interest. Do you remember the boy I showed you in the photo with Nancy? The boy she'd met on the trip to Bodie?"

Sorry, Nancy, Gabriel said to himself. *I have to tell your secret now.*

"His name was Christopher Rand. Nancy was seeing Chris back at home."

The Lewickis looked individually shocked and then shared a doubtful look.

"We would have known if she had a boyfriend," Pauline informed Gabriel.

"From what I've been told, Nancy was worried that you would prevent her from seeing him. Apparently, she would meet Christopher at the mall and record music at his house."

Off their bewildered looks, Gabriel added, "I'm sure it was an innocent crush. Surely, you can forgive a girl her first love."

Gabriel didn't know why he said that and regretted that he did. His words caused tears to materialize in Pauline Lewicki's eyes. She went into the kitchen for a paper towel. Len dropped down onto the couch, looking confused. Carmen detangled herself to put a hand on his hunched shoulder. Gabriel wondered why he felt the need to defend Nancy.

"This boy…" Gabriel began. "This boy had a father with a particular history."

Len Lewicki immediately understood. "A bad history?"

Gabriel nodded.

"What'd he do?"

"Nothing that we know of in regards to past years. But

he is currently serving time for the sexual assault of a nineteen-year-old girl."

Pauline Lewicki gasped at the kitchen doorway and scrunched the towel in her hand. Gabriel had no choice but to plow forward. He wasn't the one who had perpetrated the harm, but he needed to relay it.

"Now, I have nothing that ties this man to Nancy other than my belief that he knew her. I'm trying to get him to acknowledge that." Reaching into his pocket, Gabriel extracted a photograph that Eugenia Rand had emailed him. He handed it to the couple. "This is Walter Rand. He's standing with his son Chris at a swim meet. It's dated from around the time he would have known Nancy. Do you recognize him? Maybe you saw him loitering around Nancy's school or perhaps near your house. I realize it's been a long time."

The Lewickis eyeballed the picture, straining to recognize Rand. Gabriel could see that they did not. Even if Rand had been stupid enough to get caught stalking Nancy, too much time had passed for any remembrances.

As if in agreement, Nancy's mother and father shook their heads. They couldn't identify him.

"Get me something of his," Carmen urged Gabriel. "I can do a reading on it."

Gabriel glanced at the psychic but did not respond. Instead, he addressed Nancy's grief-worn parents. "I promise you I will be relentless with Mr. Rand until I'm convinced of either one of two things: that he had nothing to do with Nancy's disappearance or he had everything to do with it."

"What do you think, Gabriel?" Pauline asked him in a wan voice. "What's your feeling?"

He assessed the woman, her heart hanging by a thread. "I'm not making any assumptions yet." Gabriel moved to the front door. "I'll let you know what happens."

Carmen accompanied him. Again, Gabriel noticed a bit of vulnerability undermining the psychic's usual confidence.

"You okay?" he asked.

"I think somebody followed me from the studio," Carmen said. "Maybe I'm just paranoid."

"I told you to get a bodyguard at least until we have Joey Bowles in custody."

"And I told you that I'm not interested in lugging around an extra person everywhere."

Gabriel rolled his eyes at her obstinacy and opened the front door. Carmen stepped outside and immediately staggered backward into the living room, pinwheeling her arms.

Paul Lewicki followed her inside and yelled. "When are you gonna leave us alone?"

Carmen righted herself, but Paul shoved her again, and this time she fell against the side table and knocked over Paul's holiday picture. Pauline shrieked from the dining room entrance, and Len stormed over to his son.

Before Len could reach Paul, Gabriel grabbed the younger man. Holding him, Gabriel could smell the unmistakable tang of gin drifting from Paul's mouth.

"Take it easy," Gabriel told him.

Pauline slapped her hands over her reddened cheeks. "Oh, Paul, what are you doing?"

"You don't bust in here like a raving maniac," Len shouted at his son.

Paul jerked out of Gabriel's arms and rushed at Carmen again.

"Get out of our house!" He grabbed Carmen by the

shoulders and wheeled her toward the door. A violent tango ensued, with Pauline screeching, Len yelling, and Gabriel dodging around them, trying to cut in on the dance. Carmen and Paul bounced against the furniture until Paul pinned the psychic against one wall. Carmen grimaced and angled her head away as if Paul's breath would ignite her face.

"I lost my marriage because of people like you," he wailed. "Always hounding us. Never leaving us alone. Let her be!"

"Okay, buddy." Gabriel put a hand on Paul's shoulder, and the other man whirled around and punched Gabriel in the face. Carmen took the opportunity to push Paul aside and ran for safety behind an armchair.

Regaining his footing, Gabriel strode up to Paul while displaying the gun in his holster. "Take a seat and get a hold of yourself."

Len, eyes wide on the gun, darted in front of his son. Behind him, Paul Lewicki panted like a wild dog, his eyes liquor-red, his shoulders shrunken. He stood staring at Gabriel without seeing him. His mind seemed a hundred miles away.

"He's always been a troubled sort," Len explained to Gabriel. "He'll calm down. Won't you, Paul?"

Gabriel pointed to the sofa. "Sit, Paul. Let's you and I talk." He looked over at Carmen. "Are you all right?"

The psychic stood frozen but managed to nod her head.

"Pauline," Gabriel said. "I think Carmen and your son could use some water."

Nancy's mother wandered miserably into the kitchen. Gabriel gestured that Carmen should accompany her. Carmen hesitated and then followed Pauline out of the room. Gabriel turned to Len. "Paul and I need to talk alone."

Len heaved a sigh toward his son and turned to follow the women. Gabriel kept his hand on his gun until Paul took a few dismal steps and then melted into a puddle on the couch. Standing in front of him, Gabriel rubbed his sore jaw.

"Next time, you'll cool down in a holding cell. Nobody here is trying to hurt you or your parents. Carmen and I only want to help."

"Not her," Paul said in a breaking voice. "She's using Nancy. Parading our troubles in front of millions of people just to gain viewers." He looked up at Gabriel with a sorrowful expression. "You know it's true."

Gabriel appraised the younger man and then walked over to the fallen photograph. As he bent down to retrieve it, he said, "You have two sons. You want to wreck their lives?"

"My wife doesn't let me see them," Paul muttered.

"Yeah, well, maybe she would if you didn't act like an asshole."

"Fuck you," Paul told him. "I don't care if you're a cop."

Gabriel set the photo upright on the table. "How much more pain do you want to cause your parents?"

"I don't care. It's always been about their pain."

Gabriel took a seat on the couch next to Paul. "So, you want to do your part and add to it. Maybe even beat out the pain Nancy's disappearance caused them."

"Go to hell."

"I'm just curious. Is that what you're trying to do? Is this a bid for attention?"

Paul tried to get up, but Gabriel grabbed his arm and pulled him firmly back down to the couch. "It's time to grow up, Paul. Apologize for your bad behavior. Tell you what; I'll give you a minute to sit in the shit hole that you're used to sitting in, and then you let me know when you're ready to move forward."

Gabriel released Paul's sleeve and folded his hands on his lap, waiting.

Looking at him, Paul muttered, "You're a real joker."

"Lay off the booze. It's a depressant. Not good for someone in your mental state."

Len held Pauline's hand as they emerged from the kitchen.

"Here's your water, Paul." Pauline broke away from her husband and went to her son's side. Tenderly, she handed him the glass.

Carmen exited the kitchen on light footfalls. Paul, glancing at the psychic, seemed to hold the water glass for support.

"I'm sorry," he said without meeting anyone's eye. Draining the glass in one gulp, Paul asked his mother if she had any aspirin. Pauline nodded, patted her son's knee to reassure him, and then headed up the stairs.

Carmen crept further into the living room and picked up her purse from where it had fallen. "I'd better get on my way," she whispered and slipped out the front door like an escaping wraith.

A few minutes later, when he stepped outside the condo, Gabriel saw Carmen standing under a tree whose roots had broken up the sidewalk. He joined her.

"It's him." Carmen's shoe softly kicked at the uneven cement. "Paul is the one who assaulted me at the studio. I know it. He has this softness about him."

"Do you want to press charges?"

She shook her head. "I couldn't do that to Pauline and Len. Could you?"

Gabriel glanced at the Lewicki's front door. No, he didn't want to arrest Nancy's brother, although he wondered if he should. The man was imbalanced enough to pose a threat to others, including himself.

"I knew I was being followed," Carmen told Gabriel. "There was this green sedan driving behind me from the time I left the studio. I should have expected this."

At that moment, the front door opened, and Paul exited the house. He kept his eyes downcast as he walked out into the street and entered his car—a black SUV.

CHAPTER THIRTY-ONE

Miguel Ramirez entered the morgue with a whispered prayer on lips. *Dios, gracias por todo que tu nos as dado.* He always whispered his gratitude for being alive when he entered this holding pen of the dead. Murderers did not frighten Ramirez. He'd encountered plenty of them during his tenure at the homicide bureau. But the supernatural, the possibility of stalkers unseen, shook him to his very core.

Ming had filed autopsy reports on a couple of his new cases, and Ramirez thought he'd pay her a personal visit to retrieve them. Besides, he had another more private issue to discuss with the county medical examiner.

To his displeasure, Ming bade him come inside one of the exam rooms to talk while she worked. As if the surroundings weren't macabre enough, someone had decorated for Halloween by sticking a scalpel in a jack-o-lantern's carved eye.

Flanked by her assistant Geoffrey, Ming used a scalpel to

cut into the torso of a naked female. The dead woman on the steel table looked to be in her early seventies.

Ramirez watched Ming bisect the woman with a "Y" incision, and then trade the scalpel for a heavier knife, which she used to remove the lungs.

"So, to what do I owe this pleasure?" Ming asked. She held the right lung aloft and commented into a microphone hanging above the table that the organ appeared to be healthy. Handing the lung to Geoffrey, her red-haired assistant, Ming then extracted the left lung.

"I came to pick up some reports," Ramirez said.

Ming weighed the lung's mass in her hands. "This one's engorged." She moved to the small table positioned over the splayed out legs of the dead woman. "My guess is hypostatic pneumonia. Geoff, let's take a culture." Ming held the lung toward Ramirez. "Hepatization. See this mottled appearance? Looks more like a liver, less like a lung, doesn't it?"

Ramirez grimaced. "If you say so."

"The cause of death appears to be lobar pneumonia," Ming said as she cut off a specimen. "But we'll soon see if anything else got her."

"Look how he sees you." Ramirez shook his head at Ming.

"Who?" She dropped the small section of the organ into a jar Geoffrey held out for her.

"Your fiancé."

Ming's eyes dropped to her gore-stained scrubs. She exchanged looks with Geoffrey as she handed the lung to him. Putting her gloved hands once more into the opened torso of the dead woman, she pulled out the liver. "I don't go out to dinner like this."

"Yeah, but..." Ramirez lifted his arms and framed her

within his two hands. "This shit leaves a lasting impression on a guy."

Ming placed the liver on the table and began cutting pieces from it. "Miguel, why are you bothering me?"

Geoffrey stood by watching them, amused, and saying nothing. He held out another jar to Ming. Ramirez, averting his gaze from the dissected body, moved a step closer and said, "I have a proposition for you."

The day after the altercation with Paul Lewicki, Gabriel ate chiliburgers again with Walter Rand in the prison's interview room. This time, the inmate treated Gabriel as if he were an old friend.

Between bites of hamburger, Rand prattled on about his past hunting and fishing exploits and how much he anticipated his impending parole. His voice and mannerisms drooped when he spoke of the depression that filled his confined hours, and the "thing" on his foot, which made his life a misery. To add to that, Rand was sure the prison doctors were conspiring to drug him into stupidity.

After pretending to concentrate on the other man's monologue for a respectful period, Gabriel interrupted Rand.

"You loved your son very much, didn't you, Walter?"

"Call me Walt, Gabe."

"Walt." Gabriel smiled amicably, just two friends having a casual conversation. "It's nice you had a chance to go on trips with him."

He gave the prisoner a few moments to mourn his son

and then said, "From what I can gather, Chris liked Nancy Lewicki pretty much."

Rand snapped his greasy fingers. "Oh, I know who you're talking about now. She was that girl that ran away, right? It made all the papers back then. I remember reading about her."

Gabriel moved his chair closer to the other man, again lessening the space between them. "The lead investigator on the case died recently," he said. "His name was Harris Brody. Do you recall his name from the papers?"

Rand shrugged, but his shoulders were tense. Gabriel suspected the inmate knew very well the name Harris Brody —just as he did Nancy Lewicki.

Gabriel continued in a relaxed voice, "My superior had a close relationship with Detective Brody. He asked that I talk to people who might have known Nancy to see if we can help give closure to her parents."

Rand's eyes penetrated Gabriel's. Perhaps he wondered if a piece of evidence had surfaced that would implicate him. Let him look, Gabriel thought. Let him wonder.

"You know something?" The big man leaned his bulk toward Gabriel. "I do think that Chris knew her. I remember he talked about some girl that ran away. What do you guys think happened to her?"

"Nobody knows for sure. It's terrible to lose a child, as you can attest to, Walt. Her parents are craving any information." He eyed Rand. "Anything at all."

"There's no accounting for kids," Rand said. "The darndest things will make them run away."

Gabriel fought to keep the frown off his face. He knew he had to play nice, but the time had come to up the ante.

"Nancy was planning a party for your son, Walt. Did you give her money for it?"

"Sorry, Gabe. Like I said, I don't remember knowing her personally. I just can't recall from that long ago." He leveled a pudgy finger against his skull. "The old noodle is not what it used to be."

Gabriel studied the inmate. Rand behaved as if he had nothing to hide and nothing to fear, which was a show of control. Gabriel had no intention of letting the other man win a battle of wills.

"I'd really like you to think it over, Walt. There's no law against knowing someone. Tell me what you know about Nancy, and I can close this case and be done with it."

"Sure wish I could help you," Rand said. "But, I can't."

Gabriel nodded but kept his eyes steady on the inmate. So far, Walter Rand had been lucky in his life. His only indictment had been with a nineteen-year-old, a young woman old enough to be considered an adult. Meghan Wright had fought off Rand and escaped. She could do it because the big man had grown older and softer, but what kind of mischief did Rand perpetrate in his younger years? Gabriel could only speculate, but it didn't take a vivid imagination to envision Walter Rand as a more youthful, stronger, and more dangerous sexual predator.

Rand ran a paper towel over his lips to clean them of chili and tossed it on the table. "Wish we could have a little beer to wash the burgers down with, huh?" He gave Gabriel a compatriot's grin and belched approvingly.

Gabriel rose and collected their dirty plates as if he were preparing to leave. He figured that the inmate, fed and entertained, wouldn't want the party to end.

The maneuver worked, for Rand said, "That girl you're

talking about—you know, I didn't put the two together at first. I do remember she used to hang out with Chris. But like I said, he had a lot of girls, and I can't picture each and every one."

Gabriel retook his seat and produced the restored photograph of Chris and Nancy, the one taken at the ghost town of Bodie. He held the picture in front of Rand's bulbous nose.

"We're only talking about this particular girl."

The man went bug-eyed upon seeing his son, and then his eyes narrowed as they slid over to Nancy.

"It looks as though Chris was pretty happy to know Nancy, doesn't it?" Gabriel asked. "You took this picture, didn't you, Walt? You saw Nancy in 1987 when you were on one of your fishing trips."

Rand lifted a hand and scratched the back of his head, throwing another waft of body odor up Gabriel's nose. "I never seen that girl there, and you can't prove that I did."

"Nancy was throwing your son a surprise party. Did you help her out with it?"

"I can't remember." Rand rubbed his scalp a bit harder. "Yeah, maybe I contributed some cash."

Gabriel placed the photo on the desk, where the verity of the pictured young couple could beam up at Rand like a spotlight.

"What exactly were your plans for Chris's party?"

"I wasn't making any plans." Rand waved a hand in the air. "I may have offered up some cash, that's all."

"I was told by a source that you sent Chris away to Texas at the time. Is that correct?"

"I don't know. Maybe."

"And the surprise party was to take place when he returned?"

"Why the hell does any of this matter? My boy's gone. He ain't having any more birthdays."

"How'd you get the money to Nancy?" Gabriel pressed. "I'm assuming you didn't wire it to her."

"No." Rand offered Gabriel a wicked smile. "I didn't wire it to her. I guess we met."

Bingo. Gabriel tried to appear as harmless as possible. "Where did you two meet?"

Like a gecko, Rand seemed able to change his colors at will. "How am I expected to remember that, Gabe? Do you remember where you met someone years ago? I only remember that girl because she made the news. But she was just one in a long line that chased after Chris. Do you want to know what probably happened to her? I think that Chris wasn't the only dude in the picture. I think she might have chased a lot of dudes and finally took off with one."

Gabriel quelled an unexpected rage that flashed within him. A predator blaming his victim hit too close to home. He wanted to grab Walter Rand by his throat and shake him until he passed out.

Stowing his anger, Gabriel struggled to keep his features relaxed and said, "Nancy kept the receipt from the party store, so she must have gone out and bought supplies. She didn't keep the supplies, so she must have given them to you, right?"

Rand blew out an exasperated breath and rolled his eyes.

Gabriel was undeterred. "Tell me what you remember about the time she gave you the stuff for Chris's party."

"The Tasty D-Light, okay?" Rand said. "That's where we met after school. The Tasty D-Light."

Green ice cream with dark bits in it. Gabriel kept his eyes welded to the other man. "Did you buy her ice cream?"

"Maybe." Rand drew a hand across his mouth. Was the man back in 1988, wiping the ice cream as it dribbled down his chin?

Gabriel continued to stare at Rand and felt the warmth of a long-ago sun.

The sunshine bounced off the hood of the parked car, a blue Cadillac Eldorado. A couple of high school floozies exited the store; their little pink tongues licking the head of an ice cream cone, teasing him, making him yearn.

She got in, smelling like vanilla lotion and the cherry flavored lip-gloss she wore. She was full of energy, reaching over the seat to put the bags of party items in the back. She went on about a music tape she'd made for the party, but he noticed only her creamy skin, the candied smell of her, and the fresh and boundless innocence of those small breasts under her shirt.

"It's hot out," he said and shifted his body to hide his erection. "Want some ice cream? It's my treat."

Gabriel blinked and faltered. He could imagine what happened in that car so clearly as if he sat unseen between Rand and Nancy like a ghost himself.

Rand heaved a sigh. "I met her so she could give me the party goods, okay?"

"She got into your car." Gabriel found himself verbalizing what he'd imagined. "She put the bags in the back seat."

For the first time, fear caused Rand's expression to become guarded. "I can't remember."

"She got in your car," Gabriel repeated.

"You gonna walk all the way home by yourself?" Andrew asked a seven-year-old Gabriel. A shudder ran through Gabriel as the

voice of his attacker interrupted the interview. Like the clown jumping out of the Jack-in-the-Box, Andrew Pierce suddenly sprang from the dark corners of Gabriel's mind with open arms. Gabriel tried to concentrate on Rand, but Andrew cajoled him. *Come on. Get in.*

Rand said, "All I remember is that we met at the ice cream place."

Gabriel gave a hard shove to his dreadful memories, but they were too heavy to move and blocked his progress. *"I'll drive you home, Little Buddy," Andrew said as he opened the door.*

"What time did you meet?" Gabriel's voice cracked like an adolescent's.

"I told you. After school. Three-fifteen or thereabouts."

Icy fingers tapped Gabriel's shoulder at the mention of the hour.

Rand, unaware of the battle Gabriel waged internally, heaved himself up from the chair and lumbered toward the door. "I gotta take a leak."

Gabriel called the guard to accompany Rand out of the room and gazed at the empty chair in defeat. He had hoped the reminders of Christopher would break Rand down, but the prisoner's cold heart refused to warm. The only time Gabriel had gotten a rise out of the man was when he brought up Nancy getting into Rand's car. That, however, was only a well-placed guess inspired by Gabriel's overactive imagination. Further hindering his progress were Gabriel's demons, which distracted and demoralized him.

A small groan escaped his lips. Whatever excuses Gabriel might invent, he realized the truth of the matter. Nothing on earth was going to make Walter Rand confess to foul play with a missing teenager, not with the door to freedom about to swing open.

CHAPTER THIRTY-TWO

The spotlight hit a woman with an incredibly hot body and caused her turquoise-colored evening gown to sparkle. As "Dream On" by Aerosmith played in the background, the woman sauntered to a pole onstage and demurely unzipped the side of the gown. The dress fell in a glittering cascade to the floor.

The invitees to Gabriel's bachelor party stood below the stage and cheered on the dancer. Bozos, booze, music, naked girls, and flying money contributed to the chaos of Jumbo's Clown Room. Ramirez had paid off the deejay, and the dancer cavorted specifically for Gabriel. Rick Frasier pressed Gabriel against the edge of the stage and encouraged him to "make it rain" by pouring various denominations of money on the dancer.

Although he'd dreaded the evening and nearly bowed out when Rick picked him up, Gabriel had to admit the woman's body was a pleasant diversion from his frustration with Walter Rand. The stripper, her apparel now reduced to a lacy thong, grabbed the pole, wrapped one long leg around it, and leaned back to allow her lithe body to swing.

Red lights bathed Jumbo's Clown Room as the dancer onstage performed sexual acrobatics with the pole. She certainly aroused Gabriel's whiskey-fueled body, but the frenetic circus atmosphere was quickly wearing on him. A camping trip in the mountains or a hearty dinner would have suited Gabriel better. But who knew anything about him? Gabriel's journey to knowing himself had only recently begun.

He glanced at Ramirez, who stood next to him. His boss was having a ball.

"*Ven, Chica,*" Ramirez called to the long legs and tight ass and waved money at her. "*Aye, estas bella.*"

After the girl ended her dance, and before the next exotic dancer took the stage, Ramirez clapped Gabriel on the back and steered him away.

"I've got a special treat for you, *Cabron.*"

He pushed Gabriel into a VIP room. Gabriel watched the door slam behind him and figured Ramirez had bought him a private lap dance. As his eyes adjusted to the dim, magenta lighting, Gabriel spied a female lingering in the shadows. She wore a long dress and hid her features behind a silky veil. The woman lifted a finger and pointed at a low-back chair positioned in the center of the room. Gabriel walked over to it and wished he'd imbibed more whiskey.

He sat with his hands on his knees. A moment passed, and Gabriel decided to tell the stripper to save her performance for the next guy. He reached for his wallet, figuring he owed the woman a decent tip.

He was too late. The dancer moved toward Gabriel and thrust her long hair into his face. *This one needs practice,* he thought and flicked her hair away. Maybe she'd be glad for the break. Gabriel held out two twenties.

"Take this, and don't worry about the show," he told her.

Ignoring him, the woman maneuvered behind the chair. Gabriel heard the sound of a zipper and figured she was stepping out of that long dress. He felt her presence close behind him, and then her hands went to his face and ran sloppily over his cheeks and forehead.

"Okay," Gabriel said as his lips contorted under her fingers. "You can stop." He pushed her fingers away. "The face rub isn't necessary."

The dancer swung around in front of him and pressed her palms over Gabriel's eyes. He felt her pelvis drop onto his lap and knead his groin. Gabriel shifted in discomfort. He likened her gyrations to rubbing out a difficult stain. Besides that, the woman's hands squished his eyes, and he was beginning to see stars.

This gal is a total lead-foot, Gabriel thought with some amusement.

The dancer hopped from his lap and moved to his side. She thrust out her hips and bumped Gabriel off the chair and onto the floor.

"Okay." He laughed and waved the money like a white flag. "Great job. Can we be done now?"

"What a jerk," the woman said.

Gabriel paused as he placed the voice. Getting to his feet, he strode over to the dancer and pulled the veil from her face. Dr. Ming Li stood before him in a satiny vanilla-colored bra and matching thong panties.

Gabriel looked his fiancée up and down. "What are you doing here, and why are you undressed?"

"I'm giving you a lap dance, moron. What does it look

like?" Ming pushed Gabriel toward the chair. "Now, sit down and enjoy it."

Gabriel regarded Ming in astonishment, his mind still attempting to register that she stood before him. Ramirez must have arranged this. Still, the Ming Gabriel knew would never agree to a striptease. Ramirez must have blackmailed her, but with what? Why would he do it? It dawned on Gabriel that the other man must have sensed Gabriel's apprehension and gave him a reprieve. That consideration put his lieutenant in a new light.

Gabriel glanced at the door. Did the other guys know of Ming's presence here tonight? They couldn't know. Ming would never risk getting caught with her professional pants down. This scenario must be a tightly kept secret between Ramirez and his fiancée.

"Is this better?" Ming began a dance that was comically reminiscent of "The Macarena." She boogied forward and tossed her long hair into Gabriel's face. "Are you turned on yet?"

Gabriel fanned her hair out of his eyes. "Would you cut it out? Having my eyeballs whipped by your hair is not a turn-on."

"I thought you liked my hair."

Gabriel leaned forward, grabbed Ming, and sat her down on his lap. Smiling, he said, "It's you."

She grinned. "It's me. Are you disappointed? Do you want me to find someone more slutty?"

He shook his head. "No, but don't quit your day job."

Ming clucked her tongue. Wrapping her arms around Gabriel's neck, she lifted her lips to his and gave him a luxurious kiss. He stroked the satin covering her breasts and felt the nipples stiffen under his touch. Feeling the hardening in his pants, Gabriel pulled gently on the bra strap. "Is this new?"

"Bought for the occasion," she whispered. "Do you like it?"

"I like what's under it better."

Ming stroked the bulge in his jeans. "Shall we leave this fine establishment, or do you want to stay?"

"What do you think?"

———

Ming wore him out, perhaps in defense of her sensuality. After they made love, Gabriel slept hard. He could barely move when, in the middle of the night, something roused him from his sleep.

All around the mulberry bush, the monkey chased the weasel.

He propped himself up on one elbow and listened. Gabriel swore he heard the silvery music of the Jack-in-the-Box. He glanced next to him and watched the peaceful rise and fall of Ming's chest. She didn't hear it. Fully awake, Gabriel strained his ears. Now, he heard nothing. Did he dream it? Rising quietly from the bed, he pulled on a pair of sweats and walked down the hall to his study. He switched on the light.

The Jack-in-the-Box sat innocently among Nancy's belongings. He swept the toy into his hands and wondered why he would dream of the thing playing on its own. Broodingly, Gabriel turned the crank.

All around the mulberry bush.

Walter Rand crept into Gabriel's mind, a most annoying remembrance. Gabriel yearned to return to bed and hold Ming's sleeping form, yet the painted clown called to him from inside the box. It wasn't merely the clown's round face and the wily grin that reminded Gabriel of Walter Rand. It was the fact that Rand had the upper hand. All Gabriel could do was turn the crank of their conversations. Rand could choose whether to reveal himself or not.

The monkey chased the weasel. The monkey thought t'was all in fun—

The lid popped open, and the clown stood up triumphant, its arms stretched out to the sides; its red, black, and white face wore a wide grin. A round face, like Rand's.

Gabriel's eyes fell to the side of the toy, where the rusting lion tamer held a whip and a chair to the faded, snarling beast. Why choose a whip and a chair to do battle with claws and teeth?

Maybe the choice had something to do with reaching into the lion's personal space. Reaching in, but not touching. A bluff. A psychological game.

Gabriel yawned, leaned against the desk, and gazed at the image. The lion tamer's chair served as a distraction, he decided. The four legs poked and irritated the lion and caused the beast to forget that he could rip the tamer apart. The occasional sting of a whip tricked the lion into thinking the human ran the show.

Gabriel pushed the clown back into its hidey-hole and pressed the lid until it closed with a click. He glanced at Nancy's photo.

I need a chair and whip, he mused. Gabriel then realized where he could find both.

CHAPTER THIRTY-THREE

"How would you like to play a larger role in the investigation?" Gabriel held the phone to his ear and tapped a pen against his desk in Commerce.

"You already know the answer to that question," Carmen replied. "But whatever role I play, the deal is that I can talk about it on my show."

"Within reason," Gabriel warned. "You can say whatever you want within the legal limits."

"Why don't you come over tonight to discuss it? I'm making dinner for Brad, and I'm sure the District Attorney can advise us on what I can say that won't undermine the case."

"Sounds like a good idea," Gabriel said.

"You can bring your girlfriend, the county coroner, right?"

Oh, how Ming would snarl at that remark. She was her father's daughter, after all. *Medical Examiner is what I am. I worked hard to get that title.*

"Ming won't be able to join us," Gabriel told her. "She's taking her parents to the airport tonight."

"Do you need to say goodbye as well?"

"Nope."

Carmen paused over the phone. "Then come solo. I'm cooking southern."

Gabriel perused the cornucopia of mystical adornments and talismans that adorned Carmen Jenette's home. His eyes traveled over dozens of half-burned pillar candles, masks, ceramic saints, bejeweled skulls, beaded necklaces, multi-colored crystals, and decorative glass bottles filled with herbs and oils. Gabriel's gaze came to rest on the person of Brad Franklin, who poured drinks behind a beautifully restored tavern bar.

"Who's her decorator?" Gabriel asked. "Harry Potter?"

Brad chuckled. "It's all Carmen."

It's all you, too, Gabriel thought as he spied a large political sign propped against a barstool that displayed Brad's face. Underneath were the words, "Brad Franklin for Attorney General."

Brad gestured to the drinks. "Help yourself."

Gabriel shook his head. "I'll take a soda if you've got one."

Brad reached under the bar into what Gabriel guessed was a small refrigerator. The DA popped the top on a can of lemon-lime cola and handed it to Gabriel.

"How's the campaigning?" Gabriel asked. "Did Carmen give you a prediction?"

"She says I have to win so that she can have dinner with

the Governor."

"To dinner with the Governor, then."

"I'll drink to that." Brad downed one of the drinks on the bar.

Sipping his cola, Gabriel turned away from The White Knight and perused the many interesting objects Carmen collected. Unapologetic ambition made him uncomfortable. Was he the only person alive who didn't want to set the world on fire?

Gabriel inspected the books housed within an antique, glass-paned case. *Numerology, History of the Occult, Palmistry Rediscovered...* Several little sachet packets fronted the books. When Carmen entered from the kitchen, Gabriel pointed to the sachets. "What are these?"

"Gris-gris charms."

She joined Gabriel at the bookcase and pointed to one charm wrapped in satiny purple cloth. "The one inside this is called Aa'maal. A charm is written on the hide of a deer to keep the wearer safe from the evil conjures of others. And this one..." She opened the glass door, reached inside, and picked up a tiny suede bag sewed with red thread. Holding it aloft, Carmen said, "This one contains words you recite after sunset, which protect you from venomous snakes, devils, and evil people. Would you like it?"

"I don't have much fear of snakes and devils."

"What about evil people? How do you protect yourself?"

Gabriel opened his jacket to reveal a gun in his holster.

"You brought a gun to my dinner?" Carmen asked incredulously.

"Technically, I'm on duty," Gabriel explained. "Here on company business."

Brad wandered over from the bar to peer at the gun.

"Is that a Ruger?"

Gabriel nodded, and Brad said, "That's not the usual choice for cops, is it?"

"It's my choice. You know your firearms," Gabriel said with appreciation.

"Ugh..." Carmen waved the two men away from her. "Weaponry. How people orgasm over their guns. I'm afraid all the firearms in the world won't work against devils, though, Detective."

"For that," Gabriel said as he turned toward her. "There's always therapy."

Carmen replaced the charm in the case and closed the paned door with a gentle click. She dimmed the lights and began lighting a few candles.

"Speaking of evil people," Gabriel said to her. "I'm assuming you've got this place alarmed now."

Candlelight flickered off the bottles and crystals; it caused a twinkling in the empty eye sockets of the jeweled skulls.

"I'm locked and loaded." Carmen cozied up to Brad. "Honestly, how much safer could I be with the future Attorney General and a gun-toting detective in my house?"

Brad draped an arm around her. The couple exchanged tender looks and clinked glasses. Gabriel left the couple to their show of affection and meandered over to an aged-looking table covered by a Moroccan style cloth. A stack of tarot cards leaned against an unlit candle. A few of the cards were laid out.

The fool, the magician, the lovers. The medieval images evoked a sense of crossing a mystical threshold where hopes and dreams were realized.

"Is this where you work your magic?" Gabriel asked.

"It's not magic." Carmen gave a vivacious toss of her dark curls. "My practice is more grounded in nature than you think. Would you like me to give you a reading after dinner?"

"I'll pass."

"Honestly, Gabriel. What are you afraid of? Millions of people believe in the Immaculate Conception and that Moses separated the sea with a staff, but spiritual guides and a sixth sense are the stuff of fantasy."

A bell went off in the kitchen, but Carmen ignored it. "If you believe in God, why can't you believe in this? Is it because females can master this art? Does that idea offend your patriarchal values?"

"If you knew my fiancée," Gabriel said, "you'd know I have no problem with strong ladies."

"Then get enlightened, Gabriel. You say you have had therapy. Maybe this is the next step for you."

"Carmen," Brad began, "the food will burn."

Carmen gave both men a crusty look and moved into the kitchen. Her long skirt billowed in waves behind her.

Gabriel and Brad exchanged glances and followed the psychic. She slid oven mitts over her hands and removed a casserole dish from the oven. Gabriel lifted the lid off a bubbling pot on the stove.

"That's gumbo in there," Carmen told him. "I hope you like seafood." She placed the steaming, heavy casserole dish on a wire rack. "This is a sweet potato casserole. Doesn't it smell good? I've also made an okra and tomato dish."

"How domesticated of you." Gabriel winked at Carmen, and she rolled her eyes. Still, a smile lifted her lips. Gabriel spied a mile high cake sparkling under a glass-enclosed cake platter and said, "Whoa."

"That's called a communion cake," Carmen said. "It's made with caramel icing, which is very tricky. Four sticks of butter in the batter. Four sticks of butter in the icing."

"That's not a cake," Gabriel stated. "That's a heart attack."

"It's nirvana on a platter, trust me."

"She's amazing, isn't she?" Brad asked Gabriel.

Gabriel bowed his head in agreement but kept his comments to himself. Carmen served them up heaping platefuls, and the little party sat down at a butcher-block table covered with a vintage checked cloth. A bottle of wine stood at the center of the table.

Gabriel took a bite of the gumbo and found the savory bits of seafood in the hearty stock to be a delight. Next, he tried the sweet potato with the toasted pecans. The food was heaven in his mouth.

"This is terrific."

"Southern cooking is in my blood." Carmen poured herself a glass of wine. "So, why are you seeking my assistance? I thought I was only in the way."

Gabriel swallowed a bit too quickly, which killed his effort to come off as self-possessed. "As you already know, I have a suspect in Nancy's disappearance."

Carmen chewed slowly. Brad took a sip of wine. They waited.

"I'm convinced that this man, this Walter Rand, knows what happened to Nancy. I don't have any proof, but I'm sure he's involved."

"How can Carmen help?" Brad asked.

Carmen spoke ahead of Gabriel. "If you give me something of his, I could –"

"I'll do you one better," Gabriel interrupted her. "You can

meet with him face to face. I need you to do this right away."

"Of course," Carmen said.

"I want you to make it seem that you are communicating with his dead son."

"Are you kidding?" Brad gaped at Gabriel. "That's a little unorthodox for an interrogation."

"I'm desperate," Gabriel admitted. "This guy walks free in a couple of days."

"Do you think he would believe her?" Brad asked.

"I think he'll want to." Gabriel reflected on the lion tamer's use of the chair. "It's a mental game. Walter is grieving over his son. That's his weakness. I think he'll be interested in speaking to a medium. You're also a celebrity and a good-looking woman. You'll rock his world."

A rosy blush tinted Carmen's cheeks at Gabriel's compliment.

"You're taking quite a gamble." Brad's words had an edge to them.

Gabriel supposed the DA didn't appreciate another man's commentary on his girlfriend's looks.

"Carmen isn't trained to deal with criminals." Brad regarded his girlfriend. "If this person is responsible for Nancy Lewicki's disappearance, then he's dangerous. Haven't you been traumatized enough? You don't have to meet with him."

"I can't wait to meet with him," Carmen said. "If he gets tough with me, I know self-defense." She laughed, but Brad's somber expression darkened his face. Carmen clasped her boyfriend's hand in reassurance and then addressed Gabriel.

"When do I begin?"

CHAPTER THIRTY-FOUR

Gabriel entered the prison interviewing room with Carmen. Rand peered attentively at the psychic.

"You know, Walt," Gabriel said as he pulled out the chair for Carmen, "I got to thinking about you and Chris, and I thought that I'd bring a friend of mine along today. Perhaps you recognize her. This is Carmen Jenette."

Rand looked the young woman up and down hungrily like he'd caught her scent but didn't appear to recognize her. Carmen's features were relaxed. Gabriel had warned the psychic not to extend her hand in greeting.

"Am I supposed to know you?" The inmate ogled Carmen.

"Miss Jenette is a famous psychic," Gabriel answered for her. "She has a television show."

"Really?" Rand brightened. "Are you gonna film me?"

"We'll see." Carmen gave the inmate a cryptic smile as she took her seat. "I hear you are a Southern man."

"Righty-O," Rand said with a wink and looked beyond

Carmen toward the door, perhaps in the hopes that a cameraman would enter.

"My grandmother was a *traiteuse*. Do you know what that means?"

Rand returned his attention to Carmen. "Haven't heard that word for years. I had a nanny growing up. She practiced the arts."

Gabriel idled against the wall, hoping to fade into the background. He had feared Rand might not open up with him in the room, but the man appeared delighted with the Psychic to the Stars.

Carmen placed a tiny bag on the table. "Gabriel told me you were ailing, so I made you a gift."

She pushed the gris-gris across the table to him.

Rand lifted the charm with his shackled hand and eyed it with wonder. "What's in it?" Holding the little bag to his nose, he inhaled the fragrance.

"Something I made specifically for you when Gabriel told me about your health issues. There's cinnamon, basil, and rosemary to ward off sickness, plus a piece of quartz for healing and to draw out pain. I added mugwort to cure disease, and inserted a talisman spell of my own, which my *grandmere* passed down to me."

Rand closed his eyes and took a deep whiff of the gris-gris again. "Smells wonderful." He opened his eyes to leer at Carmen. "Just like you."

Gabriel's eyes shot over to Carmen. He worried Rand's lewd gawking would put her off, but the psychic remained unruffled.

"The magic begins with you, of course," Carmen told Rand. "It is your energy and belief that gives the gris-gris its power. I advise that you focus your concentration on the outcome you are hoping to manifest. The more energy you send out to the universe, the more likely you are to attract the desired outcome."

Gabriel hid an amused grin and flashed a look at the two-way glass. He knew Ramirez stood behind it, watching the interplay and probably laughing his ass off.

"I could use some pain relief," Rand told her. "Because this is what I'm dealing with."

The big man leaned forward over his stomach, an action that caused him to groan, and he removed his right sandal. Stripping off his sock, Rand displayed his foot to Carmen.

To her credit, the psychic didn't flinch, but a sudden rush of saliva into Gabriel's mouth made him nearly spit on the floor. Dry gangrene on four of Rand's toes gave them the appearance of dried twigs, mottled red and black, with white striations and gray toenails.

Gabriel knew that type of rot mostly afflicted people with diabetes and occurred when the loss of oxygenated blood caused the tissues to die. No doubt, Rand was in a lot of pain.

"These asshole doctors want to take my foot." The large man viewed his outstretched limb as one might consider a bulging tumor. "I can't walk good enough as it is, but they want to cripple me. Let me tell you something. I'll be walking outta here on both of my feet."

Rand winced as he pulled the sock over his foot. Gabriel glanced at Carmen. A thin sheen of perspiration had broken out along her forehead.

Finished, Rand rested his elbows on the table, folds of flesh peeking from under his short sleeves. Carmen pulled out a stick of gloss from her pocket and applied it to her lips. Rand nearly melted in his seat, but Gabriel knew her action signaled that he could leave the room.

Pretending to check his phone, Gabriel said, "Damn. I've got to make a quick call. Be right back."

He might as well have been talking to himself for Rand didn't notice Gabriel leave. The inmate's eyes intently followed the wand as it left mauve wetness on Carmen's lips.

Gabriel closed the door, nodded to a corrections officer waiting outside, and joined his Lieutenant in the monitoring room next door. To Gabriel's surprise, Brad Franklin stood at the glass window next to Ramirez.

"What are you doing here?" Gabriel asked the DA.

"I'm here because someone I care about is alone in a room with a convicted rapist."

"Sexual batterer," Gabriel corrected him and went over to a computer monitor that showed a live video feed of the two in the next room. "It's a controlled situation, Brad."

"With you in here? I certainly hope you know what you're doing." Brad turned his attention back to the window.

Ramirez drew a cigarette from his pack of Winstons. "You don't have to stay," he told Brad, and without asking permission, he lit up.

Brad frowned. "I want to say for the record that I am not comfortable with this."

"So noted," Gabriel muttered. He focused the camera lenses to obtain the best view of Carmen and Rand. Truth be told, Gabriel wasn't comfortable either, putting a civilian in a cage with a predator like Walter Rand.

In the interview room, Rand twirled the little gris-gris bag in the air. "So, you're a witch, huh?"

"My grandmother was considered a spiritual healer. I'd like to think I've carried on with her traditions."

"I say you're a witch." Rand's eyes mauled Carmen's breasts through her shirt. "And a damned sexy one."

Gabriel rubbed his thumb against his lips as he eyed the monitor, vigilant for any signs that Carmen needed assistance. Rand probably considered his lewd overtones complimentary. Gabriel speculated that the man had fallen into a subconscious habit of slicing at a woman's underbelly until she weakened, and he achieved control. Maybe this was Walter Rand's rendition of a lioness-taming act.

At the window, Brad crossed his arms and fumed.

The psychic responded to Rand with a condescending smile. "I've provided many people with answers to difficult questions. Maybe I can answer the questions that you have. I'm aware that you lost your son, Mr. Rand."

The big man stiffened for a moment and then ground his teeth behind closed lips. Gabriel observed his gnashing jaw and silently congratulated Carmen. *Nice parry.*

"I'm sorry," Carmen said to the inmate. "Would you rather I not discuss this?"

Rand looked away. "He died of cancer, my boy. Too young."

"I'm sorry," she repeated. "Perhaps I could help you with your grieving."

"Do you want me to be a guest on your show or something?" Rand perked up.

"We'll see. In the meantime, I'm happy to try and make contact with your son."

Rand sat thickly in his chair. Gabriel figured the inmate was disappointed that Carmen would not qualify his Hollywood aspirations.

"It's nothing to be afraid of." Carmen stretched her arms toward him. "Give me your hands."

Rand reacted as though Carmen had opened her legs to him. He slid his arms across the table and seemed electrified the moment she took his heavy hands into her delicate ones.

In the monitoring room, Brad murmured an unintelligible Mayday alert, and Ramirez waved a finger from Gabriel to the interview room. Gabriel rose and headed out the door.

Carmen felt befouled the moment she took Rand's hands. The petty flirtation in his eyes was easy to ignore because his lust most likely originated from enforced prison celibacy. What Carmen couldn't ignore were Walter Rand's more potent emotions.

Spiritual danger signs were posted along the path she traveled to go deeper and deeper into the crawlspace that was Rand's soul. *Caution: Hazardous Material.*

The goodness in him hung as if crucified. Love existed, Carmen perceived, but nails pierced it. The death of Rand's son had hammered in a spike, along with a betrayed childhood and a failed marriage. The hunt of young women partially salved Rand's dissatisfaction with himself. Carmen sensed that well enough. Rand interpreted the fear in their eyes and the trembling of their mouths as proclamations of his power.

Rand's palms wetted Carmen's. The ache radiating up her right arm seemed related to Rand's mummifying foot, and the black blood Carmen felt percolating under his skin seemed to signify disease.

At that moment, the door opened and Gabriel entered. Rand didn't bother to hide his scowl.

"Buzzkill." The fat man released Carmen's hand.

She stealthily wiped her palms on her skirt.

"Why did you interrupt us?" Rand asked Gabriel.

Before the detective could speak, Carmen said, "I could do a better reading with tarot cards, Walter." She paused a moment. "Or better yet, could you possibly provide me with something that belonged to Christopher?"

"I don't have anything in here."

"Is there a place I could go to find something then?"

Carmen caught a glance of admiration from Gabriel, but she kept her eyes pinned on Rand.

The inmate ground his teeth, apparently sizing up the situation. Finally, he said, "I'll have a buddy o'mine bring you something that belonged to Chris." He looked at Gabriel. "If that's okay with you, buzzkill."

Gabriel gave him a nod.

CHAPTER THIRTY-FIVE

G abriel sat in the Jacuzzi with the pool light on and peered nonstop into the water. Across the tub, Ming watched him in concern.

"What are you looking for?" she asked.

"Nothing."

"Liar. You didn't accidentally crap in here, did you?"

Gabriel laughed. "No. I fell asleep and had a nightmare. I thought I saw a corpse."

"That's your nightmare? Come visit me at work." Ming waded over to her lover and sat on his lap. "When *are* you going to visit me at work? I miss you. Are you going to work cold cases forever?"

"Not if I can't solve any of them." Gabriel held her lithe body against his. "At this point, I'll throw anything against the wall to see if it sticks."

"Is the pretty little palm reader sticking?"

He gave his fiancée a look. "Ha ha."

The wind chimes rustled in the night breeze, light and

airy like Nancy's voice when she softened on a song. Ming's long hair undulated in the water and tickled Gabriel's skin.

"I think I've found a place for our wedding," she told him. "It's called Rancho del Rey, and they have an opening in a couple of months."

"Rancho del Rey," Gabriel repeated absently. His mind was on Carmen. Maybe the psychic could tell Rand that Chris couldn't "rest" until the issue with Nancy was resolved. Would Rand believe her?

"It's a private hacienda in the Malibu hills that overlooks the ocean," Ming said. "They had a cancellation and can accommodate our time frame. Isn't that great?"

"It's great."

"We'll have an early spring wedding."

"Good."

"I thought you'd be happy."

"I am."

"You don't seem happy."

Gabriel shrugged. "I'm happy. I'm just thinking about the case, is all."

"Can you take a break for two minutes and talk to me? I mean, we haven't even decided where we're going to live after the wedding."

"We've got time to work it out."

Ming huffed and climbed out of the Jacuzzi. She wrapped a towel around her and headed toward the house.

"Where are you going?" Gabriel asked.

"Why do you care?" she replied.

Gabriel watched the door close and, in defeat, allowed his body to slide under the water.

The next day, Brad, Gabriel, Ramirez, and Carmen met at the prison to flesh out their plans.

"I want you to make him vulnerable by talking about his son," Gabriel instructed the psychic. "Tell him Christopher needs closure in regards to Nancy."

"No." Carmen shook her head. "I can't do that. I can't lie."

"We're running out of time before he gets paroled."

"I'll buy us time." Carmen addressed Brad. "What are the legalities of putting Rand on my show? The man wants attention, and I could appeal to his ego. Once he's on the show, I'll bring the questions around to Nancy. Rand could implicate himself. Robert Durst admitted to murder during the filming of a documentary. It can happen."

The DA didn't look convinced. "It's shady," he said. "During a trial, the defense could argue that the television producers were working in conjunction with law enforcement. Detective McRay is dealing with an open case, after all, and you and he have been in obvious contact. Even if Rand did implicate himself on the show, you couldn't claim that you notified authorities after the fact."

"But it's worth a shot, right?" Carmen asked.

Brad leveled a steady gaze at his lover. "I think the sooner you extricate yourself from the likes of Walter Rand, the better."

"I can't do that," Carmen told him. "Not now."

A guard came in. "He's waiting."

Gabriel looked at Carmen. "It's showtime."

The gold disc was embossed with an arc of stars above a

diving platform and swimming lanes. Engraved on the back: *Christopher Rand, 1987 Champion, 200-medley relay*. Carmen closed her fist around the medal.

"I'd sort of hoped you brought a camera crew with you today," Rand said.

Carmen didn't respond. *She heard a faint splash of water and the echoed laughter of young men. Someone called out a name, but she couldn't make it out. It sounded like "Opie." Nor could she identify the caller.* Carmen likened these inner sensations to feeling the sun's warmth without seeing the originating ball of flames.

"I'm getting an 'Opie.' Something like that. Is that familiar to you?" Carmen asked Rand.

In the monitoring room, Gabriel thought, it's familiar to me. She means "Bodie." He then berated himself for getting suckered in. Dr. B had warned Gabriel about that. Shaking off the supposed connection between an "Opie" and Bodie, Gabriel crossed his arms and kept his concentration focused on the video feed.

"Opie?" Rand made a face. "Wasn't that the kid from the Andy Griffith Show? I thought you were contacting Chris."

"I'm getting a lot of images," Carmen said, "only they don't seem connected."

In the interview room, Gabriel felt a cold draft brush by him. The air conditioning, he reasoned. Tell yourself it's not the suffering ghosts of dead prisoners or the reckless energy of hundreds of hardened and impounded men.

Brad and Ramirez watched from their places affronting the two-way mirror. Brad scratched his chin in agitation, while Ramirez quietly puffed on a Winston.

Carmen kept her eyes closed and her fist tight around the medal. "I'm sensing a mountain area." *Green shade and air so fresh it tastes sweet on the mouth.* "My guides keep referencing this to me in regards to Nancy."

"What about Chris?" Rand pressed. "I thought you were getting in touch with him."

A deer on a dirt path. A sound startles the animal, and it darts off.

"I'm seeing animals," Carmen said. "And danger." She opened her eyes. "Were you a hunter? Did you hunt with Chris?"

"Yes." Rand smacked impatient hands on the table. "Is he here? Tell him—tell Chris that he wasn't crazy. Tell him that, okay?"

Behind the glass, Brad Franklin shook his head at Gabriel. "Your prisoner is getting riled up."

Gabriel prayed Carmen would pry into this new revelation about Chris. Why did the young man think he was crazy?

To Gabriel's disappointment, Carmen closed her eyes and pressed the medal to her chest. "I'm getting the letter D and a number. Eleven, I think. Does that mean anything to you?"

Rand's fist hit the table again, which caused Carmen's eyes to fly open. "Forget that! Tell Chris I didn't mean to make him sick."

Holding her composure, Carmen said, "Mr. Rand, I am relating to you what is being referenced to me. I see the letter D and the number eleven. Do they mean anything to you?"

In the monitoring room, Gabriel scratched his scalp in frustration. Who cares about a letter and a number? Why did Christopher think he was crazy? Why did Walter feel guilty over it? Gabriel exchanged disheartened looks with

Ramirez. He didn't even bother to look at Brad. Acrimonious sparks were flying off the District Attorney.

"D11..." Rand began to deflate like a leaking inner tube. All at once, he puffed up again. "Oh, D11! That's a code for a hunting tag. D11 is the code for the Angeles National Forest. We hunted mule deer there. Sure, that was like a second home to us. I used to rent a..." His voice trailed off.

"You rented..." Carmen repeated and waited for Rand to fill in the blanks.

He kept quiet. In the monitoring room, Brad, Gabriel, and Ramirez perked up, waiting for the inmate to divulge something they could use against him.

"Something about the Angeles National Forest?" Carmen prompted.

Rand pursed his lips together and sat like a corpulent statue.

"Mountains. Forest." Carmen's smooth voice invited him to continue.

Gabriel stared hard at the video monitor and tried to will Rand into confessing. Speak, you son of a bitch. Say what you know.

All at once, a high-pitched whine permeated the monitoring room, and Gabriel nearly jumped out of his skin.

"What the fuck?" Ramirez whirled around.

Brad clicked a button on his cell phone. "Sorry. It's my Theremin ringtone."

"Sounds like a *pinche* alien attack." Ramirez pointed at the phone. "Shut that thing off."

Brad suppressed a laugh and set his phone to vibrate. Gabriel blew out a huge breath to calm his heart, which had now grown fists that pounded against the wall of his chest.

Brad's smile faded as he peered through the window. "Hey, are you sure they can't see us?"

Carmen Jenette stared directly at the men through the two-way glass.

A spooked Ramirez frowned at Brad. "Nobody can see through the damn glass, okay? She's talkin' to ghosts in there, and you had to add sound effects."

In the interview room, Rand's puffy eyes watered with exasperation. "This isn't working," he complained. "Chris isn't coming because he doesn't want to see me in here."

Carmen rose from her seat. "I think I need to take a break."

"I was a respected man," Rand continued. "People in the community looked up to me. I had a business. I employed people. I am not a bad guy. I didn't do nothing to that waitress."

A lopsided smile broke on Carmen's face, and like a damaged robot, she moved to the door and knocked for the guard.

"I shouldn't be in here!" Rand bellowed.

Gabriel met Carmen out in the hallway. "What's wrong?"

The psychic put a hand to her forehead. "I don't know. I have a terrible headache."

"Oh." Gabriel couldn't hide his discouragement. "I could scout out some aspirin for you."

"I think I'd better stop for today."

"Are you sure?" Gabriel eyed the door behind which sat Rand. "Look, you're getting him to talk. Ask him what he meant about Chris thinking he was crazy."

Carmen shook her head.

"Can't you tough it out?" Gabriel pressed her.

"No."

He placed a hand on her arm. "Come on, Carmen. You can do this. Meeting with him is what you've been bugging me about for days."

The psychic yanked away from Gabriel's grasp. "Did you ever think that we're not getting anything from Walter because there's nothing to get?"

"He's responsible for Nancy's disappearance. I know it."

Carmen's green eyes disassembled him, and words began to spill from her lips, unwarranted. "Your work is the only place you feel secure; the only place you can pretend to have control over bad things. That's why you get impatient to solve your cases because you need to make the bad things go away. Only they don't go. The coldest case lives inside you, and you can't solve it. Right now, you have no leads, no forensic evidence—nothing! All you can rely upon is the voice inside your head, but you don't trust it because it lives side-by-side with the bad things."

Carmen appeared to wither from the effort of her speech. She held the wall for support.

A trickle of sweat descended Gabriel's brow. "A hunch can't convict a criminal," he said. "Just ask your lawyer boyfriend about that. Rand goes free in two days, and if I don't get something evidentiary from him, he's going to drop off the radar for good. Nancy will go back to a rotting file, and her parents will go to their graves with all their questions unanswered. Is that what you want?"

"Carmen?" Brad stood at the end of the hallway, the judgment evident in his eyes.

"I'd like to go home now," the psychic said. "I don't feel well."

Brad walked over and gently took hold of her arm. He turned to Gabriel.

"I'm taking Carmen home. She can't afford to get sick from this because she has a show to do. It's obvious you're not going to get anything useful from that cretin. It was a good effort, Detective, but I'm afraid neither of us can lend you any further help."

Brad signaled to a guard, who accompanied the couple down the hallway.

Ramirez peeked his head out of the monitoring room. "What happened?" he asked nervously. "Did Carmen see a ghost?"

CHAPTER THIRTY-SIX

When Gabriel arrived home from the collapse of Carmen's interview with Rand, he sifted through Nancy's belongings in the hope of finding something he may have missed. Had Nancy left anything he could use to detain his suspect?

Thumbing through the Pee Chee folder, Gabriel's fingers paused on Nancy's English essay. *No man is an island.*

Some men are, he thought and let the paper fall from his fingers. Sitting cross-legged on the carpet under slumped shoulders, Gabriel ruminated over a salient point Carmen uncovered when she tore into his soul. Was it true? Did Gabriel's compulsion to live for his work stem from a deep-seated need to eradicate the victim in him? Maybe.

The District Attorney and Psychic to the Stars, however, shouldn't act so high and mighty. Despite their claims of being compassionate public servants, Brad and Carmen stopped short of being humanitarians. Anyone could see their egos took center stage.

Gabriel looked at his bookcase, barren except for Nancy's photo.

We're too weak, Nancy. I failed you because I can't punch down my demons, and Carmen is blinded by the stars in her eyes. We're only human, and it's not good enough.

The marine layer had migrated from the ocean to the land and created a milky dusk outside the window. Inside the study, a sense of failure made Gabriel tired.

A text caused his cell phone to chirp, and he hoped it came from Ming. She'd spent the night after their uncomfortable discussion in the Jacuzzi but didn't say much. In the morning, Ming left without saying goodbye, and the two hadn't spoken since.

Looking expectantly at the text, Gabriel saw it was from Pauline Lewicki. *How's it going with that man? Did he say anything about Nancy?*

Gabriel wished Pauline hadn't asked. He replied with a lie. *Making progress. Will update you soon.*

Nancy's mom immediately texted back. *And you? How are you holding up? Been thinking about you. Here if u want to talk.*

What a nice lady, Gabriel thought. *Doing fine. No worries.*

Imagine Nancy's mother asking after him. Gabriel felt useless that he couldn't bring closure to her, Len, and their troubled son. He glanced again at Nancy's photograph. Her smile encouraged him. *Don't give up.*

At that moment, Gabriel's landline rang, and he picked up the receiver.

"Hello?"

Ramirez was on the line. "Can that voodoo queen come back and talk to Rand?"

"Seeing that our last chance is tomorrow and Carmen is sick, the answer is no."

"Bringing her in wasn't a bad idea, McRay. Rand reacted well to a psychic. Maybe he'll stick around town because she dangled the chance to be on TV in front of his face. We could still get to him."

"The conversation between them turned in circles. You heard it."

"I still say it was a good try. Harris would have been proud."

Gabriel appreciated the compliment. He paused and then said, "I don't think I ever thanked you for putting on the bachelor party, Miguel. Thanks for that and—and the other thing. The thing with Ming. I don't know how you got her to do it, but I hope all the other guys had as good of a time as I did."

Gabriel waited for Ramirez to respond, but heard only silence. Was the Lieutenant about to spear his underling with an emblematic wisecrack, or did the pause suggest that Ramirez felt touched?

Taking a chance on the latter option, Gabriel asked, "Would it be a conflict of interest if you were to stand as my best man?"

"Who cares?" Ramirez barked. "I was wondering when the hell you were going to ask me."

***

Across the city, Carmen's key slid into her lock, and she disarmed the house alarm. Brad accompanied her inside.

"You sure you can't stay?" she asked her lover.

"Work is calling, but I'll come back and bring you dinner."

"That's not necessary." Carmen smiled. "My White Knight."

She clambered toward the bedroom, and Brad followed. "I do have a whopper of a headache."

"You spent all day confined with that creep." Brad went into her bathroom to search the medicine cabinet. "I have a headache, and I wasn't even in the same room with him. Any preference for pain relief?"

Carmen let her clothes fall and pulled a burgundy-colored peignoir over her head. She might feel like hell, but she didn't have to look like it, not in front of Brad.

"Something with a sleep-aid," she replied.

"Can I use the cup with the toothbrush in it for water?"

Carmen crawled under the sheets. "Sure."

Brad returned, sat on the edge of Carmen's bed, and handed her a pill along with a glass of water.

"You're too kind," she said.

He leaned over and kissed her. "I'll say goodbye and leave you to dream."

Brad pulled the covers over her; shut the light and the bedroom door. Carmen listened to his footsteps diminish along the hallway. A moment or two passed, and she heard the front door creak open and close.

A strange sense of confusion clouded Carmen's thoughts. When she tried to think coherently, her brain battled her. Her inner vision seemed blocked, and Carmen lacked the strength to pop the cork trapping her gift. Sleep... Sleep would free her mind.

The Santa Ana wind nudged a tree outside, and its branches scratched at the window glass. Out in the surrounding city, a siren howled. Carmen drifted off. She might have slept. She wasn't sure.

Awareness assaulted her with the ringing of a cell phone. Berating herself for not silencing the damn thing, Carmen groaned and heaved her bed-warm body toward the nightstand. She grappled for the device, distressed to realize the pain in her head hadn't abated.

"Hello?"

"You're right," Gabriel McRay said. "I am impatient to solve cases, but I've been thinking about it, and I don't think that's a bad thing."

Carmen put a palm to her aching head. "Are we truly having this conversation right now?"

"I'm sorry, but we need to talk about Rand. You've mentioned the mountains more than once. Maybe you've got something there. Look," Gabriel coaxed, "it's not very late. Can I come over and talk with you?"

"No. I've taken a pill."

Carmen heard his very audible sigh. Detective McRay... A man who wore his heart on his sleeve, but refused to acknowledge the mortality hanging there.

"Fine," she said. "Come over; but come now, because I need to sleep."

"I'm in the car, already on my way."

That figured. Carmen ended the call, threw back the covers, and trudged to her bathroom. How could Gabriel feel she had locked into something? Carmen's visions were erratic with Rand.

Standing over the sink, Carmen groaned at the sight of herself and ran a brush through her hair. She splashed water on her face in an attempt to wake up and brushed her teeth. Upon returning to the bedroom, Carmen stood at the dresser and tried to decide what to wear.

She tugged on a pair of leggings and settled on an old

flannel men's shirt. Why bother to impress the detective? Carmen then moved over to the antique wardrobe to view herself in the old mirrored doors. As she buttoned the flannel, Carmen froze. She saw the man with the head injury reflected in the speckled glass.

"Leave me alone," she told him. "If you won't speak, then go."

The apparition turned his face toward the open doorway to the hall, displaying to Carmen the glaring, seeping wound on his head.

As she looked toward the doorway, a sudden light pierced through the clouds in her mind. Didn't Brad close the door to her bedroom when he went out?

Her heart dropped. The door stood wide open. Did Brad know the home's alarm code? Probably not, which meant that nobody set the alarm. Carmen glanced at the wounded man, but he was gone. Her breath took on physical matter, and the air hurt her throat as she inhaled and exhaled.

"I have a gun!" she yelled and strode to the bedroom door. Carmen slammed it shut and twisted the lock.

Joey Bowles stood exposed where the open door had concealed him. As Carmen's mouth opened into a surprised "O," he hefted a lead pipe in his gloved hand.

Carmen reached for the doorknob as Joey swung the pipe. She ducked away and sprang onto the bed. The pipe whizzed down onto the mattress only inches from her body.

"Help me!" Carmen screamed and hoped the neighbors would hear. The pipe went up again, and Carmen pitched forward off the bed. *Where do I go? What can I use to—*

The pipe caught her left upper arm, and pain, like a hundred burning needles, stabbed her flesh and radiated up and down the side of Carmen's body. She raced toward the door, but the pipe swung again and caught her on the same shoulder. Carmen fell to the floor with a loud thump.

"What do you want?" The question tore from her chest in a ragged sob. "What do you want from me?"

Crawling backward, Carmen kept terrified eyes on her attacker. Bowles wore an irritable expression as though the task of killing Carmen exasperated him. A furious sound, like a doorknob shaking, made a strange accompaniment to Carmen's sobbing and Joey's even breathing.

He lifted the pipe once more.

I'm going to end up like the man with the broken head, Carmen thought wildly. *His warning came too late. They'll find my brains on the wallpaper.*

Two shots were fired. The first broke through the lock on Carmen's bedroom door, which flew open. A voice yelled, "Drop your weapon!" but Joey Bowles swung the pipe in a wide arc to hit the new arrival. The next bullet entered the left ventricle of Joey Bowles's heart. The discharge echoed loudly through the small house, and outside, a dozen neighborhood dogs barked from the sudden bruising of their ears.

Inside Carmen's bedroom, Gabriel stood on the threshold, pointing a gun at the still-staggering Joey Bowles.

CHAPTER THIRTY-SEVEN

Gabriel and Carmen gave their report of the incident in Brad's downtown office the following day. Carmen, her arm supported by a sling, sat in a chair opposite her boyfriend's desk. Her gaze didn't focus on any one thing, and Carmen's fingernails absently scratched at the adhesive label on a bottle of pain pills she held in her hand. Gabriel, who had been down this path before, stood expressionless against a row of look-at-me photos and civic duty awards hanging on the District Attorney's wall.

Brad's elbows rested on his desktop, his clasped hands cemented against his mouth. His eyes wouldn't leave Carmen. Joining the trio was robbery detective Adam Bonin, who sported a long-sleeved t-shirt bearing the visage of Che Guevara.

"Joey had a receipt on him from a no-tell motel in Desert Hot Springs," Bonin informed the group. "He'd been living down there for the last few weeks with his bags packed. Looks like he was aiming to get out of town." The rocker detective regarded Carmen. "I guess he wanted to pay you one last visit."

"How'd he get past the alarm?" Gabriel asked Carmen.

"That would be my fault." Brad let his hands drop to the desk. "I didn't even think about setting the alarm."

"I never gave you the code." Carmen defended her lover. "I forgot. I wasn't myself."

"You shouldn't join me tonight," Brad said to her. "I think you should rest."

"I want to support you. If you don't mind me wearing this over my gown." Carmen indicated her sling.

Bonin stood up and stretched. Gabriel noticed for the first time that he wore an earring. "Kudos to you, Miss Jenette, for being in a mood to party. That's the spirit." He winked at Carmen. "Pun intended."

She managed to smile but dragged a fingernail down the pill bottle's label.

"You no longer have to worry about your stalker," Bonin said. "Thanks to Detective McRay's good aim."

Gabriel viewed Brad's wall of accolades so he wouldn't have to respond nor meet anyone's eye. Dr. Tom Li now had one more affirmation of his future son-in-law's proclivity to violence. Gabriel hadn't wanted to kill Joey Bowles, but he didn't want to get smashed with a lead pipe either.

Brad escorted Bonin out of the office. When the two men departed, Carmen regarded Gabriel from her chair. "I know you don't believe in spirits, but I saw the injured man again —the one with his face crushed, right before I saw Joey Bowles."

"What of it?" Gabriel continued to appraise the wall photos.

"Well, I thought you could do some detective work on him. Couldn't you pretend he wasn't...?"

"A ghost?" Gabriel finished for her. "Isn't that more your line of work? Why don't you do a séance? Why don't you contact Joey Bowles? Ask him why, if he fawned over you, did he seem so intent on ending your life?"

Gabriel faced the psychic. The shadows encircling her green eyes implored him. Supposing he owed Carmen a favor, Gabriel relented and pulled out his notepad.

"Describe your injured ghost to me," he said. "Is there anything more you can tell me about him, other than the fact he's missing half his face?"

"It's ghastly—as if a ship dropped anchor on his skull. It's hard to see anything else."

Gabriel remembered what Lopez said about human faces being symmetrical. "Tell me what you remember about the half of his face that isn't damaged."

Carmen chewed at her lower lip and her eyes traveled from one corner of the room to the other. "His eye is blue, I think. He looks about thirty-five or forty. Maybe there's hair on his upper lip. Yes, I think he must have a mustache. He's a little rough around the edges, a blue-collar type of guy. He wears a uniform—not a jumpsuit, but a work shirt with pants."

"And he never speaks?"

"Not a word. But he always shows up before trouble." She looked at Gabriel earnestly. "I think he must be connected to Joey Bowles."

"Well," Gabriel said as tucked the notepad away. "Now that Bowles is dead, you won't be bothered by your damaged ghost."

"Why did you say that I ought to try and make contact with Joey?" Carmen asked.

"I was being sarcastic."

"No, you weren't," Carmen said. "You want to know why he wanted to kill me. Did he need a reason?"

"No. I suppose he didn't," Gabriel said. "He could have been mentally ill. Like I said, you're a celebrity, and this is the price of fame."

Carmen simpered, having caught Gabriel's jab. "But you don't believe that, do you?"

In reply, Gabriel turned back to the photographs and awards. He did not believe it. A mental imbalance had never been referenced in Joey's storied criminal career. Nor was he known to have abused drugs. But what did it matter? The stalker was dead, and his reasons died with him.

Gabriel shoved his hands in his pockets and perused Brad Franklin's many awards. This evening, the White Knight would hang out with other beautiful people at a fancy fundraiser. Gabriel would go home tonight with a higher body count on his conscience.

He gazed at Brad's arm-in-arm photos with famous politicians, sports figures, and actors. To the DA's credit, the majority of the framed photos depicted a younger Brad in the act of community service. Gabriel paused under a picture taken of Brad at Camp David Gonzales, a high-security facility for juvenile offenders.

At that moment, the DA reentered his office. "I just heard that the Judge ordered no probationary period for Walter Rand because the assault on Meghan Wright was his first offense."

"First offense, my ass," Gabriel said, wheeling around. "Rand was never caught before, that's all."

The District Attorney could only shrug.

"So when does Rand board his flight for Manila?" Gabriel asked. "Within the hour?"

"It's done, Gabriel," Brad answered. "Stop torturing yourself."

Late in the afternoon, Gabriel waited with his office phone to his ear, hoping Jenna Goldman Klein would pick up his call. He hoped Nancy's old friend might recall something, *anything*, about Walter Rand. Unfortunately, the call went to Jenna's voicemail. Did that woman ever answer her phone?

Checking his calendar, Gabriel was relieved to see an appointment with Dr. B scheduled for the evening. He could do with a venting session. The idea of Rand sailing the high seas while the Lewickis pined for their daughter distressed him to no end. Ming had distanced herself, a psychic had filleted his soul, and the White Knight's pristine past managed to spotlight Gabriel's recent role as a killer.

He leaned back in the chair and dug his thumbs into his temples. Something drifted at the edge of Gabriel's consciousness, and he felt sure he'd missed something, but what? The background noise of the bureau distracted him; the buzzing voices sounded like the gathering of flies.

His cell phone chirped, and Gabriel pounced on the device, hoping either Jenna or Ming had left a message. He read the caller ID and felt his heart rate hike: *Dash*.

Gabriel listened to the voicemail message and then pondered his next move. A few minutes passed, and then he rose from his desk to meet with his ex-partner.

CHAPTER THIRTY-EIGHT

I n the Commerce Casino, Gabriel bypassed the card
tables and headed toward the Arena Bar and Grill. He
found Dash sitting at the bar with a drink in his hand.
Gabriel took the stool next to him.

"Gabe," the other man began but didn't finish.

The barkeep, a good-looking sandy-haired fellow with
taut muscles and a few artsy tattoos, took Gabriel's order
for black coffee. Only after Gabriel ordered did he regard
Dash.

Ex-Detective Starkweather had always been thin, but
there were dark circles under his protuberant eyes that
hadn't been there before. His Adam's apple, always bobbing
and distinct when he was nervous, now jumped in his
throat. Dash was drinking what looked like a vodka and
tonic. Of course, Gabriel mused. Vodka had fewer carbs than
most other liquors. Dash hadn't changed.

"Has it been ten months?" Gabriel asked him.

"They let me out early."

As he set down a cup of coffee, the bartender asked if

Gabriel wanted to order food. Gabriel responded with a shake of his head. He had no appetite.

"You want a tab?" The bartender asked.

"No." Gabriel slid a ten-dollar bill across the counter. He wasn't planning to stay long. Dash pushed the money back toward Gabriel and told the bartender to add the coffee to his tab.

Gabriel took a sip and surveyed the shelves of shiny liquor bottles across the bar. He could feel Dash studying him.

"I wanted to say I'm sorry," the other man said. "I heard what you went through."

Gabriel didn't reply. He'd had lengthy conversations about Dash with Dr. B. Discussions centering on how Dash threw the trial by planting evidence, an act that allowed Victor Archwood to go free. Although Dash couldn't have predicted the catastrophic effects of his actions, Gabriel held his ex-partner partly responsible for the torment he'd endured at Archwood's hands. Dash had been Gabriel's best friend. He would have stood as his best man.

"I never thought things would go to hell," Dash said. "Eve and I nearly divorced over it. Eventually, she forgave me."

He faced Gabriel with an optimistic glimmer. In turn, Gabriel concentrated on his coffee. "How is Eve?"

He'd always liked Dash's wife. She'd been a friend, but their friendship blew up when the bomb went off at Archwood's trial. Collateral damage.

"She's good. She misses you."

Gabriel said nothing.

"So," Dash continued, "You finally decided to take the plunge with Ming. I'm glad."

Gabriel looked squarely at his ex-partner. "What do you need, Dash?"

"Nothing." He swallowed, and the ball is his throat bounced. "I wanted to see you, that's all. I'm going to save myself the embarrassment of asking Ramirez for my job back. Going in for PI work. But I wanted you to know that I _"

"It's known." Gabriel swilled down the rest of his coffee and it burned his tongue.

"Would you like a real drink?"

"No." Gabriel shook his head. "I've got an appointment."

"I heard through the grapevine that you were working in the Unsolved Unit."

Gabriel slid off the stool. "You heard correctly."

"I did my time, Gabe. I know I fucked up, but I paid for it. Can't you spare one minute? Yell at me. Punch me in the face if you want, but get it out."

Gabriel glowered at him. "Anything else I can do to ease your conscience, Dash?"

"You can talk to me."

Gabriel wondered if maybe striking the other man in the middle of a restaurant would assuage the bitterness he felt. "There's nothing to talk about."

"Tell me about the case you're working on."

"Why?"

"For old time's sake."

Gabriel reclaimed his seat. "My suspect is leaving town, and I have nothing to detain him with except a psychic. She isn't good at seeing anything but a ghost with half of a head. That's my case."

"A psychic!" Dash appeared delighted to be off the

subject of his misconduct. "We never worked with a psychic, did we? Well, why does Casper the friendly ghost walk around with half a head?"

Gabriel hadn't intended to cut Dash a break, but he missed talking with his old friend. How frustrating.

"Unfortunately, the psychic can't ask him because he won't speak."

"Hmm. A silent ghost." Dash studied his vodka and tonic. A moment passed, and he took a swallow. "Maybe he has nothing to say because speaking would be irrelevant."

Gabriel nodded in the spirit of cordiality, but he wasn't in the mood for small talk or mending fences or whatever this was. He no longer knew why he was here and decided that he no longer wanted to be.

Getting to his feet again, Gabriel tried to sound gentle. "Please give Eve my regards."

He left Dash at the bar and drove to his therapist's office.

"Do other people have problems like this?" Gabriel asked Dr. B. "Having Ming in my life is the best thing that's ever happened to me, but she's had enough of my bullshit. I just saw Dash, speaking of relationships, and I want to throttle him but also get his take on the investigation."

Dr. B followed his patient with brown eyes made larger by the spectacles he wore. "Can we take this one at a time?"

Gabriel nodded.

"Let's talk about Dash. The answer is yes; other people miss friends who have betrayed them. You and Dash have a lot of history. Of course, you'd miss the good times. I miss

Dash, as well, to be honest. Give yourself time to sort through your reactions, now that you've seen him. Do you want to talk about it?"

"Not really." Gabriel sighed. "What for?"

"Then let's talk about Ming. Why push her away now when you are about to seal the deal on your relationship?"

"The only reason I can think of is that loving someone makes me too vulnerable. I look at what the Lewickis have gone through. What they're still going through. There's too much to lose."

The psychologist contemplated his patient. "Opening yourself up to love does make you vulnerable to loss, but maybe it's not as simple as that."

Gabriel quit pacing and let his hands rest on the back of his usual chair. "Well, apparently, I'm too thick to get it, so help me out."

"Thickness plays no part," Dr. B said. "It's difficult to identify an exact cause of fear, especially if its origin is deeply rooted. We tend to run from the scary stuff instead of examining it."

"I'd rather not wait to have an epiphany, Raymond. Time is wasting, and Ming is hurt. Why don't you tell me what your thoughts are?"

Dr. B clasped his long fingers together. "You and I both know that the molestation you suffered as a child made an enormous impact on your life. You've been going to therapy and seeking help. The wonderful progress you've made has now peeled away one more layer to reveal to you another impact of that abuse."

The therapist's words bored a hole in Gabriel's stomach.

"When trauma forces us to find ways to cope, we create

layers of protective insulation along the way. But these layers are not necessarily good for us.

At one time, you used anger to make yourself feel powerful. We like feeling powerful, especially when a trauma disempowers us. All anger does, however, is scratch an itch on a festering wound. Rage has no real power; besides, it's dangerous. Anger turned inward causes depression. Anger turned outward causes us to hurt other people."

"I've dealt with the anger," Gabriel said and then remembered the temptation to slam his fist into Dash. Wilting into his chair, he thought, *But I didn't punch him. I missed him instead.* That's progress, isn't it?

"You have dealt with your anger successfully," Dr. B affirmed. "Self-blame is another protective layer." The psychologist paused to regard Gabriel. "Are you interested in knowing how we consider self-blame to be a form of protection? Self-blame applies reason to a very unreasonable event. 'If only I had been able to protect myself. If only I had walked down a different street—' that kind of thing. Self-blame gives us a sense of control over a situation that, in reality, was very much out of our control. If you can blame yourself, you are reassuring yourself that you could have avoided the trauma. That gives you a strange kind of protection from feeling completely victimized and disempowered. This is true, especially with male sexual abuse victims. This is true for you, Gabe."

Gabriel winced inwardly and then cleared his throat. "We've been down the disempowerment road before, Raymond. Tell me something I don't know."

"I'm not finished," Dr. B told him.

Gabriel sat back in the chair, white-knuckled and waiting for the bomb to drop.

"Like I said," the psychologist continued. "These layers of insulation feel safe, but they are not healthy. Self-blame inevitably leads to feelings of unworthiness. 'I failed at protecting myself, so I must be a failure.' What do you think happens when we feel unworthy?"

Gabriel waited and listened. He didn't know what to say.

Dr. B's brown eyes regarded him kindly. "We feel we don't deserve any good in our lives. You don't fear the loss of happiness, Gabe. You feel you don't deserve happiness." The psychologist pushed his glasses up the bridge of his nose.

Was it true? Or did Dr. B peddle a different brand of voodoo? Was his therapist guilty of the power of suggestion, just like Carmen Jenette? As much as Gabriel disliked the idea, he considered the possibility that he held out a stick to trip his own legs.

"You say you love your fiancée," Dr. B said. "You say you are happier when she's around. Why wouldn't you embrace this wonderful opportunity to marry her? Why not jump right in?"

Gabriel hung his head and studied the laces of his shoes. After a minute or two, he swallowed the stone in his throat. "How do I stop blaming myself?"

"Give yourself permission to embrace a wonderful opportunity. Tell yourself you deserve good things in your life."

Gabriel guffawed. "Sure. Piece of cake."

"I didn't say you were going to believe it right away. Even if you have to say the words out loud or write them on a wall in neon paint, do it. Tell yourself you are worthy of love and goodness. If you say it enough times, you'll eventually start to believe it."

When Gabriel didn't speak, Dr. B asked, "What are you thinking?"

"I'm thinking I'll hold a seat of honor for you at my wedding."

The psychologist's grin caused his glasses to fall to the end of his nose.

CHAPTER THIRTY-NINE

When Ming Li returned home from work that evening, she saw two-dozen long-stemmed red and white roses on the glass table in her entrance hall. Putting down her purse, she went to the flowers and breathed in their refreshing fragrance. The note read, "Look in the kitchen."

Smiling, Ming walked into her kitchen and saw Chinese food cartons laid out on the granite island. Gabriel held paper plates and chopsticks.

"It was too late to make anything," he said. "But I figured we couldn't go wrong with Chinese."

"What's all this for?" she asked.

Gabriel rounded the corner of the island to approach Ming. "Because I've been wrong. I made you handle all the wedding preparations all by yourself."

She kept her distance. "I can plan a wedding by myself," Ming told him, "but I can't create a marriage alone."

"I know," Gabriel murmured. "Give me another chance."

"What brought on this change?"

"I've been doing some thinking, is all." *Exercising my demons*, Gabriel thought, even without Carmen's gris-gris.

"Can I trust you?" Ming asked.

In answer, Gabriel pulled her to him and kissed her lips. His blue eyes found her ebony ones.

"You can trust me. I have only one request as far as our wedding is concerned."

Ming appeared to brace herself. "And what's that?"

"I pick the caterer."

Carmen wore an off the shoulder, lacy gown of green, which highlighted her eyes. Her curling hair tumbled around her pretty face. The gown's tight fit accentuated her bust and her flat stomach, and its train made an elegant statement when Carmen walked. Even with her arm in a sling, she looked stunning at Brad's side tonight at the fundraiser. Most of the attendees knew her face, and the Psychic to the Stars reveled in their attention.

She should have been on her usual high, what with a fair amount of fans in the room, but Carmen couldn't shake the oppressive feeling that once again assailed her.

Joey Bowles was dead, she reasoned. He no longer posed a threat to her, so why did her senses feel dulled?

"You alright?" Brad must have picked up on her fatigue. "Do you want to leave?"

Carmen shook her head. The District Attorney looked elegant in a custom-fitted tuxedo.

"After all you've gone through," Brad whispered. "You're a trooper to be here."

"I'm fine," she assured her lover.

If Carmen wanted to be one half of this power couple, then she needed to pull herself together. The election was only days away, and the campaign had gone into overdrive. Speeches and meetings jammed Brad's calendar for the upcoming week, and she wanted to be a force at his side. Brad put an arm around Carmen's waist.

"It's up to me to keep you safe now."

"And how do you intend to do that?" Carmen tossed her long curls over one shoulder—a perky gesture, designed to conceal the drag on her vitality.

He nuzzled her. "By never letting you out of my sight."

Carmen's heart skipped a beat. She had manifested a dream come true. She should have felt electrified, but, Carmen couldn't muster up the energy to jump for joy.

A man and woman, two donors, approached Brad. Immediately falling into the role of a friendly politician, Brad released Carmen's waist and spoke with the couple. Carmen felt the cell phone vibrate in her jeweled clutch. Bringing it out, she saw the call came from her producer.

"I have to take this," she whispered to Brad and moved a few steps away.

She spoke for a moment, trying to hear her producer amid the surrounding conversations and clinking glasses. When the phone call ended, Carmen's gown swished as she strode back to Brad. Energy once again surged through her.

She waited for Brad's supporters to walk away and then grasped both his shoulders. "You're never going to believe this," she told him, nearly breathless.

"What?" Brad looked pleased to see his girlfriend reenergized.

"Walter Rand contacted the show's producer. He's not leaving town." She gave Brad's shoulders a triumphant squeeze. "He wants his fifteen minutes of fame. Mr. Rand has arranged to meet me tomorrow to discuss his guest appearance. I can't wait to tell Gabriel. He's gonna flip."

As Carmen slid a festive arm through Brad's, her mind began to formulate a plan of attack. She'd have to plant seeds relating to Nancy Lewicki and hope they sprout.

Carmen's eye caught a figure standing stock-still and staring at her from among the moving mass of glittering guests. The smile faded from her face. Her previous elation fell to pieces at her high-heeled feet.

You should be gone.

The man with the crushed skull did not go. Blood and brain matter smeared his work shirt. Dirt covered his khaki pants. His one eye seemed to accuse Carmen from his frozen position amid the crowd.

CHAPTER FORTY

The following day at work, Gabriel received a callback from Jenna Goldman Klein. After a brief exchange of pleasantries to avoid appearing too impatient, Gabriel said, "I found out who Bodie was. You were right, Mrs. Klein. He was a sophomore at Taft. Bodie's name is Christopher Rand."

"Christopher," Jenna stood the name upright to see it better. "Wow. How is Bodie? Where's he living now?"

"He's not living," Gabriel said before he remembered to be patient. "He died of cancer a few years back."

Jenna gasped. "Oh, no."

Gabriel figured Jenna would use that information to bolster her opinion that the world was going to hell.

"So many of my friends have died," she murmured. "It's tragic."

Debbie Downer didn't disappoint.

"Christopher's father is a man named Walter Rand," Gabriel told her. "Did Nancy ever mention Walter Rand or talk about Bodie's father?"

"I can't remember."

"If I emailed you a photo of Mr. Rand, could you try real hard to remember if you ever saw him around Nancy? Hanging out at the mall with you guys, maybe. Picking her up from school. She met him a couple of times at the Tasty-D-Lite."

"Nancy did?" Jenna sounded astonished. "I don't think she ever mentioned that to me. But of course," Jenna assured Gabriel. "Of course, I'll try to remember him. It's been so many years, though. Can I ask you why you bring up Bodie's dad now?"

"He's a person of interest."

"Carmen Jenette didn't mention him on her show."

"You watch the show?"

"I do now. Nancy was my best friend. I would think, if you have a suspect, the psychic would say something about him."

"She's not at liberty to mention anything that would put the investigation at risk," Gabriel said. "Please check your email for Mr. Rand's picture and call me immediately if anything comes to mind."

Jenna promised that she would.

As soon as Gabriel hung up, he emailed Rand's picture to her and then stared at the blank screen of his computer, wondering what else he could do.

A voicemail message came through on his cell phone. Carmen Jenette. Gabriel listened to her message and, before he could take a breath, headed straight for his Lieutenant's office.

Rand arranged to meet Carmen at a Starbucks in Studio City. California has a two-party consent law in regards to wearing a wire, so to record their conversation without telling Rand would be illegal. If Rand confessed information in a public place, however, he would be unable to claim any expectations of privacy.

So Gabriel, wearing off-duty attire: jeans, a t-shirt, and a baseball cap, sat a few tables over from Carmen, where he planned on eavesdropping. If Walter ended up noticing him, Gabriel would simply say, "Hello."

Rand walked into the café with a noticeable limp, having traded in his prison sandals for extra wide tennis shoes. His slacks were cleanly pressed, and he wore a blue buttoned-down shirt over his paunch. He appeared almost respectable.

When Rand spied Carmen, he plunked himself down at her table. Carmen asked if he'd like a coffee or a pastry, to which he shook his head.

"Nah," Rand told her and pulled out a syringe. "I'm watching my sugar intake these days."

Sitting at a nearby table, Gabriel supposed that impending fame had tempted the big man into healthfulness.

"Why'd you disappear on me?" Rand asked Carmen.

"Well, they paroled you, and you told Detective McRay that you were off to the Philippines. I didn't think our paths would cross again."

"But you promised to put me on your show and said you'd contact Chris for me."

"And so I will," Carmen said. "Are you excited to be a guest?"

"What do you think, girlie?"

Carmen laughed, and then she sobered. "I'll do my best to communicate with Christopher, Mr. Rand, but you must tell us a little bit about Nancy Lewicki?"

Rand waggled his head. "Look, I want to clear this up once and for all. I did not kill that girl. I don't know anything about her, other than the fact that she and my boy were friends a long time ago."

"But the fans are very interested in –"

"Don't you get it?" Rand asked her. "I've been in prison. You know how embarrassing that is? It's time people hear Walter Rand's side of the story. That girl, that Meghan Wright, is a goddam lying bitch and she should rot in hell for ruining my life. Just a stupid bimbo looking for a sugar daddy, that's what she was. I put a hand on her boob, so what? Does that sound like sexual battery to you? Does that sound like three years spent living in a six by eight cell?"

Gabriel rolled his eyes. So, this is why Rand sought the spotlight. He wanted to clear his name publicly.

"I was an upstanding citizen." Rand poked his finger against his bulging chest. "And I was a good father, too. We're gonna contact my Chris. I'm gonna make things good with him, and then I get to start my life over." Rand leaned back and slapped his hands on his swollen legs.

"Whatever you say, Mr. Rand," Carmen said.

Hearing her, Gabriel could tell the medium had grown weary of the ex-con's tirade.

"Do you need any funds to tie you over until the taping?" she asked. "We could help you with a hotel or send a car for you on the day of the show. Where are you staying?"

Gabriel strained his ears to hear the answer. A mother and child had taken the table on the other side of him, and the child loudly voiced his demand for a ghost-shaped cookie.

"I got a hotel," Rand said to Carmen. "Don't worry about that. I'll come to you. I got money, okay? Walter Rand don't need to beg, borrow, or steal from no one."

"Alright, then."

The child's voice escalated from a whine to a full-blown temper tantrum, and Gabriel had difficulty hearing what Carmen said.

"Here's the address of the studio." Carmen pulled a card out of her purse. "Along with the date and time you're supposed to get there."

"I'll be there," Rand said as he hoisted himself from his seat. "You watch, girlie. Your show will hit number one with this ol' boy featured."

He limped off toward the exit.

Only when Rand was out of sight, did Carmen turn to regard Gabriel. They waited a full ten minutes before he rose and walked over to join her.

Carmen leaned forward. "It's going to be tough to corral him into talking about Nancy. Did you hear him? Walt has no intention of discussing the case and claims he didn't kill her."

Gabriel eyed the psychic. "No one ever said that Nancy died."

CHAPTER FORTY-ONE

Encouraged by the fact that Rand would stay put until his scheduled appearance on Carmen's show, Gabriel inserted a flash drive into his computer at work. It contained the last interview between Carmen and Rand, and Gabriel hoped to catch any information he might have missed. He forwarded the video to the place where Rand began getting agitated.

Tell Chris he wasn't crazy!

Gabriel wondered what that meant. Eugenia had said that Chris returned to Madison feeling burdened. Had he become mentally ill?

Gabriel reviewed the interview scribbled in his notepad. Eugenia had mentioned that she'd advised Chris to see a psychologist. Turning his attention back to the video, Gabriel viewed Carmen gripping the swimming medal as if she were trying to squeeze secrets from its round mass.

"I'm getting the letter D and a number? Eleven, I think?"

A quick thump as Rand's hand slammed the table. *"Forget about that! Tell Chris that I didn't mean to make him sick."*

Gabriel skipped through the recording.

"That's a code for a hunting tag. D11 is the code for the Angeles National Forest. We hunted mule deer there. I used to rent a…"

Gabriel watched as Rand suddenly became guarded. Carmen had prompted him.

"You rented…"

But Rand had raised his inner drawbridge at that point, which left them floundering in a moat of question marks. To her credit, Carmen had tried one more time.

"Something about the Angeles National Forest?"

"What else are you getting about Chris?"

"Mountains. Forest."

At that point, Gabriel saw Carmen jerk her eyes to the observation window. He paused the video on her bewildered, deer-in-the-headlights expression. Gabriel remembered Ramirez's hopeful, "What did she see? A ghost?"

No, Gabriel thought. Ghosts did not exist except in the jagged avenues of an impaired mind or, perhaps, in the crevice of a broken heart. But something did make Carmen sick. Curiosity prickled Gabriel. What did she see?

He ejected the flash drive and carried it into Ramirez's office. After his lieutenant reviewed the video, Gabriel asked, "Did you notice how Rand clammed up right after he mentioned a rental in the mountains? What do you think shut him up?"

"I don't know," Ramirez answered. "Could he be talking about gun rentals? An off-road vehicle rental?"

"I think he meant a cabin rental."

"Nah," Ramirez countered. "Why rent a cabin? He didn't live that far away."

"Far enough away," Gabriel mused. "I don't believe he'd rent a gun. Avid hunters pride themselves on their equip-

326

ment. As for a car, he most likely owned the kind of vehicle that could get him into the great outdoors."

"Well, check out cabin rentals and do it fast. You see, McRay? No effort is wasted."

Ramirez must have been hit with the nice stick again.

Gabriel returned to his desk and compiled a list of cabin rental agencies near the Angeles National Forest during the 1980s.

Hunters were afforded sparse offerings in the local California mountains. Still, Gabriel discovered a group of cabins called the Little Hollow Rentals that stood on the edge of the parkland. He called the number listed and hoped the company had survived.

He rubbed his jaw as he waited for someone to answer. Even if Gabriel did find out that Walter Rand once rented a cabin, what did that prove? What tied him to Nancy? Rand admitted meeting Nancy at the Tasty-D-Lite when Chris was in Texas. Then what happened? Gabriel felt his hope fade as he waited for someone to pick up the line.

Then, to his relief, someone answered, "Little Hollow Cabin Rentals. May I help you?"

Two hours later, Gabriel wound his way up the mountains. The San Gabriel Mountains shielded Los Angeles from the Mojave Desert. With the drought in force, much of the wilderness surrounding the route consisted of lowered water tables in the lakes and meadowland burned with patches of brown. Once-proud trees stood saturnine against the side of the road.

The Little Hollow cabins were spread along a lake near Crestline. Gabriel pulled up in a dust cloud in front of a wood cabin painted with green trim. A sign reading "Rental Office" hung from an awning over the entrance. The autumn sun, angled low, sent shafts of light through the trees that glinted brightly off the cabin's windows.

Gabriel walked through the door and heard a bell clang above his head. A husky teddy bear of a man emerged from a back room, holding a no-spill coffee holder. He introduced himself as Sean Kupersmith, owner and manager.

Gabriel explained the reason for his visit. He showed Sean a photo of Walter Rand and asked if he could get access to past rental information.

The owner explained that the cabins had been in the Kupersmith family since the 1960s.

"We switched to keeping records on computers in the mid-nineties, but before that, we documented the rentals in a ledger."

"Could I see the ledgers from 1988?" Gabriel asked.

Kupersmith took a slug of coffee and shook his head. "I wish I could say yes. Unfortunately, the Bridge Fire destroyed all our ledgers. It wiped out seven thousand acres back in 1999."

Gabriel nodded, disappointed.

"A couple of the old cabins burned, and we took that as a sign that it was time to renovate. The good news is that we used the same cement foundations. The floor plans of the cabins are virtually the same as they were in the eighties. Come on," he said. "I'll show you around."

Kupersmith toured Gabriel through the vacant cabins.

Most were one and two-bedroom, but some, which the manager referred to as Family Cabins, slept four to eight people.

"Do hunters stay here?" Gabriel asked.

"Hunters, skiers, hikers, anyone. It's beautiful country, isn't it?"

───────

As Gabriel headed home on the freeway, a red sunset glared at him. He brooded that for every step forward he'd taken in this investigation, he'd fallen two steps behind. Carmen was right. Gabriel had no solid leads, only hunches. He couldn't be sure that Rand had rented a cabin at Little Hollow. He couldn't be sure Rand had rented a cabin at all.

Stopped in traffic, Gabriel rested his forehead on the steering wheel. No matter how hard he tried, he couldn't budge warmth into this cadaver-cold case.

───────

The following day, Gabriel met with Ramirez to discuss closing the case.

"It's like trying to start a car with a dead battery," Gabriel complained. "I've exhausted every lead I have."

Ramirez absently rubbed the shirt pocket holding his cigarettes. "I suggest not closing it until Rand appears on the show. Who knows? He may blow it. But I'll leave the decision to you."

Gabriel's cell phone rang, and he reached into his pocket. Glancing at the phone, he told Ramirez, "It's Carmen." He answered her call.

The psychic sounded frantic. "I need you to pick up Walter Rand. Now!"

"Why?" Gabriel asked. "I'm the last person he wants to see."

"You don't understand," Carmen said. "The staff is freaking out. He was supposed to be here half an hour ago. We've had interns calling every motel and hotel within ten miles of Studio City. We finally located him at the Radisson in Burbank. I'm worried something bad has happened, Gabriel. Can you please check up on him and bring him over?"

Gabriel agreed to fetch Rand.

For a sickly ex-con, Rand had made his gate money from prison go a long way. The Radisson was a nice hotel. After speaking with the front desk, Gabriel went up to the man's room and knocked loudly.

"Walt, it's Gabriel McRay. Open the door. Carmen wants me to bring you to the studio." He waited a minute, and then knocked again. "Walt?"

Muttering to himself, Gabriel went to search out a maid and her passkey.

When housekeeping unlocked Walt's door, Gabriel stepped into the room and saw the bathroom door closed. He heard the shower running.

Dickhead, he thought and then boxed his annoyance. He

strode over to the door and said in a stern voice, "Walt, you're late. Hurry up."

Gabriel gave the maid staring at him from the doorway a few dollars and then dismissed her. He surveyed the room and walked over to a duffle bag lying on the unmade bed. With one eye on the bathroom door, Gabriel rummaged through the bag.

He inspected a Philippine Airlines ticket, one-way from Los Angeles to Manila. No surprise there. Gabriel produced his cell phone and took pictures of the ticket. Why not? This was his version of practical magic.

Reaching into the bag again, his fingers separated a few articles of clothing, some plastic containers of medication, and a couple of pairs of shoes—nothing else. Gabriel spied Rand's wallet lying on the bed and flipped it open. An expired driver's license. The key card to his hotel room. A wallet-sized photograph of Christopher. The other card slots were empty but worn. Gabriel wondered what might have filled them. Credit cards? Photos of teenaged girls?

He scowled. "Let's go, Walt." He strode to the bathroom door. "You'll miss your big moment." Gabriel gave a hard rap on the door, and it swung open on impact.

Initially, Gabriel felt a rush of embarrassment when he saw Walter Rand halfway out of the tub. Then his brain registered that Rand lay in a perverse imitation of Janet Leigh's character in the movie "Psycho."

Walter Rand's face lay squished against the tiled floor with the one visible eye accusing Gabriel. Rand's bare rump draped over the edge of the bathtub as if he were expecting a spanking. The man's flesh resembled white paste as the water sailed over his body. In the tub, twisted upwards from the fall, Rand's blackened foot poked up like a flag.

CHAPTER FORTY-TWO

So many of us dead.

Jenna's words littered Gabriel's mind, blown around by the prevailing wind of his current feeling: despair.

I did not kill that girl.

Gabriel hated loose ends. Of course, Rand killed Nancy. With Rand's death, however, the why, how, and where would remain a mystery.

He left his cubicle to get a coffee refill and to give himself something to do. Rick Frasier met Gabriel at the condiment tray and commented on how he was looking forward to the wedding. Gabriel acknowledged the sentiment with a half-hearted thumbs-up and returned to his desk in time to see his office phone line light up.

The caller was Jenna.

"I took a couple of days to think about it," she said. "I'm sorry, but I don't remember anything about Bodie's dad. His face doesn't strike a chord with me. Like I said, Nancy and I never played music at Bodie's house, only Nancy did. I cannot remember his father at all."

Gabriel had thought as much and thanked her for trying.

"I'm still in shock to hear that Bodie passed away. Cancer, was it?" Jenna clucked on the phone. "Too many people are dying of cancer. It's got to be our air. Pure poison."

Gabriel dropped his face into his hand.

"The older you get," Jenna continued, "The more you realize how harsh life is. First, Nancy disappears, then Toby dies, and now I have to hear about Bodie. It's depressing."

Lifting his face, Gabriel asked, "Who's Toby?"

"One of Bodie's pals. The one I told you about when we first spoke."

Gabriel squinted wearily as he reached for his notepad and flipped to his interview with Jenna. "Your boyfriend?"

"Please, Detective. He wasn't a boyfriend. I liked him. That was about it."

"He's dead?" Gabriel tapped the notepad against the top of his desk.

"Yes. He moved out of state when he was around twenty, as I recall. We kept tabs on each other throughout the years and used to Instant Message back in the day. Then I heard he fell off a crane or something and died."

Gabriel cocked his ear at that. "He died from a fall?"

"At work. Right on his head," Jenna said for maximum impact. "Thank God Toby didn't suffer. They say he died on impact in a pool of blood."

Gabriel ignored the melodrama and considered the rest of Jenna's information. Taking up his pen, he asked, "What was his full name, this Toby?"

I'm getting an "Opie," Carmen had said. *Something like that.*

"Toby Dillingham."

"Tell me about him, Mrs. Klein."

"Why? Are you thinking Toby had something to do with Nancy? How stupid. Toby was an adorable –"

"Just tell me about him."

"O-*kay*." Jenna sneered. "Toby went to Taft, like Bodie. He might have been one of Bodie's teammates. Toby played bass, but we never got to jam together. Our dreams of starting a band ended when Nancy went missing."

"Anything more?"

"Only that he was adorable and nice, just like Bodie. I was bummed when I heard Toby died. You never forget your first love, do you?"

"I suppose not. Thank you, Mrs. Klein, for all your help. I appreciate it."

Gabriel ended their call and realized he'd hung up on the woman again. He guessed Jenna had one more complaint to lodge in her end-of-the-world file.

Accessing his computer, Gabriel typed "Toby Dillingham head injury" into Google.

An article dated November 23, 2007, appeared: "Belvedere Pit Worker Falls Fifty Feet to His Death."

I saw that injured man again.

"An employee of Belvedere Pit died when he slipped off an elevated conveyor.

The company, which runs a landfill for construction items, issued this statement: 'We are saddened to confirm that one of our employees, Toby Dillingham, fell today while performing routine maintenance.' Dillingham, thirty-five years of age, had worked for the company for three years. The coroner's preliminary findings rule the fall as accidental."

He looks about thirty-five. Rough around the edges, as if he were a blue-collar type of guy.

334

Gabriel laced his fingers behind his head and leaned back in the chair, thinking.

It was a strange coincidence, wasn't it? Carmen described a ghost with a severe head injury, and a young man whom Nancy might have known suffered similar physical damage. Gabriel didn't believe in ghosts, but he didn't believe in coincidences, either.

He researched Toby Dillingham the way he'd done with Christopher Rand; only he found more information on Toby. The boy had indeed gone to Taft High School. Gabriel called the school's registrar, who said she would scan and email a few photos from the 1987 and 1988 yearbooks to him.

Gabriel drank coffee and waited for the email. His heartbeat quickened, whether due to the caffeine or to Toby Dillingham, Gabriel didn't know.

When the photos made their digital arrival, Gabriel studied Toby's high school picture and the photograph he'd seen of the 1987 swim team, which featured Christopher Rand. Gabriel identified Toby Dillingham standing in the same row as Christopher. Jenna was right. Toby and Christopher had been teammates and friends.

Pins and needles again unsettled Gabriel, as if he'd missed something important.

Was the ghost with the damaged head Toby? Carmen insisted that the visitation alerted her to danger, to her near-fatal encounters with Joey Bowles. She felt the ghost and Joey were connected.

Toby Dillingham, however, couldn't have known Joey. The two men were years apart in age, and according to Jenna, Toby had left the state when Joey was a baby.

Gabriel kneaded his hands against his face as if the friction on his flesh would spark a clue. He had gone so far afield from finding Nancy Lewicki. Reduced to investigating phantoms, Gabriel wondered if he should call it quits to preserve whatever sanity he had left. Carmen claimed that Nancy was sending Gabriel clues. With nothing else to go on, Gabriel wished he could believe that. If Bodie's friend Toby was a clue and served as a light along the path to Nancy's whereabouts, Gabriel didn't know how to follow it.

CHAPTER FORTY-THREE

That night, Ming did her level best to prepare dinner for her future husband. She'd chosen something simple: brown rice with sautéed red snapper. Now grease splattered the stove, spilled rice littered the counter and floor, and the kitchen smelled like something that died in a conflagration.

Through the kitchen window, Ming could see Gabriel working in his garden. He plucked two healthy orange pumpkins from a neat row growing along the fence and stepped carefully around the planters filled with edible vegetation.

The garden reflected the care that Gabriel tendered it. Ming sighed and looked down at her culinary creation. The rice had overcooked into sticky balls, and the snapper looked like strips of fish jerky.

Her fiancé entered at that moment and presented Ming with a fat pumpkin.

"This is yours," Gabriel said. "We're going to have a carving contest."

"You'll lose," Ming told him point-blank. "Carving is what I do every day."

"Ah, but you don't make designs on dead bodies."

"How do you know?"

Gabriel shook his head. "Don't be disgusting." His eyes roved over the kitchen mess. "Did a bomb drop?"

"Very funny." Ming ladled the food onto a serving platter. "It's fish and rice."

Gabriel squinted his eyes at the platter. "Where?"

"Maybe we ought to go out to dinner," she said. "I'm not sure this won't kill us."

Chuckling, Gabriel tousled Ming's hair. "I appreciate the effort. It's still a bit early to go out, though."

"Then let's get carving." Taking up a knife, Ming said, "Ready when you are."

Gabriel dramatically pulled another knife from a drawer. "I'm ready."

The couple went to work on their pumpkins. While Gabriel created a typical grinning Jack-O-Lantern, Ming made hers with an open "O" for a mouth and a surprised look on its face. She finished off her design by spooning cranberry sauce into and out of the open mouth as though the pumpkin was vomiting.

"That's disgusting," Gabriel told her in a matter-of-fact voice.

Ming looked smug. "Face it. I win with shock value."

"It should be puking the rice and fish you made."

"Watch it, McRay."

Gabriel walked over to Ming and put his arms around her. "I'm only jealous. I accede to the better butcher."

His cell phone pinged with an arriving voicemail message, and Gabriel released his fiancée to listen to it.

Moments later, when he set the phone down, Ming asked him who called.

"Kupersmith," Gabriel told her. "The guy from the Little Hollow Rentals. He left a message saying that his father remembers Walter Rand. It turns out the father knew Rand quite well because he'd been a good customer for many years. Rand rented a family cabin for both the hunting and fishing seasons. Kupersmith's father is unclear of the starting year but remembers that Rand broke his lease in 1988 and never returned."

"How could he remember that?"

"He couldn't find a tenant to replace Rand and ended up losing money on the deal."

Ming unceremoniously dumped their fish dinner into the trash. "It's funny, the things we remember." She moved to the sink and began to wash the dirty pots and pans. "I, myself, enjoy holding grudges. Does the information help?"

"I don't see how now that Rand is dead." Gabriel took up a towel and began drying the dishes. "It is curious that he broke his lease the year Nancy disappeared, don't you think?"

Ming shrugged a shoulder. Gabriel thought it curious. In 1988, a teenager named Nancy Lewicki met Walter Rand at the local Tasty-D-Lite under the pretense of planning a party for Rand's son, who was conveniently out of town. Nancy vanished, and Rand quit renting a cabin that he'd rented for years.

What about Toby Dillingham? Did the dead pit worker matter? Toby knew Chris and, according to Jenna, Toby knew Nancy. Gabriel methodically rubbed a towel against the pot in his hand.

"Would you mind if we went to dinner in West Hollywood?" he asked Ming.

"Why?"

"Because I want to stop at Carmen's house. The only lead I have left in this case is a ghost with a crushed skull, and I want to vet it."

Upon entering Carmen's den of voodoo, Ming's eyes went wide. Nudging Gabriel, she said, "Are you seriously going to talk about a ghost? Have you lost your mind?"

Gabriel didn't reply. Instead, he introduced Ming to Carmen, and the couple followed the psychic into her living room. Carmen offered them wine from behind her restored pub bar.

"What a fabulous addition," Ming said, admiring the piece.

"Its original home got knocked down by Hurricane Katrina."

"And what are these for?" Ming fingered an array of costume evening gowns draped over the countertop.

"Oh, sorry." Carmen pushed them aside, effectively clearing a place for Ming to rest her drink. "I'm trying on various outfits for a Halloween bash tomorrow night. It's a town hall meeting really, part of Brad's campaign. Do you know Brad Franklin?"

Ming glanced over to Gabriel, who stood near the curio cabinet with his nose in a gris-gris bag. "He's our DA, isn't he?"

"Yes, but he's running for Attorney General. We're dating, actually." Carmen tried to mask her joy. "Anyhow, the costume party is at the Theater in the Ace Hotel. Pretty cool, right?"

Ming nodded and sipped her wine.

"I'm thinking of wearing one of these." Carmen held up two gowns, one reminiscent of Marie Antoinette's court and the other, an ankle-length fairytale dress of white lace. "Which do you think?"

"They're both beautiful." Ming pointed to the one with the white lace. "This looks like a wedding dress."

"Does it?" Carmen asked, a little flustered.

Ming smiled.

Carmen's cheeks reddened. She set French courtier dress aside but kept the one that resembled a wedding gown in her arms. "What are you two doing for Halloween?"

"I'm dressing as a witch," Ming said. "Gabriel, I mean Detective McRay, thinks he's too cool for a costume, so we're staying home and handing out candy."

Gabriel wandered over to join the two women at the bar. Reaching into his jacket pocket, he pulled out Toby Dillingham's picture and showed it to Carmen. "Is this your ghost?"

Carmen paused in surprise and then peered at the photograph. "He looks like the guy. What is his name?"

"Toby Dillingham. He died from an injury similar to the one you described."

As Carmen inspected the photo more closely, Gabriel continued, "He was on Christopher Rand's swim team, and they were good friends. Supposedly, Toby was going to be in the band with Nancy."

"I see." Carmen smoothed the mock wedding dress draped over her arm. "I wonder why he came to warn me when Joey Bowles showed up." She walked over to a clothing bag that hung from a barstool and unzipped it. "Toby has got to be connected to Joey as well as to Nancy." Giving the ivory-colored gown one last, loving look, Carmen zippered it into the clothing bag.

Ming took another sip of wine and gave an amused wink to Gabriel, which he ignored.

"I see Toby's connection to Nancy," Gabriel said, "but not to your stalker."

Ming blew out a breath. Her eyes widened at Gabriel, and she nodded toward the exit.

Carmen shook her head. "Joey Bowles wasn't a stalker. You know it, Gabriel. It's bothered you since the time he first attacked me. Joey showed up only after I started discussing Nancy on my show. He wanted to shut me up. I'm sure of it. I think Toby served as a bridge, a way to connect the dots from Joey back to Nancy."

"Oh, come on," Ming said. "I'm not even going to discuss your 'ghost.' But you can't make a connection where there isn't one. Joey Bowles was a baby in 1988. He couldn't have had anything to do with Nancy's disappearance."

Gabriel nodded thoughtfully. "But he might have been hired by someone who did."

"Your palm reader is angling to get married," Ming said to Gabriel over lobster rolls at Connie and Ted's. The West Hollywood eatery, not too far from Carmen's home, was known for the rich and delicious sandwiches.

Gabriel chewed a French fry in contemplation.

Ming snapped her fingers. "Hey. Over here."

Gabriel focused on her. "Sorry. I keep thinking about what Carmen said."

"You don't believe in ghosts, do you? Do you honestly think she saw a dead friend of Christopher Rand's in her house?"

"How else can you explain it, Ming?" Gabriel reached for another fry. "It makes sense, doesn't it? Maybe someone did hire Joey Bowles to –"

"To kill a psychic for talking about a thirty-year-old cold case on TV?" Ming narrowed her eyes at her fiancé. "Do you hear yourself? If Nancy did meet with foul play, the perpetrator was never caught. I seriously doubt that this person today would draw attention to himself or herself by hiring a hit man to kill Carmen Jenette." Ming noticed Gabriel's crestfallen face, and her tone grew gentler. "Look, you found a perfect suspect in Walter Rand. Everyone assumes he was involved with Nancy's disappearance. Unfortunately, he's gone now. You may have to be content with that, Gabriel." She reached across the table and took his hand. "Stop searching for skeletons in the closet."

CHAPTER FORTY-FOUR

The gentrification of downtown Los Angeles had seen a boom of high-rise, high-end condominium complexes and mixed-use developments, which combined residences with retail establishments. Brad's condo was in one such building on Bunker Hill.

A doorman admitted Carmen into the lobby, and she took the elevator up to Brad's floor.

The District Attorney welcomed her with a kiss. "You look like the beautiful ingénue from *Phantom of the Opera*."

Carmen giggled. She'd left the wedding dress behind and wisely chose to wear an aristocratic-looking gown with a feathered and sequined Venetian mask, direct from her collection. Brad wore an expensive-looking suit.

"I know, I'm boring," he told her. "But I'm putting on sequined suspenders after the speech, along with a fedora. I'll be a 1940's crook to your Christine Dae."

"You'll look cute," Carmen said.

"It'll be fun. We'll party at the rooftop bar after the speeches." He moved past the kitchen toward his bedroom.

"I need to finish up. Pour yourself a glass of champagne if you like."

"Oh, I can wait until the party," she called after him. Carmen didn't feel like drinking alcohol. The slightly stricken sensation had returned. She took deep breaths to stabilize herself and meandered around Brad's apartment in an attempt to take her mind off her malaise.

"We can always break the bottle open when we come home," Brad said from the bedroom.

Home, Carmen repeated silently. Was Brad becoming serious about her? A smile broke through Carmen's wan features. She walked over to the window with a renewed purpose and let the magical lights of downtown cheer her.

"I guess you don't get many trick-or-treaters up on this floor, do you?"

"No," he answered from the bedroom.

Carmen surveyed Brad's apartment. There was a guest bathroom near the front door, and down a short hallway, she could see a bedroom. A spiral staircase wound up to a loft above her head.

Carmen climbed the stairs, which emptied into an ample space that served as Brad's library and study. Books, photos, and awards filled the shelves, and lots of campaign posters lay about. Two guitars, one acoustic and one electric, were propped against the desk.

"Do you play music?" she called to Brad downstairs.

"Once in a while."

A jagged pain suddenly coursed through Carmen, as if lightning sliced her body. She gripped the railing for support and tried not to fall as she descended the steps. She hurried into the guest bathroom. Closing the door, Carmen stripped off her mask and appraised her disheveled hair and the dark circles growing under her eyes. For the first time, she considered that she might be seriously ill.

Carmen once had a dear friend who experienced signs of influenza for weeks. When she finally consulted a doctor, the friend learned she had leukemia. Christopher Rand crept into Carmen's mind, and she felt a terrible empathy for the unfortunate youth.

Closing her eyes, Carmen once more tried to achieve that inner clarity upon which she prided herself. A vision hit her with both barrels.

A deer on a dirt path. A sound startles the animal, and it darts off.

She'd received that same impression when talking to Rand. Keeping her eyes closed, Carmen envisioned standing in a mountainous area.

The car has stopped, and I'm frightened. It's pretty, but I don't belong here.

"Carmen? Are you okay?"

Her green eyes flew open. Swallowing a wave of pain, Carmen rifled through her small clutch in search of an antacid.

She had to pull herself together! Campaigning with Brad would provide Carmen a fantastic opportunity to publicize the Psychic to the Stars brand to non-believers. This was the wrong time to fall ill. Carmen fluffed her hair with agitated fingers and made to exit the bathroom. Only, the door wouldn't open.

She tugged at the knob, but the door remained stuck. Carmen pulled and pulled. Finally, she called out in exasperation, "Brad, I can't get out of here."

"I'm sorry," she heard him say. His footfalls approached, and she sensed his presence on the other side of the door.

"The door sticks," Brad said. "Just give it a little push, then pull real hard."

Carmen followed his directions, and the door swung back and nearly knocked her into the toilet.

"You okay?" Brad asked again and grabbed her arm to steady her.

Carmen nodded but felt the strangest sense of *déjà vu.*

"I'm fine." Carmen ran her hands down the bodice of her gown, an attempt to either neaten the material or tamp down the sick feeling lodged in her solar plexus.

Pine trees looked down from impossible heights above her. A ribbon of blue sky ran between the treetops. She breathed air so fresh it tasted sweet on the mouth.

Brad extended his hand, and Carmen, who could swear she smelled mountain air, gave him hers.

"Trick or Treat!"

Gabriel handed out candy to a group of little ones, mostly dressed like popular animated movie characters. Behind him on the kitchen counter, the carved pumpkins glowed with candlelight. Ming, wearing her witch costume, lay on the couch watching a scary movie, and the sounds of screams permeated the house.

Gabriel came over to the couch and held out the basket of candy. "Want some chocolate?"

Her head shook under her pointy hat as the doorbell rang again. Ming bounced up and took the basket from Gabriel. "My turn."

A group of teenagers, sans costumes, stood at the front

door. Ming looked them up and down. "Trick or treat!" they yelled impudently and thrust out their paper sacks.

Ming dropped a single candy into each bag.

A kid scowled at Ming. "That's all?"

"One per customer. Next time dress for the occasion."

The teens groused and complained as they scattered from the porch. The same kid yelled, "Fucking cheap, bitch!"

Ming's jaw fell open, and she turned to Gabriel. "Did you hear that? Can I hit him with my broomstick?"

"They're just kids," Gabriel called from the couch. On the television, Gabriel watched a gore-flecked ghost stand behind a young woman and reach out a hand.

The doorbell rang. Ming opened the door.

"How about a treat, babe?"

Gabriel caught the edge of a leer in that teenaged voice and looked toward the front door.

Ming said, "How about a tick?"

Gabriel saw Ming wipe a wooden spoon against the sleeve of the young male, which left small brownish things on the fabric. The kid blanched in horror at his jacket and cried out. Slashing the material with his hand, he nearly stumbled down the porch steps. His mates laughed as they ran and left a stream of insults and obscenities behind them.

"Happy Halloween," Ming called after him with glee. She turned around to find Gabriel standing behind her with his arms crossed and a frown on his face.

"What did you just do?"

Ming tried to hide a spoon covered in leftover brown rice behind her back. "I'll only do it to the bratty ones, I promise."

Gabriel plucked the spoon out of her hand. "And then

their bratty parents are gonna show up with lawsuits. Hand them candy, and only candy."

Ming grabbed the bowl of sweets. "Fine."

From the kitchen counter, Ming's disgusting pumpkin caught Gabriel's eye. The candle heat had caused part of the face to cave in, which reminded Gabriel of Carmen's alleged spectral visitor with the smashed head.

If Carmen saw a ghost, and the ghost was Toby Dillingham, why didn't he speak? Why didn't he mention Nancy?

"They say there's a meteor shower tonight," Brad told Carmen as they rode in the back of a limousine.

"That will definitely make the rooftop party," Carmen said.

Brad rolled down the window to behold the night sky. Suddenly, the ear-splitting sound of a Theremin caused gooseflesh to run down Carmen's arms.

"Sorry," Brad said, as he grappled for the eerie-sounding phone. "I've got to change my ringtone."

Carmen watched Brad as he took the call. The ringtone was familiar to her. She'd heard it before—and not on a B-movie horror flick. Carmen tried to place the sound.

When the limo pulled up to the Ace Hotel, Brad took her arm and helped Carmen out of the car. The debilitating feeling spread through her at his touch, and this time, Carmen didn't rationalize it away. The night breeze fanned against her face, and the clouds in her brain parted.

She remembered that the sticking of a door and the sound of the ringtone manifested themselves to Carmen the first time Joey Bowles had tried to kill her.

CHAPTER FORTY-FIVE

Maybe he has nothing to say because speaking would be irrelevant. Funny, that Dash would take that perspective on the silent, injured ghost. Then again, Gabriel's ex-partner had always been the philosophical type.

Toby the ghost didn't speak, but he apparently wanted Carmen to see him. Maybe the significance lay, as Dash suggested, in not what the injured man said, but who he was. Okay, then. Toby was a member of Chris's swim team. He also knew Nancy.

Gabriel left Ming to handle the trick-or-treaters and went into his study. Outside the window above his desk, a magical night beckoned Gabriel with falling stars. Too focused on his task to make a wish, Gabriel spread the photo of the 1987 swim team beneath his fingers. Two rows of bare-chested athletes smiled at him.

Christopher Rand stood next to Toby Dillingham.

What is it? Gabriel thought. *What more can there be?*

His eyes scanned the faces of the boys and froze on a

swimmer standing in the back row behind Toby and Chris. His name was Bradley Franklin.

───────

If there ever existed a building in Los Angeles to make one feel transported to a distant time, the United Artists building from 1927 was it. Built under the patronage of silent screen stars Mary Pickford and Douglas Fairbanks, Jr, The Theater in the Ace Hotel sported eye-candy architecture and old Hollywood glamour.

Carmen sat in the front row of the Spanish gothic masterpiece, with her eyes lifted upwards to view the stage. The White Knight stood behind a podium and told his supporters that the good work he did for the county of Los Angeles, he could do ten-fold for the state of California.

Applause erupted around Carmen. She did not clap.

On the stage, Brad waved a hand at his patrons. He caught Carmen's eye and winked. He made a subtle gesture instructing her to meet him backstage.

Carmen drifted upwards from her seat.

───────

Nancy hadn't been mindlessly doodling, Gabriel berated himself as he rifled through Nancy's personal items.

She walked with confidence.

Nancy was a girl who strategized—always.

Nancy was a planner.

Gabriel recovered the Pee-Chee folder and inspected the cover. What he had mistaken for random doodles drawn in boredom was a blueprint of Nancy's plans. He studied the cartoon musicians on her crudely drawn stage. Chris sat behind the drums. Jenna stood at the microphone. Nancy played a synthesizer. And there were two other male figures.

Toby played bass.

Grabbing his phone, Gabriel punched in Jenna's number.

"Hello?" she answered.

Surprised that the call didn't go straight to voicemail like usual, Gabriel blurted, "This band you were forming, who was in it?"

"Who is calling?" Jenna purred.

"You know who."

"That's right, I do. The rudest man ever. Like I said, Detective, we never formed a band. It's not important."

"Let me worry about what's important," Gabriel told her. "There was another boy besides Toby, wasn't there?"

"Who cares?"

Gabriel wanted to shake the woman. "I do, Jenna. Was there another boy? What was his name? Was it Bradley Franklin?"

Her silence created a subtle hum on the line. Finally, Jenna spoke. "He called himself Brad."

Gabriel made sure he said goodbye before ending the call. He still had one item to crosscheck. Probing the file on Joey Bowles that he'd taken from Detective Bonin's office, Gabriel confirmed what he suspected.

Joey's lucky break of beating a murder charge as a juvenile came from a generous, civic-minded young prosecutor named Brad Franklin.

Gabriel fumbled for his cell phone and texted Carmen. *Be careful. Brad knew Joey. On my way.*

"I could use a drink before I schmooze more," Brad told Carmen as they waited in the elevator that would take them up to the rooftop lounge. "Wait 'til you see the view. There's a Jacuzzi up there, too."

Carmen's phone vibrated from a text, but then the elevator doors opened, and Brad steered her outside. A sweeping view of downtown Los Angeles met her eyes. A few partygoers frolicked in a roiling hot tub; the art deco tower lit them from above. Carmen felt the warm Santa Ana wind caress her face despite the transparent glass safety fences. Supporters immediately descended upon Brad, but he managed to grab Carmen's hand and escape them. He and Carmen hustled over to a flower-draped, low cement wall, by which stood an open table and two chairs.

Carmen was grateful to sit down. The pitched voices over the hot-tub jets, mingled with loud music, exacerbated her anxiety.

"What can I get you?"

She shrugged. "Anything."

Brad regarded her. "Are you sure you're okay? Too breezy for you?"

"No." She did her best to give him a bubbly smile.

On his way to the bar, people approached Brad. Watching them heartily shake his hand, Carmen felt something break inside of her. Perhaps it was her heart. The cell phone vibrated again, and when Carmen read Gabriel's text, she knew with certainty that her heart had broken.

Brad, who must have felt buoyed after his speech, returned with a bounce in his step, holding two Singapore Slings. He was high on life. Supercharged on fame, the way

Carmen used to feel, but Carmen couldn't lie to herself anymore. *The truth is humble.*

Brad saw her face and grew concerned. "What is it?"

The wind pushed Carmen's hair into her eyes, and the curls became damp with her tears. "Why did you hire Joey Bowles to kill me?"

Brad guffawed and smiled, but his eyes darted in their sockets like two pinballs. "What on earth would make you say that?"

"Nothing on earth, that's for sure." Carmen sighed and said, "Look, Brad, throughout my life, people have accused me of either being a fake or being crazy. I might possibly be a fake, but I am not crazy. You're connected to Joey. Gabriel knows it, and I know it, too. Why did you hire him to kill me?"

The DA glanced at the partygoers milling around. A neon sign from a nearby skyscraper cast Brad's face in blue light. "Because you were talking to Walt, and he believed in you."

"Walt?" Carmen repeated in a monotone. "I see. So, you knew him, too."

"I care for you, Carmen." Brad reached a hand across to hers. "I honestly do. It's been a terrible conflict for me." His fingers tightened around hers. "But I couldn't afford to have you learn of Walt's secret."

Carmen gazed at Brad's grip on her hand. Images began forming. "Walt was a father figure to you. The Rands were the family to whom you owe your success. Am I crazy, or am I correct?"

"You're correct," Brad whispered. He swallowed and glanced at the huddled groups of people sharing the rooftop.

Brad turned a frenzied eye toward Carmen. "I'm sorry. I have too much to lose."

He dragged Carmen upwards from her chair and propelled her to a place along the low wall where the safety fence ended. Shoving aside a potted tree blocking the spot, Brad shoved Carmen into the aperture and pushed. The lights of downtown whirled around Carmen as she struggled to keep from toppling over. She had not foreseen this death and refused to give it credence. Summoning up her reserve, Carmen gave Brad a quick thrust with her elbow, which caused the District Attorney to stumble backward. She followed this with a swift kick to his groin. Brad doubled over into a ball on the floor and moaned.

A young man ran up to Carmen, asking if she were all right. A crowd quickly formed around Brad. Carmen's pretty gown hung in tatters on one side where her body had connected with the wall. She supposed a bruise would form there. Carmen grasped the edge of a table for support. She couldn't look at Brad.

The District Attorney crouched on his hands and knees. He lifted his head to see the astonished stares of witnesses, the hands that covered their open mouths. He heard the whispers. A few young people produced cell phones and now memorialized Brad on video. With an anguished cry, Brad lunged toward the low wall. Hopping onto it, he dangled precariously over the edge of the roof.

"Brad, don't!" Carmen cried, now realizing the identity of the man on the rooftop ledge and the loss he hoped to forget.

Brad swerved around toward the city lights, and the wind caused his clothes to flap. He surveyed the street below and swayed. Shutting his eyes, Brad began to fall forward.

A hand darted out, grabbed Brad's arm, and jerked him like a marionette back onto the stone floor of the deck.

"I don't think so, Brad," Gabriel said to the man lying at his feet. "I'm unable to speak with the dead, so you and I need to hash things out before you kill yourself."

CHAPTER FORTY-SIX

Gabriel sat in Lieutenant Ramirez's office opposite the District Attorney. Ramirez stayed behind his desk, while Donovan Thorne loitered nearby with his arms folded across his chest. Carmen had installed herself in a chair next to the door as though she felt safer near an exit.

Gabriel displayed a framed photograph to Brad Franklin. "I asked Donovan to take this from your office wall."

The picture showed a more youthful Brad befriending the juvenile offenders at Camp David Gonzales. Brad had his hand on the shoulder of a teenaged Joey Bowles.

"You didn't press murder charges against Joey when he was younger," Gabriel said. "I guess you believed in his rehabilitation at the time. Apparently, you changed your tune when you asked him to get rid of Carmen. Tell me, did you have to pay him, or did you simply call in the favor?"

Brad laid his face in his hands.

"We can tie you to Joey Bowles," Gabriel said. "As we speak, Detective Bonin is going through Joey's cell phone records. We'll find calls between you and him, won't we?"

Brad's fingers dug into his hair.

"I also took the liberty of going through your apartment this morning." Gabriel produced a file folder and extracted three wallet-sized photos: a shot of Brad, one of Christopher and Brad taken in a boat, and a picture of Walter Rand and Brad holding hunting rifles.

"These came from Rand's wallet, didn't they? These put you, Walt, and Chris together in one happy family. By the way, when did you steal these photos from Walt?"

Brad didn't reply. He kept his face hidden.

Gabriel then brought out the swim team photograph and placed it before Brad. Gabriel tapped the photo. Brad lifted his head.

"What exactly was your relationship with Chris and Walter?"

"Chris was my best friend," Brad said. "I needed a family, and Chris offered me his. Walt gave me a home."

"And for that, you'd protect him even though you knew he was a murderer."

Brad entreated Donovan, Gabriel, and Ramirez. "I had to protect him. He was like a father to me. I couldn't turn him in."

Carmen, the one person in the room Brad had refused to acknowledge, spoke up. "You're lying."

The men looked at her in unison.

"Walt didn't kill Nancy," Carmen said. "He's telling me that you did."

Brad stared at Carmen and shook his head. Ramirez's brown skin turned the color of milk. Gabriel gave Carmen a warning look. He'd allowed her to witness the interview with Brad but told her to keep quiet.

Catching Gabriel's drift, Donovan turned toward his sister-in-law. "Carmen…"

"Walt gave you a home," she said. "And this is how you repay him? By letting him take the blame for a murder you committed?"

Observing the expression of despair on the District Attorney's face, Gabriel asked, "Is it true?"

Brad looked at Donovan for help. The deputy DA kept his mouth glued in a thin, stern line.

"If you work with us," Gabriel told Brad, "you won't go down in flames publicly. Whatever you can do to help us with the Nancy Lewicki case, Donovan is ready to make a deal."

"Donovan is ready to step into my career," Brad said in a jagged voice.

Gabriel shook his head. "You don't have a career anymore. Think about it though. If you hold out, we'll let the press mutilate the reputation of The White Knight."

"But I can't go to prison," Brad entreated Gabriel. "Do you understand how many men I've put away there?"

Gabriel leaned back in his chair. Finally, he had a proper bargaining chip in an interrogation. "Like I said, work with us, and we can paint you as a remorseful man who stood up and helped the investigation."

Resigned, Brad asked, "What do you want to know?"

Gabriel leveled his gaze at the other man. "Everything."

We're dancing to the beat, and I'm telling the crew that we'll be on that stage someday.

"Chris, Toby, Jenna, Nancy, and I used to go to concerts.

Each of us played instruments, and Nancy had the idea to form a band.

"I lived with Chris and Walt at the time. Nancy would come around the house to practice music, but she and Chris practiced locking lips a lot more than playing music."

Gabriel remembered witnessing that romance on tape. He thumbed through the file folder and held up the photograph taken in the ghost town. "Did you take this picture?"

Brad swallowed hard. He forced the words from his mouth. "We'd gone fishing up at Convict Lake. Chris knew Nancy was going to Mammoth with her folks that summer, so we planned to meet up with her in Bodie."

Ramirez finally spoke. "What happened to Nancy?"

The DA appeared listless, like a drifting boat on a shoreless sea. "Walt got me my first job," he murmured. "He helped me go to law school. But he had this sickness. Walt tried to keep it a secret, but Chris and I knew. How could we not? Boys sneak into their father's cabinets once in a while. We saw the kind of pictures and videos he liked. We also knew that once in a while, he had to pay off a girl."

Brad looked earnestly at Gabriel. "Walt didn't hurt anyone. He just liked them young. But Chris couldn't deal with it. Walt felt bad, but he couldn't stop. Chris's sixteenth birthday was coming up, and Walt wanted to do something nice for him. He'd already bought Chris a drum kit. When Chris went off to his grandparents, Walt asked Nancy if she'd help plan a party for him."

"Walt became attracted to her?" Gabriel asked.

"She was his type." Brad glanced at Carmen, who met his eyes. He looked away. "Nancy was the right age. When Chris left for Texas, Walt made his move. We had a cabin near Crestline. We'd hunt in the season and hike and do water sports at other times of the year. Walt drove Nancy there.

"I was supposed to be at home, but I felt sorry for myself. Chris had grandparents to visit, and I had no one. I decided to drown my sorrows up at the cabin. I'd gone hiking, and when I returned, I heard Walt's voice. I hadn't expected him to be there. Then I heard another voice and went cold. Nancy was there."

Brad dropped his gaze to the floor. "Walt had made a pass at her. I heard her screaming at him. She told him she was going to report him to the police. I saw Walt's face through the window. I'd never seen him so frightened. He knew what this would cost him with Chris. He begged Nancy to be reasonable; that it was all a big misunderstanding. He promised to take her home right away."

"Nancy wouldn't calm down. I was afraid people would hear her. Before I knew what I was doing, I got my Winchester rifle from the locker and walked into the main room, where Nancy stood with Walt. I remember glancing out the window to see if anyone was coming, and to my surprise, I saw a deer." Brad looked up to address the assembled party. "A deer stood outside the cabin window. He was a beautiful animal, two hundred and fifty pounds of full-grown buck with a thick crown of antlers. All those times we hunted without spotting any game, and there he was but a few feet away from me. But I didn't shoot the deer. I shot Nancy instead."

Carmen's sigh, heavy with emotion, filled the room. Brad didn't seem to notice.

Gabriel pushed the Pee-Chee folder in front of Brad, and when the District Attorney saw Nancy's crude drawing of her band, tears filled his eyes.

"I'm not evil, Detective McRay. I've been trying to make it up to Nancy my whole adult life."

"And her parents?" Gabriel asked. "Her brother? How did you plan on making up for their misery all these years?"

Brad's trembling lips closed together in response. Gabriel leaned forward in his chair. "You can begin by showing me where you and Walt buried Nancy."

CHAPTER FORTY-SEVEN

The search party consisted of Gabriel, a cadaver dog along with his trainer, forensic technicians, crime scene investigators, and a pretty, brown-haired forensic anthropologist named Ann Carter. Ming, who wouldn't miss a chance to work with her favorite detective, joined the group. A squad car transported Brad Franklin to the dig site.

Carmen had asked to come along. Gabriel granted her request, although the psychic seemed to drag herself with every step.

Low clouds moved in as the company followed Brad's directions and drove a couple of miles away from the Little Hollow Cabins.

They rolled along an uneven fire road, passing dry chaparral, and climbed higher in elevation, until they arrived at a dense group of parched pine trees. Beyond the grove of trees, the ground dropped into a small canyon, where a poor excuse for a stream trickled.

While the technicians erected a tent to serve as a makeshift headquarters, the cadaver dog put his nose to the ground. He pulled his trainer to various points around the area.

Gabriel looked over at Carmen, who reminded him of one of the pine trees, once proud, struggling to stand erect, and slowly withering. He walked over to her.

"I owe you an apology," Carmen said. "I'm a fraud. I have no vision. I couldn't see through Brad at all."

She inclined her head toward the DA, handcuffed like a common criminal in the back of a squad car.

"You didn't want to see through him," Gabriel told her.

A tear tracked down Carmen's cheek. "My grandmother warned me, but I was so cocky." She sniffed and wiped the tear away. "Are the handcuffs necessary?"

"He's on suicide watch."

Carmen, again, observed her shackled lover. Ming stepped up to the conversation and regarded the psychic in concern. "Are you all right?"

"I'll live." Carmen pulled her eyes from the squad car. "I'm still reeling from the fact that he hired someone to kill me. Do you think Brad had something to do with Walter's death?"

"It's a possibility," Gabriel mused.

"I'd like to examine Rand's remains," Ming said. "An overdose of insulin or a heart stimulant would do the trick. Either one could push a man in Rand's health to the point of death."

Gabriel nodded. "True. Brad could have done the deed at the Radisson and pulled those photographs from Rand's wallet at the same time. I think I ought to interview the hotel personnel."

"Absolutely," Ming said. "And I'll start the application process to exhume the body."

Gabriel and Ming studied each other for a moment and then shared a smile. After a moment, he turned toward Carmen. "That was a good move you made, telling Brad that Rand's ghost spoke with you about the murder."

Carmen's drooping shoulders straightened, once again a proud tree. "That was no move. Walter appeared to me."

A laugh escaped Ming, but she quickly suppressed it. If Carmen noticed, the psychic didn't show it.

"Walter is with Chris now," Carmen said. "They are coming to terms on the other side."

Ming raised an eyebrow. "Oy."

Gabriel dismissed her with a gentle wave. "What about Nancy? Still getting nothing from her?"

"Like I've said, Detective. I'm not the one she's reaching out to." With a swish of her trademark, airy skirt, Carmen left Gabriel and Ming to check on the progress of the dig.

Ming faced Gabriel. "Is it a full moon? Why would you encourage her like that?"

"I don't know," Gabriel said. "Maybe I'd like to believe life holds a little magic."

Ming snorted, opened her mouth to retort, but then reconsidered. She reached out, took her fiancé's hand, and squeezed it. "What we've got is magic."

His sapphire eyes found hers—onyx, the gemstone that releases sorrow and grief.

A commotion near the team turned their heads. Gabriel and Ming rushed over to the dig site.

"What did you find?" he asked Ann.

The anthropologist squinted up at Gabriel from her kneeling position in the dirt. "Nothing. We thought we'd discovered a few bone fragments, but they're only ceramic shards."

Gabriel nodded, his hopes dashed. He raised his eyes to petition the heavens and noted that gray clouds now obscured the treetops. Zipping up his jacket, Gabriel meandered toward the dry creek bed. A border of sand and rocks indicated that, in pre-drought years, the trickle might have passed for a good-sized stream. Water had featured so prominently in his dreams. Could there be a connection? Before he could apply reason to his action, Gabriel strode over to Ann and instructed her to dig close to the stream.

"Why?" The anthropologist surveyed the upturned earth on which her team currently worked. "Isn't this the spot where Mr. Franklin indicated?"

"It is, but I want you to dig near the streambed."

With a collective sigh, the crew picked up their tools and set up near the stream.

Ming tapped Gabriel's shoulder. "Why did you tell them to move?"

He shrugged in response. She would not understand.

As the couple watched the team dig along the perimeter of the creek, Gabriel said, "I've decided to put my house up for sale. You and I should live in Los Feliz. Your place is closer to work, and, as you said, it's bigger."

Ming buttoned her sweater against the cooling temperature. She took a moment to absorb his words. "But we cook in your house," she said finally. "We play there. I'm at your house ninety-nine percent of the time. Besides, you love your garden."

"I'll plant another garden. You have a backyard."

Ming chewed her lip. "No. It doesn't feel right."

"Ming."

"No. We're going to rent my place out. It'll bring us extra income."

"But what about your things, all your furniture?"

"We can rent it out furnished. If not, it's okay."

Gabriel crossed his arms and appraised his bride-to-be. "What about your library? All your medical books—those Latin books, for God's sake. Where are we going to store them?"

Ming rolled her eyes. "Please, who even reads Latin? We'll donate them to a library. Look, maybe someday, we'll move back there with a couple of rug rats in tow."

Gabriel grinned and took her in his arms. "You with kids. I'll have to see it to believe it."

Ming rested her head on his broad shoulder. At that moment, Gabriel felt a drop of water hit his head. He looked up. Another drop splashed into his eye.

Squinting like Popeye, Gabriel heard Ann Carter calling his name.

A gust of wind buffeted Gabriel and Ming as they made their way over to the team. Rain began to fall and pattered on the tent and their clothes.

Ann Carter fervently brushed at the earth. Kneeling, Gabriel spied what appeared to be an elongated piece of dried mud. After Ann gently prodded the object, the ground released its captive. The anthropologist used a soft cloth to clean off the grime and then handed the object to Gabriel. It was a white vinyl purse.

The rain fell harder and the team mobilized to erect a shelter. The ground, compacted in its dry state, at first refused the rainwater like the belly of a starving man that rejects solid food. A torrent of water ran across Ann's brush as it next unearthed a pair of headphones, which she gave to Gabriel. The foam ear protectors had long since disintegrated.

Ann then uncovered a small, earth-caked rectangular box. "A Walkman," she announced appreciatively as she cleaned and inspected it. The younger interns and technicians gawked in amazement as if the forensic anthropologist had opened a portal to a bygone era.

Indeed, time had been arrested on a fateful spring day in 1988. Gabriel took the Walkman from Ann and turned it over in his hands. A teenage girl had owned this music player, and those earphones had touched her flesh. They testified to the life of a girl who sang, laughed under a California sun, and loved a boy.

Ann's brush next touched what appeared to be a large round stone. The water, finally soothing the stubborn earth, washed the dirt away from the object to reveal a human skull.

Gabriel felt Ming's hand come to rest on his shoulder, but he could not tear his eyes away from the wet bones materializing in the softening earth.

Hello, Nancy.

CHAPTER FORTY-EIGHT

While the forensic team labored at the dig site, Gabriel took the vinyl purse to a worktable and laid out its contents. He inspected a cassette tape enclosed in its plastic case. Written on label were the words, *"Bodie's Birthday Mix."*

Gabriel set down the tape and fingered a Bonnie Bell lipgloss. Inside a small, plastic coin purse, Gabriel saw a couple of dollar bills molding alongside a folded piece of paper. He extracted the paper and could make out numbers next to names. Was this the missing invitee list of Christopher's friends?

Also in the coin purse, partially protected by vinyl and plastic was a high school identification card. Although it was damaged, Gabriel recognized the blonde hair and the winning smile: Nancy Lynn Lewicki.

The sense of satisfaction he'd expected eluded Gabriel. He'd found Nancy, yet one more task remained for him to complete.

Ming asked if she could accompany Gabriel to the Lewicki home. Perhaps her forensic viewpoint would be welcome. People often asked questions about the final moments before death. Once Gabriel pulled into the guest parking spot, however, Ming changed her mind and opted to wait in the car. This was, she decided, Gabriel's show. She watched her fiancé walk up the path through a steady rainfall and knock on the front door.

The Lewickis had been expecting him, as he had called to make sure they were home. They were home. Len and Pauline had been waiting at home for this moment for over thirty years.

Gabriel dove right in, of course, speaking as soon as the couple opened the door. Ming smiled, shaking her head. *Oh, Gabriel,* she admonished. He could be so brusque at times. Way too enthusiastic.

And then Ming watched Pauline collapse into Gabriel's arms. She heard Pauline repeat Ming's words loud enough to be heard through the car's water-streaked window.

"Oh, Gabriel!"

But Pauline's outburst was far from reprimanding. The woman seemed filled with gratitude as her desperate fingers crushed the sleeves of Gabriel's jacket.

Ming's fiancé stood firm in the face of that overpowering emotion. He held Pauline assuredly and without judgment, and for that, Ming swore to adore him always.

Len Lewicki extended his hand, and Gabriel, still supporting Pauline, shook it heartily. Putting an arm around Gabriel, Len ushered him into their home. They closed the door.

Ming sighed against the headrest. This is what her father did not know about Gabriel. This was the book underneath the cover that her father too quickly judged. Her fiancé was a hero today. He represented a knight in shining armor to the Lewickis, exactly as Gabriel did to Ming.

They buried Nancy next to the grandmother with whom she had been close. The storm had cleared, and a brilliant sun warmed the funeral party. Gabriel, Ming, Carmen, and Ramirez stood at one side of the grave as people came forward to share their remembrances about Nancy.

Paul Lewicki spoke first. Gabriel wondered if the man would fall apart behind the podium. Nancy's brother, however, appeared to walk in a state of mild astonishment, as if this long-awaited moment served as bolt-cutter on the lock of his emotional prison.

Jenna Goldman Klein, in particular, appeared buoyant. She put aside her ills to give an animated speech about how Nancy's enthusiasm for life had once inspired her, and then how Nancy's disappearance disillusioned her. Jenna admitted to losing the ability to follow a dream. Hopefully, she said, she would reclaim it now.

After her talk, Jenna walked over to Nancy's casket, and Gabriel saw her face crumble. "I've missed you," the woman said in a wavering voice and held a tissue to her eyes. "You always knew how to make life fun, Nancy."

Giving the woman her privacy, Gabriel walked over to Carmen. He gestured toward the plaques in the ground. "I guess someone like you gets information-overload at a place like this."

The psychic seemed uncharacteristically reticent.

"Your ratings ought to shoot up when you divulge your part in the case," Gabriel coaxed. "You might even become a worldwide sensation."

"I'm not going to divulge my part in the case."

Gabriel raised an eyebrow at that, and Carmen smiled.

"It's one of those beautifully orchestrated life lessons," she told him. "Complete with cosmic irony. If I wow my viewers by publicizing my entanglement with Nancy's murderer, then I have to admit how easily I was blindsided. Who would ever trust me as a psychic? Jesus, I barely trust myself right now." Carmen let her eyes settle on the group of people gathered at Nancy's graveside. "Besides, a girl's private life ought to be respected, don't you think?"

She moved off, and Gabriel reflectively stuffed his hands in his pockets. He caught Pauline Lewicki waving at him from a group of supporters. She wrangled free of them and approached Gabriel.

"I didn't have a chance to say hello." Her blue eyes were gentle. "How are you doing?"

Gabriel couldn't understand it. Her daughter lay in a nearby grave and, once again, Pauline enquired after his health.

"I'm fine," he replied.

Pauline laid a comforting hand on Gabriel's arm. "I think about you a lot, ever since the séance."

"I find it amazing," he said, "that you manage to put aside your own problems to care about a stranger."

Nancy's mother gave him a perplexed look. "Why would that amaze you? You did the very same thing."

She gave his arm a squeeze and then left Gabriel alone to lay all his little ghosts to rest.

In the days that followed the funeral, Gabriel returned to her parents the rest of Nancy's belongings. He hesitated to remove the photograph from his bookshelf. He'd grown used to seeing Nancy's smiling face every day.

Gabriel decided that whenever the evidence lab was through with the original birthday cassette, he would mail the tape to Eugenia Rand. Perhaps she would place it on Christopher's grave because Nancy would have wanted Bodie to have his music.

When Gabriel offered the Jack-in-the-Box to the Lewickis, Pauline told him to keep it. The novelty had worn out its welcome with their daughter, and they had no use for it. Stuck with the stupid toy, Gabriel wondered whether to throw it in the trash or rebury it on Summit-to-Summit Road in Nancy's honor.

A few days before the wedding, Gabriel went into his study to ponder the fate of the Jack-in-the-Box. Hefting it, he intended to throw the damned thing into the wastebasket, but then reconsidered. With solemnity, he placed the Jack-in-the-Box on the empty shelf of his bookcase. It would serve as a reminder that the items, people, and events that frighten or agitate us are often the very sources from which we draw our strength. Gabriel positioned the box with the best view of the lion tamer.

CHAPTER FORTY-NINE

A harpist played "Morning Has Broken" by Cat Stevens as Ming walked down the aisle. She held tight to her father's arm. Despite her efforts to appear elegant and demure, a gleeful smile sprouted on Ming's face, lessening the regal entrance she attempted to make. As Gabriel's bride made her approach toward him, he waited before the Justice of the Peace. He wore a well-fitting blue tuxedo, which accented his shoulders and highlighted his eyes. Janet stood across from her brother, having taken her place as Ming's matron of honor. Her two children, Liam and Amber, assumed the roles of ring bearer and flower girl, respectively, and stuck close to their mother's side. Gabriel's best man, Miguel Ramirez, stood, upright and proud, next to him.

The Rancho was perched on a bluff in Malibu that overlooked the mountains and the Pacific Ocean. A celebrity had lived in it and then sold it to an investment group, who now rented out the property for events. The assembled crowd numbered under fifty, but every soul present meant something to the bride and groom.

Gabriel's father and mother sat in the front row next to their son-in-law Michael. Behind them gathered Gabriel's friends from work. Ming's mother and assorted friends of the Li's sat on the opposite side of the aisle. Geoffrey, the red-haired deputy coroner and Ming's confidant, sat with a few coworkers from the ME's office. Jonelle winked at Gabriel when he caught her eye and gave her partner a subtle thumbs-up.

Gabriel waited, his black hair curling around his collar, and watched Ming walked along a path strewn with white rose petals. He recalled the countless times they'd put their heads together over a case and how much of a friend she had been to him.

Glancing at his mother and father, he met their smiles and hoped that his father recognized him. Pete McRay appeared quite happy. Mrs. McRay blew her son a kiss, which he acknowledged with a grin.

Ming arrived at his side. Her father, Dr. Li, released her arm and shook Gabriel's hand. The elder Dr. Li then took his seat next to Ming's mother, who beamed at the couple. Years later, Gabriel wouldn't recall much of what the Justice of the Peace said, but he would remember the kiss that sealed their marriage.

The party after the ceremony went on well into the night. From the way the guests tore into the food, Gabriel's menu evidently pleased them. He'd chosen to serve root vegetables, grains, herb-encrusted tri-tip, grilled flank steak, roasted chicken, and vegetable lasagna. The only complaint came from Rick Frasier, who asked why Gabriel didn't include sushi.

After dancing with Ming and dancing with Mrs. Li, Gabriel took his mother's hand. Her Irish blue eyes twinkled as they danced. When Gabriel led his mom off the dance floor to where Pete McRay waited with Janet, the older fellow stepped toward his son.

"May the road rise up to meet you. May the wind always be at your back. May the sun…" Pete trailed off, searching for the words.

"Shine warm upon your face," Gabriel finished for him.

A wide smile brightened Pete's face. "You know it. Are you Irish?"

Gabriel felt the breath stop in his throat but managed to nod his head. "I am." Before Mrs. McRay could cover for her husband, before Janet could guide their father away, Gabriel put a tender hand upon his dad's shoulder. "Thank you. Coming from you that blessing means a lot."

Pete McRay nodded and allowed Janet to lead him toward the dessert table. Gabriel leaned over to give his mother a reassuring kiss and told her not to worry. Sample the desserts, he told her. He'd handpicked them. She should tell him if he made good choices.

Gabriel watched his mother go and wiped a tear on his tuxedo sleeve. No sooner had he done this, Ramirez and Rick Frasier caught him by the arms and steered Gabriel over to the bar where shot glasses of tequila awaited. Martin Lopez was there, along with Dr. B.

"My man!" The criminologist slapped Gabriel's back with gusto. Was this the same lab rat Gabriel had encountered in the photo studio?

Lopez pushed a brimming shot glass toward Gabriel, who knocked it back. He quickly bit a lime and shook his head as the liquor went down. This was a strange new world, being "one of the guys." Dr. B clinked Gabriel's next glass and gave him a wink. "Hearty congratulations—on many levels."

Gabriel nodded as his throat sparked from the tequila. At least he could breathe again. Jonelle joined the men who insisted she take a few drinks.

"One shot," she said, holding up a single finger. "I gotta drive home." Jonelle lifted the small glass toward Gabriel. "To a great partner. Treat your wife with respect because women rule."

The men jeered at that, but Gabriel clinked Jonelle's glass and drank. He spied Carmen and waved her over.

After declining multiple offers to drink tequila shots, Carmen addressed Gabriel. "The answer is yes," she said.

"Yes, to what?" he asked.

"Yes, you will have a happy marriage."

Gabriel reflected on that and then tossed back another shot.

"What about me?" Carmen asked him. "Do you see a man in my future?"

Gabriel eyed the young woman. "You'll do all right, I guess; if you pick a man with your heart and not your ego."

Carmen gasped. "That was very profound, Detective. See? You do have inner sight."

"No." Gabriel poured himself another glass of liquid celebration. "I've simply had a lot of therapy. You want to meet my oracle? Doctor –"

Gabriel swiveled his head to see, not Dr. B, but Lopez, slightly red-eyed, admiring Carmen. With a grin, Gabriel stepped back from the bar, leaving the space between Lopez and Carmen empty—and open to possibilities.

Feeling punchy with the taste of salt and lime on his lips, Gabriel stumbled over to his new wife.

Ming, looking radiant in her white gown, smirked. "Last call for alcohol, babe," she said in a decent imitation of his voice.

"I need air," he told her.

"We're standing outside."

"I think I need more air." Gabriel looked around. "Wanna take a walk with me? Have a romantic moment near the ocean?"

She considered that and then shook her head. "There's something I've got to do first. You take a walk, but don't fall off the cliff. I would really hate to become a widow on my wedding day."

Gabriel nodded and wiped the perspiration from his brow. "I'll be careful."

Ming watched Gabriel walk beyond the party lights and the crowd. Once her new husband was out of view, she approached Miguel Ramirez at the bar and tapped him on the back. He grimaced upon seeing Ming.

"I need another drink," he teased.

"I want to call in my favor," she said.

Ramirez downed the drink in his hand. "What favor?"

Plucking the glass from his hand, Ming said, "I want you to strike up a conversation in Spanish with my mother."

Ramirez stared bleary-eyed across the dance floor to an archway bedecked in twinkling lights, where Dr. and Mrs. Li stood conversing with another couple.

"Your father looks a lot meaner than you."

"I did you a favor, Miguel. You owe me."

"You did your husband a favor."

Ming pushed him. "Go."

"*Aye, mujer*. Don't touch me. I'll make a complaint."

She pushed him again. "Go!"

"I'm going!" he barked and brushed her away. Smoothing his hair for courage, Ramirez ambled over to Ming's parents.

"Hi," he said in a booming voice to Dr. Li and the other couple. They stared at him. Ramirez faced Ming's mother. "*¿Está disfrutando?*"

Tom Li frowned. Mrs. Li eyed her husband, and her fingers rubbed together in shyness. Ramirez glanced at Ming, who watched the dialogue from a safe distance.

"I, um," Ming's mother began, and then she nodded. "*Es una hermosa boda.*"

"*Claro,*" Ramirez agreed with a slight bow of his head. To Dr. Li, he asked, "Would you mind?"

Taking Mrs. Li's arm, Ramirez escorted her to the dance floor. Ming's mother appeared perplexed by this encounter, but then she brightened. Her brown eyes grew excited, and her voice became animated as Ramirez conversed with Elena Li in her first language and swung her around the dance floor.

Watching the fountain of words spill from her mother's lips, Ming lifted a wine glass in a silent toast and, in perfect Latin, uttered a phrase by Terence, "Forest Fortuna Adiuvat." Fortune favors the brave.

———

A month's worth of rain caused Gabriel's shoes to sink a little as he walked. Life had returned to a thirsty southland, and nature rejoiced. Gabriel made his way to the edge of the yard, and here the plants grew wilder. Blooms of purple sage poked from the ground. In a couple of weeks, the flowers would reach as high as a man's chest. For now, mustard flowers topped them to create a carnival of yellow and lavender. Sprigs of Blue Dicks and white lilies added to the show. Nature had always soothed Gabriel. It was an organic, easily available gift that he treasured. He inhaled deeply, feeling content and a little buzzed from the booze.

The property ended at a cliff overhanging the ocean. The moon hung suspended over the water, a bone-white ball that bathed Gabriel's face in cool light.

The fission theory held that the moon had once been a part of the earth and, at some catastrophic point, became separated. Eyeing the faraway orb, Gabriel wondered if that was true. If so, what a shame for the moon, banished to a lonely outpost, barren and uninhabited, forever separated from its livelier self.

He could relate. Until recently, Gabriel had felt like an outsider looking in, a man forcibly separated from a happier self, doomed to a life of isolation. He'd done a lot of work, though, to come to terms with—

Gabriel stumbled on a rock and, as he glanced downward to watch his footing, he caught sight of something attached to his pant leg. Peering closer, he spied a butterfly perched above his right knee.

How odd. Were butterflies active at night? Gabriel gently shook the material of his trousers, but the butterfly would not detach.

Interesting. Was this unexpected guest like Poe's raven, an omen sent with portents of loss to lead him into a life without hope? No, Gabriel didn't think so. There was a benevolent quality about the pretty insect, which seemed content to hang out with him. Smiling at the rarity of the visit, Gabriel jiggled his leg. Since the butterfly did not budge, he sat on a nearby boulder to take stock of the insect.

What would Dr. B make of this? Did Gabriel's tiny companion have significance? Would Dr. B say that Gabriel's mind needed to assign a meaning to the event? Probably. Maybe the therapist would suggest that, to Gabriel, the butterfly signified an emergence from a chrysalis, a new life in a different form. Certainly, Gabriel felt more contented these days. If he could pinpoint a time in which he could stretch his wings, the start of union with Ming was it.

What about Carmen Jenette? Oh, what a field day she would have with this lovely creature. No doubt, she would claim that the butterfly was a messenger sent from the spirit world. But sent from whom? Christopher Rand? Toby Dillingham? Harris Brody?

Gabriel studied the insect in its perfection. The moonlight gave the red and black wings iridescence. Again, he agitated the fabric of his trousers, but his new friend held fast. The delicate wings rose up and down in a slow, almost hypnotic motion.

If Gabriel could allow himself a little fancy, if indeed the world held a tiny bit of magic, he would like to believe that Nancy was behind this evening's visitation.

Maybe one too many tequila shots were taking effect, but Gabriel found himself entranced by the butterfly's wings as they rose and fell with the tempo of the breaking waves. He let his mind wander. What if Nancy had found a way to reach out to him?

From a distance, Gabriel could hear the festive sounds of the wedding party, the band's music playing amid cheerful and boisterous voices. Gabriel should return and leave the ocean to its starry canopy of night, only... What if, in fleeting moments, barriers were broken and messages conveyed? Gabriel imagined what Nancy would want to say, and he decided to respond in kind.

"You're welcome," he whispered.

All at once, the butterfly took flight. Gabriel watched in wonder as the colorful creature disappeared into the night with the joyful eagerness of an angel that discovers wings or a man who realizes he can embrace the moon.

＼＼＼＼

Would you like to see
more of this detective?

Let Laurie know at
http://www.lauriestevensbooks.com

For updates on new releases follow
Laurie on Facebook at
https://www.facebook.com/lauriestevensbooks

ABOUT THE AUTHOR

Laurie Stevens is an award-winning novelist, screenwriter, and playwright. She lives in the hills near Los Angeles with her husband, two snakes, and a cat. To learn more about the author visit her website:

http://www.lauriestevensbooks.com-

Made in the USA
San Bernardino, CA
16 April 2020